SQU
CL

T0101959

PUSHKIN
VERTIGO

Winner of the McIlvanney Prize
for Scottish Crime Book of the Year
The Times Crime Book of the Month

'A manic tale of blood and suds told with laconic humour and warmly engaging characterisation. McSorley is definitely a talent to watch. I knew within a page that I was in good hands'
Chris Brookmyre

'An absolute knockout of a debut! Pitch-dark and yet dripping with warmth. Packed with brilliantly drawn characters, laugh-out-loud humour, and lots of blood'
Caz Frear, author of *Sweet Little Lies*

'Shattered from staying up until the daft hours finishing this. Loved it… A serious talent'
Kevin Bridges, author of *The Black Dog*

'An uproarious, sardonic noir thriller from the Glasgow depths… Brutal, wonderfully humorous and a great addition to Tartan Noir, this novel unveils a terrific new talent'
Crime Time

'McSorley writes with a wonderfully light touch... There is humour on every page, too – this really is a very funny book despite the dark material. Both main characters are works of genius, and I very much hope there will be a sequel'

Scotsman

'A fast-paced thriller with a dark sense of humour, a grisly crime caper in the vein of *Breaking Bad* and *Guilt*'

Sunday Mail

'An absolute blast... reads like a brilliant mash-up of Irvine Welsh and Alan Parks... I can't recommend this one highly enough'

Raven Crime Reads

SQUEAKY CLEAN

CALLUM McSORLEY

PUSHKIN
VERTIGO

Pushkin Press
Somerset House, Strand
London WC2R 1LA

Copyright © Callum McSorley 2023
Extract from *Paperboy* © Callum McSorley 2024

First published by Pushkin Press in 2023
This edition published 2024

3 5 7 9 8 6 4

ISBN 13: 978-1-78227-838-2

Designed and typeset by Tetragon, London

Printed and bound in the United Kingdom
by Clays Ltd, Elcograf S.p.A.

www.pushkinpress.com

For Lisa

PROLOGUE

PROLOGUE

The ash was shot through with burnt scraps of newspaper, lumpy where the hammer had failed to smash the charred bone to dust, and slushy like dirty, roadside snowmelt where the shoebox had started to let the damp in. Faint, pish smell of a doused fire—spent charcoal and blackened meat.

The logo on the side belonged to a brand of shite trainers— the kind worn by bully victims and the lonely, sexless men they grew into. Of all the fucking indignities, McCoist thought, suppressing both a manic smile and the coffee burning its way back up her gullet. She peered at the contents, eyes snapping shut with every flash of the camera, opening again dazzled and scorched but fixed on the grey powder mulching in the corners of the cardboard, the gloved hand of a SOCO sifting it as if looking for gold.

"Is it?…"

"Cannae say till the tests huv bin done."

"But is it?…"

She couldn't see the SOCO's face for his surgical mask and the hood of his paper suit, after-image spots dancing where his eyes must be. Other bodies moved around outside the tent erected over the shallow hole they'd dug in the ground, shadows going about bad business.

"Cannae say," he said.

. . .

They had a recorder and a microphone, they had glasses of water and a jug between them, they had thick folders stuffed with papers lying perfectly parallel to expensive-looking pens. They had laptops and tablets and severe silences at their disposal. On the other side of the table, McCoist had a chipped mug full to the brim with cold coffee. The words on the side—faded by a thousand quick scrubs of the ancient, hairy Brillo that lived by the sink in the office mess—declared her the World's Best Maw. The lanyard she wore said Detective Inspector.

It was three on one. A fifth—a greying man with crowns on his epaulettes and glasses hanging from his neck by a chain—perched on the window ledge. Referee? Lifeguard? Executioner? McCoist didn't know. He hadn't opened his mouth since the inquisition started, not even to speak his name for the DIR. Officially, he wasn't there. Unofficially, he lurked and listened and scratched his balls now and again.

The old goat in the middle seat straight across from McCoist was also a superintendent. He licked a finger and leafed through some loose pages. He was a man who could make rustling paper sound very loud indeed. "And these remains, DI McCoist, whose were they?"

McCoist touched the handle of her mug, turned it slightly, but didn't pick it up. "The remains were of an unborn child belonging to the murder victim, Dannie Gibb, sir."

"The lab results don't confirm that."

"No, sir, but Mr Knightley stated so as part of his confession." *Which is in the paperwork right in fucking front of you.*

"And you trusted completely in what he said?"

"Every word, sir."

"Why?"

10

McCoist followed the man out into the garden, keeping her distance. He lumbered along in an old T-shirt and joggies, smelling unwashed and sour. If his head weren't naturally inclined to slump towards his chest, his shoulders hunched, he'd have had to duck to get through the door. The sweat on his back was a dark continent which tapered into an arrow diving into the cleft of his arse crack, the valley exposing where everything was spilling out between the gap of his too-tight clothes.

There was filthy plastic furniture on a paved terrace buckled by weeds. Beyond was a jungle, the dilapidated shed a half-hidden outpost in the bush. He walked to an island of fresh soil in the middle of the overgrown grass. He turned to face her and, with a shy smile, dug at the patch of earth with his heel, like a child trying to break through an iced-over puddle. "Right here," he said.

"Mr Knightley, I need you to wait inside while I make a phone call." She didn't worry at all that he would try to run away. While she waited for the cavalry to arrive and the return call from the sheriff about the warrant, Knightley offered to make her a cup of tea in his poky kitchen that smelled of microwave macaroni and the overstuffed bin. A greasy window looked out onto the garden and what was buried there. "No thank you, Mr Knightley," she said, her voice hoarse and dry in the too-close kitchen, palms slick and fingers wriggling out the excess energy firing through her.

"Dye mind if a huv wan? There's biscuits in the tin an aw." He tapped a clumsy rhythm on a shortbread tin with long, ragged nails. He had large, fleshy hands. The skin looked soft but hid the power of an industrial vice. The rest of him was the same—a gentle, blubbery overcoat on something more powerful than he could control. "Maw goat this when she wis in Edinburgh wan time an kept it full ae bickies ever since. A try tae…"—he wheezed then coughed into his hand with a phlegmy rattle from the bottom of his lungs—"…try tae keep it up, ye know? The…"—his chest made a noise like a stone being sucked up the hoover—"…scuse me. The tradition."

"I had no reason to believe he was lying."

"Is that so? For someone of your rank and experience that strikes me as somewhat naive, DI McCoist." The super's eyes were large in thick glasses, showing off red cracks and gunky corners. They didn't blink enough. "Didn't it strike you as odd he didn't try to hide what he'd done?"

"Well, he'd certainly hidden Dannie Gibb's body. If it wasn't for the tip-off it could have been weeks till she was found."

"This tip-off—who did it come from?"

"Anonymous, sir."

The super sighed in a way that made it clear this was some-how McCoist's fault. "You didn't try to track the caller down?"

"Of course, sir—"

"The caller could have been Knightley himself. Isn't that right?" The man on the super's left—a DS with the wet-look haircut of a teenage boy and the sulky eyes and flushed cheeks to match—cut across her. *Wee prick*. McCoist made sure there was none of the deference she gave to the super in her eyes or manner when she turned to address him.

12

"No, that is *not* right, Sergeant. The officer who received the tip-off was played multiple examples of Knightley speaking and confirmed he was not the caller."

"Confirmed?" The DS smirked. "This officer, a PC…"—he made a show of looking through his notes, a clumsy imitation of his boss—"…Kirsty Ravani—she's got a good ear, does she? A big music fan is PC Ravani, eh? Not exactly a scientific test."

"Mr Knightley has a distinctive voice," McCoist said (pitched too high and nasal for his size and with a breathless rasp—just the memory of it gave McCoist a shiver, fingertips squeaking across the skin of a balloon), but the DS ignored her and continued.

"Look, as soon as you show up at his door, he admits—without pressing—the whole charade with Miss Gibb and points out where he's buried the baby. Let's just admit there's a good chance he tipped you off to the body's location in the first place."

"*Charade?* He battered and throttled that woman to death then cut out her—"

"We know what he did, Inspector," the super said, sounding almost bored.

"Then why are you asking me to explain it all again?!"

Less than silence—the sound of five pairs of buttocks clenching tight. The super slid his glasses up onto his expanding forehead and glared with the small, hardened, beady things he'd revealed. McCoist stared back, her left hand clamped to the arm of the chair to stop it trembling, the right snatching up her old mug and slugging a mouthful of room-temp Nescafé instant—no milk, no sugar, undissolved granules dredging through her teeth. She grimaced and wiped her mouth with her cuff. The woman on the super's left, a DCI, failed to hide a smirk. The DS had to look away, his cheeks flushing even more, jaw jutting out as he struggled to keep his gub clamped, desperate to say something, to have a go at her, but knowing it wasn't his place. In the corner of her eye, McCoist caught the mystery man smile—the same surreptitious twitch with which he scratched his nads from time to time.

The super's shoulders heaved up and down in a deep breath, his glasses sliding back onto his nose with it. "Detective Inspector McCoist, watch your tone, please."

"Sir," she mumbled.

"So you took this man at his word?"

"The Macadam Street girls said he'd been a customer of Miss Gibb's and that he was strange. He was hanging around, pestering her. Complaints had been made against him by other women. Miss Gibb's belongings were found in his house and the remains of the foetus were buried in his garden where he said they would be. I took his word only because it was corroborated by other sources and the *evidence*, sir."

"The evidence…"

The DCI pushed her tablet towards the super and flicked through some slides. McCoist saw a flash of jewellery on the screen. "Items found in Stuart Knightley's house that belonged to Dannie Gibb," she said. She looked younger than McCoist, despite her rank. Her voice was pure private-school blazer brigade—an accent impossible to lose. You can fake upwards but not downwards, McCoist knew. "Confirmed by DNA matches and supported by witnesses—women who worked at the brothel on Macadam Street with Miss Gibb and allege to have seen these things in her possession."

"All quite neat then, wouldn't you say?" The super looked back up at McCoist.

"The procurator fiscal was happy enough," McCoist said, trying to get some steel into her voice.

"The fiscal have some questions to answer themselves," the DS chipped in, leaning forward in his chair and uncrossing his legs so they now splayed out, a hand resting on each knee, the bulge caused by the zip of his trousers pointing at her. The super placed a hand on his shoulder and he sat back again, folding himself away.

"You didn't feel the need to explore other avenues?" the super asked.

"At the time, the evidence seemed clear." McCoist kicked herself. *At the time. Seemed.* Too close to admitting fault.

"You didn't think to look into the possibility of a link to organised crime?"

McCoist shuffled in her chair, now feeling aware of how stiff her back was, the blood sitting heavy in her legs. "This is… this is all hindsight. There was nothing that hinted in that direction." She jabbed her finger on the desk to emphasise each point as if laying it all out on the table between them: "Knightley was the victim's customer, he'd been seen hanging around her at the time of her disappearance, he had her belongings in his house, the ashes in his back garden, and he confessed to the *whole thing*." (Double tap.)

"But the brothel was *owned* by Paul McGuinn!" The DS slammed his hand down on the table, as if to wipe out McCoist's invisible schematic.

"Says who?!" she snapped back. "Show me his name on the lease, Sergeant. Go on. Get me a utility bill. A bank statement.

Get me a Tesco Clubcard catalogue that puts *that* name with *that* address."

The super put a hand on the DS's shoulder again, firmer this time, signalling McCoist to back down with his other. "That may well be, DI McCoist, but do you think if you hadn't been in such a rush to charge Knightley and close the case, had you asked yourself whether Stuart Knightley might have motivation to confess, you might have come across such a connection?"

McCoist had to turn away, her face twisting into a painful smirk at the absurdity of a senior officer suggesting a slower approach would have been acceptable. She wanted to ask him what that would do for the targets, the numbers, the public relations, the politics, the bullshit. She turned an escaping chuckle into a cough and sniffed hard, her eyes starting to sting as they watered up, her bottom lip threatening to pout. *These fuckers. How dare these fuckers?* "No, sir," she managed.

"Let me ask you outright, were you truly just being naive here or were you being wilfully ignorant in order to close the case quickly?" the super said.

The look on the DS's face showed the younger man believed neither of these things, thought that it went deeper, that McCoist was rotten at the root, that she'd bungled it on purpose.

"I worked the case I had in front of me," she said. "I worked with the evidence. I couldn't have done any different."

"Was it yours?" McCoist asked, head tilting at the window— steaming up as the kettle boiled—and the garden through it.

"Wit? Eh…" His brows furrowed, drawing creases across his forehead as thick as corduroy piping. A Simple Simon look.

"Well, now ye says that, a, eh…" The kettle clicked and he stood much quicker than his large frame would seem to allow, making McCoist flinch for the first time since she'd come into his home—this glaikit man who had committed an atrocity, with the strength to choke the life out of a woman, saw her open, and then…

"Did you do it because you thought it wasn't yours or because you thought it was?"

Knightley seemed to be puzzling this out, huffing as he mixed his brew—half water and half milk with three sugars. He drank with the teabag still floating in it then fell into another fit of crackling and wheezing. He faced McCoist, face red and dripping. "Either. Either wouldnae be good, would it?" He pawed through the biscuit tin, sieving and turning the Penguins and Viscounts and Blue Ribands.

The heating was up high; McCoist felt her skin prickle with it. She felt the stuffy, swampy existence Knightley lived within the confines of the two-bedroom council kip he'd shared with his maw. She was out living in some pensioner pen now but the decor looked as if she'd never left. Only Knightley's bedroom was a reprieve from seventies faux walnut and swirling floral fabrics in washed-out pinks and blues and oranges.

Most of the space was given over to a bed with a caved-in mattress, the floor hidden by trampled clothes, the walls by sun-bleached film and fitbaw posters with the odd Page 3 plastered here and there. A dusty shelf displayed Celtic bobbleheads (players long retired), cans of Lynx and Right Guard and tubs of hair gel, and an action figure of Al Pacino as Tony Montana, posing with his "little friend". It smelled like a gym changing room and gave McCoist a creeping fear that the prickling she felt wasn't due to the sweaty heat but because there were mites crawling around under her clothes.

After Knightley had been taken away, no need for cuffs, Scenes of Crime turned the room over. They had the benefit of gloves, booties and coveralls that could be burnt afterwards. Didn't take them long to find the hammer (still dusty) and a long kitchen knife rusted with dry blood. The team working the old shed found a recently used barbecue stinking of burnt meat and white spirit, scraps of newspaper kindling in the bottom.

"Thank you for your time, Detective Inspector McCoist," the super said, sliding his glasses up, business done. The DCI was putting the papers back in order while her junior fumed silently and continued to stare McCoist out. "You may be called upon again to answer further questions before the inquiry is concluded. We will be in touch."

"It's been a pleasure," McCoist grumbled, her voice hoarse, hands sweating and shaking, starting to come down from the adrenaline her panicked body had been drip-feeding her throughout the meeting.

She snatched the door open, but before she could get through it a voice called her back. It was the grey-haired mystery man by the window, Mr Itchy Baws. He held out her mug to her. "A detective's most important tool, don't lose it!" His voice was pleasant—chipper, even—his face long and thin but unthreatening. With those specs hanging from their chain he reminded McCoist of a librarian.

"Thank you, sir."

He winked and wiped his forehead with the back of his hand, miming the word *"phew"*.

NOVEMBER

1

He was waiting outside the closed shutter at 7 a.m., a Mr Big type: shirt open down to his freezing nips revealing a heavy gold chain nestled in greying chest hair, fag resting between the sovvy rings on his thick fingers, tailored jeans and pointed black shoes, both expensive and dated, the dress of the middle-aged working class gone wealthy. Behind him, a gunmetal Range Rover, engine idling, exhaust smoke fogging the early morning air. Its vanity plate read: V1P MCG.

"We're no open yet," Sean said, taking the padlock keys out of his pocket as he arrived at the car wash. Sean was the owner, a wiry and shrivelling forty-year-old with skin like tanned cowhide, who spent most of his time during winter in the office chaining joints and watching Russia Today. In summer, he took a folding chair out front and sunbathed while the boys worked.

"A know," the man said. "Sorry fir turnin up so early, pal, it's just am in a bit ae trouble here." He took a fast, hard draw on his cigarette.

Sean snuck a look past the guy's shoulder. The headlights were blinding but Sean couldn't make out any damage on the four-by-four's bumper, and it didn't look particularly mockit either. "It's a big motor, it'll cost ye twenty just fir a wash." Overpricing was a method Sean often used when he wanted a customer to get to fuck.

"Actually am lookin fir a valet an aw. The full hing. Seats shampooed and windies polished. The lot."

"Ye want the seats cleaned?"

"Aye, how much will that cost?"

Sean laughed, a broken-throated, cackling honk. "At seven in the mornin? Fifty quid, easy."

The guy sucked the fag down to the filter and tossed it onto the road. "Sure hing, pal."

Fucksake. Sean wasn't one to hide his thoughts from his facial expressions. His hard-living eyes, sunk deep in their sockets, rolled in disgust. "Look, the boays will be in at half past, can ye wait that lang?"

"Ye goat a kettle in there?" He pointed at the shutter.

Fuck. "Aye, moan in."

The guy's name was Paul McGuinn and you might have heard of him. At least, that's what he seemed to think. "Call me Paulo. Am fae Brigton, originally," he said, meaning that although he didn't live there any more his roots were still in the east end, meaning he was one of the lads, not some posh cunt like his car might indicate. He was rich the way a footballer was rich, not rich the way a Tory was rich. That's the impression he wanted to give anyway. "Yersel?"

"Possilpark."

"At least ye didnae say Easterhoose. Fuckin blacknecks!" He laughed and Sean returned a grimace. Up close in the cramped, gyprock office Sean had built at the back of the unit—it had no desk or filing cabinet but did have a couch, television, fridge, kettle, microwave and George Foreman grill—Sean could smell Paulo's aftershave and a hint of BO underneath. In the harsh light of a bare light bulb, he could see sweat stains on Paulo's white shirt, seeping from under his arms and spreading out

22

from the small of his back. Hair gel was slowly being washed down his forehead and onto his red face. "Here, can a smell grass?"

Of course he could: Sean puffed through five or six joints a shift. The earthy stink of weed had soaked into the couch cushions and the carpet (a patchwork of car mats) and seeped into the plasterboard walls like damp.

"Mind if ye roll wan up while we wait? Been oan the gear aw night an I could dae wae chillin oot a bit." He tapped his nose when he said "gear" and winked.

Sean sighed. "Let us put the kettle oan first."

2

"What time d'you call this, Davey Boy?" Tim tapped an invisible watch on his wrist. He'd already straightened out the hoses and dragged the water barrel with the lances in it out onto the street, and now he was stacking up sponges and mitts and topping up various bottles of polishes and degreasers. He tossed Davey a clean rag. "You're late so you're het for mopping up the jizz."

Davey looked over the mammoth four-by-four under the powerful halogen work lamp beaming down from its bracket above the shutter. "Christ. We dain inside an aw?"

"Full valet, detailing the plastic and everything."

Usually Davey would take the piss out of Tim because of the way he said "val-*lay*"—without the "T", like it was French, rather than pronouncing it to rhyme with "mallet" like a fucking normal person—but it was still before eight o'clock and some prick was already wanting his monster truck washed, so Davey found he wasn't in the mood. Especially not on top of the phone call from Sarah that morning—the reason he'd been late leaving the flat. Annalee had been up during the night puking, and as she'd been visiting with him the day before, this was obviously his fault.

"The fuck are ye feedin her?!" Sarah screeched.

"Mushrooms a foond growin in the gerden."

"Wit?!"

"Chicken nuggets and chips, fucksake! It's a stomach bug, aw weans get stomach bugs."

He'd had to run by the time he got her off the phone but had still missed the start of the shift. And now, as Tim had called it, he was having to scrub cum stains off the back seat of a big bastard tank. A much easier task with leather seats but, in this case with fabric upholstery, Davey was having to shampoo the seats. There were handprints on the nearside window, footprints on the far. "Should bloody well leave wan ae them fir his missus tae see," Davey grumbled.

"Check this out." Tim was in the front with the hoover. He pointed the nozzle at the pocket behind the handbrake, where a fine dusting of white powder had gathered in the corners. "Big man's had a heavy night."

"An doesnae want his bird tae know aboot it. Cannae go hame wae spunk aw oer the seats an charlie oan the mats."

The guy in question was pacing around the unit passing a joint back and forth with Sean, who was having to answer a barrage of questions about soaps and waxes and running costs and was looking more fucked off by the minute. "How's that degreaser shite fir dissolvin stuff? The neighbours ever complain aboot the noise ae the washers? Ye goat a meter fir how much water ye use or is there a way roon it?" He was indeed a big man, all muscle turning to fat, but still looked capable of ripping heads off shoulders. He'd made a point of introducing himself to Tim and Davey, grabbing their hands in turn with a sweaty paw and crushing their knuckles. "Am Paulo, fae Brigton. Originally." He said it like he knew his reputation preceded him but wanted to be polite and appear humble, the way a celebrity might. Every so often he would give Sean a break and come to check on the boys' progress. "Daein a bang-up joab there, lads! Mind an dae under the mats an aw, right?"

"Will do, sir," Tim said.

"Sir? Call me Paulo, fucksake, am no a million year auld! Am no even auld enough tae be yer da."

Davey snorted. Paulo's face and clothes put him mid-forties at least, and his attempts to spike up his dyed hair to make himself appear younger only made it worse. In short, he was old enough to be a grandad if he was, as he said, from Brigton. (Originally.)

"Yeez huv goat it awright here, int ye? Gaffer sparkin up joints an that, no bad at aw, right? How's that seat lookin, son? Am needin the whole hing back tae factory-fresh, get it?"

"So yer wife doesnae find oot wit yev bin up tae?" Davey said. "Or is it yer girlfriend?"

Paulo's face fixed itself into a red-cheeked mask. His jaw jutted out, eyes boring into Davey's, who struggled not to look away, cold fear suddenly swirling in his belly. The Voice of Reason squealed in Davey's head: *Why the fuck would ye say that? This gakked-up beefcake could crush ye like an empty can ae ginger, ye fuckin eejit!* Then Paulo grinned. "Baith," he said.

Tim squeezed out the shammies once they'd finished; Davey gave the back windows a final check.

"It's gleamin, boays, gleamin!" Paulo took a tour around the shining SUV. "Fuckin toap-shelf joab yev done there. Ach, ye missed a bit!" He pointed to the front door panel. Even after eighteen months of working at the car wash, with anywhere from two to five arseholes a day pulling this one, Davey still fell for it. Maybe because Paulo's massive, coke-jittering bulk had put him on edge, or maybe because he was distracted thinking about Sarah and Annalee. Either way, he craned his head for a closer look and Paulo clapped him on the back and burst into moronic laughter. He nudged an elbow into Tim's ribs and Tim had to join in, though he hated that shite patter as much as Davey did. "You missed a bit" was second only to singing "Car Wash" by Rose Royce as the most common and irritating "joke" that customers and passers-by made them suffer.

To the boss's credit, Sean didn't laugh. He just held out his hand and said: "That's fifty quid, pal."

"A bargain!" Paulo took a thick, folded wedge of notes from his pocket and slid a few out into Sean's hand as if he were dealing cards. There were five twenties. He then turned to Tim and Davey. "Cannae forget the boays who dae aw the work!" He pressed a score into each of their hands and jumped up into his Range Rover. "Cheers, lads, yev saved ma life the night!" The engine roared to life and the radio began pumping out a heavy, thumping dance beat, all bass with no discernible melody. "Cheerio!"

The tyres spun as he screeched off, spraying fresh, oily black tyre-shine all over the wheel arches.

"Wit. A. Fuckin. Dick," Sean said.

3

A detective's most important tool. Brown frothy liquid in a paper cup, oversweet and bubbling with synthetic jizz which passed for cream, a post-Starbucks-invasion coffee-machine horror. McCoist took her coffee shite but this was something else. Still, she drank it down, rubbed her dry, stinging eyes, made something in her neck crack as she stretched.

If caffeine was the detective's most important tool then the computer and its eyeball-burning screen was the second. She'd been trawling through grainy CCTV footage of the Southside for nearly two hours, though it felt longer in the gloomy, blinds-down Operations Centre. The glare-reducing under-script lighting from the consoles bathed everything in a deep-blue glow which only made her feel more sluggish, as if she were sunk in the depths of the sea. Beyond her own terminal, the huge screens beaming in footage from all over Glasgow floated in the semi-dark, her fried eyes unable to pick out more than shadows of the uniforms working along the front desk, silhouettes on a rippling, shifting patchwork collage of the bustling city.

Before, she would have had somebody else do this, but now there was rarely anybody available to take her orders. Every DS and DC in her office had a full plate. Busy bees, every one of them. Apparently. In fact, *before* she would never have been investigating a brick going through a shop window at all, never mind sitting there at Eastgate, melting into an overengineered, ergonomic throne as she chased a suspect of petty vandalism camera to camera, screen to screen. It was fucking ridiculous. Her warrant card still read "Detective Inspector Alison McCoist, Major Investigation Team" but the fallout from the Gibb/Knightley inquiry had, in McCoist's case, severely broadened what could be called a "Major Investigation".

"This could be a hate crime, DI McCoist, and Police Scotland takes that very seriously indeed," Robson had said, the first part of which at least was true and made it even more irritating—that his sabotage of her career had a well-justified cover. "Get to work." The gaffer wanted her to quit. More than the stench of failure or the suspicion of corruption that caused all her colleagues to observe a radioactive exclusion zone around her, Detective Chief Inspector Robson was pissed off that she'd undermined him by going to the fiscal with the Knightley evidence over his head. But the inquiry had cleared her of wrongdoing, so he couldn't fire her—he'd need to wait for her resignation. And, watching this wee bam with a scarf over his face and his hood pulled up pan in Mr Chandra's window again as she started the trace from scratch once more, she might just give it to him. Staple it to his ever-growing forehead. *Prick.*

The window shattered inwards as the brick passed through it and the wee guy in his matching hoody and joggies sprinted out of the camera's field of view. Seconds later, Mr Chandra himself appeared outside, brick in hand, chasing the lad down the street. Mr Chandra, sixty-nine years old, bald on top with a wiry white beard, had explained to her: "I was goin tae feed it tae the wee bastart!" He didn't tell McCoist the exact words of the stream of obscenities he hurled at the vandal as he attempted to catch him up on arthritic knees, but Mrs Chandra filled her in in great detail, her soft, Indian-inflected Glaswegian giving the torrent of filth a gentle lyricism. "And I agree with every word," she'd finished.

So did McCoist after hours squinting at screens, trying to follow the bampot through blind spots and busy streets—the big problem being him diving into Queen's Park, leaving her to scour the surveillance in the areas around every one of its exits trying to find him again. Pure grunt work. Punishment. And all because Stuart Knightley had looked at her with thick, cow eyes and calmly told her how he'd sliced open Dannie Gibb, torn out the baby inside her and torched it on a barbecue. She'd believed him; she was wrong.

When she finally got outside Eastgate—a modern, boxy glass cupboard of a council building, which in thirty years would have the same sad bearing as the brutalist efforts from the seventies—the morning had been completely lost, her early start amounting to nothing. Hopefully local uniforms would pick the guy up based on his description. Guys like this were frequent flyers: the polis around there would be on first name terms. Part of the young team, probably, headed for the real gangs, the big boys, if he could be of use to them. Most likely as a stooge of some kind—it was always good to have brainless fodder to take a fall and do the time for you. People like Stuart Knightley, McCoist thought. (Today was obviously a day for dwelling. Sulking.) The tedious, soul-crushing, mind-numbing CCTV trawl had really made her feel the depths she'd sunk to; it was no surprise she kept returning to the object of her undoing.

Knightley hadn't had any personal ties to gangs though, other than frequenting the brothel on Macadam Street allegedly owned by Paul McGuinn. Paulo. The Big Man. Brigton's best and brightest, McCoist scoffed, but he'd beaten her in a game she hadn't even realised she was playing. Not until it was too late.

She sighed and her breath plumed in the cold air. *More coffee.*

4

The rest of the morning had been quiet, with only a few more customers coming in for a quick wash on their way to work, all of them regulars who mercifully waited inside their cars while Davey and Tim worked and only spoke to say "Thanks" before handing over their money.

Tim finished at noon and headed off for afternoon lectures. He was studying at Strathy, working his shifts around his uni timetable for beer money. Tall and skinny with long, floppy hair, bumfluff decorating an ever-present and earnest-looking smile, Tim wasn't the type Sean would usually employ but he seemed trustworthy and never complained about anything. Plus Sean needed the extra pair of hands—something was wrong with his shoulder, or maybe his back, and he needed a break from manual work. He was supplementing his usual medication (weed) with diclofenac the GP prescribed him.

"Al jump in if it gets busy, Davey Boy," Sean said. "Just geez a shout."

"Nae worries," Davey said, watching the gaffer slope off into his office. That was unlikely anyway—the weather was pish. A continuous, misting drizzle fogged up the air, making everything damp and chilly. Not many folk would be wanting their cars washed in this weather. Still, a couple of valets would be good to see him through the rest of the afternoon, otherwise he'd just be standing there by the shutter door with his joints getting cold and stiff, trying to space out the cups of tea, waiting for the inevitable point where he'd cave in and ask Sean if he could steal some baccy to roll a fag. Every day was quitting day; every day he relapsed.

He got what he wanted and a few punters turned up for hoovers, keeping him busy, keeping his mind off the fags and Sarah. In the afternoon he was on his knees, sponging brake dust off the burnt alloys of an old silver Merc—the kind driven by fairly well-to-do retirees—when a pair of scuffed, black Oxfords appeared in his view.

"Excuse me, are you the owner?"

Davey looked up at a thirty-something heavyset geezer in a cheap suit, the kind you borrowed off your da if you had a court appearance. "We don't dae shoeshines," Davey said.

The guy smiled—Davey could tell he was masking his irritation but he joined in the crack: "That's too bad, these old loafers could do with a polish, I work them hard."

"Ye sellin somethin?" Davey stood up and tossed his sponge into a tub of greasy black water.

"More in the way of collections, actually, Mr Prentice. This is about something you've already bought." He held up the ID card on his lanyard for Davey to get a closer look.

It took a monumental effort for Davey not to grin but he managed it. He shook his head. "Mr Prentice is the gaffer. In the back there." He pointed to the closed office door at the back of the unit.

"Cheers, big man," the guy said and strode away. Davey almost felt bad for the bloke until he turned round, halfway there, to shout, "You missed a bit!"

The guy knocked on the door and Sean yelled, "Moan in!" The guy stepped inside and closed the door behind him.

Davey had counted all the way to five by the time the screaming started—Sean must have had a decent buzz on already, five seconds was pretty laid back. Through the plasterboard walls Davey heard Sean's greatest hits: "It's no a fuckin *law*, it's a fuckin *act*!"; "Al pay fir it when a start watchin the shite!"; "Am no fundin some corrupt state broadcaster"; and "After wit they did tae us wae the Indyref? Ye should be fuckin ashamed tae work fir they cunts!"

The door flew open and the TV-licence bloke beat his retreat with Sean following, still yelling. "Come back here an al huv the polis dae ye fir harassment. It's a fuckin racket, that's wit it is! Aw just part ae the West Minister criminal fuckin empire! RT, that's the real fuckin news! That's the real world!"

When the licence-fee collector was back outside on the street, Sean appeared to let it go and stomped back into his office. The collector puffed his cheeks and blew out a long, steamy breath. He caught Davey with a look and raised his eyebrows. "What a fucking headcase," he said. The office door slammed open again, jumping on its hinges, and Sean came striding out with a dangerous-looking, long-barrelled air pistol which he'd bought from a guy down at the Barras to up the ante in his war of attrition with the local pigeons. (The pigeons, who roosted under the arches of the nearby railway bridge and seemed to particularly love crapping on freshly cleaned cars, were the other great enemy of Sean's life and times.) The collector took off running.

"Smarmy cunt," Sean said and spat on the ground. He sloped off, leaving an alarmed-looking pensioner in beige trousers and matching sport coat in his place. The old man turned from Davey to the retreating figure of the fee collector and back again.

"Bloke said the prices were too high," Davey said by way of explanation. He handed over the keys to the Mercedes he'd been washing and said, "That'll be twenty-five quid then."

5

"I can't just skip out the door whenever I please, Mark," McCoist hissed into her phone, hunched down behind her computer terminal, stacks of paperwork and printouts providing extra screening on the sides.

"But you're out and about all the time on work anyway—and it's not like I'm asking you to dog it just to go for a coffee," Mark whined. McCoist glanced over at the weeks-old collection of empty paper cups lining the edge of her desk ("World's Best" mug currently in her other hand) and swivelled her chair around so they were out of sight. "I'm asking you to pick up your child from school."

"Funny how you only seem to remember she's *my* child when—" She cut herself off as DI Jarvis passed close to her desk. She caught his quick, averted glance and drilled him with a glare in return, causing an ever so slightly speedier step in his walk to wherever he was off to—the kettle or the bog or to polish the gaffer's boots with his tongue, the triumvirate of Jarvis's working day. "Why can't you go?"

"I have a meeting and I can't cancel—it's already been rescheduled once. I'd ask my mum but she hasn't driven since Dad—"

"Fucksake, Mark, don't bring your dad into it, that is *so* cheap."

Mark's chuckle scratched through the phone line. "Come on, Alison. You're always saying you want to see the kids more."

"Stop talking." She took the phone from her ear to take a deep breath. "What did the nurse say was up with her?"

"Eh, I think she said she was having, um, cramps. You know? Pains down—"

"I get it... Shite. That..." *That hasn't happened before.* The dumb thought finished itself in McCoist's head in a sluggish, spaced wonder.

"Sounds like she's pretty upset, there was blood and—"

"I know how it works, Mark." Tess was thirteen, so while it should have been somewhat expected, McCoist still found herself taken by surprise. Something tugged in her chest—it was like seeing an old photo of yourself and being amazed and horrified that so many years had passed without you noticing.

"You should go."

"Shite... right, yeah. Do you really have a meeting? Don't answer. I'd better go home first and pick up some spare—"

"DI McCoist?" DCI Robson—a fifty-something with a red-wine face and a steak-and-chips body—was standing over her, a beady eye roaming the mess of her workstation and taking in her half-folded posture, which betrayed a personal call during business hours. "If you're not too *busy* I have a statement that needs following up on—a man says he was shot at with an air pistol at a car wash on Bell Street."

McCoist strained not to roll her eyes, not to groan out loud. Yet another bollocks "case" to add to her workload of other bollocks cases—her stock-in-trade ever since the Fuck-Up last year. Farmers didn't work with as much fertiliser as DI McCoist did. The idea of spending the afternoon running around the east end quizzing red-eyed, tracksuited teenagers who would rather throw themselves under a bus than be seen talking to her (other than to rip the pish out her name) was deeply unappealing. Especially after the morning's fruitful fun at Eastgate.

She heard Mark's tinny voice calling her through the phone speaker—she hadn't hung up. "Actually, sir, I need to pick my daughter up from school. She's not feeling well." As the gaffer started to reply, McCoist jumped in front with a two-footed tackle: "She's just had her first period." She plastered a big *Songs of Praise* smile on her face and clasped her hands together. "We're so proud!"

Robson found something interesting to look at on the wall, cleared his throat. "Oh well, yes, um… Get back as soon as you can and get down to Bell Street. The details are, um…"

"First thing tomorrow!" McCoist beamed, snatching her coat from the back of her chair.

Tess—wearing too-big lost-and-found trousers, a bag containing her own balled-up clothes immediately handed to McCoist—didn't speak from the school infirmary to the car. Setting off, she stared out the window, eyes not seeing anything whipping by, studiously ignoring her mother's attempts to cheer her up.

"You know, when I get mine I like to eat steak. Red meat. It's silly but I feel like I'm replacing all the iron I've lost, you know? Maybe you could have dinner with me tonight and I'll cook us a couple of nice, fat steaks. Just you and me. Cam can go back to your dad's and eat beans on toast. No boys. We can have a talk about—"

"I'm *vegetarian*," Tess said with a look that suggested McCoist was a very slow-witted person indeed, possibly the dumbest on

38

the entire planet. And the tone of voice, where had she learnt that? Where do all teenage girls learn it?

"Since when? Last time you were over you—"

"*Muuum*, just…" She finished the sentence with a huff, did the job better than any words she could have said.

"Bacon butties have meat in them, you know." McCoist knew she was winding her up now. *Stop then.* McCoist never wanted to be that parent who belittled their kids' interests or took the pish out their clothes and tastes and phases—so why could she not help doing it now? Mark wouldn't have. Bad cop at work, bad cop at home too.

Back to the window.

"What's so interesting out there?"

Tess dumped her jacket and bag on the hallway floor and marched into the living room, flopping down on the settee, grabbing the telly remote.

"You want a cuppa?"

Slight nod of the head.

"You still drink milk or?…" *Stop for fucksake.* No answer. Tess flicked through the channels too fast to see what was on any of them. "I'll take that as a yes."

McCoist checked her personal phone as she boiled the kettle. A couple of messages from Mark asking after Tess, all very concerned now he could deal with the situation from a distance. Her work phone had the details of the car-wash thing. Looked like the complainant—a TV-licence-fee collec-tor (McCoist's stomach turned a little at that, *filth*)—wasn't actually shot at with the air pistol, only scared off at the sight of it. Still, those things could be dangerous, especially in the hands of some wee heedbanger. Guy's name was Sean Prentice:

owned a car wash, some minor this and that on his CHS file from a while ago, hadn't paid his TV licence in some time. A real prize, a collar to get you into the history books. McCoist gave her phone a bitter smirk and filled the cups.

Another email pinged—from Robson. The subject said "Special Assignment", punctuated with an emoji of a paw print. *Whatever fucking next.*

She put the mugs of tea down in front of Tess, who kept her eyes on the telly. "Can you take me home?" she said.

6

The rest of Davey's shift was uneventful and quiet, not counting the half-hour of Sean's seething, rambling BBC-induced rage that followed the fee collector's appearance. ("These fuckin animals, Davey Boy! Fuckin parrots, just spewin back aw the shite the government feeds them! And we're *forced* tae pay them fir that? Fir wit?! Fuck off!")

Sean paid Davey at the end of every day, cash in hand, and with Paulo's bonus on top, it wasn't bad for a none-too-strenuous day's work—though it was still pretty far from good. Davey had come to the car wash after being made redundant from the big Tesco's where he'd worked night shift on time-and-a-third, forty-five hours a week. The car wash was a fair step down but not many places would hire Davey, an unskilled labourer with a short, potted CV of menial work that was only slightly longer than his criminal record, which itself showed little ambition in that direction either. Theft, assault, vandalism, drug possession—the list hadn't been added to in a good number of years, since around the time Annalee was born. Steady work and a decent wage at the Tesco had been good for him too, though the unsociable hours had done their part in breaking up his relationship with Sarah.

He took his money and walked home in his wet jeans and hoody, feeling the chill set in even through the thermals he wore underneath. He was splashed with mud from hosing tyres and the sweet smell of car soap hung around him in a cloying but not unpleasant cloud.

He lived in a second-floor one-bedroom flat in a housing estate near an abandoned plot where the cattle market had been back in the day—now a weedy, dug-shite minefield surrounding the skeleton of an old warehouse where they used to hold the auctions. Every one of its windows had been panned in, its doors battered down, their padlocks rusty and broken. Sheets of corrugated iron were peeling and the roof was almost completely gone, showing off its bleached wooden frame. It was a den for kids and druggies. Some nights Davey would walk by and see flickering orange light from a fire going inside. Polis were always chasing people off, mostly homeless folk with nowhere else to go at night.

Sarah was waiting for him outside his door. "Answer yer fuckin phone!" she said.

"Hows aboot fuckin 'hello'?"

"Fuck up, av bin callin fir oors!"

Davey checked his phone—it had been on silent. Ten missed calls from Sarah and five from his maw. His stomach went cold, the same way it had that morning when he thought Paulo was about to lamp him for asking about his wife.

"Wit's happened?" He licked his lips, his mouth and throat suddenly feeling dry.

"Annalee's in the hoaspital."

"Fuck."

"Fuck's right! A stomach bug ye said! She's goat some fuckin parasite. Somethin she picked up in that shit pit ye live in!" She kicked his front door and hurt her toes. "Fuck!"

He was about to question how she knew that for sure, then stopped himself. "Am goin tae see her," he said instead.

"Naw ye arenae. Ma maw's wae her the now an am headin back the night, eftir a pick up some clathes fir her. *You* stay away, awright? That's wit a came tae say."

"Wit? Ye cannae stoap me fae—"

"Aye a can. Stay the fuck away." She pushed past him, car keys jangling in her hand.

7

Davey was early the next morning—couldn't sleep. He chased himself around the bed most of the night, seething at Sarah, scared for Annalee. *Howsit ma fuckin fault? Howsit it always ma fuckin fault?!* He must have dropped off at some point but his eyes were open before the alarm went off, red and unrested.

He put on yesterday's clothes, which he'd hung on the radiator—any foosty smell of sweat completely blitzed by the car soap, which never seemed to wash out anyway—and walked to work. He stood waiting at the shutter in the cold and dark. He'd given it a rattle in case Sean was in already—he sometimes dossed on the couch in the office if he was too stoned to be arsed going home—but there was no response.

Tim arrived with a Starbucks cup in his gloved hand. "Morning, Davey Boy."

"Wit fancy drink ye goat the day, Tim?"

"Eggnog latte—they've got the Christmas drinks out already."

Davey snorted. "Christ, it's no even December yet. Wit the fuck is eggnog?"

"It's some American thing—I think they make it with alcohol over there."

"Any in that yin?"

"Unfortunately not."

"Sounds rank."

"Tastes good but." Tim took a sip, a smugness coming over his face from the warmth of it—bliss on a cold bastard morning.

"Just mind an drink it up before Sean appears—it'll set him aff. He'll be bangin oan aboot tax dodgin fir fuckin oors an a cannae be arsed wae it the noo. Av goat a splittin heedache."

Tim laughed. "He is right though, I shouldn't be giving them my money, it's just it's the only place open on my way here."

"An yer a fuckin addict an aw."

"That too." He took another gulp and a cloud of sweet-smelling steam emanated from his mouth.

"Ah, Tim, wit's that shite yer puttin in yersel?!" Sean already had a joint hanging from his mouth, stomping towards them with his bent-backed swagger. "Thoat ad fuckin telt ye aboot they fuckin crooks!"

"Fucksake, here we go," Davey said.

Tim chuckled.

Sean unlocked the shutter and hit the switch, the door grinding its way up in a racket that reverberated down the street, bouncing off the dusky yellow stone of the closed factories currently in the process of being converted to luxury flats which made up most of the buildings from the car wash to High Street. "Am no huvin ye bringin that shite intae ma shoap, ye better drink it oot here an go find a bin somewhere else fir the cup."

"I know the rules," Tim said.

That didn't stop Sean launching into his usual tirade—one that eventually ranged, in a raging stupor, into all sorts of areas of politics and ended up lambasting the UK government and celebrating the bare-chested, horse-riding Vladimir Putin, hero of RT—"the real fuckin Don".

"You're het fir any jizz the day, Tim," Davey said. "You an yer fuckin eggnog latte."

"Back in a minute." Tim ran off down the street to the nearest bin while Davey set up for the day. Once he had the hoses laid out—snaking out the shutter door, down the street and looping back to where the big blue barrel held the lances—he didn't bother delaying hitting up Sean for some baccy. He wasn't even going to pretend to quit today.

"Wit's the matter wae ye?" Sean asked. "Yer rattlin like skeletons shaggin in a biscuit tin."

"The wean's in the hoaspital."

"Fuck, man. Wit's wrang wae her?"

"Don't really know yet, Sarah willnae let us see her."

"Shite… Ye needin time aff?"

Davey rolled a cigarette—Sean didn't even have a light-hearted grumble about him stealing his tobacco.

"You not well, Davey?" Tim came into the office, pulling off his hat and gloves, his long, lazy student hair falling into his face, which he swept back behind an ear.

"His wean's in the hoaspital." Sean answered for him while Davey smoked his life-preserver. "The ex willnae let him visit."

Tim didn't know what to say to that. He never knew what to say about any troubles Davey had—separations and sick kids were very far removed from Tim's current situation and experience in life. He put on a serious face and managed: "Sorry, David."

Davey and Sean's eyes snapped together, smiles widening. They looked back at Tim, who took a beamer.

"*David?!* Ye ma maw noo?" Davey said.

"Fuck you guys!" Tim said, red-cheeked. The three of them burst out laughing.

"Fucksake, Timmy, put the fuckin kettle oan fir us. Sean, could a huv wan ae yer tablets? Ma heed's bangin."

"They're up oan the shelf there, *David.*"

"Fuck the pair ae ye."

Tea, fags and painkillers evened Davey out, made him functional. They had some steady work in the morning: a decent chain of washes and a couple of valets that weren't too manky. Tim didn't seem to want to start any sort of conversation and that was fine with Davey—they had work to get on with anyway. He didn't feel he needed to supervise the lad either—he was a good one. It wasn't that washing motors took much skill, but at the same time anybody who said it was a piece of pish was generally doing a crappy job of it. There was a line to walk between attention to detail and getting it done fast and Tim had the knack of it. You had to have a pattern, and once you had a solid pattern, your body could work through it mechanically without missing anything—no stripe of dirt along the lower door, no muck in the corner of the alloy spokes, no soap scum left to dry on the bumper. With a good line of cars to get through, you could get into this rhythm, move fast, and your mind would drift away and wander while your body did its thing.

Davey's mind went places he didn't want it to go. Annalee, white-faced and frail in a too-big hospital bed, sheets too stiff, machinery and tubes and bleeps and buzzes—all this purely his imagination as he hadn't been to see her. *Couldn't* go to see her. Wasn't allowed. *Wisnae fuckin allowed—says who?* Says Sarah. Sarah's word was law for now, but she'd made plenty of threats to take it higher up, to go to the courts. He was waiting for that hit to come, he knew she was winding it up already, could feel it in the anger coming off her last night in radioactive waves. It wasn't that Sarah was quick to get nippy—she was never usually one for unnecessary aggro, always the peacemaker on the drunken nights out of their not-too-distant youth—but when she did get angry, holy fuck, it was cataclysmic. And where the subject of Davey and Annalee was concerned, she had very little patience and the whole thing strung with so many trip wires Tom Cruise could use it as a set piece in his next film.

Davey was valeting a rusty red Ford Fiesta—scrubbing away at the layer of dirt on the inside corners of the door with a rag—when he finally noticed Tim saying his name.

"Wit?!"

Tim was standing with a woman in a long coat, dyed brunette hair showing grey at the roots, face prim and puckered like a schoolteacher's.

Davey launched into his spiel: "A wash fir a wee car is a fiver, any bigger an it's six or seven, dependin oan how much bigger. A hoover is a tenner, a full valet and yer twenty. Ye want the seats shampooed ye can bung another fiver oan tap."

"I'm not here to have my car cleaned." Her accent was only just middle-class, maybe self-taught.

"Well, we don't dae anythin else."

"Detective Inspector McCoist." The woman held out her warrant card at arm's length, lanyard wrapped around her fist. "Is Mr Prentice in?"

"That's me." Sean was marching across the unit towards them. His eyes were cracked red, a cloud of earthy grass smell washing over them as he approached. The detective's nose wrinkled further.

"Mr Prentice, I'm Detective Inspector McCoist." She showed her ID again.

"Alison McCoist... Yer name's Ally McCoist. Is this a wind-up?"

"It's not. No jokes, please, I've heard them all." (Davey felt some sympathy—all the shite car wash patter foisted on him every day, she must get it just as bad.) "Is there somewhere we can sit and talk?" She looked towards the door of the office.

"Aye, course." Sean sat down on one of the Kärcher pressure washing units. "Wit's the problem?"

The detective's mouth was tight, her jaw stiff as she gave both Davey and Tim a bracing look meant to drive them back to their work. They stayed.

"A complaint has been made against you. Yesterday, a man called Dominic Bower reported that he came to speak to you about your TV licence and you chased him away with an air pistol."

Sean shrugged. "A mind a guy comin here tae threaten me, tryin tae *illegally* squeeze money oot me fir a service a don't even use. Maybe a should be the wan makin the complaint."

"It's illegal to own an unlicensed airgun and even more so to threaten to shoot somebody with it."

"Actually, that depends on the power of the gun," Tim butted in. "A pistol under the legal limit doesn't require a firearms certificate." All of them were now looking at him and his face was turning red again. Davey knew Tim was studying law but hadn't ever really asked him anything further. "How's the study-in goin?" was an accepted formality, not an actual question to be answered in any sort of depth.

"Well, let's see this gun then and we'll find out if it's above or below the legal limit," the polis replied. Under the full force of her gaze, Tim's face blistered. He'll need tae get that under control if he's gonnae make a decent lawyer, Davey thought, though he was impressed at how forthright Tim had sounded.

"Do you have a search warrant?" Tim asked.

"What's your name?" the detective countered.

"Am I under suspicion of doing something wrong too?"

"Maybe. Were you here yesterday afternoon when Mr Bower was chased—"

"*Allegedly* chased."

The detective let out a sigh and Sean grinned.

"And no, I wasn't here yesterday afternoon."

"A wis," Davey piped up. "An a didnae see Sean wavin any gun aroon." He found himself looking to Tim to see if he'd made the right move or not but the boy had such a riddy his face was impossible to read.

"And you are?"

Davey looked at Tim again. Tim looked spent now, as if the whole ordeal was a great strain on him. Davey realised the lad had probably never been spoken to by a polis before. Not like this anyway.

"If you want to make a witness statement you have to tell me your name," the detective said, obviously fucked off now, not caring to hide it.

"Davey Burnet. A wis workin here yesterday when the man showed up. There were raised voices, aye, but certainly nae threats or guns."

The detective bored a hole into him before taking out her phone. She looked like she could do with a cuppa, a fag and a couple of pain pills herself. "I need an address and contact number for you."

When she was finished typing it up, she stuffed her phone into her pocket, washing her hands of the situation, keen to get the fuck away from the three of them. As she reached her car—a silver Skoda, a taxi-driver's car—Sean called out: "Hawd oan a second, hen!" She turned, looked ready to clock him. "If ye want a wash, a dae a decent blue-light discoont."

DECEMBER

8

Tis the season at the car wash: on the 14th, Sean hung an air freshener shaped like an evergreen tree on the handle of the office door. "Season's Greetins, boays!" he said.

"Al be the wan greetin lookin at that sad hing," Davey said.

"Good to see you finally getting in the spirit!" Tim was wearing a Santa hat with the Coca-Cola logo stamped on the furry white band. He'd been wearing it since the first of the month, when Sean ripped it off his head by the bobble and tossed it into the freezing water barrel that held the lances. They were giving them out for free at the student union—he got another one. And another, the second being launched up onto the roof of the office. The third stayed on his head.

Sean took a long draw on his joint. He grumbled "Ho-ho-ho" as he puffed out earthy clouds of weed smoke. "Speakin ae spirits, av goat yer Christmas prezzies here." He gave them each a bottle: Buckfast for Davey, red Aftershock for Tim. "Didnae know wit yer drink wis, Tim, but a thoat aw you students would be intae takin shots an that."

"Cheers, Sean!" Tim smiled like an older child who didn't get what he wanted but pretends to be pleased because he knows his parents are doing what they can. "I don't think I've had this flavour before."

"Merry Christmas," Davey said. He hadn't drunk Bucky for years—rocket fuel, he blamed many of the bad decisions in his life on it, knew he was just scapegoating. He unscrewed the cap, sniffed the sweet, medicinal smell of the tonic. There was something festive about it, nostalgic. He thought of Greg and Hammy and McCrory and wondered where they'd be this Christmas. He'd heard McCrory was in the jail for something. Christ, it had been a long time... Davey felt a physical bolt of loneliness—the spirit of the season—and swallowed it down with a mouthful of wine. "It's a sweet yin, must be a good number."

"I've never drank Buckfast straight before," Tim said.

"Ye hud it bent?" Sean chuckled; Tim made himself join in.

"I mean, I've had it in a cocktail."

"Wit?!" Davey and Sean both gaped.

"It's becoming quite trendy as a mixer."

"Fucksake, take a swally." Davey handed him the bottle. "Keep ye warm at least." It was bastard cold out, the pavements pensioner-crippling icy, the air fogged with steam from people and car engines and dog turds, which blended nicely into the melting grit spread everywhere.

They washed a couple of cars, the foam the closest thing Glesga would get to a white Christmas this year. Paulo's now-familiar SUV rolled in near closing time. As ever, he gunned it forwards and skidded to a stop, splashing mucky, soapy water from the gutter all over Davey's and Tim's boots. He'd become a weekly wonder since they'd helped him hide his shagging around from his wife (and girlfriend). He liked the job they'd done and he liked to keep his massive Range Rover clean. More than that, he liked to talk a load of bollocks, and while Tim and Davey worked on his car, they were forced to listen to him.

"Awright, lads!" His bulk dropped down from the high seat. He tossed the keys at Tim, who fumbled them—he always fumbled them. Paulo honked with derisive laughter. "Ahhhh, watch yersel, Michael Jordan! How are ye, Davey Boy?"

"Am awright, Paulo, cheers. Yersel?"

"Happy as a man wae a twelve-inch stawner can be—that's an inch fir every day ae Christmas, aye?! Am aff fir a night in the toon, can yous make the motor sparkle? Goat tae impress the wee burds, ye know?!"

Tim blushed.

"Sure hing, Paulo," Davey said.

"Sean in the office?"

"Aye—"

"Is that a bottle ae Bucky?" Davey had left his bottle on the shelf with the sponges and polishes.

"Help yersel," Davey said. No chance he'd be saying no to Paulo, who was jittering and fired up, face half demonic with the gear, big and unpredictable. Sean had been telling them some wild shit he'd heard through his dealer, Rusty, about their newest loyal customer. Rusty wasn't a reliable source by any means, but gangster or not, it didn't change the fact Paulo was big enough to smash all three of them to paste if he had a mind to, and when he said "Scratch that motor an al scratch yer face", with a smile every time he dropped his car off, it was impossible to tell if he was joking or not.

Paulo checked the number on the bottle. "Might put a shoat in ma cuppa—ye heard ae Irish coffee? This is Glesga tea!"

As Tim and Davey got to work on the four-by-four they heard the echo of Paulo's joke repeating inside the office—*This is Glesga tea!*—followed by his moronic laugh.

"Told you it was popular in cocktails," Tim said.

Davey was in the front smearing window polish on the glass

with a sponge. He put the heater on and cranked it up. "Up tae anythin the night?"

"Maybe meet a few mates for a drink."

"Uni pals?"

"Nah, most of them have gone home already. It'll be folk from school. How about you?"

"Quiet yin fir me." That's what Davey always said. He hoped Tim would stop turning the question around on him every time. Simple solution was to stop asking in the first place but it was easy small talk. "Here, dye like tae go oot an get blootered oan Christmas Eve?"

"Nah, I just go for a couple. Can't ruin Christmas dinner with a hangover—the food's the best part of the whole thing. You?"

"No any mare. It'll be a coupla cans in front ae the *Father Ted Christmas Special* fir me.*" Davey used to love going out on Christmas Eve, in the pub till chucking-out time, then wandering the streets with his pals, singing, high as all sweet baby Jesus. Ruining Christmas dinner didn't enter his mind at all—his maw couldn't heat up Uncle Ben without burning the bastard, let alone manage a turkey and all the trimmings. (He shuddered at what would be in store for him in two weeks' time.) It had been a long time since one of those wild nights. He hadn't consciously broken away from his friends, but getting his life together when Annalee came along—getting a stable job, cutting down the drink, completely binning the drugs—seemed to come at that cost. Christmases after that had been bed before midnight, him and Sarah being elves, putting together toy kitchens, playsets, a bike, eating Auld Saint Nick's mince pies and taking a bite out of Rudolph's carrot. Which sounded idyllic now but at the time he'd resented it, felt stuffed and suffocated—he and Sarah nipped at each other over complicated instructions, every present under the tree was a money worry needling them, Davey would say they should just have a Chinese this year instead of doing a big meal and Sarah would storm off to bed.

They spent the rest of the job on Paulo's car quoting from the *Father Ted* special in awful attempts at Irish accents. ("Wit's that, Ireland by way ae Bangladesh?") The Big Man came in and out the office for a natter—"Ye ever huv any problems wae the drains here? Aw that soap scum an shite pourin doon them, never gets clogged up? Here, if a put a UV light oer they seats would they still show up aw ma spunk an that or huv ye cleant the DNA away? A take it when ye want tae clean the unit up yeez can just blast it wae the hose, aye?"—in between cups of tea while he waited for Sean to roll another joint. Sean's face was a picture of beatific suffering (blazed Christ on the cross) as he listened to Paulo laugh at his own jokes and pester him with questions about where he ordered his supplies from and how he managed his books considering it was mostly a cash business. "This place could be a real money-spinner," he always said. "Bags ae potential!" (It was just a wee hand car wash, Davey thought whenever Paulo said this, so the potential must be for cleaning something other than cars.)

Davey handed the keys back and Paulo was as effusive as ever with his praise. "Stunnin, lads! Here's yer wee Christmas tips!" He gave each of them a hundred-pound note peeled from the money clip in his pocket—many more folded bills remaining. "Mind an no stick those in the bank, awright? Ye don't want tae know where they came fae, get them spent! Merry Christmas!"

9

Winter was rough. In summer, the punters wanted the flies and bird shit washed off their motors; in winter they wanted the salt and grit hosed off before they started eating through the paint. So work was steady but the days were bastard cold. Davey and Tim wore layers of T-shirts over their thermals, two pairs of socks inside their boots, and what Sean called a "glove sandwich"—disposable latex gloves both over and under a pair of thick, mountaineering ones—to try to keep their hands dry and warm as they scrubbed and polished and hosed, rinse and repeat, rinse and repeat. "Wax on, wax off," as Mr Miyagi said—another piece of shite patter customers foisted on them regularly.

Paulo had dropped his motor off that morning on cue—one week exactly since his last visit. Mercifully, today was one of those days he handed over his keys and fucked off into town saying he had business to attend to. He never said what kind of business, though it was very clear he wanted them to believe it was in some way illicit. Rumours continued to leak through to Sean that Paulo was actually as heavy as he thought he was, up to his neck in all sorts, running the schemes of the east end and Lanarkshire, a bogeyman to small-time dealers and those who couldn't pay their tick. "Aye, so Rusty says," Davey would always mutter, though he was sure to do a good job on Paulo's car every time. "He geez good tips," he said whenever Sean pointed this out. "Am no shitein it fae guy wae vanity plates."

Davey and Tim had already finished polishing Paulo's colossal schlong surrogate and parked it in the small yard across the road which belonged to the car wash. It sat by itself, Paulo being the only customer dropping in for a valet that morning.

"Christ, a hope it's a quiet wan the day," Davey said. "Ma hawn's killin me." He flexed his right hand, stiff and aching inside its glove sandwich. "Sometimes when a wake up, ma fingers are stuck like this…"—he curled his fingers in towards his palm—"…as if am hawdin the trigger ae the lance. Goat tae pry them loose again. Fuckin sore."

"Sounds it. It'll be worse in this weather too," Tim said, Santa hat keeping his ears warm, making him look like a pillock. "If you want, I could do all the hose stuff today, you can scrub."

"See how busy it is. Hope it's fuckin quiet." Davey folded his arms, sticking his hands under his armpits.

Sean came out the office, hands tucked inside the waistband of his joggy bottoms, cupping his balls. "Am gonnae go get us some rolls an square fae the shoap, lads, be back in a bit."

"Yass!" they called after him as he set off down the street.

Davey and Tim stamped their feet and watched the road for cars.

"Fuckin Baltic," Davey said.

"Yeah, it's chilly all right…" Tim agreed. Their breath fogged up the air. "Bit of work might be good to get the blood pumping."

"Aye, right enough…"

"Will be good when Sean gets back with the sausages. That'll warm us up."

"Aye, Sean's sausage will warm ye right up!" They laughed a little then fell back into silence. They scanned the road. No sign of any cars indicating to come in. "How lang ye goat aff uni fir the holidays?"

"Not back till the second week of January."

"Fucksake, it's awright fir some." Davey chuckled. "University ae Life doesnae huv holidays." Christ, Sean needs tae get the bloody stereo fixed, Davey thought. *University ae Life? Listen tae yer fuckin sel.* They used to pump tunes loud from an old ghetto blaster Sean had picked up at a charity shop but the speakers had blown out last month—probably committed suicide rather than play *Definitely Maybe* one more time. Now Davey and Tim were stuck trying to make small talk in between jobs. In years there wasn't a huge gap between them, but in life experience there was a gulf. Davey hardly knew what to say to the lad.

"An how is the law school goin?"

"It's not really *law school*, not like, you know… I'm studying it along with politics and sociology."

Davey had heard this before, probably. "Ye dae exams—" Davey's phone rang (*thank fuck!*) and he stepped away from Tim to answer. He pulled a glove off with his teeth.

"Maw, am at work, a cannae—"

"At work?! Wit the fuck ye daein at work, Davey?"

"Wit dye hink?"

"Yer sposed tae be at the fuckin courthoose! It's almost two an yer no here yet!"

"Wit?" Davey's stomach was twisting. His brain was gibbering *Nonononono.* "Maw, calm doon. The hearin's oan the twenty-first—"

"It *is* the fuckin twenty-first! It's the day!"

"Naw, it's the morra. Am sure it's the morra… Tim!"

"Aye, Davey?"

"Wit's the date?"

"Twenty-first."

Fuuuuuuuuuck!

The 21st of December at 2 p.m., Davey was due at the family court to discuss access to Annalee. He hadn't seen her or Sarah since the night the wean was taken into hospital. Annalee had recovered well but her mother hadn't. Things went as Davey had half expected, the summons arriving with numb shock and long-awaited finality, like a diagnosis of terminal illness—everything was ending, just sooner rather than later.

Davey's maw was having a meltdown over the phone line. "Twenty minutes, Davey, ye better get here or—"

He hung up. "Fuck! Fuck! Fuuuck!"

"You all right, Davey? What's the problem, mate?"

"A need tae go!" He started to run down the street then turned and came back. The court was across the town. If he ran, there was no way he'd be there on time. He could see the look on Sarah's face if he turned up late in his scabby, wet work gear, red-faced and pishing sweat, the rest of them all sat there dressed in prim office wear.

There was one way he could maybe, just maybe, make it...

The Voice of Reason wasn't in his head this time; the part was being played by Tim: "Davey, pal, you can't do that! Fuck, please don't! What will I tell Sean? Come on, mate. *Please*. Run down the street and see if you can get a taxi. I'll come with you! What if Paulo gets back before you do? He'll fucking kill you, man! Come on, Davey! Davey?!" But it was all a backing track, drowned by the screaming buzz in Davey's brain as he took the keys to the Range Rover off the hook.

10

Davey swerved the walloper-on-wheels onto the road. It was an automatic, so he hit the pedal and the thing moved, lunging forward, engine growling with steroidal aggression. He'd parked it for Paulo a few times now but he'd never had a *proper* shot of it. He could see immediately what someone like Paulo liked about it, and he'd probably have enjoyed it too if his heart weren't climbing up his throat and his brain weren't going on a mountain-slope slalom between *Drive faster, ten minutes left!* and *Scratch this motor an Paulo's gonnae rip yer insides oot an use ye fir a pish pot!*

He kept it at a baw-hair over thirty through the built-up streets—he was in a hurry but the last thing he needed was to get stopped or flashed by a speed camera in Paulo's car. The Voice of Reason kicked in: *This is fuckin stupit, this is really fuckin stupit.* But it was too late, pointless to turn back now. Him showing up now could be the difference between seeing Annalee every weekend or every Boxing Day. He wasn't a bad man and he wasn't a bad dad, just a bit careless sometimes. Sometimes his mind slipped from what was important, and who isn't guilty of that? He found himself praying at stoplights. *Moan tae fuck, turn green! Just get me there. Get me where a need tae be, big man, an al be in church every Sunday, front pew, right by the aisle. A tenner in ma poackit fir the collection box. Al quit smokin, quit drinkin, quit watchin porn. Ma only leisure activity will be readin the Bible. Al tidy the flat an learn tae cook a proper meal.*

Al buy every fuckin book Jamie Oliver's ever written, just please, please, pretty fuckin please turn green!

He crossed the Clyde and turned onto the road that ran parallel, the court just blocks away now. According to the clock on the Range Rover's touch screen, he had just under five minutes. He pulled his phone out, wanting his maw to tell him exactly where he was going inside the building. He was scrolling for her number, mobile in his lap, eyes flicking up to glance at the road. Light ahead was green—*thank fuck*—but he didn't realise the car ahead wasn't moving until he almost smashed into the back of it. He slammed the brake and the behemoth screeched to a stop in a spray of grit and cloud of black rubber.

There must have been an inch between the nose of the four-by-four and the bumper of the red Corolla in front, if that. Davey, heart racing, exhaled slowly. The car wasn't waiting at the light, it was parked just before the junction on double yellows. "Absolute cunt," Davey said aloud. He reversed to give himself some space to move out of the lane but there was another squeal of tyres and the buzz-saw roar of an engine being gunned and the car behind—a luminous-green boy-racer bellend-mobile—pulled up alongside him and stopped, blocking his way.

"Moan tae fuck, man!" Davey yelled at the driver—sure enough, a young lad in peaked cap and gym gear, tank top (in December, in Scotland) showing off full-sleeve tattoos on both arms. "Oot ma fuckin road ye prick! The fuck ye daein?" The gym gear wasn't just for show—the guy was built like Arnold Schwarzenegger in his statesman years (still fucking huge), and these days Davey knew better than to have a go at someone like that, but he was desperate. He was minutes away now, metres from the place, and stuck. His hands were white at the wheel. "Get the fuck oot ma way, ye absolute chopper!" The guy didn't seem to be listening anyway. He looked round, peering into the car but not at Davey, who was still screaming out the driver's-side window. "Fuck's yer problem, man?!"

Then Davey felt a blast of cold air and turned to find the passenger door open and another tracksuited hulk climbing into the Range Rover. Hatless, the guy showed off a shaven skull, a broken boxer's nose, and matching cauliflower ears. All in, he was a brutalised slab of meat, and although a bit more weather-worn than the driver, they definitely swam in the same gene pool.

Davey's stomach dropped away from him, like he'd fallen in a dream only to jolt awake to a nightmare.

"Hi-aye!" the baldy boxer said. "Follow that motor there, go when it goes, stoap when it stoaps, aarighty?" He pointed to the green car with the tip of an eager-looking lock-back knife, the wood of the handle worn smooth to a dull shine.

Davey nodded.

The courthouse receded in the rear-view mirror, Davey's hope sinking out of sight along with it. Though it later seemed a selfish thought, he decided his problems had received a free upgrade right then, and his mind focused on keeping his sweaty hands on the steering wheel—*dae as am telt, hawns visible, nae fuckin aboot, nae funny business…*

"Keep up, laddie," the shaven gym gorilla in the passenger seat said. His brother drove—as the (pea)souped-up Corsa suggested—like an arsehole. He revved his engine at red

66

lights, the de-mufflered engine a wailing testament to steroid-shrivelled testes, launched forward as soon as they flashed amber, then came screeching to a halt at the next inevitable set of reds. With Davey "keeping up", they bunny-hopped their way down the streets until they turned into a long, narrow alley between a decrepit storage warehouse and a high, crumbling wall that blocked off an embankment leading down to railway tracks.

The driver wearing the cap got out and strolled over to the Range Rover, no hurry, his stride confident but waddling in the way of the overblown bodybuilder.

"Oot," the knifeman said.

Davey had no sooner opened the door than a pair of hands grabbed him by the collar and yanked him out onto the ground, where he landed face first in wet gravel. He tasted dirt, felt grit between his teeth. He rolled over to see a thin strip of cold sky between the leaning brick walls on either side before it was blocked out by a rain of kicks and punches which thundered down on him. Screaming, Davey rolled over, curling up in a ball to protect himself from the attack. Sparkling pain blitzed most of his thoughts but somewhere under it all was the memory of the blade and a hysterical chant of *gonnae get stabbed, gonnae get stabbed, they're gonnae fuckin stab ye…* He felt piss washing hot down his thighs.

"There it is!" one of the goons said. "Stoap, noo, stoap, that's it there!" They both started laughing. "Held oot nae bad actually—Croaker said the loon fancied himsel as a bit ae a hard man…" It was the voice of the older, baldy one with the knife. He had a kind of teuchter accent—not from around Glesga, but not from the proper Highlands either, somewhere north-east, maybe Dundee or Aberdeen. "Aarighty. We'll stoap hittin ye noo, mannie, as lang as ye put this bag oan yer heed, OK?"

Davey looked up through one good eye—the other already swollen shut—and saw the man was holding a black sack, the kind of sack that's only purpose seemed to be to go over a hostage's head. Davey wondered, in his addled, frightened state, where you'd even get something like that—*is there a shoap that just makes heed sacks fir hostage-takin?* He almost giggled then saw the knife was still in Baldy's other hand. Davey nodded.

"Fit wis that?" Baldy said.

"Aye," Davey croaked. "Nae problem."

"Nae problem?" They both chuckled again. "He says it's nae problem. Gid! That's fit a like tae hear."

The bag went over Davey's head, putting him in the dark. Then someone stomped on his face, putting him somewhere even darker.

11

Davey shivered and woke up. Rain was dripping down the back of his neck. He couldn't see and started gulping in panic breaths but there was something covering his mouth and he couldn't get the air in properly. He began wheezing, trying to call out.

"Boay's awake," someone said. The voice brought everything back—the big boxer bastart jumping into the car, the knife, the beating, the black sack over his head. That was his voice—the baldy one.

"Fit's that sound he's divvin?" said the other one, the younger brother. "Like hiccups or somethin."

"Havin a panic attack, a reckon," said the older brother.

"Will this help?" Davey took a hard kick in the stomach and spewed his ring up into the bag over his head.

The brothers burst out laughing. "Fucksake! This guy's a fuckin riot, pissin himsel an pukin everywhere. Must be a richt good laugh oan the toon ae a Seturday nicht—" The younger brother was cut off by a third voice, one Davey hadn't heard before:

"Ho, Mince an Mealy! A hope yer no bein mean tae oor pal here," it said. A man's voice—deep, local accent, thirty-a-day habit evident in the roughness of the throat, the phlegm crackling in the vowels.

"Fit like, Mr Croaker?" said the older brother.

"Bad back fae too much shaggin but other than that a cannae complain, Mince," Croaker said.

"Sounds as if ye shouldnae be complainin at aw, like," said the younger brother—Mealy, by default—with a stupid laugh.

"Aye well, complainin is an auld man's prerogative, son. Go and sort oot the motor. Noo... let's see him."

The pure darkness was torn away; Davey found himself on the ground in the freezing rain. The sun had gone down. He was in an industrial yard, abandoned by the looks of it. By two pairs of car headlights—the green Corsa and a black sedan he didn't recognise—he could see buckled shutters, Heras fencing in various states of disrepair, old barrels and other bits of general detritus that build up in these places.

A man crouched in front of him, his face coming so close Davey could smell ash and garlic on his steaming breath. The skin of his lined face hung loose like a mask, his features shrouded by wrinkles and the lank hair that curled down almost to his shoulders. The stark white of the headlights caught the greys and made them shine, a halo around an ugly angel.

"Who the fuck is this?" Croaker said. He stood up. "Mince! Mealy!"

The older beefcake brother waddled over.

"Who in fuck's name is this guy?!"

"Fit dye mean, like?" Mince said.

"A mean, that's no Paulo McGuinn."

"Well, if that's no Paulo McGuinn then fa is he?" Mince said.

Croaker stared at Mince until the muscleman had to look away. When he spoke, he spoke softly, making Mince get closer to hear him. He separated his words, overenunciating: "That is wit a just asked *you*."

Mince tried to speak but couldn't find the words. He looked like he was chewing something.

"Ye tellin me ye mistook this wee cunt fir Paul fuckin McGuinn?"

"Well, a thought he maybe looked a bit young, like, but… A dinnae know fit the cunt looks like."

Croaker turned away and closed his eyes, kneading his forehead with the heel of his hand. "Ye don't know wit the cunt a telt ye tae kidnap looks like?"

"Well, ye didnae say… we had his car make an reg an that so a thought—"

"Yev no heard ae fuckin Facebook?!"

"Well—"

"Ye useless, sheep-shaggin prick!" Croaker screamed, his voice wheezing. Mince scrunched up his face as spittle sprayed over him. "Go an fuckin stawn oer there away fae me. Go!" Mince slunk off towards the green car.

Croaker crouched down in front of Davey, who had pushed himself up into a sitting position on the wet ground. "Right, yer no Paulo, so who the fuck are ye?"

Davey started to tremble. He felt sick and hungry at the same time. His limbs were weak and insubstantial and he wasn't sure what would happen if he tried to move them. "D-Davey Burnet."

"Davey Burnet?"

"Fae Carntyne." It had been a long time since Davey had lived there, back when he had friends to run around with. His name wouldn't mean much there any more.

"Davey Burnet fae Carntyne. Paulo's goat himsel a chauffeur noo?"

Davey shook his head. "A don't huv anythin tae dae wae Paulo, a barely know the guy."

71

"But ye dae know him then. Yer no just some stupit fuckin joyrider."

"A wis just borrowin the motor! A needed tae get tae the court—" Sarah and Annalee popped into his head then. Christ, he might never see them again. What if this mad bastard was going to kill him? He started to sob. "A wis late, a needed tae get tae... tae get tae—"

"The court. Ye said."

"So a took his motor—"

"This motor?" Croaker moved out the way and pointed past the two cars with their headlights on. Davey could make out the shadow of the big Range Rover in the distance and the other bodybuilder—Mealy—standing next to it. Suddenly, he was lit up by a bright orange flame. He started running. The flames licked their way up a short length of rag soaked in petrol, hanging from the open cap of the four-wheel drive's fuel tank.

The explosion lifted the car into the air—the doors flew off, the windows shattered into vapour, the burning shell clattered to the ground on melting tyres. The noise was visceral, as if something else had exploded inside Davey's chest. The shockwave knocked him over again. He cracked his head against the concrete. Blood dripped from his left ear; a piercing whistle muffled the roar of the flames which lit up the abandoned yard and blotted out the night sky.

Davey saw feet crunching over gravel and weeds towards the remaining cars.

"Fit we gonna div aboot the laddie?"

"Fuck aw. He's a naebdy, might even be a fuckin civilian, Christ Awmighty. No worth huvin tae clean up his body an aw, yous huv made enough mess as it is the night."

Headlights swept over Davey as the cars turned and drove off. He cried because he was alive and he cried because he was in deep, deep shit.

12

The sound they made was pathetic but they looked cute. Too cute to resist, apparently, as DI McCoist grabbed one of the whining brindle puppies and tucked it inside her long coat, close to her thumping heart.

McCoist had been asked to chum along with the uniforms and an SSPCA inspector to close down a front for a puppy farm being run out of a spacious suburban home in Cathcart—the sting being the "Special Assignment" she'd been promised. Once again, it wasn't really a task for someone of her rank, but little McCoist did lately was. Not since the Fuck-Up. So she found herself chasing down vandals, getting into games of verbal soggy biscuit with eejits at dirty little car washes and, currently, getting into the hair-covered passenger seat of a Transit van that reeked of dog pish next to the baldy SSPCA guy, who seemed to be angling for a place on one of those daytime reality programmes on Channel 5—*Authoritarian Pedants Given a Little Taste of Power vs the Working-Class Scum*.

They parked down the street and around the corner from the house to talk tactics. "You have your boys get round the back and over the fence and me and you will go up to the front door. If I knock and nobody answers, I've got the authority to have the door opened—the legal right to get it open any way necessary, even if we have to take it off the hinges—"

"They're not boys," McCoist interrupted.

"Sorry?"

"PCs McClelland and Mannan are both women."

"...Right." He huffed and thankfully stopped talking until they were ready to go.

McCoist took out a radio, hit the button. "Now," she said. The SSPCA man slammed down on the accelerator, tyres screaming in a wheelspin as they took off round the block and came wailing up to an average-looking family home—could do with a fresh spray of roughcast, a lick of paint on the porch timbers.

Ross Kemp snatched the handbrake, bringing them to a jerking stop, and jumped out of the door. He had a stab-proof strapped on and some plastic cable-tie handcuffs which he let dangle conspicuously from his belt hook.

McCoist signalled lazily to her officers. "Round to the back door."

"Yes, ma'am!" they chorused. The pair were fairly fresh but even they weren't as excited as the Mitchell brother charging up the path. He was attempting to adopt a mask of steely determination but if he'd had a tail (like the hostages they were about to liberate) it would have been wagging.

"Plenty of dog shite in the grass there if you're needing to collect evidence." McCoist smirked, following him through the front garden.

There was no need to batter down the door and no dramatic on-foot chase for the uniforms—still, Dug the Bounty Munter was proud as a pistol with his big bust, as he narrated his way around the house, counting the puppies in cages: "These are being sold as cockapoos—very trendy, popular pets—but there's no real way to tell what mix is actually in these ones... Miniature dachshunds, these have a street value of fifteen hundred pounds sterling, and see the colour of them? Double dapple—that's bad breeding, should be on the banned list, they have all sorts of genetic problems... Not seeing any illegal breeds, though we do have some Staffies, popular in dogfights, can be made vicious if they're not trained properly, not looked after... We need to talk to the homeowner, see if she'll tell us where they're coming from..."

McCoist let him take care of it. The woman who was selling the dogs took him into the kitchen to talk—McCoist heard him turning down a cup of tea as if it were a bundle of hundreds stuffed in a brown envelope—while McClelland and Mannan conducted a search of the property.

A snub-nosed wee pup with brown tiger stripes and a white belly was keening at the bars of its cage, its front paws attempting to scrabble up the wire, its pink nose pushing out through the gap. The cage stank—there were ten more pups crammed in beside it, all of them living in their own filth, scrawny from having been taken away from their mothers before they were ready to wean.

McCoist held her hand out to it and its tongue shot out to lap at her, slurping away, almost as if it wanted to suckle on her fingertip. She felt the nibble of razor-sharp teeth and pulled her hand back. "You wee dick!" She reached out again, smile on her face, the tongue ticklish against her skin. "Do I taste nice?"

A thought struck her.

No, it was wild. *Crazy.* But Tess and Cam had always wanted a dog—years 5 through 9 had been a constant barrage of pleading, whining, crying, demanding, wheedling, cajoling. Sure, it had been a few years now since she last recalled the twins mentioning it—had they asked since the divorce?

Maybe not—but that kind of desperate want didn't just go away, did it?

Stupid.

The puppy nibbled her again. The reasons she'd always refused them before came back: who would clean up after it? Who would walk it every day? Who would train it not to be a menace? "We will, we will!" No, *I* will, she knew. But what was to stop her from doing that? She certainly had the space. Some company might be nice, a bit of exercise to unwind…

Crazy.

She heard the uniforms stomping about upstairs. She could get in trouble. She could get fired. So fucking what? The job was relentlessly pish since it all went tits-up last year with the Knightley thing. Demotion in all but name, made to scoop up all the shite as an unofficial punishment. She still kept her desk in the MIT office, but now it was a shrine to incompetence, a public naughty step. Everything deemed too unimportant for any of the other detectives to waste their time on came filtering down to DI McCoist, the gutter. It was embarrassing, ridiculous, and everybody could see it. Even before then it had been shite, hadn't it? Nearly twenty years of slogging through the figurative (and occasionally literal) sewer pipes of Glasgow—and Alison McCoist was one helluva name for a polis in Glasgow. It brought smiles to faces in the Rangers neighbourhoods but in the Celtic ones she might as well have scrawled "Fuck the Pope" across her forehead. People weren't forthcoming with the police at the best of times—the name often did not help. She'd climbed the ladder, but didn't things just keep getting harder? Getting worse? She didn't get through a single day without thinking of packing it in.

Mental.

She tickled its tummy through the bars and it toppled over, paws kicking the air. It would likely get put down. There were so many of them, they couldn't all possibly be rehomed. ("It's a sad part of the job," she pictured Donal Macuntyre saying, displaying his stoicism in the face of grim reality, looking like a shaved testicle.) It was three days till Christmas and she hadn't been shopping yet. The twins wouldn't be over till Boxing Day but it wasn't like that actually gave her any more time.

Fuck it, they won't miss one dog.

She flipped the catch on the cage door, reached in and grabbed the puppy by the scruff of its neck, stuffed the kicking thing inside her coat. She bent over, awkwardly, the dog's warmth against her, its smell rubbing off on her shirt, and ran out the door and down the street, all the way to where she'd left her car.

She popped open the boot, had a quick look over the shoulder, and tossed the animal inside. She closed the boot—a pang of shame at the muffled squealing—and ran back to the house.

"Ma'am?" PC Mannan was staring at McCoist, puffed out and red-faced in the doorway.

"Thought I saw something odd out the window, went to take a look—it was nothing."

Mannan gave her the kind of placating smile McCoist used on her deranged old auntie whenever she started banging on about whoever she believed to be stealing her teabags this week. Young officers treated her to this often. Her reputation preceded her—the Dannie Gibb murder was still echoing around the city a year after Stuart Knightley's sentencing, mostly due to its gruesomeness, his soft, gormless face still popping up in the papers now and again because another inmate had had a go at him or he'd been given Netflix privileges or some bollocks—but they were too junior to display their contempt openly, so they offered false sympathy instead.

The SSPCA inspector finished his bit and began loading the dogs into his van with the help of the uniforms—they put the seller in their own car.

"See you back at the station, ma'am?" Mannan asked.

"Yeah… later."

Mannan stood watching her, that condescending concern on her face again, then tipped the peak of her cap and got into her car.

McCoist let them get out of sight before returning to her own motor and opening the boot. The puppy's rotten fear scent wafted out at her—it had also taken a sludgy crap, which it was now standing in.

"Fuck."

Its front paws scrabbled on the lip of the boot, trying to get out. It *was* cute though.

The dog sat in McCoist's lap on the drive back to her house. She'd spread her jacket over her knees, which was now covered in poo. The pup clambered up at the steering wheel and up McCoist's chest trying to lick her face, pushing its muzzle into her hands to get her to pet it as she attempted to push it down out of sight. You could get a fine for having an animal loose in your car—you'd get worse if you were a polis and the animal in question was evidence from a dog-mill operation that probably had its roots in organised crime in some other country.

Once home, she scooped the dog up in the bundle of her soiled jacket, ran straight through the door, up the stairs, and dumped the whole load into the bathtub. She hosed both dog and jacket down with the shower nozzle, crap melting and sliding down the drain, the smell of warmed-up shit making her gag. The dog scrambled up the side of the tub, slipping on the porcelain, yelping as if it were being tortured.

Drying it off didn't go very well either. It slipped out of the towel, skited out the bathroom on wet tiles and began shaking itself, spraying water all over the walls, then rubbed itself on the carpet, which was apparently a better way of getting the job done than the towel.

It bounded down the stairs, tripped and rolled the last three, shook itself again, then set about sniffing, nibbling and scratching everything in sight.

McCoist had to get back to the station—she left the dog with a cereal bowl full of water and half a pack of cold meat on a plate. "Be good!" It howled miserably as she closed the door. A sinkhole of worry opened up inside her—*You've done it again, another fuck-up.* Not on the same scale as the Knightley thing, at least, but one more fuck-up on top of the Fuck-Up could finish her. Well, if she could no longer have the job she wanted, maybe she could have the home life she wanted instead—and that little looted dog just might be the key.

When she got home from work after skipping out early—not as if she had anything important to do; they'd only miss her if a blocked toilet needed investigating (in fact, they probably wouldn't even trust her with that in case the clogged-bog inquiry turned out to be a Dennis Nilsen situation)—she found the kitchen swimming in urine and studded with turds. The puppy, delighted to see her, splashed its tail in the puddles.

13

"THREE HUNNER AN TWENTY-SEVEN FUCKIN THOUSAND POUND!" Paulo bellowed. The gyprock walls vibrated. Paulo took huge, deep breaths, nostrils wide, shoulders moving up and down, his body puffing up like a hissing turkey about to peck some cunt's eyes out. Davey wasn't sure if Paulo had finally run out of steam after ten straight minutes of screaming and swearing and elaborating on the various ways he might torture and murder Davey and then defile his corpse, or if he was just taking a quick break. Paulo licked his lips and a smile crept over them. Dropping nearly to a whisper he added: "An sixty-four pence."

Davey's body had the consistency of a cheese string. "A swear, Paulo, it wisnae ma fault—"

The Big Man lifted a huge bear paw to strike him and Davey flinched, throwing his arms up over his face. The blow didn't land; Davey wasn't smashed through the wall. Paulo's fist hung there above him, a row of sovvies as big as two-pound coins flashing in the stark light of the office. "Ad kick yer cunt right in, wee man, if somebdy hudnae done such a good joab ae it awready."

Sean glowered from the other side of the room, hands trembling over a *Street Fighter* video-cassette case where he kept the day's grass and skins, his grinder and poke. He sure as fuck wasn't going to jump in for Davey but nor did he want a man being killed in his office. So he did what he could: rolled a fatty.

Paulo continued: "An a still might, if ye don't tell me exactly wit a want tae know. Ye understawn?"

Davey nodded, head bobbing like a dashboard toy. "A-aye, Paulo."

"Hawd back anythin an al take the missus' GHDs tae yer fuckin toes. Right?"

"R-right."

"Act fuckin smart an al put the nozzle ae that Kärcher right up yer arse an pull the trigger till the water's comin oot yer mooth like a fuckin fountain. Followin me?"

"Aye, a get ye, Paulo."

"An Uncle Paulo doesnae believe in lube, son."

Davey nodded, swallowing hard, throat dry, the reek of the bifter Sean had sparked stinging his eyes, fighting back tears.

"So, ye bumped ma motor. Then wit happened?"

"A didnae bump it... A wisnae gonnae—a just needed tae get tae the court cause, cause—" The slap made his ear ring again, burst the inside of his cheek open against his teeth.

"That's gettin smart. A don't want tae know why, the noo a just want tae know wit happened. Get tae it."

Davey went through the hijacking, the knife, the journey to the alley by the tracks where they beat him and black-bagged him. Waking in the rain in the industrial estate, the blinding, deafening explosion as the car (all £327,000.64 of it) went up in flames. Paulo asked for detailed descriptions of the teuchters—Mince and Mealy—and Croaker, their accents and mannerisms, the cars they drove. Davey did his best, his memory occasionally jogged and clouded by another slap or a flick to the nose.

When he was finished, Paulo folded his arms and leant his bulk against the IKEA unit which functioned as the car wash's canteen—microwave, grill and mini fridge among a sea of crumbs and spilt milk. His eyes bored through Davey to the wall behind him, unblinking. Looking beyond him, brain turning over, pistons pumping as hard as the supercharged V6 of his now-exploded car.

The silence was growing unbearable. Davey waited for another kicking. Eventually he chose to speak up and snap the tension even if it meant bringing it upon himself. "Al gee ye the money back, Paulo. A will, a swear a will."

"How, Davey Boy? How ye gonnae get ma money? Sell a kidney? Huv a bake sale?"

"Al hink ae somethin, Paulo, a will." In his desperation, Davey was entirely earnest, but already the obstacles were falling in front of his scattered train of thought. He had nothing in the bank except the money for next month's bills. He had no house to sell, no car. His telly, his clothes, his furniture would add up to a fraction of what that motor was worth.

Paulo let him squirm under a long, heavy-browed gaze which then opened up into one of his chummy smiles. "Look, Davey Boy. It wis just a motor. Some sheets ae metal and a bit ae rubber. Wit's important is *you* are awright, son."

Davey had a stupid smile on his beaten face, clinging to the almost believable sound of concern in Paulo's voice while the Voice of Reason groaned in disgust at his wretchedness, his wilful gullibility.

"We'll hink ae a way ye can pay me back. Plenty ae time, we're aw pals here." Paulo turned his smile on Sean, whose stoned face was slack and dejected. "Put the kettle oan, gaffer."

14

Davey was chaining fags in the office, Sean working his way through another joint. They sat in silence, the weight of the world-ending reaming-out Paulo had delivered still a physical presence in the room fifteen minutes after the Big Man himself had left.

A blast of fresh air came in with Tim. "All right, lads! How…" He didn't finish the sentence, read the room: Davey chewing on a rolly, eyes on his boots—his face a patchwork of livid bruises—Sean glowering at him, his staring, bloodshot eyes looking more paranoid than at the end of an eight-joint shift. "Fuck, Davey, what happened to you?"

"Tim, yer sacked," Sean said, without looking round.

"What?"

"I said yer sacked. Fired, canned, witever. Pick up yer tea mug an fuck off, son."

"But—"

Sean took a wad of cash from the small lockbox he used for the day's takings and stuffed it into Tim's hand. "Severance pay. Now go."

Tim looked hurt and pissed off but he was too polite to tell Sean to fuck off; he left without saying anything, his Santa hat scrunched up in his hand with the money. When the door closed the weight settled in again.

"Ye gonnae say anythin?" Sean said, finally.

"A fuckt it," Davey mumbled.

"Fuckt it? *Fuckt it?!* Yev goan an hud its bastart inbred weans! Paulo McGuinn owns us now. He fuckin owns us. Every penny this place earns is headin aff the books an intae his poacket."

"A know it wis an expensive motor, Sean, but al pay him back eventually. Wan day it'll be oer."

"Wan day?!" Sean hoofed the wall, making a massive hole in the gyprock. "There is no fuckin day! Ye never pay this kind ae debt back, ye fuckin eejit! Ye understawn that? Never. That cunt is never gonnae let us go, we're part ae his fuckin *empire*. An now av hud tae fuckin gee Tim the sack an aw—a don't want him involved in aw this, it's no his fuckin mess."

"A know, Sean, a know, awright! It's mine!" Davey started pacing. "An it's no just Paulo." His voice was cracking. "Sarah… I missed the fuckin court, am no gonna get tae see—"

Sean held up his hand. "Just fuckin get oot there an get tae work. Someone's goat tae earn some fuckin money roon here."

It was a slow afternoon, which was good because Davey's body was aching all over from the doing he'd got the day before. At least it was the last shift before the Christmas break. Washing cars was a physical job, and with every stretch to reach a roof or bend to scrub a wheel, something hurt. When he'd finally got home last night and stripped off his rain-soaked, vomit-caked, piss-damp clothes and jumped in the shower, he found brown and purple bruises already blossoming all over. His face was unrecognisable it was so beat and swollen. If the image in the mirror wasn't bad enough, the voicemails Sarah and his mum had left him offered a whole new world of brutality.

While he worked, slowly, trying to ease himself around the cars gently, his mind switched tracks between the morning's debriefing with Paulo—where he'd extracted every single thing Davey could remember about the day before like a mouthful of rotten teeth—and Sarah's words coming small and tinny from his phone: "A didnae want a big fight, an a guess a goat that, but a… a thought yed at least want tae show up. Say somethin fir yersel, fir Annalee…" He had wanted to say something. To stand up in front of them all and say how much he loved his daughter, how much he needed her in his life—certainly more than she needed him in hers. Was it too late to say it now? Would the words even come out his mouth if he had the chance again?

A numbness set in that every so often would be shattered by a sudden flush of adrenaline and an immediate, desperate warning in his head that he was about to be attacked—but nobody was there. *Get a fuckin grip*, he told himself.

A silver Focus pulled up to the kerb and out scrambled a woman in an expensive but worn-out jogging suit—clearly not worn-out from jogging though: the car's suspension groaned as she struggled out of her seat. She handed over her keys and said something about going to the shops or the Barras or maybe the bank or something—Davey, still preoccupied and pinballing between numb and edgy, wasn't really listening, but he gathered that she wanted her motor hoovered and all the rest.

As soon as he opened the passenger door, he knew from the smell what kind of car it was. There are people who show up every week who can't bear even a splash of mud on the wheel arch, and there are people who treat their car as a mobile bin. This was the second kind. There was fag ash on every surface, so much dog hair on the seat it looked like it had been covered by a rug, and the car mats in the footwells couldn't be seen for the empty bottles and McDonald's cartons piled up in a grotty impression of a ball pit at a kiddies' soft play.

"Fuck me, what an absolute, rank —" Then Davey noticed the child sitting in the back seat. A boy, he looked about six or seven years old—a bit older than Annalee—and was tapping away at a Game Boy while carefully avoiding looking at Davey.

Sean blew his lid. "She's left her fuckin wean wae us? While we hoover her fuckin car, she's gone an left her wean here."

"Wit dae we dae?"

"Well, yel huv tae get him oot the fuckin hing while ye work."

"He's goat nae shoes oan, he's in his jammies."

Sean flapped his arms. "Well, a dunno, fuckin hoover roon him then, fucksake!"

Davey tried chatting to the boy while he worked—"That a Game Boy? Back when a wis your age a Game Boy wis the size ae a brick. A real, proper brick, ye could build hooses wae them. That hing could slip through a crack in the pavement. Looks mintet though, ye still get Mario an that oan it? Gettin any new games fae Santa?"—but he got nothing. The boy just kept his eyes on the screen and his mouth shut, but he moved obligingly from seat to seat as Davey hoovered and polished the windows around him. Unlike his mother, he was a skinny thing and slid without trouble between the front seats and over the handbrake.

When Davey finished, the woman still hadn't come back. Usually he'd just park the car over the street until the customer returned but with the boy still inside Davey was reluctant to move it too far away, despite Sean's command: "Get it tae fuck. This isnae a fuckin crèche."

After half an hour, the woman came back laden with shopping bags. "How much?" she asked.

"Twenty fir the valet," Sean said, "plus fifty quid fir the childcare."

The woman might have laughed if Sean had been smiling when he said it, but he wasn't, and when the woman replied "Wit?", Sean exploded at her. The two of them went at it for five minutes. Davey hung back, kicking his feet, watching the lad still sitting there in the back of the car, playing his Game Boy, ignoring the screaming and bawling going on outside.

As the woman sped off, driving angry, Sean screamed, "Don't come back, ye cunt!" He stomped off just as another (familiar) customer returned—a beige-suited pensioner who'd dropped off his old silver Merc for a valet that morning.

"Here's a little extra," the man said, slipping another fiver in over the price.

15

"I don't see how a burnt motor with no burnt people inside it is a major investigation and therefore my job," McCoist griped to the SOCO who was taking pictures of a blackened machine husk which had been left in an industrial yard overnight. Scenes of Crime had little involvement in the office politics of detectives so were safe to gripe to.

"Well, looks like it was a pretty *nice* car," the SOCO said.

"Aye, a human life, an expensive car, pretty much same-same." She drank a mouthful of the terrible coffee she liked. The polystyrene made it taste better. Of course, she knew why she was being asked to look into a gubbed motor rather than a murder. Same old answer: the *eff-you-see-kay-you-pee.* "There's definitely nobody in the boot?"

"Afraid not."

"Shame."

"It's not all bad though—looks like I've got a partial plate for you here."

"Partial. Yippee." She followed him around the shell of what had been a massive four-by-four—the kind that was too big to park properly anywhere and deserved every single door-panel ding it got. A Range Rover, the SOCO had said, promising her the model and year later. The tyres had blown out, the seats charred to ash, the plastics melted into a rigid ooze like cooled magma, stinking like nothing else, you could taste it as much as smell it—acrid and chemical. The smell of something gone wrong, of trouble. The windows had been turned to sand and the layers of paintwork blistered off, revealing its gnarled skeleton. At the back, hanging off the bumper, was a twisted and half-blackened strip of yellow licence plate. The front one was completely buckled and illegible.

"Looks like 'MCG' at the end there. Maybe part of an 'R' before that? Maybe a 'P'? See what we can do about cleaning up the chassis and engine numbers when we get it back. Hopefully give you something to go on."

"Hopefully, yes…" McCoist knew how this one would go. A quick look at cars recently reported stolen and bingo, there it'll be. Case solved, Sherlock Holmes can put his feet up for a bit, go back to playing the violin on crack or whatever it was he was into. (In McCoist's case it would have been eating, reading, sleeping and watching whatever shite was on telly alone between fortnightly visits from the kids—making her relinquish the TV remote for a weekend—but had now become chasing after a small dog whose sole purpose seemed be the entire destruction of her home and sanity.) And if there *was* any hint it was more than just a joyride with a bit of pyromania thrown in from the local young team, it would be reassigned to somebody supposedly more capable. Truthfully, she knew her own cynicism and despondency was as big a block as her lack of good cases, but it was getting harder and harder every day to give a fuck.

The recovery lorry had arrived to take the leftovers away— the charcoal carcass of a Christmas turkey worthy of McCoist's own culinary efforts.

She got back into her car and turned the heater up. She wanted to go home and see the dog, prayed he hadn't chewed up the rest of her remaining skirting boards, the little shit. McCoist hadn't checked whether it was male or female when she pinched it—she found out when he cocked his back leg and took a piss up the leg of the kitchen table. God, how she hoped he would make the kids happy, because at the moment he was driving her crazy, and on top of the constant worry she'd be found out and fired any day she was certainly regretting her rash decision. *Rash? Utterly moronic more like.* But if Cam and Tess fell in love with him, well, Merry fucking Christmas and a better year ahead for all.

16

Davey went round to his maw's for his lunch on Christmas Day, just the two of them in the flat where Davey had grown up. His bedroom was gone, replaced by an overcrowded and dusty gym with little space to move between the exercise bike, rowing machine, gym ball, punching bag and step machine—all of them decorated in cobwebs, home and hunting ground to spiders who'd been there so long they should have been paying digs. The rest of the place was fresher, his maw being a keen amateur in interior design, though she didn't have the money to get rid of the Artex on the ceiling or the chipboard on the walls, spiking her best efforts at replicating the rooms in the home and lifestyle mags that were stacked on the coffee table, years of back issues piled up in a magazine rack ready to fall apart under the strain. There were sun-bleached pictures of Davey as a boy on the mantelpiece, ones of his da taken in the eighties before he was even a twinkle in the man's bawsack. The many thousands of photos of Annalee were all on her phone.

Mercifully, she'd been to Iceland and bought in stuff she could just throw in the oven—no fucking about.

"Decent gravy, Maw."

"Aye, splashed oot oan the good stuff fir ye, seen as it's just the two ae us this year."

Davey grunted, filled his mouth with a chunk of hard, dry stuffing (an unwanted workout for his swollen jaw and loose teeth) so he couldn't reply. She'd asked him what had happened to his face and wasn't happy with his explanation about falling down the stairs at the flat, but he'd told her straight up to drop it for the sake of a quiet Christmas, and it was certainly quiet.

"Toap up?"

"Aye, please," Davey said through another mouthful. His maw was drinking Buck's Fizz but he was sticking to the tinnies as it was still quite early.

"Goat a Viennetta fir eftir an aw."

"Nice wan."

"Ye wantin it straight eftir or ye want tae wait till a get back?"

Davey kept his eyes on his plate, kept his knife and fork working, chewing something tasteless that he couldn't swallow so he just kept chewing. "When ye goin?"

"Sarah said the back ae three. A willnae be lang, back aboot four fir the puddin, if ye want tae dae it that wae roon."

Davey chewed and nodded. "Mind an take the bag wae ye." Davey had brought presents for Annalee, the poor wrapping job supplemented and structured by most of a roll of tape.

"So ye want tae dae the Viennetta eftir?"

"A want tae finish ma meal before a hink aboot puddin." Davey saw the hurt on his maw's face, felt the words bubbling up between them: *Ye sound just like yer faither when ye speak like that.* He relented. "Yel probly get some cake or trifle or somethin oer there, will ye no?" His maw was invited over to Sarah's to have a drink and see the wean after they'd finished their lunch. Davey was not, as per the new, legally binding arrangement.

His maw necked her drink. "Wait till am back, we'll huv puddin thegether."

"Aye. Sound... Turkey's nice."

"Watch the bag, right? Don't leave it oan the bus or somethin."

"David, will ye stoap worryin?"

"Yev hud maist ae that bottle ae Prosecco, am just sayin—"

"A huv no! An there's no even any buses runnin, am walkin oer. There somethin expensive in it or that?"

"See ye later, Maw." Davey closed the door, cracked another can and dropped onto the sofa in front of the telly. He flipped through the usual shite looking for a film to watch. That one with Dudley Moore as the elf was on. When Davey was wee, the scene where the rich girl gives the homeless boy a plate of dinner and a can of ginger always made him ache for an ice-cold Coca-Cola—proper Coke, real Coke, in a can, the Christmas-red tin with white, swirly script—but his maw only ever bought the shop-brand shite. He flipped on, sipped his lager.

He couldn't settle on a channel. He still felt as if he had fingers stuffed in his ears after the explosion, thoughts of hard faces and flashing knives overloud inside his skull. He turned the volume of the telly up again and again, though he wasn't watching anything. The smell of cold Christmas dinner wafting through from the kitchen seemed mixed with flaming petrol and redolent of his own sour breath under the too-tight black bag. He had an urge to get one of those nose hair trimmers that dads get given as gifts and jam it up his beak to see if he could cut the smell out. A line or two of something would do it—he felt a nostalgic pang for the chalky burn of coke in his nostrils, claggy in the back of his throat. No idea who he could even buy gear off any more (Sarah had been a good source back in those days—she always knew someone who had something). Paulo McGuinn, maybe. His new boss, his creditor, his owner. Three hundred grand and change in the hole to a gangster, what would a few hundred more for a bit of gear matter? Acid roiled in his stomach, a bitter taste of metal in his throat from the tinnies.

When he'd finished the cans in the fridge, he checked the cupboards for something stronger— there was plenty to choose from, though some of the bottles had been sitting there since Davey's childhood. There was an unopened bottle of Glayva with the stamp from a NAAFI shop still on it—the latest it could have been bought was in the early nineties when his da left the navy (and still lived with them). He chose a half-full bottle of gin with a less questionable vintage and filled the other half of the bottle with lemonade.

It was past four and his maw still hadn't returned from Sarah's. He slugged from the bottle of pre-mix he'd created, choking for a fag. Whose idea was it that he had to quit? His own? Sarah's? Sarah smoked until she got pregnant and didn't go back to it afterwards. Same with the drink. She could be so fucking pious about it. *Ye don't hink aboot yersel but at least hink aboot the wean.* Same story with food—she'd become obsessed with eating right and crowed on about nutrition and vitamins as if she hadn't spent every weekend of her twenties firing down kebabs and chippies after a night on the bevvy, or eating nothing at all for days at a time while on the gear. Davey had once seen her tackle a King Kebab—absolutely refusing his help with the massive thing, grease running down her chin, fingers and arms, congealed into yellow pools in the tin foil it came in by the time she'd stuffed the last of it in. She'd been a good laugh back in the day.

Back in the day! Davey thought, the Voice of Reason slurring in his head. *Listen tae yer fuckin sel, ye sound like wan ae they sad bastarts whose best years were in secondary school, afore they've*

even hud a real fuckin life. Golden age, glory days, it's aw bollocks.
Get a fuckin grip.

Davey choked down more dusty gin and lemonade. It was nearly five—where was his maw? Laughing it up with Sarah and his "in-laws" (they were never married, but it all amounted to the same thing), siding with them, the fucking enemy, over her own son. All so she could play with her granddaughter—*his* daughter, who he hadn't seen in a month. His eyes stung. Who had the right to tell him he couldn't see his own daughter? Nobody but God, and even then Davey would have a square go if that cunt said anything.

Past five now. Davey looked out the curtains. It was dark— no sign of her on the street. He lurched into the kitchen and rifled through the freezer, pulling out bags of peas and boxes of crinkle-cut Micro Chips and tossing them onto the floor. The Viennetta was solid as a brick so he put it in the microwave, stabbing at the buttons until the thing started humming. He sat on the floor and polished off the bottle while he waited.

By the time the machine pinged, the Viennetta was half soup, half lumpy cream. On the plate, it looked like a clump of wet clay on a pottery wheel. He went at it with a spoon, barely tasting it—some bites were chilly and hurt his teeth, others were roasting hot. The ice-cream puddle grew, spilt over the plate onto the kitchen counter. He was eating as if it was a competition. *Finish the hing—finish the whole bastart hing!* He choked as a still-frozen chunk caught in his throat, hacking and coughing until it came back up. Raging, he threw his spoon at the wall then smashed his fist into the Viennetta. It exploded, splattered the walls, the counter, Davey. A second punch shattered the plate and cut open Davey's knuckles.

He yelped and sucked the blood from his fist. "Bastart!" He shook his hand, splattering drops of blood on the floor.

Tears and bile were bubbling up inside—the alcohol, gravy, ice cream lying rotten in his stomach.

He stormed out the flat and down the stairs, the cold slapping him down as he stepped outside, fresh air going to his head, making him feel the drink—legs heavy and uncooperative, head spinning.

He waited for a while on a bus that never came. When he remembered there was no service on Christmas Day he started booting the scratched and graffitied glass of the bus shelter. It kept his anger frothing. The noise of a solitary car engine behind him made his heart stop, the wash of its lights as it passed by sending him diving to the ground, laughing in drunk hysterics, verge of tears, as he tried to gather himself up, pressing the flat of his hand hard into his chest in the hope of slowing his heart. *Wit did ye hink was gonnae happen? It's probly just Chris fuckin Rea oan his way hame.* The Voice of Reason making merry.

He stomped all the way to Sarah's, teeth chattering, the street weaving in front of him, the mouth of every turn and alley and underpass stoking up his fear and anger. "Moan then, fuckin moan then," he whispered under his breath.

Davey knocked on the door even harder than he meant to. Hard enough that nobody immediately came to open it. A head peeped out of the living-room curtains, a jagged face like some deep-sea crustacean—Sarah's maw.

"Angie! Angie, hen, it's Davey, gonnae let us in?"

The head popped back in, curtains closed.

Davey slapped his open hand against the door, feeling his palm sting, pain dissolving into pins and needles. "Sarah! Sarah!

It's Davey! A want tae see her! She's ma wean, a want tae see her!" His face was against the wood of the door. "It's fuckin Christmas! Moan tae fuck!"

The door flew open and Davey almost fell right on his face on the doormat.

"The fuck's yer problem?!" Sarah hissed. She was beyond furious. Hair done and face made up, she looked like the girl Davey had met at the Savoy seven years before. (*She's a stunner. Al go an ask her if she wants tae winch ye, Hammy.* But Davey had ended up winching her himself.) The girl who loved dancing, who always bought an extra portion of chips for the homeless guy in his sleeping bag outside the takeaway, who took her heels off to run over the top of parked cars, Davey half cheering her on, half terrified she would slip and fall.

"A just want tae see Annalee. Ye cannae keep her fae me, she's ma daughter."

"Ye cannae turn up here like this, Davey. Pished intae the fuckin bargain an aw. A telt ye tae stay away an a meant it. Wis the court order no clear enough?!"

"Annalee!" Davey started to yell past Sarah into the hall "Annalee! It's Daddy, Annalee!"

She slid through a crack in the door—his wee girl, dressed as a princess, a Christmas present, probably, Davey didn't think he'd seen this costume before. "Awright, doll?" He sank to his knees. The look on her face was inscrutable—dreamy, confused, the glaikit stare that children get when they're turning something over. "Merry Christmas, hen." Davey was full-on crying now, sniffing hard, snot rattling in his nose.

"Annalee—back in the livin room. Noo!" Sarah snapped. "Go oan. Dae as yer telt."

Both of their maws appeared next. Angie took Annalee's hand and tried to pull her back into the living room. Davey's maw came to him. "Moan, son, let's head back up the road." She put a hand on his shoulder. "Sorry aboot this, doll," she said to Sarah. "He just misses her that's aw."

"He's drunk is wit," Sarah shot back. Now she had the face on—full of disgust and disappointment—the one Davey had grown to hate so he wouldn't have to hate himself.

"Fuck does that matter?!" Davey exploded. "Ye cannae dae this tae me! Ye cannae just keep her away fae me. She's ma wean. She's ma fuckin wean!" He staggered up onto his feet. Sarah flinched; his maw put her hand against his chest, firm.

"Leave noo or am phonin the polis," Sarah said.

He almost fell again as he backed out the door.

"Wait a second, son, al come wae ye, just let me get ma hings—"

But he was already marching away, bumping up against the walls as he went. "Bitch! Ye fuckin bitch!" he screamed. Faces peered between the curtains in the houses all around, the whole block looking down on him. "Cuuuunt!" he screamed, his throat raw, shredding the night air.

17

McCoist had been to the shops on Christmas Eve to get bowls, food, treats, chews, toys, pee pads, a lead, a bed, a book on training—the whole works—then nipped to the supermarket for a bit of elbow-jabbing, last-minute food shopping, managing to snag herself a turkey-and-stuffing microwave meal for the big day. She was ordering a Chinese for her and the kids on Boxing Day—they'd be having the full shebang at her ex-mother-in-law's the day before anyway and she had no desire to inflict her own cooking upon them (or herself).

She worked Christmas Day with the other divorcees. They even shared a dram in the evening—McCoist's disgrace let go for the moment in the company of other fuck-ups, men and women whose home lives deteriorated due to hours worked, obsessive personalities, controlling tendencies, cynical minds bruised by constant exposure to society's worst side. Missed birthdays, missed anniversaries, cancelled holidays, dinner going cold because of last-minute overtime, their presence at home reduced to a sulky poltergeist who shouldn't be disturbed. McCoist ate her compartmentalised Christmas feast at her desk.

Her neighbour, Edith, was checking up on the dog for her throughout the day—the auld biddie's low estimation of her as a mother living alone was balanced out by her being a police detective, so she was able to do McCoist a friendly favour while also looking down on her.

Boxing Day morning she put up the Christmas tree and tidied the gaff, which was hard with the puppy chasing her around, barking at the hoover and continually creating more mess to clean up. "You better be fucking worth it," she grumbled. "Make them love you hard." He wagged his tail, licked her ankle. "I'll take that as a promise."

When she saw Mark's car pull up outside she grabbed the puppy and stashed him in the kitchen. She'd slapped a bow on his collar which he was trying to chew.

"Sorry we're late," Mark said. Mark was one for non-apologies. "My mum came over and made pancakes for breakfast. How was work yesterday?"

"Fine." She smiled at the twins—diverging as they entered their teens, Tess in a black hoody and ripped jeans, Cam in gym gear which he seemed to live in. "Merry Christmas!"

"Merry Christmas," they said, awkward hugs and kisses in turn—Cam because he was a teenage boy, Tess because they were, as ever, in the middle of a running argument about nothing/everything and even the birthday of Jesus Christ Himself wasn't a good enough reason to take a break from it.

"Well, I'll see you in the morning then," Mark said. His breath clouded the air; he didn't move from the doorstep. He had a stupid smile. His hair was noticeably greying, his belly growing out. Looked as good as ever.

"How's your mum doing?"

"Really great, actually. I think. I mean, she was really enjoying herself yesterday. Seemed to be, anyway. It's tough this time of year, that's when you really miss people, you know?" Stupid smile.

"I know. How are you holding up?"

He shrugged, huffed out a puff of steamy breath. "I've got the kids to look after me."

"You do."

He hovered and smiled. Since they separated, Mark had grown completely insensitive to McCoist's barbs, or tried very hard to ignore them. He didn't like confrontation—even in the days when it became apparent their marriage was over, there were no blazing rows. Mark suggested it was time for a divorce as if meekly handing in his two weeks' notice along with an apology for the inconvenience it would cause. Truthfully, it stunned McCoist that he was the one who had finally called time. She had got comfortable with the idea they would continue living under a cloud of silence loaded with unuttered resentments for ever—or at least until she let the thunder crack and the rain fall herself.

"Not too early tomorrow, have a lie in," McCoist said. It's hard to break off a doorstep conversation politely when you're the one holding the door.

"Sure, sure. Will do… Sounds good." He stuffed his hands under his armpits for warmth. He was about to say something, then turned instead and looked at his car as if just noticing it there—engine idling, exhaust spewing sweet, poisoned smoke into the winter morning (fineable offence)—then looked back, another smile.

"See you then?"

"Yeah, see you then."

She shut the door.

"Mum! Mum! What is that?!" Cam said. He was looking from her to his sister with a glint of childish glee that made him seem like a wee boy again. There was scratching and barking coming from behind the kitchen door. Wee bastart had given the game away.

"*That* is your Christmas present," McCoist said.

"Nooooo. No way! It's not—really?" Cam was grinning. This was it, this was what McCoist had been waiting for. Pleasurable warmth was coursing through her veins—the fucking Christmas spirit.

"For goodness' sake, open the door and see before it scratches its way through!"

Even Tess was starting to smile. She took a mobile phone from her pocket which McCoist didn't know she had and started to film her brother.

Cam threw the door open and the pup came bounding out. He squealed—"No way!"—and dived down onto the floor. The dog set about licking his hands and face, clambering all over him as they rolled about on the carpet.

Tess watched it on her phone screen, smiling to herself.

"What are you doing?" McCoist asked.

"Filming his reaction."

"Why? Go and see the dog."

She shrugged slightly, not moving her eyes from the screen. "Because it's funny."

"Did your dad get you that phone?"

"We both got one."

It was an iPhone. Expensive, connected to the internet, to social media, to all the horrors within that world within a world. McCoist's mind immediately went to scams, grooming, revenge porn... "Your dad should have run that by me first."

"Mum, just..." Tess let out a sigh.

Cam had his own phone out now, snapping photos of the puppy up close. It pawed and licked at the camera. "What's his name?"

"That's up to you two. Have a think and come up with something you agree on. Shouldn't be difficult." McCoist laughed at her own joke—Cam ignored it; Tess treated her to another exasperated sigh.

"Dad is gonna freak when we bring him home," Cam said.

That hit McCoist right in the belly. She couldn't speak for a moment, had to collect herself. "The dog is staying here, Cam."

"So what, you bought *yourself* a dog for *our* Christmas present?" Tess said.

McCoist was dumbfounded; she almost snapped back, *I didn't buy him!* She looked from one to the other. "You can see him every time you visit." It sounded lame, lame the way Tess would say it, full of disgust.

They called the dog Bruce.

18

Davey came to in the hospital. The winter sun sliced through the blinds and pierced his skull. His mouth was dry and sticky as if he'd been chewing moths and tasted just as sweet. His headache throbbed with his heartbeat, which was too deep, too fast, and as soon as he tried to sit up he whitied out a glorious, bubbly concoction of beer, gin and what remained of Christmas lunch.

The nurse who came to clean him up and change the sheets did little to hide her revulsion. Who could blame her? She picked up a chunk that was still clearly a half-digested sprout. When she was done she gave him water and painkillers.

He closed his eyes, tried to sink back into oblivion, hopefully never to wake up from it. Snatches of the night before came to terrorise him. He remembered ice cream on the walls of the kitchen—explained the bandage on his hand. At least he hadn't been fighting. Sarah's face hovered behind his eyelids, a wave of seasickness as the thought *At least ye didnae hurt yer hawn hittin her* passed insidiously through his mind. *Ye were angry enough*—the Voice of Reason, kicking him while he was down as always. *The way she looked at ye, the way she always looks at ye, ye could ae done it this time, couldn't ye? Knocked that look right aff her pus.* But no, it was the plate he'd punched, the plate which had cut open his knuckles. He'd never laid a hand on Sarah—never. But he had no illusions about his temper. The idea he might one day really fly off the handle and do something he could never take back was a fear that nagged him in dark moments. *Blame the booze if ye want, stupit cunt.*

As he drifted in and out, he heard snatches of a conversation.

"Can we get him tae fuck?"

"Not yet, psych wants to see him. Polis brought him in last night. He was wandering down the middle of the road."

He remembered catching his reflection in the wing mirror of a car and hoofing it—the mirror shattering, the whole plastic unit cracking back the wrong way like a snapped wrist, tearing off, left dangling by its electrical wires. High-vis uniforms closing in. *The fuckin sodjers.*

A doctor woke him again. She didn't look like they do on the telly. She was in plain office wear—no coat, no scrubs, not even a stethoscope around her neck.

"The police officers who brought you in said you were very upset, Mr Burnet. Do you remember that?"

Davey shook his head—his brain rattled like a pea in a cup and he decided it was best to stay still. "Naw, no really." His voice was so raspy he sounded like a soap-opera villain.

"They were worried that you were deliberately trying to get hit by traffic."

"No much traffic oan Christmas Day." He tried to smile.

"Have you had thoughts of hurting yourself in the past?"

Davey couldn't meet her eyes.

"Have you ever had suicidal thoughts, or even just entertained the idea of taking your own life?"

"Am feelin a bit dodgy fir aw this right noo."

"Can you tell me why you were so upset? Has anything happened recently that might make you feel like this?"

Of course there was. There was the obvious incident and

then there was the worst of it: he'd been cut off from Annalee, he'd all but lost Sarah, that naive glimmer of hope that maybe one day… but he was just kidding himself, he'd known that for a while. That life was as good as gone, he'd had it and ruined it all too quickly, all that was left to do was cling to whatever he could get under his nails—to see Annalee, be part of her life, even if it was only for a day or two a week. And now he'd thrown that away too. "A wis just drunk," Davey said, getting angry but not sure why. "That's aw it wis. Drunk, bein stupit. A should head noo, stoap bein a waste ae space."

"Nobody's a waste of space, Mr Burnet," she said.

"A meant the bed an that. Free up the bed fir somebdy who actually needs it."

19

Paulo sang a bit of Andy Williams's classic Christmas cracker, hamming it up, his voice pretty decent—Elvis out of Brigton. "A love Boaxin Day even mare than the big wan itsel. The weans are either oot wae their pals or busy wae their toays an ye can stick Mickey Bubble's Christmas album oan an get doon tae some eftirnoon shaggin wae the missus. Halle-fuckin-lujah! Amaright, boays?"

He was holding court in front of a small crowd of goons, each one bigger and more muscular than the last, like a set of massive, ugly, chib-marked Russian dolls. Hard cunts. Real hard cunts, each one of them proven killers. They snickered at Paulo's blowhard bluster.

"Ye start aff wae the gentle stuff, whisperin in her ear an aw that, but by the end ye make her feel like the Virgin Mary bein drilled by the fuckin donkey!" He laughed and they laughed with him, the sound of idiotic, laddish guffawing bouncing around the warehouse. "Wit's the matter wae you cunts?" Paulo turned to address the four men hanging by their ankles from the tines of two raised forklifts parked side by side. Their faces were like battered, swollen beets from the blood lying heavy in their skulls and the rough handling they'd already endured: snatched, subdued and strung upside down. Below, a tarpaulin protected the floor. "Didnae get any this year? Were ye no good wee boays fir Santa? Did the big yin huv nothin in his sack fir yeez? Didnae slide doon yer chimney?" He gave them each a big, chummy smile, back teeth grinding a little from the couple of bumps of coke he'd taken to get him in the festive spirit.

He pushed each of them in the chest, one by one, making them swing and groan. The bawbag on the far right—Jamie "Stone" Mason—was sniffling, tears running into his hair, pish leaking down over his body to his neck. "Naughty, naughty. Well, Uncle Paulo hasnae forgotten yeez. Don't worry. He's goat a new game fir ye, fir yer Christmas prezzie." He held out a hand and one of his men handed him a prybar. The others were holding an assortment of tools—hammers, chisels, drills, saws, angle grinders, the shadow board on the wall of the warehouse all but empty. "It's called 'keep yer kneecaps'." He patted the hooked end of the prybar against an open palm, beating a jaunty rhythm. "Tell me wit a want tae know an ye win. Lie tae me an ye lose. Simple as that. Understawn?"

By the time they were done and the last man had slipped away in a rattling gurgle, blood drooling from his toothless mouth, Paulo and his hard cunt Russian dolls had stripped down to their undies—to keep the blood off their clothes but also because torturing information out of people was sweaty, thirsty work. And it had all been for nothing. Four captains from a host of his rivals dead and not a single one had known who had tried to kidnap him, who had torched his car. And it wasn't because they had successfully held out on him. Paulo made sure of that. When he'd degloved Andy Bannerman's cock with a Stanley knife and a pair of pliers and Bannerman had admitted to setting up the whole thing, he knew they were innocent of this. That they really knew nothing at all.

"Get them doon an get fuckin rid ae them!" Paulo bellowed at his exhausted men, who couldn't look in his saucer-eyed, gurning face, shining with sweat and blood spray. His arms were red from the elbows down. The boss's jovial mood had leaked away with the pints of blood they'd spilt and they were all now on the receiving end. The night had gone sour, the steamy air in the warehouse thick with the stench of shit, a post-climax sense of shame creeping around their bare bodies. "An dae a proper fuckin joab ae it an aw. If a hear aboot a single wan ae their baw-hairs showin up it'll be yous hangin up there next time an a willnae go so fuckin easy oan—"

A phone started ringing. They all began wiping their hands on rags and kicking through the bundles of clothes they'd left on the floor. "It's mine, probly the fuckin missus…" Paulo grumbled. He fished his phone from his trouser pocket but it wasn't his wife calling.

The men watched as the smile—vicious but genuinely happy—spread over Paulo's face again. Boxing Day might have been a dead end (in several ways) but a new lead had come in: the green motor had been sighted.

JANUARY

20

"Good afternoon, Mr Burnet." He was hosing soap off the roof of a car. He looked round at her and kept working. He moved the water in a quick arc, rinsing away, the edge of the spray catching her as she approached, stepping around frothy puddles. He had healing bruises on his face, crusty cuts on his lips and brows.

McCoist shouted over the noise of the pressure washer. "Do you remember me?! I'm Detective Inspector McCoist!"

The water and the machine noise both stopped abruptly, leaving McCoist bellowing her name in the sudden silence. Burnet leant into the window that was sliding down. "Five quid, please… Cheers!" The car revved up and rolled away, dripping.

"You don't do a shammy dry?" McCoist asked.

"Only if they ask," he said.

She held out her warrant card for him again. "I was here about the air-pistol incident back in November."

"A mind. Ye want tae speak tae Sean?"

"I do, but first I'm going to ask what happened to your face."

"Hud a bad fall," he said. Burnet was going the way of his boss, shrinking and ageing before his time. He already had a slight slump in his shoulders from lugging drums of soap around. The smashed-up face made him seem decrepit. "Doon the stair," he added.

"Head first?"

"Hit every step oan the way doon."

"Your gaffer, he has a temper, doesn't he?"

Burnet shrugged. "Nae mair than anybody else."

"Really? A couple of days before Christmas, a woman reported that Mr Prentice screamed her out of the car wash and called her a 'cunt' in front of her young child. Is that normal behaviour?"

"Fir Sean or in general? Look, that wummin left her wee boay in the motor wae us—two guys she doesnae know fae Adam—while she went aff tae the shoap. That isnae right, an even if Sean wis oer the toap wae her, she needed tae be telt."

McCoist had looked both Burnet and Prentice up on her phone before approaching this time. Their previous evasiveness and obvious collusion had wrong-footed her and it wouldn't happen again. The CHS showed both had a history of petty criminality—drugs, fights, theft, vandalism. Most of it from some time ago, with the odd blip: Prentice with the airgun thing, and Burnet had been picked up in the early hours of Boxing Day and taken to A & E by a couple of uniforms—a marker on his PNC file flagged him as potentially suicidal. Either Burnet's perception of the appropriate level of aggro for someone to live with was genuinely warped—not unlikely—or he was covering for Prentice again. He certainly had been last time they'd spoken.

"It's a crime to lie to the police, Mr Burnet," McCoist said, "and being charged with making a false statement or obstructing the course of justice won't help you when it comes to appealing a child-custody decision." That was something else she'd dug up. He'd recently missed a court date.

Burnet gave her a look of pure venom—it was a low blow; McCoist would have reacted the same if somebody brought up her own divorce and child-custody situation to strong-arm her. But it was the kind of look you got used to as a polis. The ugly shape his face had been boxed into made it particularly disturbing though. McCoist held the stare—felt the frisson of challenge between them and the urge to smirk at the idea of being cowed by this battered wee man.

A metallic-navy Kia pulled up beside them, making the soapy water in the gutter lap up against the kerb, and Burnet broke his gaze. "Noo, ye want tae speak tae Sean? Cause av goat work tae dae."

"Mr Burnet, did he do this to you?" She pointed to his face.

Burnet laughed, a grating, nasal cackling. "Naw, Sean didnae dae this tae me. Like a said, it wis—"

"The stairs, aye, heard that one."

Burnet shrugged. A middle-aged man got out of the car and held out his keys. "Could ye gee us a full valet, son?"

"Nae worries. Hawf an hoor awright?"

"Aye, catch ye then." The man walked off through the puddles towards the city centre.

"Al go an get Sean fir ye."

McCoist cast a look around the unit while she waited, intuitively snooping, the kind of behaviour that was hard to switch off and made you an unwanted guest, even in your own home (how many polis's marriages had been wrecked by the suspicion of an affair that had never even happened?)—stone walls and floor painted white, damp mould creeping in up in the mossy corners, wooden rafters forming a floor for storage above. Shelves on the walls held washing-up gear: spare lances and hoses; sponges, mitts and shammy cloths; assorted spray bottles, polishes and waxes. Beside the yellow pressure washing units were soap drums and a bin and a couple of square, vac-packed bags of assorted rags torn from clothing and towels—patterned and brightly coloured, scraps of logos and prints. The office was a drywall cube at the back of the unit, also dirty white, paint peeling off in strips. The door opened and Burnet and Prentice came out, followed by the smell of weed and tobacco.

Burnet set about getting things ready, picking up a bottle of degreaser and tearing rags out of the plastic wrapping—a strip from a Levi's T-shirt and something that might once have been children's pyjamas, adorned with little Peppa Pigs. Prentice gave a wasted smile, teeth gnarly and yellowed. "That discoont offer still stawns," he said.

"Are you high, Mr Prentice?" McCoist asked.

"Aye. Oan life."

"Life smells quite a lot like marijuana."

"Funny, a find that an aw."

"I'm not in the mood for messing around with you today, Mr Prentice. A woman called Caroline Mackenzie has reported you for abusive, threatening behaviour towards her and her seven-year-old son."

"Is this the wummin that cannae look eftir her own wean? She goes aff tae the shoap or the pub or witever an leaves her lad in the care ae a couple ae strangers at a car wash she's never bin tae afore?"

"Are you saying she was drunk when she returned?"

"Fuck if a know, but she could ae bin. Gone fir fuckin ages an the wee boay's just sittin there in the motor. Should huv called the fuckin social masel. Fuckin Childline or somethin. An a didnae say a fuckin hing tae the boay. Davey wis lookin eftir the wee cunt an everythin—he's a da himsel."

McCoist pinched the bridge of her nose. This was going to be the end for her. She couldn't put up with it much longer— this crazy little man was going to be the one to finally push her over the edge, make her leave her resignation letter on DCI Robson's desk along with a steaming turd courtesy of Bruce.

"Mr Prentice, just… I don't want to come back here, OK?" She moved in close, almost grabbed hold of his collar. "I really don't. I don't care if you have to double the amount of grass you're already smoking, I just need you to *calm the fuck down* and stop screaming at people who come in here. Can you do that?"

He seemed to be caught off guard at her plea. "Eh, aye… A can gee it a try."

"Please do."

21

Davey had never seen Tim out of his scaffy work clothes. He looked uncomfortable in a thick wool shirt and Doc Martens, hair tied back in a ponytail. Not quite as arty as the people sitting at the tables around them but getting there. Tim had picked the place—a hybrid cafe, bar, restaurant, venue and, by the looks of the dusty bookshelves all around the room, library, in a pishy alley near Central Station—so maybe it was aspirational for him.

The customers sipping a mixture of coffees and craft beers at 11 a.m. looked in their mid-twenties, most a little younger than Davey, some probably his age or older, yet he couldn't help but think of them as weans. They were all clashing colours and clumpy shoes, an ironic shell-suit jacket worn with an oiled beard, hair cut in severe lines with shaved patches, piercings and detailed, delicate tattoos—not the thick, faded things sported by people Davey knew. All *look-at-me-I'm-different*, yet nobody standing out in the context of the cool-kid bar, a homogeneity at odds with the desperate attempt to look unique. Nonconformity was another type of uniform. Davey glared, thinking about how he could batter fuck out all of them. The thought of violence sent a shot of panic through him, reminders of wet jeans and choking on his vomit under the hood.

"Cheers, man." Tim took a glass of the pub's cheapest draught lager from Davey—it had burnt him for nearly a tenner for two fucking pints, but it was Davey who had asked Tim to meet him, and it was Davey who was wanting to ask a favour, so he took it on the chin.

"Nae worries, Tim. Cheers." They clinked glasses. The drink was bowfing, tasted as grotty as the pub tried hard to look—a dive-bar affectation, exposed ducts and pipework above their heads, rotten floorboards below their feet. Davey grimaced.

"How are you?" Tim wiped a foamy stache from his upper lip. He meant the bruises, which were deflating and yellowing.

"Aw right." Stock answer—Davey hadn't stopped jittering since his encounter with Mince and Mealy and Croaker and the verbal crucifixion from Paulo that followed, but you couldn't just say that to someone. "Yersel?"

"I'm OK." He took a deep drink.

"Cool." Davey eyed the bare light bulbs and exposed brick walls of the pub, the posters for bands he'd never heard of. "Ye bin tae any gigs here?"

"Now and again."

"Local bands?"

"Mostly—they get some touring acts from England and the US sometimes as well."

"Anybody a woulda heard ae?" Davey knew the obvious answer was no but Tim wouldn't want to say that in case it sounded like he was insulting Davey's taste. He was too nice sometimes. Saft, Davey thought, but why was there so much wrong with that? He looked again at the trendy set around them, free to chat and drink and dye their hair and play fancy dress. He could never be like that himself.

"Nobody huge," Tim said, "just, like…" He scoured his mind, eyes searching the posters for inspiration.

"The Beatles huvnae bin through."

Tim laughed. "That's it. Day off?"

"Aye, fuckin need it an aw." More true than he could really say.

Tim took a deep, bolstering mouthful of rank, expensive beer. "I was surprised you got in touch."

"Aw aye?" It was probably the only time Davey had ever messaged Tim about something that wasn't directly related to work. Certainly the first time he'd asked him to meet for a drink. He almost signed the text off with "Davey fae the car wash", then deleted it and put "Davey Boy" instead. Actually, he almost deleted the whole thing but he was desperate. He had to try something.

"Yeah, just the way things went at the car wash before Christmas, you know? What the fuck was that about? You in the shit for borrowing that car? Sean sent me home before Big Paulo came back looking for it. What happened?"

"Nothin much. Goat a slap oan the wrist. Fair dos."

"Looks like more than a slap. What did that have to do with me anyway?"

"Sean's just fuckin mental, that's aw. Ye know wit he's like. Para as fuck fae aw the weed and watchin that Russia Today shite oan the telly aw the time. Probly goat it intae his heed that yer a sleeper agent fae the CI-fuckin-A." Davey forced a thin laugh. Sean had fired Tim so he wouldn't be dragged into the shite along with them, so the gaffer would probably not appreciate Davey telling Tim the truth now. Still, it felt fucking awful shoving Sean under the double-decker. *Ye two-faced prick.* "Still, if yer needin a reference or anythin am sure he'd still gee ye a good yin."

"From that doped-up maniac? No thanks."

"Well, a can dae ye wan if it's needed aw right? Just geez a phone."

"Cheers, Davey."

Davey made a telephone with his hand and held it to his ear. "Tim is the smartest, hardest-workin, best-dressed lad av ever hud the opportunity, actually the *pleasure*, tae work wae. In aw his time at the car wash, he never wance shoved his dick in the hoover nozzle. How's that?"

"Could become the prime minister with a reference like that."

"Yed dae a better joab than maist. Hard tae catch a guy in a scandal who knows how tae clean up cum and blow eftir himsel."

Tim laughed and they fell into another slurping silence, the pints draining fast—another round almost imminent, Davey was going to be bankrupted if he didn't get to it soon...

"Tim, a wis wonderin if ye could gee us some advice? Or, at least, put me in touch wae somebdy or somethin." Davey felt his pulse quicken, heat rising in his face. It wasn't just fear of bringing up what had happened, it was embarrassment too.

"...What kind of advice?"

"Legal advice—yer a law student, right?"

"Well, kind of, I mean I study it along with other subjects, I'm not in law school."

"That's wit yer wantin tae dae though, aye? A mean, the way ye spoke tae the polis that day, it wis crackin."

"Maybe. If I can get this degree then maybe I'd be able to get into a proper law course afterwards."

"But ye know aboot hings though, right? Law hings."

"In an academic way, but I've not done any training or anything."

"No even work experience?"

"I've been trying to set something up but it's tricky… Is this about your daughter? What happened at the court?"

Davey knew it was desperate and unlikely Tim could help him but he felt disappointed anyway. After the effort of screwing himself up to ask, he was deflated. He finished his disgusting pint. "Didnae go well. Nae visitation rights at aw."

"I'm sorry, Davey." They looked away from each other. "Are you wanting to appeal? I'm sure there's any number of solicitors you could phone—I don't know anybody personally, but…"

"It's no just that, it's…" Davey tried to take a swig of his pint, forgetting it was empty. He stared at the glass like it was its fault. He traced a finger across the frothy rings formed by each gulp. "Dye know anythin aboot criminal informants? Polis protection and that sorta hing?"

Tim sat his glass down carefully on the scratched table—it was the kind of bench that might have come second-hand from an old school science class, the lacquer gouged and scarred and carved with names. His body tightened. "Is this about…" He pointed to Davey's battered pus. "What happened, Davey? Really, I mean, I come into work and you're all beaten up and Sean just fires me on the spot for nothing… What's going on? Are you in trouble? Is it Paulo?"

Tim looked very young, faint acne scars on his chin nestled amongst a sparse, fluffy goatee, the sockets of his eyes smooth, no shadow, thin laughter lines only just beginning to entrench at the corners. Maybe he had worries beyond studying and chasing burds but it couldn't touch the depth of trouble Davey was in. He realised then how surprisingly clear-headed Sean had been in firing the boy. He should never have got in touch.

"Wan second." Davey hopped out of his seat and up to the bar. The bartender didn't bother hiding the judgemental look he gave to Davey's battered face, his clothes, his weathered work Timbies—he was the freak here, he didn't belong. He came back with just one pint which he put down in front of Tim. "Here, huv this, pal. Cheers fir comin but just forget a said anythin, right?"

"Davey, what's this all about?—"

"See ye later." He was out the door and down the street, alcohol numbing the loss he felt. To be born into a different life…

"Wait, Davey!" Tim clumped down the street behind him in his heavy, fashionable boots.

"Look, am sorry, Tim, a shouldnae huv—"

"There was this guy who came to our class to do a guest lecture once—a criminal lawyer. Proper old school. He was telling us all these war stories about gangsters and cops and everything. He seemed, I dunno… He still has an office down by the Saltmarket, but. Maybe you could ask him about…"— Tim looked over his shoulder and dropped his voice—"…that sort of stuff. His name's Carter Lennox."

"Carter Lennox… Sounds like a posh prick."

22

Davey almost dropped the lance and bolted when the slime-green Corsa pulled into the car wash the next morning—the *brrrap* of the engine loud but brittle, whining like a dentist's drill. He felt his legs melt and become bendy, unreliable; his breathing started to come in great, dizzying whoops.

The doors opened and Paulo got out the driver's side—Davey hadn't seen him through the car's tinted windows. The passenger was a young guy, stout like a rugby player. The resemblance between him and Paulo was clear.

"Davey Boy!" Paulo strode over and clapped him on the shoulder as if the last time they spoke he hadn't been threatening to rip Davey's balls off and use them like scoops of ice cream in a Coke float made of blood (he also described in detail how Davey would be bled—like a pig, you hang them upside down by the feet and then just slide the knife, *like so*, into the throat...). "Goat a wee joab fir ye, son. Gee this motor a good clean, right. Spoatless, aye?" He leant in close, so when he spoke Davey felt the heat of the man's breath in his ear. "Make sure an gee the boot a good scrub."

Paulo straightened up and pointed to the side of meat he'd arrived with. "This is ma nephew, Colin—Colin the Karaterpillar!" Paulo chopped the air and struck a Hong Kong Phooey pose. "He's gonnae be workin wae ye fae noo oan, Davey, awright? Noo, Colin, listen tae wit Davey Boy tells ye, he's the expert, awright? A need a word wae the gaffer, yous two get tae work!"

"Awright," Colin mumbled.

"Ye ever cleaned motors before?" Davey asked.

Colin shrugged.

"Nae worries, it's a piece ac pish as lang as ye don't mind gettin wet."

"Wit aboot ma trainers?"

"Eh?"

"A cannae get ma trainers wet—they're new." He pointed to the spotless white Huaraches on his feet.

This is the point when Davey would have told a new-start to fuck off, but he couldn't. Instead, he smiled and said: "Maybe get yersel a pair ae boots or at least some auld gutties tae wear fir next shift. Just stawn back fir noo."

Davey checked the boot first. What he saw nearly made him fall down. His heart tried to claw its way up his windpipe, battering against the sides as it climbed. The boot liner was saturated with blood. There were dark pools of it in the corners where there was just too much to soak in. Davey slammed the boot closed and covered his mouth, screwing up his eyes and begging his churning stomach not to regurgitate the steak bake he'd had for breakfast. *Christ, aw Jesus Christ. So much fuckin blood, so much…* So much that whoever it belonged to must surely be dead. *Whoever*—whoever could be one of two people, considering the car. So would Davey be cleaning up Mince or Mealy? The thought brought him close to the edge of vomiting again.

"Make sure an hawd back the whitey, Davey Boy!" Paulo said as he passed by on his way out. "The state ae that motor is bad enough as it is!"

Sean came to have a look. "Holy fuckin shite!" He too slammed the boot down almost as soon as it had opened. "Fuck!" When he stopped gagging he pulled Davey close and hissed: "See wit yev brought tae ma fuckin door. Get the motor intae the unit and clean it as fast as ye fuckin can—al deal wae the punters the day. Wan mare hing: watch wit ye say roon that cunt." He pointed to Colin, who was keeping himself busy squeezing the various mitts and sponges sitting out by the machines—the thick bastard looked like he might just take a bite out of one to see what it tasted like. "He's no just the faimly lazycunt who cannae get himsel a joab—he's a fuckin spy. Mind that." Sean stalked away, his crazy, dope-red eyes flickering in their sockets.

Davey started with some rags. He tied one over his nose and mouth then used the rest to soak up the pooling blood. He threw these into a bin bag—God knows what they'd do with the bin bag full of bloody rags. When he'd taken that as far as it could go, he got out a stiff brush and a pail of soapy water—the liner was unfortunately upholstered: rubber would have been so much simpler. But life is never simple, so Davey scrubbed and soaked. And when he'd finished *that* stage—and tossed the brush into the bin bag with the sodden rags—he got out the machine for shampooing car seats. The vacuum head squirted out shampoo and sucked it back in. Its top container, filled with soapy water, emptied as the bottom container filled up. This is where the advert would usually show the bottom container full of minging ash-coloured water (*Look how fucking filthy your sofa is, you disgusting animal! Buy our carpet cleaner!*) but in this case the grey filth was mixed with gluey pink. Davey emptied the machine into the toilet and did it again. He did it over and over until the pink was all gone and the water being sucked back into the machine looked drinkable. Finally satisfied with the boot, he then had the rest of the whole fucking car to go over with a fine-tooth comb—a platinum-level valet, a keep-yourself-out-of-jail-level valet.

The car finished, he took the carpet cleaner apart and washed each individual piece. Then he scrubbed the toilet where he'd been dumping the bloody water. When he was done, he sat on the pristine throne and sparked a cigarette. His hands shook.

"Attention tae detail!" Paulo boomed. He was taking Colin around the car. "Look!" He pulled up the car mats, moved back the seats, opened the glove box and the storage behind the handbrake. "Fuckin spoatless! That's how ye dae a joab, Colin."

"Aye… right, Uncle Paul," Colin said, trying to pay attention.

"Looks as good as fuckin new—cept fir they alloys. Anythin ye can dae wae them, Davey Boy?"

Davey shook his head. "It's burnt brake dust. Ye can take brake dust aff as lang as it's no burnt in, but the way this lad drives—a mean, the way this person drove, they're heavy oan the brake, too much heat an that…" He trailed off, his mind going to Mealy, the younger brother with the cap, his Shrekked-up Corsa leaping between traffic lights. Davey had described the car and the brothers as best he could. Well enough, so it seemed. Him and his brother had beaten him and threatened him with a knife and would have killed him if they'd been asked, so Davey told himself: *Good. Am glad wan or—fuckin hopefully—both ae they sheep-shaggin cunts are deed.* But his twisting stomach didn't believe him. "Wit ye gonnae dae wae the motor?"

Paulo did the facial switch he liked to do, from chummy shark to stone-faced killer. "No yer problem, Davey, yev enough ae those as it is, so don't ask."

Sean paid Colin fifty quid appearance money and the boy got in the green Corsa with his uncle and sped off down the street.

There was no time for one fucking thing to be done before the next thing started:

"All right, guys! Was that Big Paulo in again?" Tim was at the open shutter, thumb pointing towards the receding racket of the Corsa. In his too-trendy civvies he looked alien in the car wash, as if he'd never worked there at all. "Still coming here after what happened with, you know?..."

"Tim." Sean gave the lad a nod and glared at Davey before stomping off and slamming the office door behind him. Davey got the message.

"Tim, ye cannae be here—"

"I sent you a few messages but you never got back to me. Did you get in touch with Lennox?"

Davey took Tim by the arm and walked him outside and away from the unit. "Naw, naw a didnae, an just forget aboot aw that, a awready telt ye tae forget it the last time. That's why a didnae reply tae yer texts."

"But Davey, I could help. Is it what happened with Paulo's car? If you're in trouble, mate, I—"

"Everythin's fine, Tim, awright? Everythin's fine as lang as ye stoap phonin me and don't come roon here again."

"But—"

"Look, ye goat sacked!" Davey shouted. Tim took a step back, rubbing his arm where Davey had been squeezing it with his work-hardened grip. The lad was taking a riddy, eyes looking watery. "Ye goat sacked, ye cannae just come stoatin back in like nothin's happened, it's no allowed. Awright?"

Tim turned without a word and went on down the street.

"Yer better aff, mucker. Yer too good fir this shite," Davey said after him, but if the words reached him there was no sign.

Davey returned to the car wash, utterly miserable, where Sean was arranging the shelves to no purpose, joint hanging from his mouth. Davey kicked at the bin bag stuffed with bloody rags. "Wit dae we dae wae these?"

23

"Yer lookin affy dry fir a man who's just cleant a motor," Paulo said to Colin, who was in the driving seat of the Corsa.

"Didnae want tae get the seats aw wet eftir they've just bin cleant an aw."

"That right, aye? Very thoughtful." His nephew was always quick with an excuse if with nothing else. The lad didn't even notice the sarcasm in Paulo's voice, just gave him a quick, simple smile. "Stoap sniffin up this cunt's arse an oertake him, will ye?" Colin put his foot down and swerved out into the right-hand lane to a barrage of honking from behind. "Christ, check the mirrors first!"

"Sorry, Uncle Paul."

Paulo give his nephew a look over. The boy wasn't even good for driving him around. If it weren't for his size and his family connection, the life would have killed him already. (It was the missus who insisted he take Colin on. "Ma sister wants him tae get the fuck oot her hoose.") At least he had some muscle, and he would never intentionally cross him. Unintentionally though, who knew? He was a helpless gobshite sometimes.

Paulo thought of the teuchter lad they'd gouged and bled and all but melted down into blubber. They'd got little out of him—all he could give them about Croaker was the man's surname and description (which he already had from poor old Davey), a dead phone number, the location of a few places they'd met (Paulo would have them watched but with little hope) and the amount of money he'd paid to kidnap yours truly, who the young man seemed to know dangerously little about. He knew now though, that was for sure. He knew the minute the edge of the knife touched the bridge of his nose that Paulo McGuinn would take his beak right off his face, that he was not a man of empty threats.

But this sheep-shagger, no matter how many bits of him Paulo cut off, said nothing about his brother. Not a single thing. There was no price you could put on loyalty like that— especially when there were men like this Croaker out there who apparently had the hairy big-boy baws to try to take Paulo down right out on the street. Colin, thick as he was, was unquestioningly loyal to his uncle, maybe not so far as to withstand piecemeal evisceration, but far enough to still be an asset. Maybe. Threats of reprisals for Boxing Day were circling, so there was a slim chance it might even be put to the test. Paulo doubted it though—he'd made sure the details of the four captains' slow deaths were known where it mattered and the Bannerman dick-slice had rightly put the shits up everyone. Still, he'd made new security arrangements, at least until the madman Croaker was found.

"Where are we takin the motor then?"

Paulo knew Colin had been hoping it was a gift for him—he was as subtle as a wean circling toys in the Argos catalogue. "We need tae get the plates and numbers changed." Colin's tail was practically wagging now but Paulo was about to break his wee heart. "Then it's aff tae the scrappy."

"Wit? But why did we clean it?"

"We?! Ye did fuck aw!" Paulo laughed at his nephew's huffy face. "We cannae take the risk ae anythin bein foond in it—it wis a precaution. Also, it's good fir the new boays at the car wash tae see who they're workin fir, tae know their place. And *you*..."—he punched Colin on the arm—"...are gonnae be there fir them as a reminder."

24

It was still getting dark fairly early, yet Davey put in some over-time until he felt it was really, really dark. Dark enough. He put the bin bag inside another bin bag and topped it up with clean rags—not *clean* clean, used but just in the normal way—and any rubbish he could find lying about the unit before tying it tight. Then he set off down the street in the direction of home.

He detoured by a livelier part of town near the brewery, where he slipped into an alley between two rows of restaurants. The first two great big bins he tried were locked; then he spotted one that was sitting slightly open because of how full it was. A quick look at either end of the alley—the fire doors that led into the kitchens were all shut over, but chefs are notorious for sneaking fag breaks so he had to work quickly—then he tossed the lid open, pulled some of the rubbish bags out, tossed his own inside and reassembled the whole mess before pulling the lid back down.

He peeled his nitrile gloves off, balled them up and stuffed them in his pocket—he'd find a bin further away to dump them. Wiping his hands on his jeans, he started down the alley, his heart pumping nervous, toxic sludge around his insides.

"Hi-aye." The man stepped out from between two luminous-yellow oil bins just before the alley opened out onto the street—an over-muscled beast bursting out of a tracksuit, head shaved to the quick, face angular and boxy from years of being broken and reshaped. The wood-handled lock-back knife caught the orange glow of a street light somewhere beyond the alley.

"Mince," Davey said.

"Dinnae *you* call me that!" the older brother said. When he said *you* he pointed at Davey with the knife for emphasis.

Davey started to back up.

Mince advanced. His eyes were bulging with stupid hate. "Ye fuckin killed him."

"A didnae dae anythin, pal, a swear. A swear oan the life ae ma wee girrul, it wisnae me!"

"Ye went an cliped tae yer mates an they came an did him in. Stole his fuckin car an everythin."

"That's no ma fault. It wis that auld bastart Croaker who sent ye tae kidnap Paulo. Speak tae him, he's the wan that goat ye intae aw this."

"Cannae spik tae him. He's gone. Disappeared, like. Maybe Paulo's killed him too, maybe he's just run away."

"Then maybe ye should go an aw, pal, eh? A willnae say anythin. Al no tell anybody a saw ye the night, gee ye plenty ae time tae get goin."

"Aye that's richt, ye willnae tell aabdy ye seen me—ye willnae tell aabdy onythin again." He started to close the distance, knife raised.

"Look, al speak tae Paulo, get him tae leave ye alane, call it even. Av goat his ear, he'll listen tae me!"

"Yer a fuckin liar! Yer a car-wash boy, yev nae idea aboot these people, or fit goes oan."

"An *you* do? Ye kidnapped me by accident, ye sheep-shaggin eejit!"

134

"Fuck—"

Davey grabbed hold of the nearest yellow bin and hauled it over. It landed with a heavy slam and a gush as the oil surged out in a greasy, stinking wave. He turned and bolted. Mince lunged through the emptying fat bin and slipped on the growing puddle of brown, used fryer oil. He landed hard on his chin, the oil soaking him as it spilt over the cobbles of the alley. He coughed and retched as the foul-smelling stuff lapped at his mouth and nose. He got up on his feet then slipped again, his trainers completely soaked in the oil. By the time he managed to get back up a second time, Davey was already disappearing around the corner at the other end of the alley.

25

It had been a ball-breaker of a shift. Two hundred covers. In a normal restaurant, two hundred covers meant six hundred plates (maximum) to wash, plus all the pans and cooking gear. But Diego, a kitchen porter since coming to Glasgow from Madrid six months ago, worked in a fucking tapas restaurant, which meant God knows how many plates per person, plus several stacks—from counter to ceiling—of wooden charcuterie boards that had to be hand-washed. And the paella pans had to be oiled after going through the machine. And all the burnt-on crud on the supposedly non-stick frying pans had to be gently cleaned off with a soft sponge. Once he'd got through all the washing and cleaned the machine itself, he then had to deck-scrub the floor.

It was already half-eleven yet Diego was miles from even getting the dishes finished, never mind the floors. The reason being that a tiny little cutting blade from inside the mincing machine had gone missing. And the head chef—a psycho-eyed alcoholic called Eduardo—blamed Diego. Diego must have carelessly dropped it into the bin when he was scraping out the machine, Eduardo said, and as such, Diego had to go through all the bins until he found it again. Otherwise, he'd be put through the mincing machine himself.

It wasn't in any of the bins still in the kitchen, so Diego headed out into the alley to check the bin bags he'd tossed out earlier in the shift. "*Puta madré*," he said over and over, under his breath.

At least he wasn't the only one having a hard night: he gave a wave to Scott, the KP from the Italian place down the street, who was trying to soak up a massive oil spill with a roll of paper towels and a broom. "What happened, man?" Diego asked.

"Some fuckin prick knocked the fuckin fat box oer. A bet it wis that fuckin gimp fae Marco's. They goat ye fuckin dumpster-divin?"

Diego nodded. "Looking for a cutting tool this size…"—he made a circle with his thumb and forefinger about the diameter of a 10p—"…in this thing." He pointed at the overflowing bin.

"Motherfuckers," Scott said.

"*Puta madré*," Diego agreed.

He started pulling out bags and picking apart the tight knots carefully so he could retie rather than rebag when he was done. After digging through the third bag of soggy, rotten food, a huge part of him just wanted to walk away, go home, pack his bags and spend the remainder of his meagre savings on a flight to Madrid.

The fourth bag was mostly full of rags, which was odd because they weren't the kind of rags the chefs used to wipe the counters and equipment, which were all cut from a roll of cloth and were off-white with a woven texture like a bandage. These rags were strips torn from towels and clothing. Digging a little deeper, Diego found another bag inside this one. He opened it up and a strange smell came wafting out. More rags, but these ones were soaking wet and stained a dark colour.

26

The crate-training lasted less than a week. McCoist now shared her bed with Bruce, who was growing exponentially. His gangly legs prodded at her back during the night; sometimes his cold, wet nose would press against her and shock her awake. Swearing, she'd lift him out from under the covers and dump him at the foot of the bed, only for him to come back up five minutes later, whining and pawing to get under the duvet again.

It was nice in the morning though, she had to admit, having his warmth close to her, his breathing steady, calming. She would bury her face in his fur, breathe in his smell. He would often ruin these moments with a well-timed fart. Silent, the rotten stink would engulf her out of nowhere, trapped in the poor ventilation under the covers. Gas attack. Also, he'd pissed the bed three times now.

He was a stubborn mutt—walkies meant having to either drag him by the collar through the rain or hang on for dear life as he chased after a squirrel or a bird in the park. On his last visit to the vet for his immunisations she carried him home in a big blue IKEA bag.

The kids loved him though. That much was going to plan. Tess and Cam bounded through the door now when they came to stay, Bruce coming to meet them in the same manner. Kisses and cuddles. McCoist was hoping that would soon stretch to her too—that the affection towards the puppy would start to wear off on her, love by association.

Mark eyed the whole thing with suspicion but he said nothing—that was his way after all—and McCoist didn't bring up the mobile phones or all the junk his mother gave the kids in the form of her exceptional baking. (Bruce offered exceptional barking, which he did at other dogs, people, cars, litter blowing in the wind and anything else that moved or made a sound. "Gonna buy one of those bloody shock collars if you don't pipe down!" McCoist said often.)

That morning, McCoist had finished a run of night shifts. Bruce had been left to his own devices in the kitchen while she was out, so she had some crap to clean up when she got home, exhausted. Bruce had a habit of standing on the pee pad while taking a dump over the edge of it.

Janitorial duties done, she lay on the floor and let Bruce lick her face, his tail whip at her. She took him into bed and he mercifully let her have a few hours before needing to go to the toilet again and have his breakfast.

The first day post night shift was always a zombie day. McCoist forced herself to push through so she would sleep at night and get back into a normal routine. At some point she had a bleary conversation with Mark about parents' evening coming up—"Tess really wants you there, you know"; "Not that she'd ever tell me herself—fucksake, she asked you to do the careers talk over me and you're in fucking admin"; "I'm not in *admin*, I do data entry"; "Christ"—then she finished dinner with a glass of wine and fell asleep in front of the telly in the early evening.

Her phone woke her. She stabbed cancel before even looking at the name and number. It rang again: work, of course. Squat to do all week except ponder and despair over that big burnt motor—CSI had managed to put together the VIN by recovering jigsaw pieces of it from the engine and chassis but it didn't match the type of car it was inscribed on, meaning the Range Rover was knocked off and given a facelift, impossible to trace, a dead-ender—and now they were calling her for something once she was finally off. It was still dark outside the open curtains. She was confused, unloosed in time and space, drool on her chin.

"DI McCoist," she said, woolly, brain and mouth sticky with sleep.

"It's Patterson, ma'am. You're needed out—"

"I'm off," she grumbled. "It's not me you should be calling."

"DI Jarvis phoned in this morning—he's not well, can't come in. I was told you were covering the shift for him, ma'am. Did you not know?"

Of course she didn't fucking know. She didn't know because nobody told her. Being out of all loops, major and minor, was part of being ostracised. They could easily just claim it was a mistake, an administrative oversight, if she complained. "Where am I going?"

Aaaand the car wouldn't fucking start. "For fuck's sake!" She kicked the tyre, freezing cold toes making the pain more intense, strobing.

She phoned Patterson back—he took for ever to answer, they all did. McCoist suspected it was some other part of her torture, that they were all on orders to slow her down, impede her progress, and generally irritate and frustrate her as much as possible.

"DC Patterson."

"I need someone to come and get me—my car isn't starting."

"What's wrong with it?"

"I'm not a fucking mechanic, DC Patterson, just send someone to come and get me."

"Will do, Inspector."

She went back inside her house to have another coffee while she waited. Bruce was as excited to see her as he had been that morning when she'd been away for nearly twelve hours. "Calm down, you crazy animal." He yapped with excitement. "Quiet, it's the middle of the night." She got out a treat for him—he spun in circles as she held it out before snatching it from her fingers and lying down on his belly to work on the chew.

She finished the coffee, scalding hot straight from the kettle as she liked it—or at least was used to—and her stomach started rumbling, its own digestive routines disrupted by the nocturnal shift pattern. She was just thinking she'd maybe have enough time to go to the toilet when the doorbell rang.

Bruce went ballistic.

"*Shhhhh!*"

He yapped and squawked and barrelled out the kitchen, down the hall, and slammed head first into the door.

"Quiet!"

Bruce scratched the door with his front paws, his barking turning into a high-pitched whine that pierced McCoist's ear drums.

"Down! Stop! No! Bruce, listen to me! Stop for fuck's sake, it's middle of the night. Bruce. Bruce! *Come here.* Come! Here!" McCoist picked him up, limbs windmilling and scratching her, his body wriggling to be free. She bundled him back into the kitchen and closed the door, grabbing a bag of treats from the cupboard to try to settle him. It drew his attention for a second, then the doorbell rang again. "Fuck off!" she shouted at the doorbell. She tossed the chew on the floor, pulled Bruce back from the kitchen door and opened it just enough for her to slip through as he pawed, licked and nosed at her legs. "Stay!" she called to the closed door. Bruce whined on the other side. "I'll be back soon. Be good."

The porch light had come on. McCoist could see high-vis yellow through the warped window of the door. PC McClelland was waiting on the other side. "Evening, Inspector."

"You mean 'Morning'. Sorry about the dog."

"No problem, ma'am—mine goes mental when anyone comes to the door as well."

"There's no way to get them to stop then?"

"Nothing worked on mine—how old is yours?"

"I don't know exactly."

McClelland gave her a funny look.

"He's a rescue. He's a pup but I don't know how old in months." She pre-empted the next question: "He's a mongrel of some kind."

"Cute. What's his name?"

"Bruce."

They got into the car—McCoist in the back, being chauffeured, McClelland in the passenger seat with PC Mannan driving.

"The inspector has got a new puppy," McClelland said.

Mannan looked at McCoist in the rear-view mirror—eyes sharp, smile slow to follow. She'd need to develop a better poker face if she wanted to become a detective, McCoist thought, sitting there behind the grille that kept the cops from their quarries, as if she were already caught. "The kids have been bugging me about getting one for years," she said. "Bloody handful. You got any yourself?"

The interior light went off, hiding Mannan's face. "Dogs or kids, ma'am?" she said.

They pulled up in an alley running between blocks of restaurants. The smell of bins and dirty, cold frying oil created an oppressive funk that complemented the yeasty stench blowing in off the brewery nearby. A constable was standing guard at a fire door that led them into a greasy kitchen which smelled like a prison cafeteria, the floors covered in offcuts and scrapings, the white plastic walls coated in charcoal dust.

A young man was working away at the pot wash, scrubbing furiously at plates, stomp and slam as he filled the racks, hosed the dishes, flipped the handle of the machine up, slid out the clean rack, slid in the dirty one. Boom, bang. He had a long way to go, the counter next to him stacked high like a losing game of Tetris.

A fat middle-aged man watched him work. He chewed on an unlit cigarette, had a bottle of Mahou in his hand, an empty one on the countertop next to him. His hands and arms were rough, hairless, mottled with burns and striated with cuts of various vintage, from weeping fresh to scar tissue. Another uniform was waiting with him. "Ma'am," he said as McCoist approached, McClelland and Mannan flanking her. "This is Mr Eduardo Amador Conejo, the head chef and owner."

"Call me Edu," he said and held out a hand deformed by decades of work damage, exposed to blades, heat, scalding liquids, onion acid and chilli pepper.

"And he's the one who found the bag?" McCoist pointed to the lad at the sink.

"Diego!" Edu screamed. "Come here!" The boy shook off his thick black rubber gloves and dried his hands on a towel tucked into the strings of a blue plastic apron which was torn at the waist where the strings met in a wet knot.

"Hello," he said in a thick Spanish accent. He held out a hand.

"This is Diego, my KP," Edu said. "He's a pot-wash athlete!" Edu grabbed Diego's upper arm and squeezed hard. The boy winced, gave an awkward smile.

McCoist had Diego take her through the story, his English competent but careful. When she asked why he'd been out raking through the bins his eyes flashed over to his boss before he began to explain about a bit from the mincing machine getting lost.

"Mistakes happen, what can you do?" Edu said. He sounded genial, his eyes were deranged.

"And this is the bag..." A black bin bag was open on the floor, the smell of grease and something rotten wafting from it.

"Both bags were tied up when I found them," Diego said. "I opened them when I was looking for the thing."

"It definitely did not come from us," Edu said. "Look, it's not even our brand of bag. We use these..."—he held out a roll of bin bags—"...without the tie handles. Cheaper. It all adds up, you know? Thin margins."

"Were you wearing your gloves when you looked in the bag?" McCoist asked. The boy nodded. "And it was you who brought them inside?" Another nod. She looked from the young porter to the boozy kitchen vet. "I'll still need both of you to provide

144

fingerprint and DNA samples for the purpose of elimination, OK?" The big man huffed.

"Diego, I need you to take me out and show me exactly how you found them," McCoist said, then to the constables: "Knock on the other restaurants along both streets, see if anybody is still cleaning up or having a lock-in." They did as she said but she saw, or imagined she saw, a reluctance in their movements, like it was beneath them to follow her orders. Even these uniformed skivvies were second-guessing her, thinking they could do a better job of it themselves, that anyone would know better than Detective Doughball here. She took some deep breaths—too little sleep and a glass of wine were making her paranoid. She let the cold, rotten air of the alley sharpen her up. Once she might have found this exhilarating, but she knew if anything interesting turned up after the lab had a look at it then somebody else would take charge (Jarvis would likely have a quick recovery from whatever he was suffering from)—only if it was deemed a dead end would it be left in her apparently incapable hands.

When she hadn't been fired over the Knightley Fuck-Up she'd rededicated herself, sworn herself to be diligent and focused and take whatever shite came her way until she'd scrambled back into her own good graces. Stupid cow, she'd admonished herself. But the zeal faded. They'd worn her down. They'd won. All she wanted now was to keep her head down and crawl through the decades until early retirement, save some money until life could begin again. A life her children might hopefully want to be part of.

McCoist let out a jaw-cracking yawn, shivering in the alley, not bothering to cover her mouth, letting the steam of her tired wine-breath fill the air. She wanted to get back home to Bruce, curl up in bed next him. (After cleaning up whatever presents he'd prepared for her.)

Scenes of Crime had arrived suited and booted, snapping photographs and now pulling rags—shredded scraps of clothing and towels—from the bin bag and laboriously separating them into plastic evidence bags for logging. The topmost rags were smeared with grime and grease and smelled of a lemon-scented cleaning product. The ones in the bag within the bag were sodden with blood, those at the bottom sopping wet with it. There were a lot of them. They also found a stiff wire brush, its bristles rusting with congealed blood. McCoist's nose wrinkled.

"What are you thinking, ma'am?" Mannan asked, watching them work.

"I'm thinking it's animal. Some other restaurant around here has been doing a bit of butchery, cleaned it up, and dumped the results in any old bin out the back."

"Cleaned it up with old T-shirts?" Mannan pointed to a scrap being lifted from the bin, dangling from a SOCO's gloved hand—Bart Simpson's shredded face just visible beneath the blood.

Coincidence probably, but the link fired through McCoist's brain like a spark hopping between exposed wires and once a connection—however tenuous—was made, there was only one way to undo it.

27

The building had probably belonged to the council once, maybe thirty or forty years ago. That was the design, anyway: grey, square, functional as a rusty razor blade. Its face was weathered concrete with bleached red plastic frames around the windows. Hammered-metal letters spelt out "Carnaby Centre" above the front door, which was painted in flaked, glossy brown, a narrow, cracked window panel running most of the way from top to bottom. The stickers by the columns of buzzers were scabby, peeled and repeeled, label on top of label with every new business started, every business folded.

There was a blank one above "Mortimer & Saint" and below "Cushings, Ltd"—whatever they were, the inscrutability was probably intended. Nile pointed to the button. "This yin's yours, if ye want tae stick yer name oan it," he said.

"Al just leave it, a hink. Don't you?" Croaker gave him that look, like he was a stupit wee boy, condescension piled on top of the usual base level of threat he always regarded Nile with. Even when he was joking or laughing or making small talk, it was always there, that edge, that thrum of potential violence. And, oh, how Croaker wanted to let him have it, the twitchy, boot-licking rat in his cheap suit and Christmas-gift-set aftershave. The day was coming. Soon, he promised himself. So Croaker broke his glare and smiled a matey smile.

"The code is 8693." Nile punched in the numbers. Croaker was standing too close behind him—intentionally—sucking him into his aura of mouldy aftershave and cigarettes.

"Who else has it?"

"The landlord, the other business owners who rent here, anywan that works fir them, anywan they've telt…"

"Secure," Croaker grumbled.

"Well, it's just a couple ae recruitment people an a wee web designer guy, it's no like there's much need fir security. There's an alarm an that, case anywan does break in, but."

"An the polis come runnin."

"Fast as they ever dae, aye."

Nile let them in—Croaker followed, carrying a stuffed sports bag over his shoulder. The carpet looked like worn, baldy-at-the-knees corduroy. Nile took Croaker up to the second floor, where the landing split in two directions. They hooked a right where two doors faced each other. The one on the left had a sign that said: "CyberGrafix". The one on the right was blank. Like the entrance door, these were painted shiny brown with a long, thin window running top to bottom and fitted with door closers.

"This is us here." Nile took a key from his pocket.

"Wit's the neighbour like?"

"Dunno, never met him. We arenae movin here fir another month—av no been back masel since a signed the lease."

"Al be oot yer hair by then."

Nile's face said *I hope so*, but his mouth said nothing.

Inside, there were new tables covered in plastic foam wrap. Further boxes of flat-pack office furniture were stacked up around the room. It was cold, the ancient brick radiators dormant. The carpet featured the kind of pattern you'd see on a bus seat.

"There's a coupla boxes ae chairs kickin aboot somewhere. A can have them made up fir ye. There'll be a kettle an microwave somewhere an aw a hink. There's a bathroom doon the hall at the end—shared wae aw the offices oan this flair."

"Lovely, like the fuckin Ritz."

"And dae us a favour—if ye need tae smoke, go ootside. There's smoke detectors aw oer an the windaes only open up an inch—they've goat these safety hings oan them."

"Am daein ye a favour awready, son," Croaker growled. "Ye askin fir wan mair?" He waited a good five seconds before laughing and letting Nile off the hook. "Course, nae bother, pal!"

"Here's yer key." Nile closed the door behind him with audible relief.

Croaker went to the bathroom and gave himself a quick wash in the sink. He took his tablets, swallowed them with a handful of water. He ran his hands through his hair, pulling it back, away from his face, water dripping from the ends down his neck. Needed a cut but he never got round to it. The choice was either an old man barbershop or a trendy young beard-trimming parlour and he couldn't be fucked with either.

He did Nile his favour by tearing the batteries out of the smoke detectors and bursting open the safety catch on a window. He sat on the windowsill and lit up a fag. He had a duty-free carton of Mayfair in his bag that he'd bought from the Barras. It took up a lot of space in his meagre belongings—a couple of changes of clothes, a toiletry bag, rolls of cash held with elastic bands. You needed to travel light in this business, and you needed liquidity.

He'd burnt his last dosshouse as soon as Mince called to say Mealy was gone. The brothers had been sharing a flat in Brigton. Mince came back from the shop carrying a couple of frozen pizzas and a crate of tinnies for dinner and the Corsa wasn't on the street where it had been left. He looked up at the curtains, saw them twitch—flash of an unfamiliar face watching the street. He'd ducked into a nearby close and sat on his crate of beer while he spoke to Croaker:

"Somethin's up, Mr Croaker. Av bin tryin tae call Mealy but he's nae spikkin, like. Car's gone. A saw some loon's face up in the window ae the flat—"

"Did he see ye?"

"A don't think so."

"Then leave. Go. Noo."

"Fit?"

"McGuinn's foond ye, get the fuck oot ae there."

"Far should a go? And fit aboot Mealy? Far is he?"

"Lose that phone an lose yersel." Croaker hung up, split his phone open (one of several), tore up the SIM card and flushed it down the toilet. His bag was already packed and he was out the door.

He was in too much of a hurry even to be angry then. *Fuckin meatbaws.* He'd picked his muscle carefully—out of town, clean records but sketchy reputations, willing to do anything for money, and easy enough to control. Maybe too easy, the fucking eejits. By the time he'd got some breathing space from the fallout of the failed hit on Paulo, his anger had drained away. Maybe that was age, maybe wisdom—blind rage was pointless, it stopped you thinking, and now Croaker was thinking again. There was no way he could do a repeat of the carjacking. Paulo would be taking extra precautions and the rumours flying around about what happened to Andy Bannerman on Boxing Day, along with a few other known faces who hadn't been seen since, had ensured it wouldn't be easy to get anybody to help him go against Paulo. There was blood in the water and fear in the air. The feelers were out for him.

The guy in the car—*Davey Burnet fae Carntyne*—how well did he really know Paulo? He didn't seem a likely gangster—and if he was, he was a pathetic one at that—but he did have keys to the prized motor. It had been Croaker's instinct to leave him be—maybe it was time to see if it was right, see if the lad could be useful after all. Worth having a look into at any rate...

Croaker shivered, couldn't work out how the old radiator worked, gave it a kick to see if that would help. He'd set up this office situation with Nile already. Nobody knew about this one—nobody yet. And he was sure they wouldn't hear about it from Nile—he had the guy pinned down and shiteing himself to boot. He knew Fred Nile's real name, he knew the sins that had gone unpunished, and that was enough to give him an iron grip on the boy. Still, it never did to stick around in one place for too long. He'd have to start making removal plans again soon. Something that would burn the kip along with Nile himself would be sweet as a nut.

He tossed his cigarette butt out the window, lit a second one as he rooted around among the boxes for a kettle. He had some teabags and packs of sugar in a plastic bag tucked in with his bathroom kit and pills. He'd need to get something to eat soon but for now a black tea and a third cigarette would do while he waited for the call.

It came, as it inevitably did, and this time he answered, but didn't speak first.

"...Bullfrog?" said the voice on the other end.

"Here."

"Where are you?"

"Just sittin oan a lily pad."

"Are you going to get more specific?"

"Sittin oan a lily pad scratchin ma arse."

"You're not at Barrowfield Street any more?"

"See fir yersel."

A sigh rustled through the speaker. "A burnt-out car was found in an industrial estate—belonged to Paul McGuinn, apparently, according to the knit and natter, though no ownership can be traced."

"Was he inside it?"

"I think you know the answer to that already."

"Ye disappointet?"

"You know what I'm going to say—there are only so many ways to phrase the word 'reckless'. Why did you decide to answer tonight?"

"Just wantet tae hear yer voice."

"If you need something then we can arrange to meet. It's overdue. Why don't we set something up?"

Croaker held the phone away from his face and rubbed his eyes with his free hand. A wave of tiredness crashed over him. He could hear the voice coming out small from the speaker.

"Bullfrog? Are you still there? Hello?"

"No yet. Mair time. Speak soon."

"Bullfrog!"

Croaker hung up, simmering. He knew himself as a man who got results no matter what—whatever method, whatever it took, approved or not, he was the genie that couldn't be put back in the bottle, he was Robin-fuckin-Williams with bloody knuckles and a permanent hard-on—and now that had been proven otherwise. And if he wasn't the man who got results then he was just some other cunt.

Fucking Paulo McGuinn. Fourteen stone of psycho muscle turning to middle-aged jelly who walked around as if Al Capone didn't die syphilitic and alone, as if Escobar wasn't gunned down on the roof of his own home and Dillinger wasn't sold out by his own burd.

These kind of men needed reminding that a crown on the head comes with a knife in the back. And if that wasn't reason enough, there were all those souls left bloodied and ruined in their wake: corpses wrapped in sheets and tarps, mass dumpsites and river bottoms, tied, weighted, chopped up, fingers removed, teeth pulled, birthmarks peeled—all the fetishist rituals of body disposal. Dannie Gibb wasn't hard to find when you knew where to look, and Croaker had pulled all his strings and levers to narrow it down. Waxy skin through clear plastic, grey insulation tape at regular intervals—ankles, knees, waist, etc.—to make a tidy, movable package. It had kept the flies off her and the wild animals out so far. He'd already heard what to expect with regard to the ragged wound down the front, what was missing from inside. But hearing was different to seeing. There were many others like her and Croaker had seen too many of them.

No, it wouldn't stand. It was time for the next plan, whatever that might be. Davey Burnet was a thin lead but he'd made more of worse.

28

Lennox & MacGillivary had a ground-floor wedge of a tenement row on the Saltmarket, crammed between a picture gallery and the *Big Issue* office. Their window front and signage didn't scream success but neither did it hint at cold-calling ambulance-chasers.

Davey stood across the street, half hidden in a close, three fag butts crushed at his feet. He'd been running it all through in his head. Croaker the kidnapper, the car torcher; Paulo the gangster, now car-wash owner. Murderer. What would he say? How would he say it? How can you tell someone you spent a day cleaning some lad's insides out of a car boot, but that it wasn't your fault? Not really. All he'd done was tell Paulo what had happened. And what they looked like, and sounded like, and what they called each other... *Fuck*. The shakes started again.

He opened the pack for another fag and found it empty. It was time. Go across the road or go home. In or out. Take the chance and see if he could get help, get out from under all this shite and just maybe find his way back to Sarah and Annalee, or turn around and wait for the next clean-up to arrive. Free valet for loyalty-card holders. Dead bodies a speciality.

"Fuck." He strode across the road, narrowly missed getting hit by a car, the driver honking furiously, Davey not taking any notice. The door was heavier than it looked and Davey slammed into it, needing to take a step back to try again. The elderly receptionist glanced up at the noise, took in the fading bruises on Davey's face, his wired eyes, then went back to her computer screen, her fingers rattling over the keys. "Name, dear?"

"Eh, Davey Burnet."

She clicked a few times and squinted. "Am no seein ye oan here."

"Av no actually goat an appointment or anythin, a wis just hopin a could speak tae Mr Lennox fir five minutes."

"Am sorry, dear, but ye need tae book in fir him. He's a busy boay."

"Just fir five minutes, that's aw." He hadn't wanted to phone ahead. He was sure if he phoned ahead he would never turn up for it. *Stupit.* "Or just wan minute, please, missus—"

"Appointments only, dear, a really am very sorry, but—"

"It's OK, Sandra, I've got just one minute." The voice belonged to a middle-aged man in a rumpled off-white shirt stuffed into a too-tight belt. His tie was loose at the collar, the tail hanging longer than the blade. He was bald on top but the grey hair still clinging to the back and sides was shaggy and unkempt. A pair of goggles and a white coat and he'd have been a mad scientist. "Coffee?" He stepped behind the reception desk to a used and abused pod machine.

"Al huv wan, dear," Sandra said. She winked at Davey. "Mr Burnet?"

"Naw. Cheers."

Lennox took him through to his office—coffee in one hand, a Hobnob in the other, a second Hobnob held in his teeth. "Shit," he said, gesturing to a chair on the opposite side of a desk stacked with paperwork. He sat his coffee on the top of a burst Manilla folder. Davey had to move a box of files to sit down. "What can I do you for?" There was a roughness to his "proper" speech that suggested he was either hiding humble origins or he'd spent too long among Glasgow's blue-collar criminals. "Have you left the other guy looking worse?" He pointed to Davey's bruises. "Hard to prove self-defence if it looks excessive."

"Naw, naw. It's…" Davey's fists gripped the moulded plastic of the chair. He looked around the untidy office. There was no window. The urge to get up and run struck him.

"Mr Burnet, was it?"

"Aye. Davey."

"Look, Davey, you've got till I finish these biscuits, could you just—"

"Ye know the name Paul McGuinn? Paulo?"

Lennox paused with his Hobnob dunked half in his coffee cup. When he finally lifted it out, the half was completely missing, melted into the hot coffee. "I certainly do. If you're meaning the, let's say 'notorious', gang leader."

"A am."

Lennox went to eat the biscuit, his teeth coming down on nothing. He stared at the remaining half of the Hobnob as if it were something entirely alien then dropped it into the coffee, pushing the cup aside. "So what about Paul McGuinn?"

Davey wanted assurances: protection from prosecution, protection from being karate-chopped to death, protection for Sarah and Annalee. The full *Goodfellas* ending. Lennox was vague but promised Davey's story wouldn't go any further than the four walls around them. Although Davey couldn't decide if he trusted the man or not, he told him. Because he had to tell someone. Because if he didn't the weight of it was going to turn him into

Flat Stanley, get him dragged into Leverndale. It burst out of him like pus from a lanced boil—nicking Paulo's motor, getting hijacked by the sheep-shagging bodybuilders, greasy old Mr Croaker and the exploding car, McGuinn taking over the car wash and turning up with a familiar, blood-soaked motor, and then, finally, Mince returning to have a go at him—and when he was done, he felt the anxiety lift from his chest for the first time in a week. Purged.

The break didn't last long.

Lennox considered everything in silence except to ask a few pointed questions, his face set, betraying no shock or disgust. He was particularly fixated on Croaker, asking Davey to repeat his description of him again as he chewed on a raggy thumbnail.

The lawyer leant back in his chair and smoothed out his tie, tucking the wayward tail into a gap between his shirt buttons. "There's no way you could get hold of the money to replace the car?" he said.

"Aye, a could go doon the Halifax wae a balaclava oan ma heed an a banana in ma jaiket poackit," Davey replied.

Lennox nodded as if he were giving it serious thought. He leant forward, closing the distance, his elbows finding space on the desk. "It probably wouldn't make a difference now anyway. If McGuinn thinks he has a good thing going at your car wash, it might be worth more to him than the money anyway…" He let out a deep sigh and sipped at his cold coffee full of melted biscuit mush. "I could set something up with the police but it will take time. And they might not think you have enough to trade for protection. They might want to cultivate you as an informant instead. They might still want you to do some time. Are you prepared for that?"

Davey pushed himself away from Lennox. His mouth was dry, heart rising up from its hollow, choking him. He massaged the pain in his chest with a hand.

"Look, just think about this carefully, OK? I want to help you but we need to be clear-eyed going in."

"Wit if a huv mare tae tell?"

"Do you?"

Davey shook his head, struggling to speak.

"Davey, why don't I give you some time to think about this? I'll see what I can line up but I won't go ahead until we speak again, OK? Davey?"

Davey almost knocked the chair over standing up. He blundered back into the waiting room. The meeting had run well over the one minute Lennox had offered him and the room was full of bored, pissed-off punters giving him the eye as he stumbled to the door and ripped it open, practically throwing himself outside as if jumping from a plane.

He kept himself steady by leaning on the windows of the buildings as he staggered down the Saltmarket, sucking in tight, painful gulps of air that weren't enough to stop his head swimming, stars prickling in his vision.

29

On her day off, with nothing to do and nobody to see (the kids were at school and stayed with Mark during the week anyway), McCoist drove to Pollok Park with Bruce in the back. As she crawled through the estate—making sure she dipped into any muddy puddles along the way—Bruce keened and pawed at the windows, wanting to get out to chase the Highland cows, whose majestic, country stink wafted through the broken window seals of McCoist's car.

She passed the police-dog training centre—idly wondering if they would let her take a position there if she decided to give up as a detective; they could hire Bruce too—and Pollok House, ignored the small, paved, car park by the burn and drove into the adjacent field which was used for overflow parking on busy days. She trundled her way through some particularly deep mud, making the wheels spin a little, kicking up clumps of dirt and earth which splattered across the wheel arches of the Skoda, slopped up the sides and clumped in the grooves of the tyre treads.

Bruce yanked at her arm as they walked. It was something McCoist hadn't been able to put a stop to yet. (Tess refused to walk him herself, the upshot being a family walk at the weekend had become a pleasant ritual, the kids silently tapping away at their phones as McCoist fought Bruce to set the pace, the lead only changing hands when McCoist had to stop to pick up poo, a total embarrassment to the human beings she'd given birth to.) She had a pocket full of chewy, gelatinous chicken strips to get his attention away from birds, squirrels, other dogs, pedestrians, cyclists and the odd horse. She let him loose in the woods and he took a swim in the stream, then they looped back round to the car. She let him into the back seat without drying him or even putting a towel down. His muddy paws padded around, digging about for a comfy seat. "Good boy," she said. She could smell him soaking into the fabric of the seats as the car warmed up on the drive home. She dropped him off with more chicken treats—he still broke his heart whenever she left, which in turn always made her feel ill, but he would get used to it. That's what she kept saying to herself. They'd both get used to it, the loneliness, the guilt.

She drove her filthy car into the town and pulled up at the car wash behind a white Beamer that was being lathered up by Burnet. Prentice was waiting with a mitt on each hand, fag hanging out of his mouth. A young guy she didn't recognise was leaning against the jet washer smoking—a pose too familiar to be a customer, she reckoned, plus he was wearing the unofficial car-wash uniform: old hoody (no zip), old jeans and a pair of Timbies on his feet. The only thing out of place was that these items were all completely dry. He was a big lad—broad-shouldered, muscular, virile-looking in a way that Burnet and Prentice were not. The two of them were shrunken by comparison, too much time in the wash.

They finished with the Beamer and it drove off. Burnet walked out onto the street and called her forwards, only clocking her as she pulled up into place. "Sean?!"

"Ahh fuck. Wit's it this time, missus?" Prentice grumbled.

"Just wanted to see if that discount offer still stood." She held out her keys. "I'm needing a full valet—seats shampooed too."

"Christ, wit happened in there?" Burnet was looking through the back window at the mess she'd let Bruce make of the seat. He stood back to take in the bigger picture, the muck all over the lower half of the Skoda. "Is that horse shite?"

"Took my dog out for a walk."

"A don't guarantee a can get aw the dug hair oot ae the seats, by the way," he huffed.

"That's all right, just do your best," McCoist said, laying on the condescension as thick as she could to make sure the mug got it.

"Twenty-two fifty includin yer ten per cent aff," Prentice said, taking the keys. "Come back in an oor or somethin."

"I'd rather stay here and wait," she said.

"It's no gonnae get nicked. Think am dumb enough tae blag a motor fae a polis?" He tapped the key fob against his hand.

"I'll not answer that." McCoist noticed the young guy perking up at this exchange. He gave her a brazen top-to-bottom that made her feel sorry for the young women of the world.

Prentice tossed the keys to Burnet. "Ye want a tea while ye wait?"

"Got any coffee?"

"Aye—milk an sugar?"

"Both."

"Al huv wan an aw," the young guy said.

Prentice glared at him. "Colin, why don't ye gee Davey Boy a hawn an we can get *Detective Inspector* McCoist oan her way as soon as, eh?"

The guy replied by lighting another fag, changing the polarity of his crossed legs. Prentice stomped away to the office muttering to himself.

Burnet pulled the rubber mats from her car and lined them up on the pavement. He sprayed them with cleaning solution and blasted them with the jet washer. "Yer in ma road, Colin," he said to the young guy as he whipped the hose to straighten it out. The guy still didn't move. Then Burnet dragged the hoover out the corner on broken wheels, unwound the cable and clambered into the Skoda, digging into all the corners and crevices of the footwell, his arse crack and the soles of his boots the only parts of him that were visible.

"You on your break?" McCoist asked the boy called Colin.

"Cannae work oan the tools constant waeoot regular breaks—cause ae vibration white finger rules an that. Health an safety. It's the *law*." He smirked.

"An ye cannae get vibration white finger if it's stuck up yer arse aw the time." Prentice appeared with a styrofoam cup in one hand and a mug in the other. "Broon finger's the bigger problem fir Colin."

"Fuck up," Colin said, taking the mug from him. He looked ready to say more but was obviously put off by McCoist's presence.

McCoist took the cup and had a sip. It was an absolute kicking of a beverage: scalding hot, sickly-sweet, painfully bitter, sour with too much heavy milk. Decent. "Cheers," she said.

Burnet was gathering up window polish, sponges, something in a spray bottle that was a caustic yellow colour from the rack. He pulled some rags from a tight plastic-wrapped sack below—this is what she came for, either to shut up the idea worming through her head or to risk opening the can fully. They were of various colours and textures, some strips from worn-out bath towels, others from clothing. She saw part of a Jack Daniel's logo on what once must have been a black T-shirt, the kind bartenders often wore.

"Where do you get those rags from?"

Prentice was gathering up some gear too, since Colin was obviously not going to help. "Fae the laundrette doon the road."

"They get recycled?"

"Aye, a shove them in a bin bag an take the dirty wans back every coupla days an they gee me a bag ae clean yins."

There was a dustbin next to the pack of laundrette-fresh rags. The bag inside had yellow tie handles. Filthy strips of threadbare tea towels and bleached clothing were piled up over the rim, Spider-Man's headless body visible under a grimy oil stain. That niggle she'd felt when she'd seen Bart Simpson's bloody face—the one that brought her round snooping—became a cartoon anvil dropping on her head. She swallowed another mouthful of acid coffee. It could be nothing—how many car washes used recycled rags like that for cleaning? How many also happened to use bin bags with yellow tie handles? Even if her hunch was correct, unless she found another Bart Simpson scrap that matched the bloody one exactly, it was of no evidential value. Still, she felt that itch in her brain insisting there was something there and the almost-forgotten excitement that went with it.

"Where do you get your soaps and other stuff from?"

"Ye startin up yer ain car wash?" Colin asked, sneering.

"Just interested."

"Just nosy, mare like."

"Nosy is my job."

"Well, don't be bringin yer joab roon here any mare, goat it?" He stood up, dropped what was left of his fag in his mug and it sizzled out.

"But you do such a good job yourself." She took a measured sip from her coffee for emphasis, holding his gaze over the mouth of the cup.

Colin did the same, copying the gesture, and choked on a mouthful of ash, spluttering all over himself.

"Fuckin eejit," Prentice hissed.

MARCH

30

"Panic attacks," the doctor said.

Davey wasn't usually one to go to the doctor but he thought he'd had two or three heart attacks in the weeks since Mince jumped him in the alley—and, of course, everything that had come before: the beating, the explosion, the bloody car, losing Annalee... Random thoughts of these incidents were causing Davey to hit the deck, unable to catch his breath, his heart rattling like it might just pop. He'd dragged his arse to the GP one morning for an emergency appointment, expecting to be told he'd had a stroke or an aneurysm, but no. "Panic attacks caused by acute anxiety," she'd said.

"So wit? It's all in ma heed?" Davey asked. Grim memories of the hospital on Boxing Day crept up on him.

The doctor chewed the lid of her pen for a moment before answering. "The cause of the attacks is psychological, but the pain and distress you feel during them is very real and shouldn't be ignored." She could prescribe something, but she wanted him to talk to someone too. "Talking therapies are very effective for anxiety." Davey didn't see how, just the thought of sitting with a bunch of strangers and telling them all his personal shite was likely to make him break out in a rash. How could he explain to people that he was edgy from watching his back all the time, jumping at every shadow, sprinting past the abandoned cattle market at nights, imagining he could smell the beasts and the butchered meat? He let her put his name on the waiting list anyway, worried she might not hand over the script if he refused.

She asked him briefly about work and home, trying to gauge potential stressors. The weather was thawing out now, so work was getting busier but more bearable—though he was often distracted, leaving muddy streaks on the cars, or a window still smeared with polish, chaining fags and feeling jittery, Colin jawing away in the background at all times. His mother was talking to him again, which was good because she (against all logic) got on well with Sarah and was still seeing her and Annalee regularly. Getting Maw back onside was a massive boost. There was no way he could disclose the most likely cause of his problems though, so it was either the doctor's prescription or self-medication, and Davey didn't think he could survive the latter. Thankfully, she gave him the pills.

Loads of Paulo's pals and associates were coming to the car wash to get their motors valeted. Many arrived in a similar state that Paulo's had that morning last year, stinking of perfume and sweat, the windows covered in handprints, cum stains on the seats. Twice, Davey and Sean had hoovered large amounts of suspicious white powder from the boot of a car where a brick had split open and spilt its valuable contents. In these cases, they emptied the vacuum's dust container into a fresh bag and handed it over to the driver of the car.

Colin didn't help because he was useless as an apprentice and he wasn't really there to work anyway. He made that pretty clear—ignoring any request for him to get off his arse and do something—so, therefore, wasn't a great spy either. When he wasn't watching the telly and smoking Sean's weed, he was chatting with Uncle Paul's business friends while Davey scrubbed the semen and hoovered the blow. "Took a wee visit tae the kaboose hoose, eh, McCready?" He was often told to shut the fuck up.

Davey kept his ears open. It was easy to gather from the work and from Colin being gobby that Paulo was running brothels and moving drugs—and yet when he'd first met him, Davey had assumed from the Big Man act that Paulo's "gangster" activities had involved nothing more than selling counterfeit trainers down at the Barras of a weekend. *Yev nae idea aboot these people, or fit goes oan,* Mince had said. Davey was pretty sure he had a good idea now. And he was keeping it all filed away in his head, later scribbling it down at home on spare bits of paper which he hid away under his mattress like some mental cunt. He hadn't called the lawyer, Lennox, back yet, but when he did he wanted to have as much ammo to bargain with as possible, enough to trade with the polis for a new life, for all of them.

Then, that morning, the truck arrived.

It was a small lorry, more like the ones home-removal businesses used rather than a full-on artic. Still, it would be a massive job. Sean came stomping out the unit as the driver climbed down. "Sorry pal, we don't usually dae big lorries, this is just a wee hawn car wash—"

"This is fir Paulo," the guy interrupted, and Sean's shoulders slumped. He dug the heels of his palms into his eye sockets and grumbled something under his breath. "Wit wis that?" the driver said. He was a big lad, saggy from years of sitting on his arse and snacking on junk food during long drives, but he still looked capable of bulldozing someone if he got moving.

"Nothin," Sean said. "Just... We'll need tae get the big ladder oot ae storage if yer wantin us tae dae the roof."

"Fuck the roof," the driver said, "just clean inside the back, awright?" He slapped a meaty hand against the side of the lorry and tossed his keys to Sean. "Ye goat a bog in there? Am dyin fir a shite."

Sean huffed. "Just roon that wee corner there by the office door."

Davey was waiting at the back of the lorry. "You're lookin inside first," Sean said.

As soon as the door swung open, the smell came wafting out. Davey and Sean both stepped back, covering their mouths and noses with their hands. The vinegar stink of stale urine assaulted them first, then billowing along on the undertow was the other kind of human waste. The mellow tang of sweat and unwashed clothes completed the bouquet.

"Christ, it smells like they've been runnin a nursin hame in there," Davey said.

"Smells like a tramp's scants," Sean said, eyes tearing up.

Colin came out to see what the fuss was about. "Fuckin hell!" He fell back as if he'd been punched. "Wit is that, the devil's fuckin Portaloo?" He started laughing. "Yer gonnae huv some fun wae this yin, Davey!"

"Ye no helpin oot, Colin? Yer usually so fuckin useful an aw," Davey said, his voice brittle, pacing and tugging at his hair.

"Wit wis that, Davey Boy?" Colin tried his uncle's trick of switching from comedian to tough guy, like a French mime sliding a hand over his face—now smiley, now frowny. It didn't quite work, but it still made Davey think about Colin's nickname, "The Karaterpillar", and wonder if there was any truth to it.

"Nothin, Colin," Sean said, getting between them. "He's just pullin yer prick. Go an roll a joint, that would be fuckin useful right noo."

"If yev goat a problem, Davey, just say it. Al stick it in ma uncle's complaints boax if ye want."

Davey said nothing.

"Thought not," Colin said.

Davey's stomach turned as he reached out to open the back of the lorry, trying to brace himself for it this time. His hand was shaking. He could feel the burbling of panic down in his guts and had to turn away, taking deep breaths, rubbing his gloved hands together as if they were cold. He noticed Colin giving him a funny look from the open office door and shot him a thumbs up. Colin replied with the vicky. *Arsehole.*

Davey lunged forward, snatched the door open, fell back coughing and spluttering as the stink of starving, suffocating, freezing bodies steamrolled him again. It was an animal smell, there was fear and desperation soaked into every cubic centimetre of the wood-panelled hold.

He attacked it with the foam gun, lathering everything in a thick layer of sweet-smelling snow, hiding the various stains and burying the evidence. Then he took the lance and power-washed inside, the foam and the filth crashing out of the lorry in a wave onto the road and down the drain at the corner of the street. He foamed it up again, this time climbing up into the box and scrubbing the floor, walls and ceiling with a stiff broom before power-washing once more. He left the doors open to let the weak spring sunshine dry it out a little.

Davey valeted the rest of the truck too while the driver waited, yacking away with Colin: "Aw, the lorries these days practically drive themsels. Get yersel oan the motorway, stick the cruise control oan, it reads the traffic, automatically slows doon and speeds up, stays in the lane, everythin. Tell ye wit, oan ma way up fae Dover a wis just sat there wae ma phone oot under the wheel, huvin a cheeky tug as a drove up the M6…"

When he'd finished, Davey tossed his gloves in the bin and handed the keys over. "Aw done."

"Cheers, pal! Transportin livestock makes a hell ae a mess!"

"Livestock? Wit kind ae animals ye carryin?" Colin asked. Everyone turned to look at him. The driver gave sideways looks to Sean and Davey, an *"is this cunt for real?"* look.

"Sheep," the driver said, and winked.

As the lorry drove away, Colin said, "Sheep? Christ, ye hink Scotland wid huv enough fuckin sheep awready waeoot bringin in mare!"

Davey shook his head and stalked away to fill up the soaps and squeeze out the sponges.

"Wit?" Colin asked.

"Yer wastet workin in a car wash, son," Sean said. "Wae a brain like yours, ye could dae anythin!"

31

It wasn't until he was back in his flat that it hit him—the deep pain stabbing into his chest, his stomach hurting as he wheezed, struggling to catch his breath, his ribcage squeezing down on his lungs and threatening to crack. He couldn't swallow the tranquillisers, choking on the water as he tried to wash them down, so he ground them to powder with his teeth and swallowed the dry, chalky mixture, forcing it down until he was nearly sick.

When the shaking stopped, he rummaged through his kitchen cupboards (he'd been making an effort to keep the gaff clean and tidy, which meant he could no longer find anything) until he found a half bottle of Glen's his maw had left there at some point. The doctor had made it pretty clear not to mix the tranqs with alcohol, but desperate times called for desperate measures—Davey's was a triple.

He choked half the enormous shot down in one—the cheap vodka burning the taste buds off his tongue and stripping the inner lining off his mouth and throat as it slipped down into his belly—and poured the rest of the bottle down the sink. Then he crashed down onto his TV chair, head whirling, body oozing into the seat.

"Wit a day, wit a fuckin day," he mumbled to himself, words slurring.

Something was beeping, and the thought drifted through his mind that it might be the fire alarm and the whole building might be burning down while he was just sat there, cosy, and after they'd put it out all they'd find was his skeleton just sitting there, chilling out in front of the melted telly, blissed out on diazepam, not a fuck to give in the world. *Might be awright…*

Davey shot awake in the dark, a sudden sense of vertigo as he struggled to understand where he was. As he calmed down, black shapes formed themselves into the familiar outlines of the couch and the telly and the coffee table. He remembered taking the pills and washing them down with vodka. Then he remembered why: the lorry, stinking of human waste. People died in the back of those things, sometimes. Probably often. If death had any smell wouldn't it be just like that lorry?

He launched himself from the chair, stumbled through to his bedroom, catching his elbow on the door frame. He pulled a holdall down from the top of his wardrobe and started stuffing clothes into it—just whipping things off their hangers without looking to see what they were and bundling them in unfolded. As he raided his sock-and-undie drawer, some part of his mind—the Voice of Reason, maybe—needled him with questions. Where will you go? What will you do when you get there? The answers snarled back: *Anywhere, anythin.* What will happen to Sean if you do a runner? They might hurt him, in your place. *He's a grown man, he can look eftir himsel.* There was, of course, one place his mind could go to put a halt to his mad dash, one thing the Voice of Reason could say to stop him from leaving, but it didn't have to…

He snatched up his phone to check the time and saw there was a missed call from his maw hours before—the beeping he'd heard. She'd left a voicemail. She was the only person Davey knew who would ever leave a voicemail.

"David, it's yer maw here…"—*well, obviously, fir fucksake*—"…just tae let ye know a wis speakin tae Sarah aboot Annalee's birthday next month an she says she might see her way tae lettin ye come tae the perty, just fir a wee bit. So just, just stay oot ae trouble, awright? Al keep talkin ye up an hopefully she willnae change her mind afore then. Get the wean somethin good fir it. A can help ye wae the money if ye need it, but get her somethin good, that way… ye know. Geez a call when ye get this."

He dropped the holdall, sagged down onto the bed. He reached under the mattress and felt around for the notes he'd taken—he hadn't written anything about the lorry yet. Some of it was indecipherable even to him, most of the handwriting so ugly it was rendered as complex as the Zodiac's code, but he still thought about ripping it all up there and then. *Fuck, if Paulo finds oot wit yer up tae he'll tear ye fae ear tae arse. It's madness, absolute fuckin madness.* Reason was so often correct but cowardly. If he wanted a proper chance at life with his family again, he would need to be brave, even if that meant doing something daft. Davey didn't tear up the paper. Instead, he switched on his bedside lamp and rooted around for a pen.

When he finished writing there was no getting back to sleep so he jumped in the shower and decided to walk to the twenty-four-hour McDonald's for a scran before work.

32

There were three boxing gyms that seemed likely. Croaker hit it lucky on the second one up in Springburn: "Ye hud a big teuchter lad in here lately? He's goat a scalped heed, a mashed-up pus, an gees it aw 'nicht' an 'richt' an 'fit like' an that."

The owner/coach was a stout wee hard man of around fifty—could have been younger though: the rough parts of Glasgow age the skin as if you're living in radioactive Pripyat. He shrugged, not telling. "How?"

"A want tae find him, that's how."

"You his da, aye?" The old boxer laughed, showing off toothless gums.

"His social worker, mare like! Cunt's bin puntin roids in aw the gyms fae here tae John O'Groats. A want tae put a stoap tae it afore he gets himsel in mare trouble. It would save ye some problems ae yer ain an aw."

The boxer glared. They might have been around the same age, both of them weathered and the worse for wear, and Croaker had the height advantage, but there was no way he could win in a physical confrontation. All he could do was face him down with an attitude of sheer vicious abandon and hope it worked.

It did. "Aye, lad like that's bin comin here right enough—*richt* enough…"—he laughed at his own joke again. "Shown up Wednesday an Friday the past two weeks. Listen, a cannae huv him puntin shite in here. Am no, like, *against* the stuff but—"

"Ye arenae the wan who decides who can sell where an wit. A get it. Al sort it, pal, nae worries."

Gym rats are creatures of habit. They've got to work out. They need it like a junky needs heroin. They'll do it bigger and more until it breaks their body. Mince was one of those guys. He couldn't stay away even though his brother had just been killed and half the city's gangsters were after him. He'd go without sex and television before he'd go without the gym.

Croaker watched him strut into the boxing gym in Springburn on Wednesday evening after dark—gym bag over his shoulder. Croaker waited ten minutes and followed.

The gym was busy—stuffed with beefcakes, the air warm and heavy and smelling of trench foot. A pair were sparring in the ring in the centre of the room, grunting and wheezing as they tested each other out.

Croaker winked at the gummsy owner as he passed the front desk, finding a dark corner to hang around in. There was Mince, working out. He skipped and punched bags and lifted weights alone. He turned red, veins popped, eyes screwed up in painful ecstasy. He could have cracked nuts open between the bulging muscles of his tensed arm. He pushed himself until his breath was ragged, his whole body shining with sweat, veins ready to burst. Good. Croaker wanted him exhausted when they spoke, just in case.

Mince had put himself through a truly brutal routine—Croaker equal parts impressed and impatient—by the time he towelled himself down and headed for the changing room. Croaker followed.

The changing room smelled even worse. Croaker felt like he was wearing a pair of three-day-old Ys over his head.

Mince was stripping off to go for a shower. Croaker waited until he was bollock naked before saying: "Fit like, Mince?"

The lad jumped. His cock and balls juggled comically. It was a fair-sized piece he was carrying. "Mr Croaker..." To his credit, he didn't try to cover himself up. That was bad news for Croaker, though—he wasn't defensive, the boy was a bull ready to charge. "A thought ye were—"

"Deed meat? Naw, that's *your* nickname, son, no mine." He gave a wheezy laugh which turned into a crackling cough, the phlegm sacks he used as lungs threatening to regurgitate themselves entirely.

"Fit ye after?"

"Time tae get back tae work. Lain low lang enough. New plan, time tae move an shake."

"Move an shake," Mince repeated. "A had tae leave the hoose wae nae money an nae clothes, like. Had thawed oot pizza fir ma breakfast the next mornin in an underpass. Ma brother is fuckin deed."

"Aw the mare reason tae take the bastart doon."

"Fit is this fir you?"

"Av telt ye, aboot ma wee Becca. Wit that cunt did tae her." Becca, Dannie and plenty of others Croaker had seen used and beaten, drugged up and pimped out by Paul McGuinn. And when they were no longer needed, they ended up face down in the mud. Heads split open, or ligature marks on the throat, or a puncture in the lung or heart. Croaker had seen a girl who'd been suffocated with a poly bag over her head, eyeballs full of blood. And Dannie with her belly opened up...

"Ye have. Yev telt me twice or more."

"Well there ye go, yev a memory like Rain Man, well done."

"Fuck up."

"Watch who yer fuckin talkin tae," Croaker snapped. He prodded a ragged, yellow fingernail into Mince's rock-solid chest, which was adorned with muscle-head tattoos: hyper-realistic animal portraits, older, greying tribal patterns, the word "Unlimitless" in script across his collar. "Ye know wit that man did tae ma wee girrul an ye know how far am willin tae go fir revenge. Aw the fuckin way. An you should too. A didnae kill yer brother. He did."

"If we hadnae got mixed up wae ye—"

"Well ye did. An it wis yer ain choice, ye cannae hawd that against me. An if ye hud done yer fuckin homework an grabbed the right guy, none ae this would be happenin."

Mince's face was all dumb hate, body tensed, every wire and rope of muscle singing tight. This was the moment where Mince would either punch him out or not...

He looked away.

"Ye were bein paid fair enough an aw. Hows aboot this: join us fir another tour an ye get Mealy's share as well as yer ain. Come oan, son, they're oot there lookin fir us baith, ye know that? We need each other. We need tae get this done noo, there's nae goin back."

"If a say aye, like, then a get tae be the een who divs him."

That hit Croaker out of nowhere. He almost burst into laughter; he felt it tickle in his belly, in his blackened and shrivelled chest. He'd been after Paulo McGuinn for years. *Years*. The attempted kidnapping was just the last and most extreme in a long line of schemes to get at Paulo, one he'd started putting together after Knightley went down and everything turned to shit. Desperation Station. In that time he'd strayed way off into the jungle in his pursuit of the big, sacred tiger—all the ones before him had been hogs and does by comparison. Lured away, obsessed, no way to return. He'd become an animal himself out there in the wilds. He'd done things he had never thought himself capable of, things that would shame the devil. He looked at his twisted and haggard reflection and saw he no longer recognised that person. They were gone for ever. This had cost him everything—and now this big, silly teuchter cunt was asking to be the one to finally bring the hammer down.

Croaker controlled himself, let a smile spread across his face. "Be ma guest."

33

Sean was incensed. He was always incensed, about the BBC, or the government, or the pigeons, or—worse than all above—the customers, but now he was *really* incensed. He stomped around the unit, eyes pinballing off the walls, fists clenching and unclenching.

"Ye awright, Sean? Ye seem a bit wound up," Davey said.

"Funny fucker, are ye?" Sean squared right up to Davey; they were almost chest to chest. This close, Davey could smell cigarettes and coffee on Sean's breath. He could see the thick, bristly hairs peeking out from Sean's nostrils as they flared. "The guy that steals a fuckin gang lord's motor, wrecks it, and leaves me payin the bill, is here makin fuckin jokes?" Davey was used to Sean's screaming matches with customers and salesmen and local jakies, but he didn't have much experience of being on the receiving end—even when the whole shitestorm started with Paulo, Sean hadn't torn him a new arsehole. He must have been too shocked, too scared.

"Am sorry, Sean, a didnae mean tae take the pish, just wantet tae know if somethin's happened…" *Christ, it cannae be worse than the lorry…*

Sean turned away, heading for the office. For a second Davey thought he might be going for the air pistol and wondered if he should start running. "Let's get the fuckin kettle oan," Sean said. As he set up a brew, he let out a deep sigh like a punctured balloon. "Rusty willnae sell us weed any mare."

"Wit?! How come?" Davey was genuinely shocked. Rusty had been Sean's dealer for years and constituted the one solid relationship in the man's life.

"Someone's fuckin bin at him, wan ae Paulo's lot."

"Ye sure?" Sean was a paranoid guy as standard, and Davey was halfway there himself, but he had to ask. "A mean, how dye know?"

"Goat a text message fae that shite-fir-brains Colin sayin him an his uncle could hook us up wae aw the grass a want. A says naw, cause av goat ma ain guy. Then aw ae a sudden, Rusty willnae sell tae me any mare, willnae even speak tae me. Am tellin ye, they've bin roon fir a word wae him. Probly mare than a word."

"Fuck… Well, a guess ye could still get weed fae Paulo at least—"

"A don't want Paulo's fuckin weed!" Sean threw his mug at the wall, where, rather than breaking, it buried itself in the gyprock. Lukewarm coffee dribbled down the wall. Davey stepped back from it as if it were an unexploded bomb. "Takin the car wash wisnae fuckin enough fir them! Noo they've goat me buyin their fuckin skunk an aw. Well, that's it, am fuckin quittin."

"But ye cannae quit, Sean, it's *your* car wash, ye own the place."

"No the car wash, ye fuckin eejit. The weed!"

Davey had to take a seat. Sean quitting the ganj. That would be something. "Maybe that's a good hing, Sean," Davey said.

"Shut. The. Fuck. Up."

Sean worked that morning. He hustled, he scrubbed, he polished, he held the lance with one hand, chain-smoking fags with the other—an army of roll-ups laid out across the top of the jet wash unit that fell one by one. Valeted cars were returned to customers stinking of smoke. They looked away from Sean's face and didn't complain.

Colin didn't turn up until the afternoon, with Paulo in the driver's seat of a brand-new monster truck, its engine making a glacier-melting roar, its paintwork a gleaming black shell, V2P MCG on the number plate. The Big Man dropped down onto the ground. "Look at that, Davey Boy, that's how a man works." He pointed at Sean furiously scrubbing the burnt-on brake dust from an Audi's alloys. "That's how ye become the gaffer. Hard fuckin graft! Knockin yer pan in!" He swaggered over and squeezed Sean's shoulder. "Take a break, pal, come oan, let's get a cuppa."

"Al be five minutes, Paulo," Sean said, not turning round. Davey caught the look flicker over Paulo's face—just a flash of anger, then back to the matey "boss-who's-yer-pal" thing he had going.

"Nae worries," Paulo said. "Finish up an come tae the office."

Davey made the teas and coffees. "Two sugars wis it, Paulo?"

"Aye, an a spoonful ae crystal meth if yev goat it, am fuckin knackered, wis up aw night ridin!" He pulled the reins on an imaginary horse and clicked his tongue, making a *clip-clop* noise.

"Fucksake, that's ma aunt yer oan aboot!" Colin said.

"She'd be fuckin lucky," Paulo said. He gave Colin the death stare then burst into laughter. The young lad forced a chuckle, not really sure exactly what was going on but getting the feeling that he could be in trouble if he didn't pipe down.

"Well, am afraid aw av goat is sugar the day, Paulo," Davey said, trying to steer the conversation back to somewhere safe, knowing it rarely stayed that way for long with Paulo. In fact, he knew for definite it wouldn't—Paulo had carried in what looked like a flight case for a musical instrument with him and sat it on the couch, where its hard, black sheen caused a shiver to run up Davey's back. There was something radioactive about it.

"It'll huv tae dae then," Paulo said, and slurped the just-boiled instant coffee black, making a lot of noise to get some cold air in his mouth with it. "Like the new motor, Davey Boy? Goat it shipped oer fae the States. The hing's fuckin bulletproof!"

Davey nodded. "Is it, aye? Nice wan." Finding words was difficult around Paulo and even the few he managed always came out thin and slightly high-pitched.

"Nice? Bit better than nice, ad say!"

Sean marched in and accepted a cup from Davey, his usual mug having been rescued from the wall with only a minor crack at the rim. "Ye awright, Paulo?" He lit up another rolly.

"Knackered, mate, been up aw night pumpin," he said, again. Sean just nodded. A lifetime solitary stoner, sex was not something that entered Sean's mind much any more. The last time he'd got laid was so far away the very idea of sex had become abstract. There were no nude calendars on the walls of the unit as you would expect of such an establishment. Not getting the reaction he wanted, Paulo changed tack. "Goat some sweet Hindu Kush comin in this weekend if ye want some? Al gee ye a good deal by the ounce. Mate's rates, aye?"

"Am aff it," Sean said, pointing to the stubby cigarette in his mouth, where usually there would be a long three-skinner.

"Aff it? Since when?"

"This mornin. A just woke up an thoat… 'Fuck it.'"

Davey was watching Paulo's face carefully, waiting for the quick reveal, a glimpse of the fury, but it didn't come. "Well, good fir you, mate. That shite rots yer brains, a should know! But if ye change yer mind…"

"Al let ye know."

"Sound!"

There was silence as the four men sipped their hot drinks. Colin was smirking, looking like he was holding in an uncomfortable laugh.

"Want me tae gee yer new motor a wash, Paulo?" Davey asked, just to break the tension—he had no actual desire to have to clamber all over that mammoth thing to clean it.

"No the day, Davey Boy, cheers. Just stoappin aff fir a quick coffee an a word. Goat a favour tae ask, actually." He drew them over to the black flight case. He popped the locks and lifted the lid. "How aboot wan ae these tae keep the bastart pigeons at bay?"

The inside of the case was padded with foam cones like the inside of an egg carton. Davey had last seen something like this when he was at school—the wee gimps who spent their weekends down at the Games Workshop used to carry them around. It was where they kept their models, the miniature soldiers and goblins and whatever-the-fuck-else those virgin-lifers were into. Davey remembered him and Hammy and Greg stealing a case like that off a dweeb called Martyn Bell(end) and tearing all the painstakingly painted figurines from their protective eggbox padding and throwing them on the ground, crushing them under their feet while the poor sod Martyn greeted. While he stomped on them, Davey thought to himself how pretty they were and, in hindsight, knew he was jealous of Martyn for having them, and for having the skill and time to paint them, and for having friends to share his hobby with. If only that's what was inside Paulo's briefcase too. Davey would gladly take a guilt trip down memory lane rather than be confronted with the insidious, oozing fear produced by the actual contents.

Paulo held it up. The gun looked brand new. A pistol made from matt-black plastic with a blocky-looking barrel and a grip moulded to fit comfortably in the hand. Davey had seen one like it in films.

"It's no quite Dirty Harry," Paulo said, "but it's sexy in its own wee way, int it?" He pushed a button with his thumb and the magazine slid out. He gave them a quick look. "Empty. Fir noo. Anybody want tae hawd it?"

"Geez a shot!" Colin lunged at it.

"Careful, dickheed, it's a gun fir fucksake, no a fitbaw."

Colin took the pistol, fumbled the magazine back into the grip like a teenage boy having his first ride, then slapped it home once it was lined up, trying to emulate the way an action hero would reload his gun. He pointed it at the wall—two-handed grip copied from *COD*—and cocked his head with one eye closed to look down the sights. "Yippee ki-yay, moth-erfucker," he said, and pulled the trigger, which made a click that caused everybody else to jump.

"Wit the fuck?!" Paulo screamed, yanking the pistol from his nephew's hands.

"Wit?" Colin's cheeks were turning red. "It's no loadet."

"Doesnae matter if it's no fuckin loadet, ye don't pull the fuckin trigger!"

"Why?"

186

"Ye just fuckin don't! Fucksake. Ye no seen aw them stories aboot American maws bein shot by their two-year-auld weans?"

Colin huffed.

Paulo put the gun back into its groove in the padding. There were two more just like it in there. "Right, Sean, a want ye tae keep this here, just fir the noo. Av goat somethin comin up an a need ye tae hawd on tae it till then. A shouldnae huv tae say this but a will: keep it fuckin hidden."

He also gave them four shoeboxes full of loose bullets.

Davey asked Paulo for a quick word before he shot off. It was the first time he'd ever been one-on-one with the man. Having his complete, focused attention without anyone else to deflect it onto was almost painfully uncomfortable. The man's eyes were not easy to meet.

"It's no ma round tae dae a favour noo is it, Davey Boy? Thoat you were still het." He did his smiling growl.

"No at aw, Paulo," Davey said. He took a breath; then, once he'd started, the words stumbled out in a nervous prattle. "But it is aboot favours. Cause aw this wis ma fault, yer right, an *a* should be taken the derry fir it, no Sean. If there's, a dunno, somethin a could help ye wae or that, ye know, tae help pay ye back. A can dae it. Sean doesnae huv tae be involved. Just me." Much as his common sense baulked at it, Davey needed to find out more, get in deeper with Paulo and his organisa- tion—a mole was called a mole for a reason. *Aye, an clipes also bide undergroond*, the Voice of Reason sniped. *Yel end in the muck wan way or the other.*

Paulo gave him a cold, searching look which turned to bemusement. He laughed. "Davey Boy!" He clamped a hand on Davey's shoulder, almost buckling his knees. "Maybe yer no such a wee fanny baws eftir aw. Good oan ye, son. But there's fuck aw a want fae ye, an yev fuck aw tae gee." He gave Davey a dead arm and hoisted himself up into his new car.

34

"Somethin's fuckin happenin, an a know where the guns are, an if that's no enough fir the polis tae step in an gee me a get-oot-ae-jail-free cerd an a joab as a rid coat in Butlins then a don't know wit fuckin is." Davey was stabbing at the crumpled, messy notes he'd written, scattered on Lennox's desk, and slurring his words. He'd taken a blue on top of his prescription meds, which, combined with coffee and fags, was making him simultaneously spacey and agitated.

Lennox sifted through the notes. The office's stark lighting gave the lawyer's bald crown a good shine. His tie was loose around his neck, his shirt open at the collar, revealing grey chest hairs and a vest below. "This is… dangerous, Davey. You shouldn't be doing this by yourself, the police should be involved. I thought you were going to think things through."

"A fuckin did, an a decided am better aff daein it by masel, then we can go tae the polis fir a good deal. Me an Sarah an the wean, aw looked eftir. Nae bullshit. Nae mare grassin, nae jail."

Lennox collected the sheets together again. "This isn't going to sort out your custody problems, Davey. They won't just stick you all in a house together down at the Lakes—"

"Wit the fuck am a sposed tae dae!" Davey slammed his fist onto the desk so hard his hand went numb. He sniffed hard, holding on to tears.

Lennox flipped through the pages again as Davey calmed down. "Did you get the reg of the truck?"

Davey shook his head.

"The guns might be a goer. Your boss could be looking at some trouble for hiding them though."

"He's no goat a choice. He has tae. An it's ma fault. Al swear tae that."

"He'll have to make his own deal when the time comes. You think he would be willing to cooperate as well?"

Davey sniggered, wiped his eyes. "Absolutely fuckin not."

"Well, that's another consideration, then."

"Ye hink a should just pack it aw in an run, don't ye?"

"It must have occurred to you. And it might be the best way to avoid hurting more people."

"Wit aboot Paulo? Ye no keen tae see him put away, big-shot lawyer?"

Lennox just smiled at the barb. "When they put away men like him, there are always others who come along to take their place. The system survives because the big things don't change. Taking down men like Paulo, really getting rid of them, would take fundamental shifts in societal attitudes towards sex, drugs, immigration, equality, you name it. Big shifts that would change the very laws we work with. But for now—for you, Davey, the person I want to help—your best chance to stay alive and out of prison is to run. Simple as that."

"A cannae dae that," Davey said. "It's Annalee's birthday soon." He gave a weak smile.

Davey went to pick up his papers, but Lennox gently pinned them to the desk with his hand. "I'll hold on to these, keep them somewhere safe. Please be careful, son."

"Aye… aye, will do," Davey grumbled, letting the door swing shut behind him. As a rule, he kept his eyes down as he walked through the waiting room—think invisible, be invisible—but he heard a voice that made him look up.

"Caramel, gingerbread *and* hazelnut? You've got it all, Sandra, it's better than Starbucks!" Behind the reception desk at the coffee machine, pawing through the sticky, half-full syrup bottles, was a young man in suit and tie. With his face freshly shaved and his hair recently cut short, he looked like a character from *Bugsy Malone*.

"A keep a wee bit ae cocoa oer here fir sprinklin oan the toap an aw," the receptionist replied. "We're proper fancy here, son."

As the lad turned, his eyes met Davey's and he gave him a sheepish grin, his baby-boy cheeks turning pink.

"Wit in the actual name ae fuck are ye daein here, Tim?!" Davey had waited down the road, watching the door for Tim to leave. He'd retreated round the corner of an adjacent street as the boy came strolling towards him with his lanky Bigfoot stride, and snatched him as he passed.

"Davey Boy! Eh, I-I was hoping you'd wait for me—"

"Don't fuckin 'Davey Boy' me, answer the fuckin question!"

"I'm doing work experience."

"Wit?"

"Work experience. Helping Lennox out at the office. Bit of filing, bit of researching, going to Greggs for him, that kind of thing."

"Bullshit."

"Speak to the staff at the Greggs if you don't believe me—they know me by name already. Man, the amount of pastry that guy consumes!" He forced a smile, clearly hoping Davey would join in, but Davey's brain was still in high para gear after his chat with the lawyer. He felt people watching the two of them as they passed by, wondering what Davey, looking rough in faded jeans, hoody and work boots, half-mad fear oozing out of his pores, could have to do with this spit-polished pup in a suit.

"Work experience... Which ye just happen tae be daein wae Carter Lennox, whose name ye geed me. Nae other offices takin people oan?" He gave Tim a manic stare. The lad chewed his lip, shuffled his feet.

"Look, Davey, you're right. I went to Lennox because I was hoping I'd at least find out if you'd decided to talk to him."

"Why?! It's no yer fuckin business, Tim. An av telt ye that. Thoat I wis pretty clear last time an aw. It's no yer fuckin business and ye don't want it tae be. Believe that."

"I just want to help," he mumbled, eyes blinking, having to look away.

"But *why*?"

"Because you look like you need it." Tim sniffed and wiped at his nose with a starched cuff. He met Davey's eyes again and there was a new strength there—it reminded him of the way he'd tackled the poliswoman, McCoist, when she'd come round to harangue Sean about the air-pistol incident. "And I don't think there's anyone else who will."

Now it was Davey's turn to look away. "That's right enough," he mumbled. He felt his loneliness like a stone in his belly. He had to step back, open the space between them as his anger fizzled out. "Yer a good pal, Tim, but this whole hing is just so fucked up—"

"So let me help."

"Am no even sure yer new gaffer can help me, never mind his scran gofer." They both chuckled with a bit of effort, sliding into the awkward camaraderie they had always shared on quiet, rainy shifts at the car wash.

"Hey, it's an important job, an army marches on its stomach."

"Is the cunt at least payin ye a few quid?"

"Is he fuck."

"Could ae guessed that fae the new shed." Davey pointed to Tim's business trim. "Looks like they cut yer fringe usin a fuckin spirit level."

35

There was nothing useful on the bloody rags or the brush ("Bupkis!" the lab tech, Specky Bupkis—not his real name—said, using his catchphrase) so that one remained McCoist's case. It was certainly human blood and therefore probably a murder, but they had no idea whose blood it might be and no bloodless bodies had turned up as a match for it. All she had was a tenuous connection with Prentice and Burnet at the car wash which was so shoogly she'd kept it to herself. This was perfect for Robson, who could no longer be accused of giving her grunt work beneath her position while simultaneously complaining that she wasn't making any progress on the one important case she did have.

The man himself interrupted McCoist's latest session of banging her head on the desk with a phone call: "If you're not busy, DI McCoist, CID need something chased up and they're swamped. A report came in about a squatter in..." McCoist's brain was already tuning out, her hand mechanically writing down the address in her notepad. She could see DCI Robson through the blinds of his corner office, mouth yammering away, his voice thrown into her ear. Her eyes homed in on the little details of his face: the dry skin on his lips, his nasal hair, the extra fold of chin above his collar.

"Yes, sir... yes, sir..." If I'm out the office, I could swing by and see Bruce, she thought. "Yes, sir."

.   .   .

She pulled out of the station car park—swinging out onto the road in front of a silver motor which had slowed down to turn in but without indicating (*typical male driver*)—and headed south out of the city into housing estates grim at one end and bland at the other, the drab sprawl hidden behind the respectable faces of the hundred-year-old tenements that lined the main streets. The building she arrived at was no creative, space-sharing business hub. The man's statement who'd phoned in—a web designer who rented an office there—had made the Carnaby Centre sound like some trendy Silicon Valley start-up co-working space, gym balls for office chairs and sleeping pods so you never had to go home. But Apple this was not. It was barely Acorn.

She hit the button for CyberGrafix.

"Hello?" The speaker blared static behind the barely audible word.

"This is Detective Inspector McCoist, can—"

The speaker fizzed again, interrupting her.

"Hello? Hello? This is the police."

The speaker stuttered and crackled; then the door buzzed and unlocked. She went up to the second floor and found a man waiting half out of an open door with the word "CyberGrafix" stencilled on it. He pointed to the door opposite his office and mouthed the words: "He's in now."

McCoist nodded and tried to indicate with her hands that he should go back inside and close the door. He did, but she could feel him watching through the strip of glass that ran vertically down the door.

She knocked on the blank door where there was reportedly somebody squatting in the office. "Police. Open up," she called. There was no response so she knocked again. "This is Detective Inspector McCoist. I know you're in there and I'd like to speak to you, please." Her "please" did not sound at all like a "please". She peered through the vertical slit of the window, pushing her face close to it to try to see as much of the room as possible through the narrow gap. She could see boxes and desks, rows of windows opposite, one open. There was a sleeping bag unrolled on the floor. She squashed her face right up against the glass, trying to see what was round to the left corner of the room when suddenly the view went black, blocked out, and she jumped back.

A man's face was looking back at her through the door window. It was sagging and shrivelled like last year's tangerine forgotten in the bottom of your Christmas stocking—framed by shoulder-length greasy hair that looked like it had been dipped in an ashtray.

A face was what had caused the Fuck-Up. It wasn't that Knightley looked cruel or vicious or evil; the trouble was more that he looked like a fucking eejit, a doddering weirdo with a gormless expression shaped from Play-Doh, and McCoist immediately pegged him as such. When he confessed in his quavering, too-thin voice, she believed him without question—that was the truth, regardless of what she told the inquiry about evidence and corroboration. Prejudice masquerading as instinct. *Silly cow.*

This face, the one staring at her behind the window, would cause no such problems. McCoist was immediately on guard. She clocked the faint scars of chib marks on the jawline, brow and cheekbones, the edges of his face chipped like an old coffee table. The eyes, buried in pouches of tired, saggy flesh, were brutal in their intensity.

He opened the door. The stale smell of cigarettes, after-shave and cold coffee wafted out. His shabby jumper and grey jeans had the pishy, damp scent of clothes that hadn't been dried properly. "How can a help ye?" His voice ground like a pepper mill.

"I'm Detective Inspector McCoist." She held out her warrant card. "There's been a report—"

"Can a get a closer look at that? Av no goat ma glesses oan."

McCoist held her ID closer and he snatched it right out of her hand—held it up to his nose. McCoist found herself going for the CS spray in her pocket, fingers gripping the small tin, palms starting to sweat.

"Detective Inspector Alison McCoist right enough." He looked between her picture and her face like a doorman, feigned familiarity in his voice. "Good name fir a polis in Glesga." He handed the card back. "Yer pals call ye Ally?"

"No." Emphatic, humourless. "There's been a report of someone squatting in this office."

"Is it the bloke oer the hall? That web designer. He never goes hame." He grated out a laugh.

"Could you tell me your name, sir?" McCoist got her notepad and pen, having to let go of the pepper spray.

"Bootin oot squatters is a bit below yer pay grade is it no? Fir a detective, a mean."

"Sir. Name, please."

"Am just tryin tae get some work done here."

"What kind of work?"

"The honest kind. A promise."

"Can I come in?"

"No." He didn't even pretend to think about it.

"I can come back with a warrant to search the premises."

"Al huv the kettle ready when ye dae."

McCoist rested her forehead against the steering wheel. She was having a slight adrenaline comedown, adding to her usual despondency. Doorstepping people agitated her much more than it used to, ever since Knightley.

He'd let her into his house—a two-bedroom terrace in a crappy estate blocks away from the high-rise flat on Macadam Street where Dannie Gibb had lived and worked—without even asking for ID. He appeared to have no guile, wasn't bothered about why a police detective might want to snoop around his house. The place needed a decent clean. She could smell the kitchen bin from the living room—a time warp of a place, everything shades of brown and burnt orange, faded floral fabrics. He had lived there alone since his mother had been moved to a care home two years before. He had no other family, friends or alibi.

The CHS showed old complaints of sexual harassment of young women and Knightley was a known face among the girls at the brothel—he creeped them out. Again, looking at the faces of these jittery, wasted young women—bored and abused and hanging on for either the next hit or nothing but hope—it didn't occur to her that they might be lying either. She believed they had cared for Dannie, that they were scared by what happened to her…

The mother's bedroom hadn't been touched since she'd moved out. A fine layer of dust had settled on the geometric-patterned bedspread, the chair by the dressing table, the shelves with their photographs and trinkets. The dressing table itself was in disarray, make-up brushes and curlers strewn about where they'd been when the woman last downed tools. A spider had set up home in the angle where the trifold mirror met the tabletop. A collection of brooches was set out. McCoist's eye plucked one from the bunch. It was out of place: no dust. She spotted something else: a hairband, a pair of earrings. All of them clean, placed on the dresser much more recently.

"Whose are these?" she asked.

"Dannie's," Knightley said, a half-smile on his face, as if being taken away by a pleasant memory.

Knuckles white on the steering wheel, McCoist thought about heading to her desk to apply for a warrant. It would be low priority and her name was mud with the fiscal—hours could turn into days and the chances of rejection were high.

Instead, she decided to go home—she really did need to see Bruce.

As she pulled out of her space, she had a fleeting feeling of déjà vu as a silver Audi Middle-Class joined the road just after, getting close as she came to a stop at a red light. She tried to get a look at the driver in her rear-view but his head was down, busy with his dash computer or a phone in his lap. He missed the lights when they changed, McCoist leaving him behind.

The dog worked his magic, lapping tongue and wagging tail. McCoist barely minded cleaning up any more—he was getting better with that anyway. She cooed at him and let him lick her face, his hot, fishy breath giving her its strange comfort. Tess found that "gross", but Cam was just as guilty of it. Bruce was certainly finding more favour with him than her daughter. Same for McCoist. Cam was just easier these days. The thought made her feel guilty, but it was true—and painful truths were her career and calling, or had been, so she swallowed the ragged edges of it.

While she boiled the kettle she called the building's landlord, came up with the name Fred Nile as the renter. Nile owned a small printing-supply company that was on the ups with a warehouse and another (presumably used) office in East Kilbride. There was little else easily available about him beyond that. He had no criminal record and no social media as far as she could see.

Off to the suburbs—McCoist knocked on the door of a tiny office above an off-licence in a square of shops and takeaways, the local pub in one corner, dog groomers in another. The woman hemmed in behind a desk—shelves and filing cabinets and a printer blocking her in on every side, so she probably had to crawl under the desk to get out—informed her Mr Nile was at the warehouse and gave her an address and mobile number. She likely also called ahead to let him know the polis were looking for him because he was ready and waiting when McCoist pulled up at the industrial estate where he kept his company's chemicals.

The suit was decent but the face was guilty. He chewed his nails—McCoist noticed nicotine stains on his fingers but no bulge from a packet in the inside pocket.

"Fred Nile?"

"That's me."

"Detective Inspector McCoist." She showed her ID. "You're renting office space at the Carnaby Centre in Dalmarnock?"

"Aye. The auld yin's gettin a bit small fir us so we're movin. Bit closer tae hame fir me an aw."

"When?"

"Aboot a month."

"So what's the place doing now?"

"Needs tae be kitted oot, gettin new office gear an that. Could dae wae an update."

"There's a man living there."

Nile became conscious of the tip of his thumb in his teeth. He pulled it out and stared at the ragged nail before folding his arm down by his side. He shuffled his weight onto the other foot and the thumb popped back into his mouth. He couldn't decide whether to deny knowledge of this or not—McCoist could tell. When he did reply his words came out slow, halting.

"He's, eh, just a pal, that's aw. Needed a place tae kip fir a bit—his missus chucked him oot. Ad huv him stay at mine but *ma* missus doesnae like him either."

"He said he was working there."

"A telt him tae say that if the landlord or anybody came an asked."

"Why?"

"Eh… Cause there's probly no sposed tae be folk livin there, ye know? Insurance or somethin?"

"What's his name?"

"Tam."

"Tam what?"

"Eh…"

"You don't know his second name?"

"He never telt me an a never asked."

"What kind of pal is he that you let him live in your office but you don't even know his full name?"

"Look, a just know him fae the pub an the fitbaw an that. He needed a favour…"

"Did you owe him one?"

"Naw... naw, a didnae *owe* him, a just... wis tryin tae help."

"So what kind of pal is he then?"

"How dye mean?"

"How well do you know each other?"

He took his time to answer again. He knew McCoist was trying to trip him up. He looked gasping for a fag to suck on, something to anchor him.

"Like a says, we just met at the pub or the fitbaw or somethin, became pals, huv a drink thegether noo an again."

"When?"

Nile shrugged, pushed his bottom lip out a little. "Fuck knows. Years ago."

"How many?"

"Two, three, maybe."

"Is it two or three?"

"Eh, *th-r-ee.*"

"That's around the time you started your business, isn't it? What were you doing before that?"

"Workin fir other companies, just daein the same hing a noo dae fir masel, really."

"What companies?" McCoist got out her notepad and pen.

Nile reeled off a list of acronyms, counting them on his fingers. Unlike everything else he'd said to that point, these names came out quick and mechanical. By rote, McCoist thought.

"Tell your pal he needs to find somewhere else to doss."

36

Thursday was late-night shopping in the town. Davey turned down the offer of overtime to head into the hoaching streets of the city centre to look for something for Annalee's birthday. His maw said he was still good to come to the party—Sarah hadn't changed her mind yet—but going out and actually buying a present almost felt like a jinx. Still, it was only a week away now so this was his last opportunity to shop. And—as his mother reminded him every single time they'd spoken in the last month—it had to be good, though she had no suggestions of what that might be. Good to her just meant "spend lots of money" but Davey felt that wasn't quite the "good" he needed.

Turning five years old, Annalee was in the full bloom of a Disney obsession. Annalee's bedroom (and most of the rest of Sarah's place too) was a cartoon riot of dolls, plushies, costumes, tiaras, stickers, Lego, colouring books and anything-else-just-name-it branded by Disney princesses in lush pastel colours, glittering head to toe. Something Disney would go down well, but that was a bit of a no-brainer and Davey had decided he needed to use his brain on this one.

Travelling the lengths of Argyle Street, Buchanan Street and Sauchiehall Street backwards and forwards, moving sideways through the pressing crowds, he eventually stumbled upon something he thought might be good: a digital camera encased in bright-coloured, durable rubber with big, simple buttons in order to be used by a wee one. Annalee loved to take selfies with her mum. They were always at it, to the point Davey used to find it irritating. Not being interested in social media himself, he failed to understand its appeal for others. What the fuck did it matter if everyone knew what you'd had for dinner, or where you went to on holiday, or how big your morning dump was? *#Myarseholesbeenrippedopen*. What did Sarah have to share with the world? She went running once a day, she watched so many films—a fresh stack of knock-off new releases from the Barras every Sunday—she couldn't remember the titles and confused the plots, politically she still asked her uncle who to vote for, and her guilty pleasure was a McDonald's now and again—a Big Mac every time, no gherkins, with a vanilla milkshake if the machine was working. (*Ye sound jealous*, the Voice of Reason jabbed. *Green as the Hulk, pal.*) He also didn't like the idea of all these pictures appearing online for so-called friends—pretty much strangers—to see. He didn't like that his absence from them would be so obvious. However, he saw the camera and knew Annalee would love it. And, almost as important, Sarah would too.

He was leaving the shop—the oversized, garish box of the toy camera in his arms—when somebody grabbed him around the upper arm and a familiar voice said: "Let me help ye wae that."

Davey tried to pull away from Mince only for another man to appear at his other side. "Don't worry," said the older man with the saggy, melted-mask face and greying shoulder-length hair. His voice had a sandpaper grain. "He willnae steal it, technology like that is far too advanced for a teuchter like him."

Mince glared over Davey's head at Croaker but didn't reply. Instead, he flashed his lock-back knife at Davey. He pushed the tip of it against Davey's arm until it was through his coat and digging into skin. Davey felt the point pierce his arm and gritted his teeth. He'd had needles put into him at the hospital before—this had the same unnatural feeling to it, one that made him queasy. That and the pain. "Dinnae say onythin an just keep walkin, aarighty?" Mince said.

They crossed Argyle Street at the bottom of Buchanan Street and passed St Enoch subway station. They came to a street round the back of the shopping centre which bore the name of the same saint, passing a kebab shop, nightclub and the rippers—none of them open for business yet. Croaker opened the back door of a dingy Volvo and Mince shoved Davey inside with the tip of the blade, pushing it deeper, making Davey squeal. "Fuck up!" Mince yelled. The blade came out with a twist.

Mince got in the driver's seat while Croaker got in the back with Davey. The door locks snicked shut.

"How huv ye bin, Davey?" Croaker asked, sounding as if he cared.

"Fan-fuckin-tastic," Davey said, his voice higher-pitched than normal, squeezing the camera box to his chest like a life-preserver, one hand clamped to the bleeding wound in his arm.

"Good tae hear! A wis worried oor last wee confab hud left ye in a bit ae a state."

Davey could feel whoops of panic squeezing their way up from his belly into his chest. "Ye bin followin me?"

"Bin keepin tabs is aw."

"A thoat yed done a disappearin act."

"A wis layin low fir a while, sure enough."

"Eftir they killt yer man's brother?" Davey felt a look from Mince bounce off the rear-view and hit him square in the face.

"That wis unfortunate, right enough, but it means there's mare reason than ever tae take Paulo McGuinn doon."

"A don't want tae be part ae this!" Davey could feel himself about to greet. "A don't want tae be part ae some fuckin gang war. A just want tae be left in peace, see ma daughter."

"Me too, son, me too," Croaker said.

They'd headed south, over the Clyde and out of the city proper, past the old tenements towards the "new" towns—far from it these days. Croaker leant forward to issue instructions to Mince, who turned off a main road into an anonymous maze of suburban sprawl, rows of terraced housing joining on to squat, single-room flat blocks arranged around the bin sheds—loose shingles, peeling paint, cars abandoned by the shoogly kerbs with four flats.

"In here." Mince pulled into a car park behind a run-down church, the weathered crucifix nailed above the front door the only sign the hall, with its seventies council-build aesthetic, wasn't just any other defunded community centre.

The window at Davey's side slid down and Croaker scooched over on the seat, pressing up against Davey's bleeding arm, so they could both see out. Davey got a waft of stale cigarettes with a hint of old-man musk as Croaker pointed past the trees that edged the car park to a block of flats that stood alone at the top of a grassy embankment. It was starting to get dark and lights were on in many of the windows, except on the top three floors. "See that?" Croaker said, pointing again, this time at the top of the tower. "Blackout curtains."

Davey nodded in dumb reply.

"Ye know wit goes oan behind them?"

"A could probly huv a guess," Davey said. He was less pre-occupied with the pain in his arm now and starting to build up a steady, cold sweat. *Kidnapped. Again.*

"An yed probly be right. The lassies who work there, they're aw hooked oan somethin. Heroin, crack, witever. The place is part brothel an part shootin gallery. That's how it used tae be anyway. Hings huv changed since he started bringin in the foreign burds. They're smuggelt intae the country illegally. He doesnae need the drugs tae control them, he has them pinned doon fae the start."

Davey's mouth was dry. "Ye mean Paulo?"

Croaker didn't answer, didn't need to. He rummaged around in the pockets of his leather jacket and fished out his cigarettes and lighter. "Ye smoke, Davey?"

"A geed it up," Davey said. Croaker handed one over anyway and Davey put it in his mouth without thinking. He lit them up.

"Some ae these wee burds, Davey, they're only fourteen, fifteen year auld. Stuffed intae boats an lorries by their maws and das who hink they're savin them by sendin them away, fae war or famine or witever else. An they end up here." He pointed to the flat again with the tip of his fag. Ash fell onto the toy-camera box in Davey's lap.

"Why are ye tellin me aw this?"

"Just want ye tae see who yer workin fir."

"Who am workin fir? Am only workin fir Paulo because ae *you*. Ye torched his fuckin motor, now a owe him mare money than al see in ma entire life!"

Croaker smiled. The bastard smiled! "Right ye are. Tae be fair tae me that wis Mince's fault, really."

"Fuck up!" Mince interrupted.

"An how are ye any better yersel?" Davey continued. "Wit, ye only enslave lassies oer eighteen fir yer sex dungeons?"

Croaker's smile became laughter. "Am no who ye hink a am at aw, lad…" He gestured out the window again. "Second flair fae the top, third windae fae the left. That's where ma girrul used tae work. Ma wee lassie. Ma wean, Becca. Seventeen year auld when she ran aff. Ended up oan the smack, workin fir Paulo up in that shitehole drug den, bein pimped oot." Croaker had become flat, with little trace of rational anger or sadness on the surface. Instead, he seemed calm, slightly absent. "Me an the missus tried tae get her oot, get her hame, get her clean, but she always went back. Sometimes ad come here an park up an just watch the tower, lookin fir a chink ae light fae a window, just tae be close tae her again, as close as a could get."

He tossed his fag out the window, lit up another. "It was ten year ago noo when she wis foond in the burn, skull caved in. The killer wis never caught, an it wis never traced back tae Paulo, though a know fine well it wis him. Maybe no by his ain two hawns, but done oan his orders fir sure. See, ma wee girrul wis gettin aulder, gettin mare strung oot. The drugs, booze, fags—they aw suck the beauty oot ae ye. Makes it harder tae pull in punters, harder tae pay back the money ye owe fir the smack ye need fae yer dealer who's also yer pimp an yer landlord. In the end, yer good fir nothin, just a liability tae be cut loose."

Davey tried to start a sentence a few times, getting stuck at the first word. In the end he managed, "Am sorry," before Croaker cut him off, ignoring him.

"An in the ten year since, it's only got worse. Half the wummin he brings in die in transit, crushed tae death or frozen in the back ae lorries in the winter. A shouldnae say wummin, really, they're bairns. Kiddies like yer ain wee yin."

"Hawd oan, pal, ye don't need tae go there—"

"A do, son, a do. Cause a need tae make a point. A need tae make ye see that ye huv tae help me. Am no fuckin gangster. A mean, am no saint, al tell ye right noo av no lived the best life, but this isnae aboot money or turf or product. This is aboot gettin rid ae a dangerous man. Cuttin open the swollen snakebite an sookin oot the poison. Davey… a need yer help."

37

He waited for two hours to be seen in minor injuries. By the time his arm had been stitched up, the polis had been called. The nurses and doctors had obviously found Davey suspicious, hadn't bought his story about catching his arm on a nail. He couldn't blame them, turning up at A & E dripping in fear sweat, clutching the toy camera still in its box, with something very like a stab wound in his arm.

A familiar face entered the ward—irritable and drawn with tiredness. "Mr Burnet, your relationship with the stairs has taken another downturn, has it?" It was that detective: McCoist, backed up by a bored-looking lad in a too-shiny Next suit, conspicuous and self-confident, boy-band good looks which didn't suit the job.

"So," she said, reviewing the yarn Davey had prepared for her, which she'd tapped into her phone, "you were taking a shortcut through the old cattle market on Bellgrove Street to get home when you snagged your arm on a nail that was sticking out from a fence you climbed. Is that right?"

"Aye."

"Do you usually cut through the cattle market in the dark?"

"Aye, sometimes."

"Is it not dangerous there?"

Davey shrugged. "Av never bin hassled."

"You'd been out shopping for a birthday present for your daughter." She pointed at the toy camera.

"Aye."

"What is it, a digital camera?"

"Aye."

"And she's going to be how old?"

"Five."

"Isn't that gift a bit advanced for her?"

"Naw, she's a bit advanced hersel." The Voice of Reason slapped Davey's metaphorical wrist. *Stay calm, keep it steady, say "aye" or "naw" or nothin.*

"I'm sure." *Patronisin coo.* "Were you not worried the present might get damaged climbing over fences and tramping through abandoned buildings?"

"Obviously no." *Watch it.*

"And this nail, what was it like?"

Davey shrugged. "Like a nail."

"How long was it? Four inches, nine inches?"

"A dunno, it wis dark, like a says."

"You didn't see it sticking out of the broken fence, and you caught your arm on it as you passed by?"

"Aye."

"And you became *impaled* on it?"

"Aye."

The detective let out a big, fake sigh. "Mr Burnet, the staff here see a lot of injuries. You can see for yourself how busy it is. They see all sorts, things you wouldn't even believe, but an injury like yours they see pretty often, especially on Friday and Saturday nights, or match days. The doctor who stitched you up was quite confident that what you have in your arm there is a stab wound, as in, a gouging injury inflicted by a knife or similar sharp implement. Did somebody stab you, Mr Burnet?"

"Naw."

"Are you sure?"

"Very sure."

"I'm not. I think somebody stabbed you and you're not telling me because you know who it was. I'm also pretty sure somebody beat you up a few months ago and you know who that was too."

Davey was squirming. He wasn't a natural liar. He pleaded guilty to everything he was ever charged with without argument. He hoped she'd put the edginess down to the stitches and painkillers. "Well, sorry, yer wrang this time," he mumbled.

"But not last time?"

"Baith times."

"Sticking to your story then?"

Davey nodded.

"David, if there's something going on, tell me now and I can help." She was being earnest now—her voice and eyes softening, reaching out to him—or trying hard to appear so. You could never tell with people in their line of work. They'd whisper a friendly word in your ear while they fucked you from behind. He focused on his shoes. "You have a child to think of. You want to be there for all her birthdays, right? Not just this next one."

When he didn't reply, she closed the cover of her phone with an ostentatious flip and a sharp exhale through her nose, her jaw wound tight, her social-worker spiel rebuffed.

As she turned to leave, the young polis stepped forward. "Ye don't remember us, dae ye, Mr Burnet?" he said. McCoist's huff dropped in an instant and she turned back to listen.

Davey was flummoxed. His mind raced through old faces, people he'd known in school and after, from playing fitbaw, from Carntyne, friends of friends, friends of Sarah's, cousins who weren't really cousins. He shrugged—it hurt.

"Christmas night, mind? Ye hud a bit much tae drink, a brought ye here. Maybe no surprisin ye don't remember actually. Maybe if a hud ma hat an yella jaiket oan." He gave a sympathetic smile. "Ad ask if ye were keepin well, but…"

"Cheers, pal, but ad had a few again an a fell oan the fence, awright? End ae story. If ye can even caw it that."

The young polis gave him a nod and said cheerio—Davey saw a look from McCoist drill through the boy. She'd be hearing all about it as soon as they were away down the corridor. No doubt.

Once the polis were gone, the nurses were keen for him to get to fuck and free up the bed. They pushed him out the ward with some more painkillers and bandages and instructions to clean the wound regularly. "If ye start gettin yella pus comin oot ae it, call yer GP, awright?"

He followed a red line painted on the wall, which led him out of the ward and through a maze of corridors back to reception.

Outside, beyond the ambulance bay, the smokers were corralled inside a large pen. Davey was on his way past when something made him stop and peer into the smoky den.

There were patients, visitors and staff crammed inside—the staff notable by their lanyards and, in some cases, their scrubs, the patients obvious from looking like shit, some of them sitting in NHS luggage trollies. There was a man Davey recognised, drawing on a king-size held in one hand, the other on the handle of a crutch. His left leg was in plaster from foot to groin. His face was a Hallowe'en mask of bloated, healing bruises with butterfly stitches stuck over his nose, eyebrows, chin and cheekbones. Davey didn't know the guy all that well, but he was familiar from popping into the car wash to see Sean now and again: Rusty.

38

McCoist got home late. Bruce was keening for her at the door, almost toppling her as he jumped up, trying to climb her, whining and excited, tail thrashing in a happiness so desperate it was almost miserable. "Hello, I know, I know, come on now, let me in properly. Good boy." She managed to get the door closed and dropped to her knees so Bruce could get a good lick at her face as she rubbed his head and back, stroking his muzzle and his chest as he rolled over for her, his paws up in the air, wiggling and ridiculous. "Oh, I'm sorry, I'm sorry, my good boy. What have you been up to today?" This was the voice she'd used on the twins when they were little. It had come back as if she'd never put it away.

Bruce's food bowl had been launched from its rubber mat and was upside down halfway across the kitchen, dry dog food scattered all over the tiles. Likewise the water bowl, which had created a sizeable puddle. In their place on the rubber mat was a perfect, cartoonish crap like a chocolate Mr Whippy.

"Right," McCoist said, grabbing a towel and putting her hand into an inside-out poo bag, "time for a walk, I think." Bruce was delighted.

She could hear Edith's telly blaring from outside as she headed down the front path into the chill, damp evening. The street lamps were on and the curtains in the houses were closed, lights glowing from within. "Just a few turns around the neighbourhood," she told Bruce, who pulled ahead on his lead, crossing this way and that in front of her, chasing whatever he'd smelled on the pavement. McCoist tried to ratchet the lead in, worried he would find something lovely to roll around in. "Settle down, for Christ's sake!" He stopped to piss against the Johnsons' garden fence and she hurried him along, quick look at the window to check nobody happened to be peering out. No Johnsons, but there was a guy out on the street, not far behind her on the other side. If he'd seen the crime he didn't say anything—anyway, he looked focused on the path ahead of him, taking no notice of McCoist or the bucking Bruce. He was wrapped up in a chunky anorak with the hood pulled up, probably giving him tunnel vision.

McCoist took the next left onto Naysmyth Bank just in case, the Johnsons' fence not likely to be the only property Bruce would defile.

Her mind drifted to Davey Burnet and his "nail" injury. First his trip down the stairs and now this. It was rotten—stank so bad Bruce would be happy to use it as perfume. DC Findlay had filled her in on his previous encounter with Burnet on Boxing Day—she'd seen the tag on his file before but hadn't heard the details.

"And do you think he was seriously at risk of suicide?" she'd asked.

Findlay chewed his lip, looked away, shuffled a bit. "A, uh, a don't know really, he wis absolutely mortal, who knows wit somebdy in that state might dae… But a wis worried enough that a thoat we should dae somethin, a mean… It wis Christmas, a don't know, ye know?" His boyish face flushed. Not a comfortable subject for a young lad in the polis, not the kind of thing they wanted to get into talking about—mental health, emotions, human feelings, etc. Not if they wanted to climb the greasy ladder.

He seemed OK, though—just assigned to her unit out of uniform, hadn't yet begun to file down his accent. He wasn't quite clued in on the office politics either—he was the new kid at school who'd been dumped on some friendless gimp. Within a few weeks he'd be desperate to break free of her, but for now he was happy to follow her orders and even make her coffee when he went to get his own. *Good guy*. Sharp too. McCoist had delegated some of the nonsense cases that came her way to him—shite rolls downhill and all that—and had him hounding the lab techs to do more tests on the bloody rags. He'd asked for her theory on that one—keen for it to be a murder he could solve—and hadn't believed her when she said she didn't have one. "It's the only lead and, so far, there's nothing. Hows about, if you can get the tests done and something *does* come back, I'll let you in on the extremely unlikely, long-shot, unicorn of an idea I have floating about in my head." That sent him bounding off with a dutiful "Ma'am".

"Bruce, will you just—" The dog had stopped to nose at an empty sandwich packet on the ground and then started getting his teeth into it. McCoist turned to pull him away and noticed, just beyond the pool of light from a lamp across the street, the man in the anorak, hood up, tapping away at his phone, his walk slowed to a crawl as he scrolled with cold fingers.

McCoist felt the chilly drip of horror-film nervousness in her belly. She was sure he'd continued on down Bell Green East when she'd turned onto Naysmyth. But there he was, hovering just outside the lamplight. Lost? He had his phone, and what was there even to look for around here? "Come on, Bruce." She tugged hard and continued down the street.

The weird feeling about the silver Audi outside the Carnaby Centre came back to her. She hadn't properly seen the driver's face, and she couldn't get a clear look at this one either because of his hood. Why the fuck would someone be following her? What had she done lately that made her worthy of being tailed? The only remotely interesting thing she'd been involved with recently was the bloody rags and the potential car-wash connection. Was she right? Was this what it was about? The man in the anorak was certainly too tall and broad to be either Prentice or Burnet. The way he carried himself was wrong too—no slumped shoulders, no labourer's back. The younger one, Colin? She'd certainly got his back up.

She took the next left towards the low flats at Henry Bell Green—yanking at Bruce's lead to get him to come to heel, being careful not to turn right around but straining at the corner of her eyes for any movement getting closer, listening for running feet—went up the stairs and along the path that ran between the buildings, coming out onto Baird Hill. She crossed between the parked cars which choked the pavement, crossed the grassy square where kids played football in the summer—using the plastic red tombstone which declared "No Ball Games" for a goalpost—and tucked herself around the hedge-lined path which led to the lock-ups.

Here, she hovered behind the hedge; then, after a couple of deep breaths, she peeked out.

And there he was—out of the alley between the flats, crossing over towards the square.

She ducked back in. *Fuck… Fuck!* Had he seen her? She pulled at Bruce but he wouldn't budge. "Bruce!" she hissed. She saw the look in the dog's eyes, his hunched back. "Not right now, Bruce, for fucksake, not now! Was one in the house not enough?!" His tail was stiff out behind him, jittering up and down slightly like the handle of a pump as he did his business. She tried to pull him but his feet stayed planted, skittering a little over the disjointed, mossy paving stones but staying firm. "Fuck!"

She felt in her pocket: keys, poo bags, alcohol gel and, finally, the round canister of CS spray. *Come on, you fucking creep, get any closer and you'll get a pus full of Nando's Extra-Hot Peri-Peri.* She'd only seen him holding a phone but his warm coat was padded enough to conceal anything—could have a blunderbuss tucked up in there and she wouldn't have noticed. The sick pounding of her heart fought with the adrenaline lighting up her muscles and filling her brain with reckless aggression—if she had to run she'd outstrip Usain Bolt, never mind this cunt. She peeked out again. He was lingering in the square, almost hidden in the shadow of a tree, but not quite. He wasn't pretending to be on his phone now.

Bruce stood up and shook himself. *"Go!"* They sprinted into the lock-ups and turned, taking the darkened, overgrown drive—a tunnel of thorny hedges and fences topped with nails—that led cars between the back gardens of two rows of terraced houses and back out onto Baird Hill, flying over the large speed bumps, Bruce thoroughly enjoying the whole thing, McCoist dizzy with panic.

As they reached the last hurdle before the street, the man in the anorak stepped out in front of her into the mouth of the alley.

They stood facing one another, McCoist breathing hard and rapid, the man too still. His eyes were hidden by the shadow of his hood, the collar of his jacket zipped up over his chin, only the tip of his nose and his mouth visible in the orange overspill of the street lamps. Bruce howled at him, straining against his lead, his collar threatening to snap. McCoist almost let him go for it—one hand clamped to the handle of the lead, the other around the can of pepper spray. *Turn and run. Turn and run.* But back the way she came was all uphill, all in darkness, over the bumps, and Bruce would be pulling the opposite way. Her legs were jelly now, all thoughts of outrunning the world's fastest man vanished—wild, panic-induced bravado giving way to the reality of her sub-Olympic physical shape.

"Dye know where the South Parish is?" he asked, after somewhere between a minute and an eternity had passed.

McCoist pointed to her left. "That way…" Her voice was breathless, throat hoarse from gulping in fiery air. She didn't know what to think, could barely get her mind to turn over at all. Up close, the sound of his voice, it certainly wasn't that Colin either… A confused numbness was creeping over her. "Keep going straight, bottom of the hill."

"Cheers, hen! Nice dug!"

Bruce continued to bark long after the man had gone on his way, until McCoist started to shiver from the chill of her cooled sweat and somebody across the street opened a window to yell: "Shut that bloody dog up!"

39

There was a collective intake of breath when Davey entered the room. It was done up for the party—streamers and banners, pictures of Annalee from over the last five years plastered on the walls, a timeline tracing all the way back to her wrapped up in the little hospital cot when she was brand new, swaddled in an orange blanket with a woolly green cap pulled down over her head (Davey had said she looked like a carrot). Wrapping paper littered the floor, torn-up Disney princesses in pinks and purples and baby blues.

The in-laws and some of Sarah's friends (not mutual) were arranged around a coffee table on couches, dining chairs, and beanbags. They were all staring at Davey, smiling but silent. Davey smiled back, held up his hand in a stiff wave. Then—

"Daddy!" Annalee came barrelling in from the kitchen, crashing straight into Davey in a hug, her head knocking the wind out his stomach and her arms wrapping around his legs. Everybody laughed and Davey picked her up for a proper hug, nuzzling into her neck, breathing in the no-tears scent of her long hair. Sarah had her dressed up in a pretty frock but she'd kept the plastic *Frozen* tiara on her head.

"Happy birthday, doll!" Davey said.

The friends and in-laws smiled and began talking among themselves again. Davey's maw came through the door just after and then it was all hugs and *how are yes*.

Sarah came through, looking all done up, checking if anybody needed another drink. She clocked Davey and gave him a nod. He forced a smile and waved, dropped his eyes quickly back down to Annalee. "Here, av goat somethin fir ye, hen. Go oan, huv a look." He handed over the present—more Disney wrapping paper—and she tore into it. At first she was confused, but excited nonetheless. "Look, it's a camera," Davey said, "so ye can take yer ain pictures. Ye don't huv tae steal yer maw's phone any mare."

"Coooool!" She studied the box, held an inch from her nose, and started walking towards her maw. "Mummy, Mummy, look! Can a open it?"

"Course, honey. Get Daddy tae help ye." A smile. *Result!*

Davey got the toy camera out and tried to show Annalee how to use it—though she wasn't really keen for anybody's help, never was. Davey caught his maw's eye, motioned towards the present and gave a questioning thumbs up. She sniffed and busied herself with the lager tops Sarah had made her. *Fuck's her problem noo?*

He fielded a few questions about work and that from Sarah's uncle—a big, auld fat cunt who drove a taxi until he became too unfit for it. He was sound though. He'd always got on well with Davey and, even now he was retired, was always sending his old taxi-driver pals down to the car wash, drumming up a bit of business. "Can a get ye another, Pat?"

"Aye, go oan then, son. Mine's a Heineken, cheers, none ae they Tennent's tinnies, please, fir fucksake."

"Nae worries!"

Davey went to the kitchen, where Sarah and her maw were getting the spread ready: sausage rolls, mini pizzas, chicken pakora (the classics), some fruit and veg for the weans (definitely not for Uncle Pat, that was sure), and assorted crisps in plastic bowls.

"Oh, hi Davey, how are ye?" Angie said with a thin smile. Davey's own mother considered him the villain of the break-up; Sarah's thought he was the Antichrist. Luckily, she wasn't the confrontational type and was happy to keep things civil. She found an excuse to leave the room.

"Can a get ye a drink, Davey? Goat lager in the fridge, some stronger stuff in the cupboard. There's ginger an aw," Sarah said.

Sarah had always looked younger than her age—still occasionally got ID'd for a lottery ticket—and she'd canned the booze, fags and gear early enough that they'd left no lasting impression. The only obvious concession to the years between their first meeting in the Savoy and now was a tiredness around the eyes left exposed by a more pared-back approach to make-up in her late twenties, partly out of changing taste and partly because she didn't have the time to spend on herself any more. Davey had always believed this everlasting youthfulness was a sign domestic life had been good for her, really, but somewhere deeper he pictured her bare feet, toes painted neon pink, leaving sweaty prints on the roof of a car and wondered.

"Al just huv a glass ae water, cheers. A can get it, nae worries—am pickin up a brew fir yer uncle anyway." Davey had given himself a good scrub, had a shave, ironed a shirt to wear. He'd had another bad panic attack that morning, collapsed on the floor with his eyes streaming, gasping for air like he'd stepped out onto the moon without a spacesuit on. Croaker's reappearance and the new kink it added to the predicament he was in had, unsurprisingly, not improved his anxiety or his general level of fucked-ness. He was a mess, but there was no way he could miss Annalee's party, so he primped and preened and showed up shiny and fresh, off the booze, off the fags—*diazepam only fir me, ma'am*—keen to pretend everything was fine, or even better than fine.

"That wis a nice present, Davey," Sarah said. "A hope ye didnae spend too much."

Davey waved her away, as well as the end of the sentence—*A know ye cannae afford it.* It was important to keep cool, keep it light. "How ye bin keepin?"

"Aye, awright. Yersel?"

"Good, cheers. Actually…"—Davey had a burst of inspiration—"…av signed up fir therapy."

"Therapy?"

"Aye, talkin therapy, in a group, ye know?"

Sarah's eyebrows shot up into her scalp, her mouth hung open a little.

"The doacter says it might be good fir me an a thought, why no gee it a try? Maybe it will."

"Ye went tae see the doacter?" Her tone and accompanying expression of pleasant disbelief would have been similar had Davey told her he'd been skydiving.

"Aye, a wis strugglin tae sleep, bin huvin a hard time ae it lately." There was an almost audible pop as the mood in the room suddenly flipped. *Shite, said the wrang hing.*

"An that's ma fault is it? That wit yer sayin tae yer doacter and yer group, eh?" Sarah crossed her arms, shifted her stance, ready to fight. "Maybe if yed shown up oan time fir yer ain daughter then—"

"—naw, naw, naw, Sarah, that's no wit am sayin, wit a mean is…" He looked away, bit into the knuckle of his thumb. "It's no aboot *you*, it's me."

Sarah looked as if she was about to ask why it wasn't about her, but instead she said, "Pat's posh lager is in the veggie drawer."

They were speaking again by the end of the party—keeping it light—and Davey managed to have a good time, playing with Annalee and her young cousins. The wean had a bit of a meltdown when it was time for him to leave, which was painful but at the same time encouraging for Davey. She wanted him there, she really did, and he would do anything to be there, to earn that place. Hell or high water—likely both, with Paulo's jewelled hand clamped to one shoulder and Croaker's yellow claw to the other.

His maw cornered him as they walked down the street together: "Are ye gonnae tell me then or are ye gonnae wait till ye huv tae call me fae the jail?"

"Wit?"

"Don't 'wit' me, David. Tell me wit yer intae this time!"

"Nothin, Maw, Jesus Christ, are ye goin fuckin senile? Av no idea wit the fuck yer oan aboot." Inside, his mind raced, trying to guess what part of all the shite he was into that his maw had managed to find out about.

"Senile?!" She clapped him on the ear.

"Fucksake, Maw!"

"Al tell ye wit am oan aboot. The other day, a get a phone call fae the polis."

"Sayin wit?"

"They were askin aboot ye. Where ye worked, where ye lived, when had a last seen ye, aw that shite."

The gears were clunking away in Davey's skull. He needed to speak. Quickly. "Wis it a wummin?"

"Aye. Wit does that matter?"

"Aw right, it'll be aboot that work hing… It wis last week, so ad forgotten aw aboot it. Sean—the gaffer—goat intae another rammy wae a customer oer somethin an somebdy called the polis oan him. That's aw, they just want tae speak tae me aboot it, get ma angle ae the story. That's aw. Av bin ignorin ma calls." Davey studied his maw's face, watched her chew over the bullshit to see if she would swallow it or spit it out.

"That aw, aye? Fuckin Sean. Here's me huvin a heart attack oer that prick. Ye need tae get yersel another joab, Davey, that guy's a nutter. An fir fucksake speak tae them when they call ye back, last hing ye need at the moment is gettin pulled in fir *obstruction* or somethin. No when yer gettin oan wae Sarah again."

"Ach, Sean's no bad when ye get tae know him. An al speak tae the polis if ye gee *Line ae Duty* a rest. 'Obstruction', fucksake!"

His maw laughed. Maybe Davey was starting to get better at this lying thing.

APRIL

40

What it amounted to was a whole lot of weird shit going on, and if McCoist could be the one to thread it all together then it just might be her way out of purgatory—a ticket back into the game. No more goober work with the uniforms, no more disdainful looks from her superiors or pitying ones from her subordinates. No more moping around, doing herself down, making herself shrink from the sudden quiet as she walked into a room. *From Fuck-Up to Fuck-You: A Motivational Guide to Redemption* by Detective Inspector Alison McCoist. Hope was a fire that could burn you up—she knew she should be wary but she couldn't help it.

She laid it out:

One—somebody was dead. From the amount of blood soaked up by those rags, somebody must have been dead.

Two—these rags (and the bin bags they were found in) were very similar, if not the same kind, to the ones used by the Bell Street car-wash goons, who may have helped cover up a murder or may even have committed one themselves.

Three—Davey Burnet, car-wash goon of the year, had been beaten up at the end of last year and then, more recently, stabbed in the arm, likely by somebody he knew.

Four—his boss, Sean Prentice, was off his fucking rocker, a paranoid android with a temper and a tinfoil hat. She wondered what he'd be like without the weed chilling him out.

Five (query)—was somebody following her? She hadn't had

229

any strange encounters since the night Anorak Man asked her for directions to the church, and she'd been keeping an eye out for strange men and silver Audis but hadn't spotted anything.

There were problems here—the major stumbling block being that a butchered body had still not been found which paired with her bag of blood—but there was enough that warranted a closer look. Not on the books though, not yet. She needed to feel it out by herself first before she took any official steps. Eagerness had burnt her before. If she hadn't been so keen to nail Knightley she might have been able to see the bigger picture before it was too late.

She began staking out the car wash whenever she could. She parked on the hill just beyond the railway bridge, where she could watch over the face of the unit and the street where they hosed down the cars. They knew her Skoda pretty intimately now, after spending a good half-hour trying to scrape up dog hair from her seats, so she had to take care not to be seen.

It was a busy wee place, and not just on weekends. As she'd observed on her previous visit, Burnet did the lion's share of the work while Prentice hopped out of the unit to help during peak times, taking care of any valets while Burnet dealt with the line of cars waiting for a quick wash. The youngster, Colin, did fuck all except talk, smoke and drink tea. His function there was hard to divine, the reason anyone would pay for the pleasure of having him hang around impossible to fathom. McCoist stuck it on the weird-shit list—it could be something.

Weeks passed. There was an irony to watching a car wash while stake-out snacking turned her own motor into a dump on wheels. If she was there in the evenings she would take Bruce with her, his nose pressing up against the glass, leaving greasy smears, his hair carpeting the fabric and the floors.

They stayed open in the evenings fairly often now the light was stretching out and even then there was a steady stream of cars, vans and taxis queueing up. Not so unusual. Slightly more unusual was the high number of fancy-and-gleaming, already-clean four-by-fours that often showed up.

One evening, she saw one such vehicle—an absolute behemoth so big it looked like it would require tank treads to move, its paint job so lusciously black it absorbed all surrounding light—pull up at the car wash. Its vanity number plate read: "V2P MCG".

McCoist sat bolt upright, nose almost pressed to the steering wheel. Her heart started throbbing, her brain sparked, atoms splitting and colliding, hands clammy. The burnt-out Range Rover from December—the dead-ender with the falsified serial number and the end half of a number plate that read "MCG" (maybe a "P" before it). The door opened and a familiar face got out. McCoist had never met the man in person, but like every detective in Glasgow, she knew who he was: Paul McGuinn.

"Fuck," she whispered. She reached out a hand to feel Bruce's fur. Paulo fucking McGuinn. Maybe it was a coincidence. Everybody needs to get their car washed somewhere. Even gang lords need their Batmobiles hoovered once in a while. But Paulo McGuinn wasn't just visiting the car wash once in a while. While McCoist sat in her car bin night after night, chewing through Snickers after Snickers, he appeared on several occasions. Presumably, the parade of other expensive or souped-up cars belonged to his associates...

McCoist had stumbled onto one of McGuinn's fronts. This could be bigger, much, much bigger than just one unsolved murder—it could be a link in a chain that led to Paulo McGuinn himself, the kind of tangible connection that always seemed to be missing. She put it together: a (missing) dead body, a bag of bloody rags and a car wash secretly owned by a notorious gangster, one who had—indirectly—destroyed McCoist's career.

It had been the shoebox in the garden that had flipped her switch, made her charge forward into overdrive, press on with the confession and the testimony of the girls in the high-rise. Her evidence was solid: Dannie's brooch, hairband and earrings on Knightley's mother's dresser, and the shoebox full of ash found under freshly turned earth in the middle of his garden. There was so little of it, so little powder, it only just coated the bottom of the cardboard, filled the corners.

"Bupkis," Specky Bupkis the tech had said.

"I thought you said they were human?"

"They're likely human remains?" (Specky B's most irritating feature among many was the upward inflection in his voice which turned everything he said into a question.)

"But?"

Specky B's rasping, high-pitched sigh scratched through the line and tickled her ear. "I can't get any DNA from it? Too much heat?"

"So you can't even tell me if it's Dannie's, let alone if Knightley is the father?"

"No?"

This was a conversation that now weighed heavily on her mind whenever she played the hindsight game.

Dannie's Gibb's body had been well hidden, only discovered because of a tip-off that couldn't be traced. The mutilated state of her corpse had been the reason the murder of a sex worker had stayed in the headlines so long. Her belly had been torn completely open, her bowels and organs left loose and hanging, her womb removed.

Dannie had laser scarring on her side—below the ribs and above the hip—from a tattoo removal. The tattoo had been a kind of branding, which led them to the brothel on the top floors of a high-rise growing in the cracks between city living and suburbia. A well-run operation like this was strictly the work of an OCG and rumours said the place was owned by the infamous Paul McGuinn, but, as ever, there was nothing concrete to tie it to him. (When a sting goes down, the foot soldiers get the hard years while the royalty are always out of reach.) Or maybe there would have been, had McCoist been looking for it, or had been open to seeing what was there.

But she wasn't. She had a shoebox full of burnt would-be baby and a man who claimed he'd lit the fire. There was push-back from others—discreet calls for her to slow down from Robson and those above him, who he wouldn't name—but the fiscal was under pressure from outside, and when she went to them, over the heads of her superiors, they jumped at it.

Everything seemed fine until a couple of months after the sentencing, when Knightley's mother was inexplicably moved into an expensive private care home. Forensic accountants worked through the tangle of transactions but nobody could find where the money had come from or continued to come from—she was still there now, having her arse wiped by top-of-the-line specialists.

There were murmurs that it had McGuinn all over it. Evidence planted, girls threatened into corroborating the false confession. It was a set-up. Knightley had taken the fall for money and McCoist had eaten the shite right up as if it were a melted Toblerone. It couldn't be proved conclusively—the final finding of the inquiry into the investigation—which saved McCoist her job, her rank and her place in MIT (though it had been a year since she'd officially touched anything approaching a Major Investigation, let alone felt part of the Team), but everybody knew she'd fucked up. Capitally.

She wouldn't rush in this time. She wouldn't be duped. She would watch and wait and follow every line and wrinkle with patience and clear eyes. Slow, steady, solid police work. She could do it. She was capable. More than capable, although she'd almost been made to forget this.

Her heart slammed in her chest. This was her chance to get it all back: her status, her reputation, her self-respect. Plus payback for McGuinn into the bargain. And she wanted it—she knew that now, felt it in every fibre that thrilled at the sight of that gangster's car pulling into the car wash. She wanted it badly.

"What do you think?" McCoist said to Bruce, patting his flank. Taking down Paulo McGuinn would be very far from easy. Obviously, because nobody had managed it yet. He was well protected, well connected and well known to be monstrous when it came to violence. The stories whispered around the station—none of which could be proven—were like something from a tawdry horror story written by a teenage boy. There was also the likely chance she was already on his radar—who else would have had her followed? It made sense now—she wasn't just being paranoid. She had shown up (unwittingly) sniffing around his operation and he'd sent somebody to check her out, even scare her a little. Maybe he even knew her from the Dannie Gibb investigation. She'd managed (again, unwittingly) to do him a big favour there. Not likely he'd return it by just handing himself in to her though. No, it would take some doing for sure. Some meticulous, intelligent, dangerous work. "Can we do it?"

41

"So wit, yer patchin me?" Davey paced the cramped office, chewing the filter of a cigarette itching to be sparked.

"It's not like you're paying me anything, son," Lennox said. He had his tie tucked inside his shirt, a blob of curry sauce down his front, empty takeaway cartons stacked on his desk. Aside from the greasy dollop of rogan josh soaking into it, the shirt was starchy and white, his trousers and the suit jacket thrown over the chair looking sharp-creased and fresh—he was just off a court day, an important one, and had met Davey after hours at Lennox & MacGillivary, the reception lights off, both Sandra and his partner away home, Tim saying goodnight just as Davey arrived, their eyes avoiding each other.

"That's it, aye? Ye cannae see any money in it—"

"Sit down, Davey. Come on." Lennox ran a hand over his bald dome and through his remaining hair, which had been slicked to his head earlier, now tugged out into its usual mad-scientist look.

Davey slumped into the chair. The mixed smell of stale sweat and cold curry was bowfing, not sitting well with the already queasy feeling of anxiety in Davey's belly and chest. He'd told Lennox everything that happened with Croaker and Mince and their trip to the high-rise.

"I didn't mean what I said. I just think this has got all too much. It was bad enough when it was McGuinn we were dealing with, now this other one is back in the picture…"

"He says he's no a gangster an a believe that." Davey replayed the rough old man's tale in his head, the earnestness in the low, gruff rumble of his voice, the pain etched into every crevice of his saggy face. "A hink."

"Well, the name's not a familiar one, anyway, which means… not much, but I would say most of the main players and rivals to McGuinn are known, so I can't discount the man's story. I asked around but apart from a few vague maybes at his description, I've not had any decent hits on him. This thing about the daughter though, that's something I could look into for you."

"Would ye?"

"If you'll consider my previous advice I will."

Davey met the lawyer's eyes, his face all patrician concern like a minister or a social worker. It made Davey want to cry or lash out. "A cannae leave ma faimly. A cannae just no see Annalee. It's no a fuckin option."

"It might be the safest thing for them. Seriously, son, think about it." The lawyer began chewing on a chunk of hardening naan.

"There's a polis who keeps turnin up at the car wash an the hoaspital an that. DI McCoist. Ye know her? She seems, a dunno… Awright. Fir a polis. She definitely hinks somethin's up but. A can tell."

"McCoist?" Lennox spoke around his mouthful of naan, working hard at it. "By reputation. I wouldn't trust her to water my cactus."

"She bent?" Somehow Davey couldn't picture the woman with her schoolteacher's tone and her *up-tae-the-eyebaws-wae-morons* expression as someone getting backhanders from the likes of Paul McGuinn. Davey was surprised at how keenly he felt the disappointment.

"Hmmm." Lennox picked at a nigella seed stuck between his front teeth. "Can't say for sure but if she's not then she's either useless or very unlucky. Or both. Let me know if she comes to see you again."

This time, it was Tim's turn to huckle Davey outside on the street corner. "So what's happening? What did Lennox say?"

Davey had reluctantly given Tim a lean version of the story so far after their last face-to-face. He told him he'd wrecked Paulo's car and that Paulo had taken over the car wash and was using it to launder money. He didn't mention cleaning up the bloody boot or hosing out the lorry container or hiding the guns, deliberately leaving the hardships McGuinn was inflicting upon him to the lad's imagination. He absolutely had not said anything to him about the Croaker complication.

"Fuck aw."

"He must have said something, come on, Davey—"

"He says am fucked, an that's aw. Am fucked an a just have tae learn tae like it." Davey stomped away, Tim trying to keep pace.

"There must be something we can do—"

"'We'? Listen tae yer fuckin sel!" Davey rounded on him, making Tim shrink under his glare, the boy's tall, skinny frame shrivelling. "There's nae 'we', just me an ma ain shitey fuckin problems. Ye no goat other folk tae pal aboot wae? Wit is this, ye nosy cunt?"

"Davey—"

"Look at ye!" Davey screamed, making Tim cringe, his eyes start to water. Davey hated himself then, let his self-loathing fuel his anger as it always did. No drink to blame this time. "Look at ye, fillin yer fuckin scants just cause am raisin ma voice tae ye. Wit dye hink it's like when it's Paulo fuckin McGuinn daein the shoutin, eh?! Man's a fuckin murderer, Tim. This isnae fuckin university or work experience or witever. The guy doesnae gee ye a bad grade if ye dae somethin wrang, son, he puts ye under the groond an yer fuckin lucky if yer deed afore he does it."

Tim's shoulders started to shake. His chin was on his chest, avoiding Davey's eyes. He had no reply this time, no rally, no appeal to Davey's loneliness or his withered need for friendship.

"Nae mare ae this, right? It's fuckin done. Leave me alane. It's the last time a ask ye nicely." Davey stormed off.

Yer a real piece ae shite, the Voice of Reason told him. He took a couple of extra pills when he got home, pre-empting the coming panic shakes.

42

"Here we fuckin go," Sean said, seeing the guy stumbling through the railway tunnel towards them. He shuffled his feet as he walked, scuffing the soles of his minging, burst trainers over the ground, his body slightly bent as if he were hiding an injury. His face was gaunt, chin and cheekbones exaggerated by how little skin there was to cover them. There was a line of scar tissue across the side of his head where hair wouldn't grow. Another old slashing had turned his right cheek into an arse crack. He had a carrier bag in each hand, and as he got closer to the car wash, Davey could see they were stuffed with random small electronics and boxes of perfume, bits and pieces from the shop.

"Awright, boays?" the guy said. His voice was a nasal drawl. He had smack eyes and speed teeth.

"We don't buy stolen shite here," Sean said, as the guy held open one of his carrier bags.

"Al day ye a tenner fir that Calvin Klein eftershave there. Goat an MP3 an aw—"

"MP3? Wit fuckin year is it?!" Colin cackled. "No heard ae Spotify?"

"Av goat some steaks in this other bag here…"—he carried on as if he hadn't heard either Sean or Colin—"…sirloin steaks, al dae ye a fiver fir two, a fuckin bargain, man."

"A said a don't buy stolen shite, so get tae fuck." Sean lit a fag and set about straightening up the mitts and rags and bottles.

"Big man, big man…" He came right up to Davey, holding his bags open. Davey could smell him—unwashed, stewing in his own bodily wastes. "…Need any perfume fir yer missus? Ye goat a missus?"

"Am awright, pal, no fir me the day," Davey said. It was pathetic, fucking sad, and he even started to feel some anger towards this guy, the way Sean was, though he wasn't entirely sure why.

"How aboot some coffee, ye like coffee?"

"A said am awright, cheers."

"Just tryin tae make a livin, pal—"

"Bumpin stuff fae the shoaps and sellin it isnae makin a livin," Sean said, visibly heating up. "Hink yer gonnae get oan the fuckin *Apprentice* wae that business model?"

Colin giggled. He had his phone out, filming them.

"That's how Alan Sugar goat his start," Davey said, maybe trying to deflate the situation, maybe just wanting to pile on. It had been quiet today and the three of them had been kicking their heels, bored as fuck.

"Can ye tap us a fag, pal?" the guy asked, oblivious.

"Naw." Sean took a deep draw and blew smoke straight into his face.

He shuffled away from them before turning back: "Ye goat any joabs goin here?"

Colin roared with laughter.

"A don't hire fuckin junkies!" Sean yelled back. "Get tae fuck or am gonnae hose ye doon!"

"He could fuckin dae wae it," Colin added. "Get the soap oan him first, but."

The guy doddered away down the street towards town.

Colin was still filming as he stoated away, veering all over the pavement. "Wit a fuckin rocket."

"Pure zoomer," Sean said.

"Feel sorry fir they cunts, but," Davey said.

"Why?!"

At the risk of sparking a Sean tirade, Davey answered: "Cause it's nae kind ae life, is it? Imagine that wis yer lot, just stoatin aboot tryin tae punt stolen shite so ye can load up oan witever cheap gear ye can get yer hawns oan."

"Well it's their ain fuckin fault."

"You're the wan always goin oan aboot the government stealin fae us, takin oor money fir themsels instead ae daein any good wae it. Where are aw the joabs, aw the hooses, eh? The fuckin purpose? They've taken it aw." He huffed. He was still feeling bad about how he'd treated Tim, couldn't help lashing out again, almost hoping Sean would have a go, tear strips off him.

Instead, Sean actually seemed to consider this. Before he could answer there was a smash of glass and a car alarm went off. A couple of blocks down the street, the jakie was head and shoulders inside a car, the exploded window lying in shining crystals all over the pavement. He came out with something in his hands which he shoved into one of his bags. He snatched them up and bolted.

"Hey!" Sean screamed and ran down the street. "Oi!" Colin was behind him, phone out.

Before the jakie got a few steps from the car, two polis who he hadn't noticed standing on the other side of the street—they'd materialised from thin air as far as the poor wee fucker could tell—came charging over and had him up against the wall, one of them going through his bags, the other patting him down.

Sean gave his spiel to the polis, Colin got told to fuck off with his camera, and they both came back giggling. "That wis fuckin class, man, didnae even fuckin see them right there."

"Am gettin this up oan YouTube, gonnae go fuckin viral!"

When a couple appeared at the motor, swearing at the shattered glass and then looking up and down the street, Sean went over and spoke to them. Davey watched as Sean got into their car and drove it down to the car wash. "Gee these seats an that a hoover, will ye, Davey Boy? There's gless aw oer the mats an aw. Nae charge, awright?"

"Ye tellin ma uncle aboot aw these freebies and discoonts yer geein oot, Sean?" Colin asked.

"If he wants the fiver fae a hoover al chip it in masel."

Davey pulled off his hoody and wrapped it around his hand, using it to clear the remains of the glass from the window frame.

"Wit happened tae *you*, Davey Boy?" Colin pointed to the fresh pink scar on Davey's arm where Mince's knife had gone in, the pinpricks of recently removed stitchwork around it.

Davey felt heat rush to his cheeks. "Eh, nothin, just… hurt it."

"A can see that. A meant how? Wit did ye dae?"

He dredged up the story he'd invented for the polis: "Caught it oan a nail, climbin oer this auld fence near ma gaff."

"Aye?" Colin's face twisted a little—as sceptical a look as he was capable of. "When wis this?"

"Few weeks ago or somethin, a dunno."

"Ye never says anythin, looks a bad yin an aw. How big wis the fuckin nail?"

"Pretty big. Look, it wis fine enough tae work wae, so... Am no wan fir complainin, Colin." He shook out his hoody and put it back on, hoping that covering the scar again would make Colin forget and move on to something else, goldfish-like.

Colin seemed to be searching for a couched insult in there—as a lazy person he was very sensitive to being called lazy. "You're wan ae they guys who hinks it's pure impressive tae never take sick days, aren't ye?"

"Ad take them if a could afford tae, fuckin believe it."

"That sounds like complainin." Bored now, Colin went back to rewatching the video on his phone.

43

The video was doing the rounds of every WhatsApp group in every police station in Scotland and beyond. The two lads in uniform who'd made the arrest were heroes of the hour and would be getting drinks out of it for some time to come. Even McCoist had seen it. Of course, the thing that stood out to her wasn't the supposed hilarity of the oblivious homeless man breaking into the car but Sean Prentice's leathery melon and his weed-fiend drawl as he wound up the assailant and the uniforms equally with his version of events. He and the cameraman—Skiving Colin, she guessed, owner of the YouTube account KaraterpillaCuntKilla, which had first uploaded the film—had chased the guy down the street after he'd broken into the car, just as the bobbies on the beat showed up on the spot, right-time-right-place. The camera swung away in the last couple of seconds and there was the railway bridge and the car wash before it, the tiny, blurred figure of someone watching from the open shutter, likely her old pal Burnet.

Movement had slowed on her "solve the red rags, take down McGuinn and shove everybody's face in it" case, with hours more car-wash surveillance not turning up anything else useful. Also, a one-person stake-out was not an effective way to do things, leaving massive holes where anything could be happening and McCoist would never know about it. She even checked at Eastgate (an eye-bleeding, skull-numbing testament to just how far McCoist was willing to go) to see if she could cover the missing time by looking back over CCTV footage, but there were no public cameras with a view of the car wash.

She was itching to get something else to go on, and the car break-in was a plausible excuse to pay another visit. (Officially she hadn't been handed this particular non-case and was almost offended. Were her approval ratings going up or slipping further down?)

Approaching the unit, she felt her heartbeat quicken, her hands clammy on the steering wheel. She took a couple of deep breaths. Things had changed since her last snoop around but she couldn't let them know that. No, she was just there to ask a few questions about the car break-in, just a routine follow-up: maybe someone had fucked up the paperwork and here she was again—star detective Alison McCoist—with another job that was beneath her. Bored, irritable, unable to hide her contempt for these idiots in their poxy car wash.

Face set, she parked—the street outside empty, no work going on, no soap in the gutter—and got out. Inside, Burnet was hovering by the office door, and when he heard her footsteps echo off the whitewashed floor and walls of the unit, he jumped back from it and spun around. His face was ashen as he approached her, eyes wide.

"Wit ye daein here?" His voice was hushed and McCoist found herself copying him.

"Afternoon, Mr Burnet, just here to ask some follow-up questions about a car that was broken into last—"

The door of the unit opened and he strode out. Six and a half feet tall but made visually shorter by shoulders so broad it squared him out, a hulking body of muscle and fat like a Roman gladiator, a straining Ralph Lauren shirt and thick, gold jewellery round his neck: Paul McGuinn. The man himself.

She hadn't seen his car outside... Panic held her tongue, rooted her to the floor. Colin and Sean appeared behind him but her eyes stayed fixed on McGuinn, as his seemed to devour her.

No, he had no reason to hurt her. *He had you followed.* There were people here, he couldn't do anything in front of them. *Aye, his three stooges, who are probably linked to this missing dead body of yours.* She was a polis. OCG captains and half-brained thugs alike wouldn't just openly attack polis without a very good reason. *But the stories, the mutilations, the missing people.*

"Look!" Burnet shouted, coming forward, putting a hand on her shoulder, shocking her out of petrification. "A telt ye awready, wummin, a cannae get the dug hair oot yer smelly motor. A geed it a brush an a shampoo an that's aw a can dae. A says tae ye a couldnae guarantee it afore an am sayin it again. Nae! Refunds!" He tried to turn her, push her back towards her car.

"Here, that's the nosy poliswummin who wis here afore," Colin said to his uncle.

"Ally McCoist, isnit?" Paulo smiled. "Wan ae ma aw-time favourites. Had yer name oan ma fitbaw jersey back in the day so a did."

Davey let go of her with a look of terrified resignation. He was saying something with his eyes but she didn't know what— all she gleaned from his stricken face was that she should be very worried herself.

"Wisnae that bad a joke, wis it?" Paulo said. Only Colin had joined in the laugh. "Guess yev heard them aw though."

"They're all pretty much the same," McCoist said, finding

247

her voice, sticky and dry as it was. "And it's *DI* McCoist, thank you, Mr McGuinn."

Paulo's smile started small and grew wider than seemed possible, as if his jaw were capable of unhinging and splitting open, with row upon row of razor teeth hidden in there. "An wit can a dae fir ye the day, DI McCoist?"

"What can *you* do for me?" McCoist clasped her hands behind her back to affect an air of nonchalance, to avoid anyone seeing them shake. Finally speaking had broken the grip of his eyes and she turned as if idly inspecting the bottles and sponges on the shelves. Face to face with a man who had tortured and murdered and ordered the deaths of unknown numbers of people, and apparently her best defence was pretending to be Columbo. "I came to speak to the owner of this establishment, who I believed to be Mr Prentice over here, is that not right? Have I made a mistake?"

"Mare than wan, fae wit a hear." The smile sank to a thin, hard line, then sprang back up, like a cat moving its claws in and out.

So he knew. He knew she was the lucky cop fucked over by the Knightley scam, who had "solved" the Dannie Gibb murder and sent the wrong man to jail. Already wrong-footed by his mere presence, McCoist found herself losing balance completely. Fear and rage fought inside her. It was like being back in the interrogation room in front of the super but with an added potential of physical violence. It had felt then like she was being flayed open—this time she knew Paulo McGuinn might make it literal. Part of her seethed. *Who does this fucking jumped-up Brigton-scheme ned think he is?!* And another trembled and wanted to run away, because she knew exactly who he was, what he was capable of.

She screwed herself up, bolted herself back together, met his gaze. "You live and learn. I'm sure you've had a few slip-ups yourself."

"Me? No likely."

She even managed to smile back at him. "Och, everybody does though, Mr McGuinn. And what's *worse* than making a mistake is not even *knowing* you've made one. Those are the ones that get you in the end. As you pointed out, I should know."

McGuinn's chummy performance was cast off. Not just his face but his whole body changed shape, glowering head sinking low like a boxer protecting his chin, chest puffing up. His fingers twisted the sovvy rings on his opposite hand. The other men had gone rigid. Burnet was squeezing a sponge like a stress ball, bits of it tearing off and sprinkling his boots with yellow fluff.

"A asked wit ye were daein here, noo tell me."

"I'm here to speak to the owner about a car that was broken into down the street a few days ago. Am I speaking to the right person?"

"A polis awready came an asked aw aboot ma video the other day," Colin piped up.

Paulo shot him a withering look then turned back to McCoist with just a hint of the old smile. "Well there ye go. Stevie Spielberg's awready answered yer questions. If yev seen the video, yev seen it aw, noo ye better be oan yer way."

"I've got to follow—"

"It's nearly the weekend, DI McCoist, better get the hoose tidied fir the weans comin oer, eh? Dugs can make a hell ae a mess. Never hud wan masel, but. Goat enough lassies slobberin aw oer ma crotch never mind dugs."

.   .   .

249

McCoist drove a couple of blocks away, swung a left before reaching High Street and parked immediately on double-yellows, hands shaking on the wheel, trying to catch her breath, which was wheezing in tight as if there were a hand squeezing her throat. Thin air and adrenaline erupting inside her left her almost euphoric. When it drained away, she was steady again but exhausted. Even fear had slipped off with the dregs of the rush.

Fuck. Fuck, fuck, fuck. What the fuck was that?! Mental. That was fucking mental. She had been followed then. He knew about Bruce. Christ, he knew about Tess and Cam. She remembered the feeling of being stalked around the neighbourhood by the man in the anorak, the feeling of all the other times strange men had followed her, starting when she was still a young girl. When would it happen to Tess? Maybe it had happened already. Wouldn't she have told her though? She was her mother; she was a police detective...

As if conjured, the huge black motor with "V2P MCG" on the vanity plate cruised down Bell Street towards the car wash, passing through McCoist's mirrors. The man driving—something about the shape of his nose—Anorak Man? Maybe, maybe not. Could be any one of the thugs on Paulo's payroll—McCoist didn't manage to see him properly. Didn't matter which it was, only that McCoist had to be on the lookout. Maybe time for a more grown-up version of the stranger-danger talk with the kids too.

The situation had got very thick very fast and McCoist still had nothing evidential to go on. *So back off or do the work?*

By the time she'd gathered herself enough to turn the key in the ignition, she'd made up her mind. "Detective Inspector Alison McCoist, Major Investigation Team." That's what it said on her card.

44

Davey had a visitor's pass back into heaven. Temporary. A guestie. It went unsaid but understood that he had to toe the line or Sarah would toe his bollocks—privileges revoked, access rescinded, don't steal anything on your way out, dickhead.

Heaven wasn't the poky but well-kept council house in the east end that he used to live in—though it was a step up from Davey's current gaff for sure. Heaven was his daughter's arms around his sides, the smell of her hair, her smile that came from her mother, the brazen cheek behind it that came from him. The sight of her toys all over the floor. He'd never thought he'd miss stepping on Lego. Her unavoidable presence, her barrage of chatter: "Pretend this is the princess an this, this is her dug… Pretend yer a monster and ye want tae eat me… Pretend this is the castle where we live, an, an, an pretend that, pretend…"

He was on the floor with her, knees and back aching and stiff from work, the car wash getting busier as the weather brightened. The healing wound in his arm didn't help things. Plus he'd just run from the bus stop because he was late—couldn't find his wallet and had to dig change out of the drawers and couch cushions. He grinned through the pain.

Sarah watched him over a mug of tea, a smiling examiner, weighing him to see if there was any diamond among the lump of coal. The performance at Annalee's party and further cajoling from his maw had led her to call him up and extend the invite on his day off.

Annalee went to her wee arts-and-crafts table to draw him a picture and he used the break to switch his attention to Sarah. "How ye bin keepin?"

"No bad. Same auld. Bin seein aboot gettin some shifts wae Tracy at the hostel once Annalee starts school eftir the summer."

"That's good. Christ, cannae believe she's startin school this year."

Sarah snorted into her tea. "A can. Am ready fir it. An please don't say, 'Where's the time goan?' A know exactly where it's goan. Every minute ae the last five year." Again, the memory of Sarah's feet running over the car came back to him, screeching like a wean as she slipped down the windscreen. *Gettin some shifts*. When they first met, Sara had wanted to become a nurse, planned to sit some highers at college to get into the uni course. What had happened to that?

Davey felt the treacherous waters, carefully rode the waves and about-turned. "A saw Pat goin intae the Goose the other day. He wis sayin aboot the surgery an that…"

"Aye, well it's no gonnae be happenin at aw if he keeps spendin aw his time at the Goose. Ma maw's been gettin ontae him aboot geein up the drink fir ages. Ye back oan it yersel seein as ye were at the pub then?"

"Naw, naw, a just bumped intae him ootside, wisnae stoappin." This was mostly true—Davey had cut way back, just the odd pint that barely counted at all.

"An huv ye bin feelin better fir it?"

An answer lodged in Davey's throat. Where could he even start with how he was feeling? The panic attacks were still regular, his prescription for the diazepam rewritten and rewritten.

Day-to-day his needle swung between completely numb and trembling wreck. Colin watched him all the time at work and he still hadn't got back to Croaker—he expected to be jumped and black-bagged again at any moment by either one. The most recent run-in with the poliswoman McCoist at the car wash and his grassing to Lennox fuelled his paranoia to Sean level and he spent so much time looking over his shoulder he could practically turn his head right around like the burd from *The Exorcist*. In truth, the only time he'd been at peace in recent memory was playing with Annalee on the floor right then and there.

Sarah was waiting. He couldn't give her the full truth but even a small slice of it might make the connection she was waiting for, one he desperately wanted to make. He could see her face sinking by the millisecond. He took a deep breath and…

There was a knock at the door.

Saved by the fuckin bell, Davey thought, as Sarah went to get it. The Voice of Reason nudged him to think—this was a stay of execution, think of something to say. Instead he knelt down next to where Annalee was working. "Wit's that yer drawin? A hope it isnae me, there's nae way ma belly is that big, yer daein me a wrang turn—"

He heard the voice through the wall and his stomach felt like he'd been force-fed a bucket of icy water. *Saved by the fuckin bell aw right.*

The living room door opened and Sarah came in first. "Davey?" Her voice was unsure. No wonder.

The Big Man himself came in behind her. Paulo was wearing a slick, pale-grey suit, collar of his salmon shirt open wide enough to show off chest hair and chain. His aftershave wafted in with him in a thick, invisible cloud. "Davey Boy, howsit goin?!" His voice boomed, sounded genuinely jovial, pleased to see him. Davey couldn't reply at first, his tongue stuck inside his suddenly dry mouth.

Sarah's eyes darted between the two of them. Davey got up off the floor. "Awright Paulo, eh, nice tae see ye… here," he managed. Davey choked on the words, tried to smile but his cheek muscles twitched and withered, as if he'd been smiling too long while waiting for a photo to be taken.

"Ye look like av just popped up oot ae a cake, pal!" Paulo wiggled his thick fingers like a magician. "Ta da!" The chunky sovvy rings he wore on them had stamped a few faces in their time—the personal seal of Paul McGuinn.

Davey forced a laugh. "Sorry, naw—it's just… how…"

"How did a find ye here?" Paulo was beaming. "Fir ma next trick…" He waved his hands around again and pulled a wallet from inside his suit jacket. It was Davey's, the one he couldn't find, the one with his driver's licence in it with the address that still hadn't been changed to his new flat, years overdue.

"How… a mean, where—"

"It wis in ma motor, musta fallen oot yer poackit while ye were valetin it." Paulo gave him a big stage wink which Sarah couldn't help but catch.

"Fell oot while ye were cleanin?" She looked from Davey to Paulo and back again. She smelled bullshit. It was as thick in the air as Paulo's aftershave. *Where the fuck did he get ma wallet fae?* If Davey's wallet wasn't jammed into his tight front pocket, it was in his bag in the office with his phone and his pieces.

"Aye, musta done. Cheers Paulo, yev saved me a load ae hassle there." *That prick Colin, he must ae taken it.* Paulo threw the wallet and Davey fumbled the catch, smooth-worn leather slipping between his clammy palms.

"Fell right oot yer poackit an intae the car an ye didnae notice," Sarah pressed. Her eyebrows twitched upwards. It wasn't the Face but it was a preliminary step towards it.

Paulo was enjoying this. Davey's cheeks were starting to turn red. He couldn't think. Pressure adrenaline was drip, drip, dripping, eroding holes in his brain. He was suddenly back at school, staring down an exam paper, barely able to write his name on the first page because his mind had gone and his fingers were too tight around the pen.

"Hawd oan…" Sarah's face was screwing up now, mind stumbling towards something—a good sign regarding the likelihood of Davey getting a bollocking, a bad sign for where the conversation was going next. "Yer no really a customer, are ye?"

Davey's heart pounded, sweat prickled his back, he could feel his blood coursing, whooshing up and down inside him, far too fast. His chest was tight, breath coming short.

"Yer fae Davey's therapy group int ye? Sorry, a mean, a know yer no allowed tae say—it's like alcoholics anonymous an that, int it?"

Paulo smiled at Davey, the way a shark might, showing its rows and rows of teeth. Skulls have had more benign grins. Armani scent rolled off him in waves, secreting from him like some predator hormone. He kept his eyes—behind the black holes the sparks in his brain plugs were firing—squarely locked on Davey's as he slowly, painfully formed an answer: "Aye that's right. Am sorry fir fibbin but it's like ye say, we're no really sposed tae talk aboot it ootside the, eh, *group*. Davey wis treatin me tae a coffee eftir the meetin the other day an left it oan the table."

Davey's throat was so tight he couldn't speak. The panic was like a fist squeezing around his neck. Thick fingers decorated in thick, gold rings. He nodded instead.

"He wis buyin *you* a coffee?" The line between a sarcastic joke and genuine suspicion was a crack as thin as a strand of spider's web.

"Aye, he's a generous lad, this yin. Insistet."

"Aw that talkin must be daein some good then. Would ye like a cuppa? Paulo, wis it?"

"Paulo, aye. Ad love wan if it's nae trouble, hen."

"No at aw."

Sarah went to the kitchen and Paulo sat himself on the sofa, his bulk making the cheap settee groan. He looked around the room, not worried about offending Davey with the openness of his distaste. *The cunt.* "A grew up in a place just like this," he said. "Made us intae the man a am the day. Determined tae get the fuck oot ae it."

Annalee had been focusing on her drawing, shy of the big man in the posh suit who smelled so strongly of perfume that it had already filled up the entire little flat. She looked round at the swear word.

"Awright, doll? Wit's yer name?"

She smiled and looked away again.

"It's Annalee," Davey said.

"An how auld are ye, Annalee?" Davey cringed at the sound of his daughter's name in the man's mouth. His nails dug into his palms, his fists crying out to swing for him. *Ma wee girrul*, Croaker's voice crackled in his head. His wee girl, filled with smack, strapped to some infested, cum-stained scratcher, man after man lined up at the foot of it. *Some ae these wee burds, Davey, they're only fourteen, fifteen year auld.*

"She's no lang turnt five," Davey answered for her again. *A shouldnae say wummin, really, they're bairns. Kiddies like yer ain wee yin.*

"Five!" he boomed. "That's a great age, five. Aff tae school then?"

"Aye, eftir the summer. Ye goat kids yersel, Paulo?" It sounded innocuous, small talk, but Davey knew there was a challenge there and the Voice of Reason berated him for the thick fuck he was.

Paulo gave him the patented one-two look—a burning stare of demonic intensity quickly replaced by a matey grin. The question *Why are you really here?* hung between them, Davey too scared and wired up to ask it. Sarah came back in and handed Paulo a mug of tea. "Cheers, hen."

"Wit dye dae yersel, Paulo?" Sarah asked.

He took a mouthful of Tetley and groaned as if he'd crawled out the desert, gasping. "A own a few businesses roon the toon."

"Nae joabs goin fir Davey? Get him oot that mingin car wash."

"Sarah—" She silenced Davey with a look. She still had that power.

Paulo laughed. "Ye know, as soon as somethin comes up yer man's gonnae be the first tae hear aboot it."

"Ye hear that, Davey?" Sarah said.

"Aye… Cheers, Paulo," Davey mumbled. He became dimly aware of a burning heat in his right hand and noticed Sarah had given him a fresh brew. The hand was clamped fast around the scorching mug in a claw he had no control over, the same way it sometimes seized up during the night after a busy shift.

"Well, ye could try an look pleased, son," Paulo said, face straight. There was a hush, a current of threat trembling in the moment—surely even Sarah felt it—before Paulo cackled again. "Am only jokin, mucker. Listen, a know a came tae return yer wallet but a also wantet tae see ye cause a wis concerned the other night. The whole, eh, *group* wis—ye don't mind me talkin aboot this in front ae yer missus, dae ye?"

Davey swallowed, mouth dry—it didn't occur to him to drink the tea and there was no way it would go down his throat anyway, it felt narrow as the barrel of a syringe needle—and shook his head. Sarah didn't correct Paulo, she was too interested. Annalee carried on drawing.

"Yev been jumpy lately, *agitated*. We can aw tell yer no yersel. Worse than when we met ye, a mean." His face was a mask of worry, charitable pity. Davey saw right through it—he was supposed to. Paulo was enjoying this. "Yer huvin a tough auld time ae it, an a wantet tae say tae ye, personally, beyond the group an aw that, ye can talk tae me if ye need tae. Talk tae me if ye can talk tae naebdy else. Big Paulo will look eftir ye."

Davey's left palm was gouged with red crescents from his nails; his right was scorched pink. He imagined he could smell burning meat coming off him in waves, from his hand, from his brain.

"Ye don't huv tae say anythin right noo, just mind it. A don't want anythin tae happen tae ye, Davey. Wit would yer family dae waeoot ye?" He slapped Davey's upper arm—his injured one, the healing wound hidden under his jumper, right where Paulo had clamped his massive, meaty fist—and squeezed hard, as if

258

with rough affection. Davey clamped his teeth together to keep from crying out, to keep the pain from his face. They sat like this for a few long heartbeats, stretched out in Davey's mind to infinity, then he let go. "Wit would they dae?" he repeated.

As he got up to leave, Annalee ran over and handed him the picture she'd been working on.

"Fir me?"

She nodded and ran away again, over to Davey where she buried her face in his side.

"That's lovely, doll, yer a wee star."

Davey spent the rest of his visit distracted, trying to keep his hands still. Fucking Colin. That fucking grass. He'd bumped his wallet and he'd told Paulo about the injury. Must have. Maybe the way he'd been that day with McCoist as well… Was he acting suspicious? *We can aw tell yer no yersel.* How was he supposed to act? He'd been kidnapped and beaten and threatened and spent his time mopping up after atrocities. Of course he'd be "jumpy". He'd tried to get rid of McCoist before Paulo saw her because, well, what if she'd tried to search the place or something? With the guns hidden there—what would Paulo have done then? What would Davey have had to clean up that day?

Sarah looked at him with wet eyes. "A didnae realise that ye were that… Look, am glad yer goin tae that group an that. Ye, ye don't huv tae talk aboot it any mare if ye don't want tae but just sose ye know, if ye do, al listen…"

A nice offer. In his current, atrophied state, Davey couldn't quite believe it to be genuine, tears or no. There hadn't been much listening when they were together—on either side. Davey could only bring himself to nod and grunt—which would usually have annoyed Sarah, being a talker herself meant she took anything approaching reservation for rudeness, but she didn't seem to mind right then. What she did mind was the way he snapped at Annalee for tugging at his jeans for his attention. The room was still thick with Paulo's aftershave, cloying and heavy, sticking to everything. It followed him right out the door when it was time to leave soon after. He had a kiss and cuddle from Annalee that he could barely feel.

"Let us know when yer aff an maybe we can sort another visit," Sarah said, watching him walk away.

45

Davey was skating. When the buzzer woke him it was like he was dropping through a hole in the ice and into freezing-cold water. He shot up in bed, gulping in air, half dreaming it was water, suffocating, heart pounding, blood in his stuffed ears. It took him a minute to fully understand the noise was coming from the front-door buzzer and not his phone on the bedside table. *Wit fuckin time's it?* It was still dark in his flat, no light creeping through the cracks in the curtains.

He crept to the intercom phone in his scants. The silence between buzzes was heavy, his skin slick with sweat, cool air prickling the fine hairs on his neck and arms. *Who the fuck is ringin the bell at this time?* Three immediate possibilities jumped to his mind, and right then the idea that it might be the polis seemed the most comforting.

It buzzed again. Davey snatched up the phone as if diving on a hand grenade. "Aye?"

"Oot yer scratcher an get yer clathes oan, Davey Boy. This is work, so no yer Sunday best, awright? Don't keep me waitin."

Paulo's stealth bomber was parked outside, sucking in the light from the street lamps, engine rumbling. The man himself was at the wheel, eyes ringed with sleep, dressed in a well-worn Gucci jogging suit, the cuffs dirty and frayed. Davey climbed up into the cockpit and the door locked shut behind him.

The familiar smell of Autosmart plastic polish washed over Davey, the hint of unshowered men with stale cigarette breath just beneath. "Goat a wee joab needs daein," Paulo said, doing a burly and tearing out of the cul-de-sac. "Mind ye were sayin yed like tae dae us a favour? Well, noo's the chance. Maybe a need ye eftir aw, eh?"

"Eh, aye, Paulo. Coarse. Wit—wit's the script?"

"Yel see." They drove to the big twenty-four-hour Tesco—the one where Davey used to work. The car park was mostly empty but for a few insomniacs' motors and hot boxes belonging to weed fiends in need of snackage. Paulo parked in a disabled space by the entrance. "Get yersel some cleanin supplies. Heavy-duty, plenty ae bleach, scourers, know wit a mean? Somethin that can get right in aboot it. An a roll ae black bags."

Davey's hand gripped tight to the ergonomically moulded door handle.

"Look, ad rather be in ma nest wae the Television X freeview oan masel but there's shite tae dae."

"The freeview? Wae a car like this an aw that, ye cannae just pay fir the channel?"

Paulo looked as if Davey had slapped him. "Am no a fuckin degenerate, Davey Boy! If a man cannae get wit he needs in ten minutes he's a fuckin wrang yin, mark ma words. Anyway, stoap fuckin aboot an get goin."

Davey stepped out on legs like wooden stilts. He prayed he didn't see anybody he knew. "Oh, an Davey boy!" Paulo called from the car. "Mind an keep yer receipts, aye?"

When Davey returned with the necessaries, Paulo whizzed them over the car park, cutting a straight line across the marked roads and spaces, and over to the all-night Starbucks. "Better get some coffee in ye," he said, ordering for Davey at the drive-thru. "Ye want a cinnamon bun an aw? Here, get it doon ye." He passed Davey a steaming plastic cup and a greasy bag with the pastry inside. "Caw that quits fir the supplies, eh? These fuckin chains are so fuckin expensive."

The coffee did little to still the tremors in Davey's body. Chunks of cinnamon bun sat in his belly like lumps of lead. He made the effort to chew it up into a paste before he tried swallowing it, nipping little bird-like bites to make it easier on his adrenaline-full stomach.

The route became familiar. Davey felt like he was strapped into a rollercoaster, climbing higher and higher towards the inevitable drop, the bottom impossible to see yet.

They pulled up outside the high-rise with the blacked-out windows at the top, stopping nearly exactly where he had the night Croaker told him about his daughter, Becca. This time, Davey knew, he'd be going in.

"Wan ae the rooms is in need ae a deep clean. Av seen yer work wae the motors, Davey Boy, it'll be a pure dawdle. Moan. An fire that doon ye, there are weans starvin in Africa!"

They stepped out the lift on the twelfth floor. The inside of the building could have been any block of council flats, except probably better kept. There was no litter in the halls, no graffiti, no smell of pish or abandoned, half-eaten munchie boxes.

They walked past rows of identical doors, occasional voices coming through them sounding like Charlie Brown's parents. They came to number 1214 and Paulo knocked in a sequence. The door opened a crack and a slice of a face could be seen.

"It's me," Paulo growled.

The man behind the door had baggy bloodshot eyes and sweat on his forehead, and scrunched his nose in a phlegmy coke sniff every few minutes. He held the door open for them as they stepped into a short, narrow hallway—one door at the end and one to the right—which was empty but for a radiator and an electric meter. The doorman stuck his head out to check the corridor before closing it behind them. "The sheriff gone awready?" Paulo whispered to him.

"Aye, PJ showed up wae the spare clathes, headed oot ten minutes ago. This yer tap valet man?"

"Aye, this is Davey Boy, he's gonnae geez a hawn. He's the fuckin expert, knows the score."

Except Davey didn't know the score. He had a nightmarish idea of it but it wasn't until Paulo opened the right-hand door and led him into the bedroom that he really knew for sure what he was being asked to do.

She was on the bed, naked but for a thin robe, lying open. Hair half covering her face, matted with something dark and sticky in the pink mood lighting of the room—a silk scarf over a bedside lamp. A smell came wafting from her—voided bowels and something else, something too rich, overripe. Fresh blood.

"Get the light oan, fucksake," Paulo snapped at the two men standing around the bed, the sweaty, coked-up guy joining them too. "Man needs tae see tae work!"

In the harsh brightness of the big light, the blood on her body was too red, cartoonish. Davey could see the dark centre of the puncture in her ribs, just below her right breast. The bruises on her face were livid and swollen but couldn't disguise how young she was. There was a blotchy tattoo on the lean curve of her hip—interlocking letters that made an indecipherable rune, like a scheme-team tag on a tunnel wall.

Davey's pus must have been green as the Grinch because Paulo gave him his shark smile and said, "Bathroom's through that other door."

Davey just made it to the toilet, regurgitating coffee and mashed cinnamon bun, almost untouched by his digestive system, into the bowl. His throat burned; his nose was choked with vomit, eyes streaming. Stars popped in his vision; the room spun. He took in deep breaths, rubbed at the pain in his chest. He flushed the toilet—there was blood on the handle, now on his fingertips. The sink was also rinsed in pink where bloody hands had been washed. There was a bundle of soiled clothes in the bathtub, a red handprint on the mould-flecked shower curtain.

"Awright in there, Davey Boy?" came Paulo's voice through the wall. "Ye fallen in?" He guffawed. There was a titter from the other men.

Davey wiped his face on his sleeve, braced himself, and went back into the bedroom.

"Maybe wan ae they baristas wiped their arse wae that cinnamon bun, eh?" Paulo said. "Ye should sue the robbin bastarts!"

Davey forced a weak smile.

"Right then, wit's oor plan, team?" Paulo looked around the men. As well as Dope Nose, there was a big bruiser with a shaved skull and Viking beard in trackies and a good-looking youngster dressed as plain as a model from the Great Universal catalogue. He was holding a plastic baggy with a bloody knife inside it. There was something familiar about him. "Deek an me are gonnae wrap her up an get her tae fuck doon the stair," he said. "We can sort that end. Malky"—he pointed to the sniff-head—"will start takin the cerpit up—nae way tae clean that—an Davey can get started however he hinks is best."

It was only when the man said Davey's name that he realised why he was familiar: the young polis in the shiny suit at the hospital tagging along with DI McCoist. The one who'd taken him to A & E in the early hours of Boxing Day, worried he was trying to get himself killed. Maybe Colin hadn't been the one cliping to Paulo about Davey after all... A look flashed between them; Davey moved his eyes to the floor.

"Sounds solid, boays, get tae work!" Paulo clapped his hands, *chop-chop.*

When the girl was gone it was easier to pretend he wasn't cleaning up a murder. Easier to keep a lid on the panic roiling in his now-empty gut. He began with the bathroom to give numb-face Malky time to get the carpet pulled up. He started at the corners of the ceilings and worked his way down inch by inch. He used a toothbrush dipped in bleach to get into the grouting around the tiles. There wasn't much blood visible in the bathroom beyond that on the suite itself but, as Davey's *CSI: Miami*-based knowledge of forensics told him, it was the stuff you couldn't see that fucked you, so he scrubbed the room top to bottom.

In the bedroom, the carpet was up and the sheets stripped—used to carry her away as she began to stiffen. There was a stain on the mattress. "That'll have tae go anaw," Davey said. With Malky's help he flipped the mattress off the bed and inspected the slats beneath for any leakage. He squinted, unsure, and cleaned them anyway. He cleaned the headboard and the posts, wiped the light switches and plug points. He went to wipe away a couple of Keith Richards rails still carved out on the bedside table but Malky grabbed his wrist to stop him. "Nae point in it goin tae waste," he said, and hoovered them up with a short length of plastic straw he apparently carried around with him. When Malky was done using his saliva-wet fingertip to pick up the residue and rub it into his gums, Davey cleaned the table.

Blood had gone through the carpet and onto the rough, unvarnished floorboards beneath. "Fuck, gonnae huv tae scrub the whole bastart flair," Davey said. At least Malky's coke-fuelled energy was useful for something, though his non-stop gabbing gave Davey a headache.

The young polis and the shell-suit Viking came back to help get the mattress and the carpet down into their van. Davey didn't ask where it was all going. Or where she went. The girl. *Only fourteen, fifteen year auld.* She looked a little older than that. But not much.

Paulo drove him home. They didn't speak until they were back outside Davey's flat, the sun coming up.

"Wit happened there, Paulo?" Davey's voice was hoarse with sleep, burnt with stomach acid.

"Ye sure ye want tae know?" There was a hint of a smile behind the sound of concern. "Yev goat a wee girrul yersel, it doesnae dae tae imagine wit can happen tae wee girruls. Wit happens tae them aw the time."

"Wit happened?"

"Punter goat rough wae her, started slappin her aboot, she fought back, hud the shank in her drawer. Ended up gettin plugged hersel."

"The punter says that?"

"Aye. Said it wis maistly an accident, didnae mean tae stab her, it wis just they were rollin aboot wae the blade an—" Paolo blew a raspberry, miming the knife going into her heart.

"An wit's gonnae happen tae him?"

"Honestly, Davey?" The Big Man fiddled with his rings. "He's an important man. That lassie deed is worth mare tae me noo than she ever wis alive. Cause this cunt, this *powerful* man, he's mine noo. For ever. An if he does wit a say, when a say it, he'll be fine." Paolo leant over, so close Davey could smell his rancid morning breath, the sweaty, up-all-night hum underneath worn-out Armani aftershave. "Ye did good work the night, Davey Boy. How are ye oan the tools by the way?"

Davey's heart hammered in his chest and he felt another round of involuntary purging coming on. "Eh, a, well… it's bin a while since av been oan a site, ye know, a—"

Paolo burst out laughing. "Don't worry, son, am no gonnae ask tae see yer tickets. When this sorta stuff…"—he pointed a thumb out the back window, to flat 1214 and the girl on the bed—"…comes up, it's good tae huv guys who are *capable*, ye know wit a mean? Guys who a can rely oan. Guys who know how tae graft. An like a says, ye did good work."

The night Croaker and Mince had dropped Davey off at the Royal Infirmary, he left the car not just with a present for Annalee but with one for himself. A gift from Mr Croaker: a brand-new mobile phone, pay-as-you-go, already loaded with ten quid of credit. The phone would have cost someone a bomb back in 1999—it had a colour display, polyphonic ringtones—but twenty years later it would've come out the Argos catalogue at under a score.

There was one number in the address book. It rang four times before Croaker answered: "Aye?"

Davey chewed his lip, listening to the man's rasping breath. The Voice of Reason was screaming, *Wit the fuck are ye daein gettin involved wae this rocket?! He's gonnae get ye fuckin killt. He's tried twice awready!* But what other choice did Davey have? He'd cleaned up the mess left by Mince, the people in the truck, and now this girl, this young girl strung out, beaten up, raped over and over then stabbed to death. He'd seen the body this time. He'd never be able to unsee it—the garish red of fresh blood against lifeless, empty skin, the cattle brand on her rump, the deep dark well of the wound. What would be next? *Oan the tools.* That's right, Paulo would have him chopping up the corpses too. On top of that, he had polis working for him, he had a sheriff and whoever else under his thumb, and he knew where Sarah and Annalee lived. No, Davey had no choice at all. It had to stop.

Davey replied: "Aye. Ye goat me intae this, an yer gonnae fuckin well get me oot ae it an aw. Wit we daein?"

46

Davey took the bus into the city centre and jumped out at George Square. He crossed the square and entered Queen Street Station, squeezed through the busy concourse—workers heading back to Edinburgh—and went out the exit at the other side. He took the long tunnel down into Buchanan Street subway, surfacing on the street itself—thronging with shoppers making their way home and people already out for the night—without buying a ticket or getting on a train. He then headed uphill into the Buchanan Galleries, zigzagged through the shopping centre, milling in and out of shops, weaving between people, and then out onto Sauchiehall Street. He doubled back down Renfield Street, kept going downhill until he reached Central Station. He went in through the grand gates of Gordon Street, shouldered his way through under the glass roof, headed down the escalator towards the low level, then exited under the Hielanman's Umbrella, which stank of frying oil from the chippy and pish from all the pools of pish. From there, he walked towards the back end of the St Enoch Centre, where he was to wait at the spot the car had been sitting last time.

The car that arrived this time was different. "Get in," Mince said. His hair was starting to grow back, thick stubble on his head. The hairline was high and there was a bald spot on his crown. It made his panel-beaten face look more human.

"Nae Croaker?" Davey asked.

"Meetin him there."

"Where?"

"Fit divs it matter? Yer goin onyway."

"Ye gonnae cover ma heed again?" Davey closed the door. The car smelled of old people. A quick glance over at the mileage confirmed it had been somebody's weekend tootle-about.

"No after last time, like. Gads!"

"Well, *you* try it an see how ye dae."

"Am sure wull aw be havin a go if we fuck this up—did ye brek the phone after?"

"Aye."

"Nae aabdy ahin ye?"

"Naw."

They headed across the Clyde, which rippled darkly in the wind below the bridge. Traffic was thick in both directions. Mince made sure to hop through every solid amber he came across, even taking a chance on the odd red if it was close enough. Not that he was driving recklessly—in his own warped way, this was him being cautious.

"Mr Croaker's speech convinced ye after aw then? Took ye a bit ae time."

"Scuse us fir takin a minute tae hink afore a signt up tae square-go Tony fuckin Soprano. Wit did he say tae ye eftir aw that happened wae yer brother? Ye really intae that revenge pish an aw?"

Mince glared at him until Davey had to nudge him: "Eyes oan the fuckin road."

"He's payin me double. Twaa shares."

"Fuck, a didnae even hink tae ask fir money."

"That's cause he's got ye thinkin that he's the een divvin ye the favour. Dinnae need tae pay a mannie fa's under pressure."

"Pressure is fuckin right."

Mince chuckled. "Listen, let me tell ye somethin. Ye dinnae want tae ken fit we'd be divvin tae get ye tae agree if ye hadnae aaready. Dinnae get tae thinkin we're aa pals here noo—specially Croaker. That's ma advice, an al only gee it ye the eence."

Davey had taken some diazepam before he left the flat—plus a couple of beta blockers he'd pinched from his maw—but even then he still felt the lurch in his stomach, the sick nerves that had been plaguing him all day.

They cruised into an industrial estate, pulled up outside a warehouse, where the shadow of Croaker was leaning against another car. His face was up-lit by the glowing tip of the fag in his mouth. He waved.

"Stay in the car." Before he got out, Mince added: "Say a word ae that conversation to aabdy an yel spend the rest ae yer life walkin aboot on yer hawns like that loon fa played ET."

Davey watched them talk for a moment, couldn't hear them. Croaker jabbed a thumb over his shoulder towards the boot of his car. Mince nodded and went round. It was unlocked. He pulled out a pair of bolt cutters.

Croaker left the boxer to it and came over. He tossed his fag end to the ground and stood on it before getting in, bringing his scent of sweat-smothered cologne and rank smoke in with him. He immediately lit up another fag and offered Davey the pack.

"Nae thanks."

"Ye quit again?"

"Quit again the day, quit again the morra."

"That's a solid motto right there, Davey."

"This part ae the plan? Are we at wan ae Paulo's places?" Mince had broken open the lock on the warehouse and was now lifting the shutter.

"Don't you worry aboot aw that, son. Wit a want fae ye the noo is tae tell me everythin ye know aboot McGuinn. Start fae the toap an tell me every little hing that's happened since ye first met him. Then we'll see wit we can dae wae it."

Mince had gone back to the car boot and replaced the bolt cutters. Two large parcels then came out—brown paper wrapped in plenty of tape—which he carried inside.

"He showed up wan mornin, end ae last year, wantin a valet…"

47

"How did you get this number?"

"Av goat ma ways—wee pigeons, tin cans oan strings…"

"Where are you? It's time we had a face-to-face."

"No yet. Am oan the move again."

"So why are you letting me know? If this is about money, I think you already know what my answer will be."

"Money's no the problem. Easy enough tae make ma ain."

"I don't want to know."

"A met a familiar polis recently. Ye mind the wummin fae the Dannie Gibb hing?"

"Christ. What did she want?"

"Probly just lookin fir mare rope tae hang hersel wae—first yin wisnae lang enough. It's likely nothin, but."

"I'll keep an eye out. Is that it?"

"Fir noo…"

"Bullfrog?"

"Aye?"

"Don't ever call me at my home again."

The line died and Croaker allowed himself a smile. Noising cunts up was always a sure-fire way to brighten his day a little. It was part of what made him good at what he did. A bit of friction, a bit of heat, and you see where the frayed edges were. Abrasion can smooth down or tear apart.

Or eviscerate, in the case of Paul McGuinn. He'd have the bastart, he'd have him soon. And it wouldn't be the jail for him this time. That option had passed. He'd given the polis their best shot when he'd led them to Dannie Gibb's body and—so he thought at the time—served up Paul McGuinn on a platter, and they'd fucked it. Sure, he'd been impressed with the audacity of the Knightley confession gambit, but disgusted all the same that they'd fallen for it. No, he'd do it himself this time. He would leave McGuinn the way the merciless bastard left so many others: Dannie Gibb stripped and throttled, wrapped up in the undergrowth, her guts hanging open and the life carved out of her; Jill McTiernan, just seventeen and sent floating down the Clyde, her body blue and bloated, OD'd on his cheap smack; Stephanie Williams, dead from exposure one winter, cut loose after contracting HIV; Becca Coleman, skull opened up with the claw end of a hammer and dumped in a burn, having been given to McGuinn by her own father to settle a debt; and the bits and pieces of many more over the years since Croaker began this hunt, the ones who couldn't be put back together, the nameless, the missing.

He finished his fag and stubbed it out on the window ledge. He allowed himself another minute with his feet up on the desk before getting his shoes on. He folded up his sleeping bag and stuffed his pills, teabags and toiletries into his holdall. With what little cash he had left, he'd bought some bin bags and antibacterial wipes and set about cleaning up—starting with all the ash and fag douts on the window ledge.

Once the office had been dighted down, he replaced the battery in the smoke alarm and fixed the security latch on the window. Job done, he selected one of his unused pay-as-you-go phones and called in the tip-off on his way out. He didn't feel bad about what would happen to Fred Nile—in fact, it made his grubby wee heart sing to think of it. Nile might be an innocent these days but he was no choirboy when Croaker first met him years before. Up to the gills in all sorts of nasty shite, then weaselled out of his full sentence by grassing on his pals. Punishment wasn't a one-and-done deal: you paid for mistakes for the rest of your life. And now the polis had come sniffing around and the boy had served his use, it was time to cut the tie and give Nile his lost time back. Happy days.

The heroin was supposed to have been burnt—the trial it was evidence for had finished—but someone on the inside had pinched it and sold it to Croaker, who got a good deal because he was happy to take it in bulk and, also, dealing with a bent polis gave instant leverage which made driving the price down easy. The seller, traced through the tiers and tangles of off-the-books business, technically kicked up to Paul McGuinn. This was unsurprising since there were only really a handful of guys at the very top (or very bottom, depending on which way you looked at it) of Glasgow's underworld, but it was a pleasing coincidence that appealed to the sadist in Croaker.

Nile's choice now was either to let himself be banged up or blab about Croaker and expose himself in the process—which he wouldn't, because a decade behind bars would be infinitely preferable to what Paulo McGuinn would do to him.

After hanging up, he opened the phone, pulled out the SIM card and split it in half. As he walked down the street, the handset went in one bin, the SIM in another. The bin bag with the used wipes found yet another resting place. He kept an eye out for a car as he strolled towards the bus station. He wanted one with a bit of space where he could stretch out on the back seat—he didn't have a new base of operations worked out yet, just a few vague notions of places he could squat for a while. The drugs had rooked him for the time being—even at mate's rates—so a hostel wasn't an option. Staying mobile might be sensible anyway. The McCoist woman turning up may have just been coincidence and might not go anywhere, but he couldn't have her fucking things up again when he was this close. (He wasn't superstitious but that woman was a walking bad omen.)

The meeting with Burnet had yielded a solid gold nugget—he'd been right in leaving him alive, his instinct had played out well, the lad was certainly making himself useful for the time being. Now he just needed to find the right opportunity.

"Tam?"

The sound of his name being called out almost made him drop to his knees and cover his head. He whirled round to face his accuser.

"Tam!"

"...Johnny."

"Christ, Tam, how are ye? It's bin…"

"Years. A know." Croaker looked over his brother's shoulder, over his own, scouted the people walking down the street across the road.

"Yer lookin—"

"Like av bin swallied whole an shat oot again."

His brother grinned. "You said it, no me."

"Well, yer no a calendar model any mare yersel."

His brother had a sweet, simple laugh. It made Croaker ache. "Even Stace wouldnae buy that calendar."

"How is ma sister-in-law?" Croaker half listened, his antennae still probing for the set-up. He'd been careful: he didn't

277

think there was any way a connection could have been found between them any more, but it was impossible to be sure. The past existed in faint pencil lines, indentations dug into the page, no matter how hard you rubbed at it.

His brother yammered away: "She's grand, aye. Wuv just moved tae the area, actually, doonsizin noo the kids arenae hame any mare. Ye bin here lang yersel? A, a didnae know where ye were livin…" He smiled again, waiting for a reply, and when none came, he charged on: "Ian's doon in Newcastle noo an Young John's—"

"Look, a huv tae go, Johnny, am sorry. Am in a hurry."

"Hows aboot ye come oer tae the new gaff soon, eh? Stace would be happy tae see ye."

"Would she?"

"Ad be happy."

"Maybe. Look, al gee ye a call soon, awright?"

"Aye, nice wan."

Croaker turned and marched away—eyes scouring every doorway and junction for the heavies who may or may not be using his brother to get to him. Probably not, but you could never be sure. The best way was to avoid giving them the opportunity at all. He double-timed. His breath came short. He pressed his fingers hard into his chest to try to soothe the pain jabbing away inside it.

Johnny's voice was fading behind him: "Hawd oan, a didnae gee ye ma number! Tam! Tam!"

278

48

Nile left the police station. His shirt collar was open, his tie balled up and stuffed into his pocket. He carried his suit jacket over his arm even though the late evening was cool. He needed to blast away the stuffiness of the cell he'd been held in for the last twenty-four hours. His shoelaces were loose and mangled, all through the wrong holes where he'd quickly put them back in upon their return to him along with his watch, keys and phone.

He thought about calling Heather to come and pick him up but didn't. How would he explain all this to her? That he was probably going back to jail. That he'd been to jail in the first place. That his real name wasn't Fred Nile.

He sat down at the bus stop—the hard, plastic bench not much worse than the bed he'd lain awake on the previous night—and it wasn't until his bus pulled in he realised he had no way to pay for his ticket because his phone had run out of battery while it had been confiscated. "Fucksake." He'd be walking back then. His heels rubbed against his loose shoes. Never had he wanted a cigarette so badly—and now he had no way to buy a pack.

They'd grilled him for hours in a windowless interview room that reminded him of the Job Centre—shiny, peeling veneer on plywood tabletops, council-grade carpet, plastic bucket chairs straight from a school classroom. He had nothing to tell them. "Nae comment." He had no idea how the drugs had ended up in his warehouse—though he did know somebody who might be able to enlighten him. It was pretty far out of the way to the Carnaby Centre but it would be worth the walk. Plus, he might be able to get some money for a taxi—Croaker owed him that much at least, especially if the raid on the warehouse had happened because of whatever it was he was up to.

He let himself in with his key fob and trudged up the stairs to the office. He rattled the door a couple of times. When there was no answer he unlocked it himself.

The office stank of smoke, dirty laundry, aftershave and disinfectant. "Clatty bastart." Some of the office stuff had been unboxed but there was no other sign of Croaker. Maybe he was out. Maybe, but it all felt wrong. Absent. Abandoned.

He went back out and knocked on the door of CyberGrafix—he could see the light was still on in the door's window slit. The wee web-designer bloke opened the door. He had a pair of big, bug-eye lenses on and looked like he'd cut his own hair.

"Awright, pal?" Nile said.

"I'm afraid it's after hours—"

"Sorry, am the guy who rents the office across the hall."

"Oh." The web designer gave him an accusatory look—he clearly hadn't been happy with his neighbour but wasn't going to say anything outright. He wasn't the type.

"A wis wonderin if yed seen the bloke who wis workin there?"

"Working?"

"Aye."

"I saw him leave yesterday, hasn't come back yet."

"Did he huv anythin wae him? Like a bag or somethin?"

"Maybe. I just saw him go past the window but he might have been carrying something, can't be totally sure though."

"Right, nae worries. Cheers anyway, pal... Ye wouldnae happen tae huv any fags oan ye?"

He wasn't going to be lucky at all tonight. No fags, no Croaker. He knew he was gone. Maybe he'd heard about the raid and thought he was best off out of it. *Eejit*. There was a part of Nile that knew he was being naive, that he'd trusted Croaker too far, even though that wasn't very. Truth was he had no choice but to go along with him, do whatever he asked. Croaker was his only remote link to his past life—the smack must have had something to do with him. Bastart might have even stitched him up himself. Some form of long-game payback for the crimes of a past life, or just for his own twisted fun. Croaker had always enjoyed holding it over him—the threat of revealing his old identity, bringing his new life tumbling down. He didn't really mean it though, did he? Just a sick joke. He wouldn't have... Would he?

Nile started trudging home to Sighthill, a mission away. He rehearsed what he would say to Heather. How he would break it to her that he hadn't always been Fred Nile, printing-supplies salesman, business owner. When he'd met her just under three years ago, he was fresh out of jail with a new identity and a clean slate he'd bought by cooperating with the cops. "Cooperating" was what the polis called grassing up your pals.

They were particularly interested in the activities of his former boss, Paul McGuinn. What he gave them never amounted to charges in the end, but he'd gone far enough that his lawyer made them keep their end of the bargain. He'd done courses on printing while in the jail and set up his own office.

The two polis questioning him hadn't known any of that though. It was protected information. His lawyer eventually got word through to the right people and they let him go for the time being—a reprieve. Any new offences weren't negated by previous goodwill.

He came to where the M8 skirted the Royal Infirmary—the speeding traffic sounded like a rushing waterfall. He wound his way up to the footbridge that arced over eight lanes of fifty-mile-an-hour tarmac. The parapet of the bridge was panelled with graffitied grey steel that rose above head height, creating a gloomy trench with buzzing sodium-vapour lamps spaced out between pools of darkness. His footsteps bounced and reverberated in confusing ways, every clack of his heeled shoes pinballing away from him in both directions.

As he came over the hump of the bridge, he saw a man under the grey light of the lamp at the far end. A hood hid his face in shadow. The blade in his hand flashed orange-yellow.

Nile's heart thudded. He felt ill with the sudden onslaught of adrenaline. He'd been plugged once, back in the day. It was pain beyond anything he'd ever experienced before or since. In the years following his stabbing he'd built it up into a phobia. Just the sight of the knife was making his skin crawl, his legs freeze up. He recalled the sickening, unnatural feel of the blade being *inside*, the pain worse than anything he thought possible.

The sound of footsteps ping-ponged off the steel plates of the parapet—not his own and not from the man ahead, who was staying put for the moment. Nile spun around—another hood heading for him, cutting off the way back. This one was carrying the kind of meat cleaver used to butcher cattle—the handle big enough to be held two-handed.

The hood at the far end started coming for him too. Moving quickly now. Footsteps clanging and reverberating.

Nile turned this way and that. He started in one direction, stopped, turned the other way, stopped again. He might cough his heart right up, it was so high in his throat he felt if he opened his mouth it would be visible. A vague warmth spread down his legs.

The river of running metal swept past below. He could hear the motors, the wheels spinning. He jumped at the wall and got his hands on the top of the parapet, scrambled with his feet until he'd got his head over it, then one leg up, hanging right on the edge. The traffic was a blur of light, a tsunami of noise.

They were running for him now.

He didn't know how long the drop was to the road, but if he hadn't felt so queasy from his bursting heart already the height would have done the trick. Though he wasn't actually thinking about whether jumping was survivable or not, or whether, even if it was, how many cars would hit him after he landed. None of that was in his head—everything was pushed out by the sight of those flashing blades, imagination choked, overloaded by the vision of them biting into his skin, hacking down to his bones.

Heather wasn't in his heart or his mind as he fell—only fear. Then it was gone.

49

McCoist was mulling it over. A lot of the time her mulling was about what a sieve full of runny shit her life and career had become and what she would or could do if she handed in her notice. Recently, though, whenever the gears were turning in her brain, it was about the car wash and how it could get her back into the premier league. The wobble caused by her confrontation with McGuinn and the confirmation she'd been tailed by him had resolved into a desperate determination, something altogether even more unprofessional than before. No longer seeking only personal glory, but revenge too.

Same old problems though: still no body. And apart from suspicious comings and goings, still nothing solid on what McGuinn had them involved in. She'd dug further into Burnet and Prentice, including speaking to Burnet's mother (a joy of a woman) and a former foster carer of Prentice who barely remembered him. Was this guy really helping someone like Paulo McGuinn do people in and hide bodies? (Then burn the evidence—like a stolen Range Rover, for instance. Another piece she knew belonged but couldn't find a place for.) She thought of Knightley and decided there was no way she could count it out.

She was tempted to rake through the old Dannie Gibb files as well but knew she couldn't do so without anyone getting suspicious. Plus, her memories of it alone still caused her to clench and turn inside out as if she'd swallowed a sour ball whole. Actually going through the case files and seeing point by point where she'd been blinded by her own hubris and misled by her single-mindedness would be masochistic, probably annihilating any sense of confidence she'd recently clawed back. Confidence she was going to need to get this new case whacked and be returned to her rightful place. She was done wallowing but still needed to keep her head down.

A lot of the work on this was being done on her own time—the gaffer had plenty of scud work for her to get on with while she was on shift, and even with Findlay helping her out she was kept busy. She was lucky the kids had taken to Bruce so well—he was practically watching them for her whenever they came over, while she trawled away in her mind through bloody rags and baby ashes. She and Tess weren't arguing so much but only because they were barely communicating at all. "You in there?" Mark had said the last time he picked the kids up, pretending to knock on a door. An old joke he used to make. It was still annoying.

She'd been pondering the tattoo removal. They were used as brands, stamped onto working girls by their pimps. Why had Dannie's been lasered off when she had apparently still been working at the Macadam Street brothel? This question, as ever, led on to the one that was really burning her up: if it wasn't Knightley, who was the father of the unborn baby? Who had cut Dannie Gibb's body open—shredding through skin and fat and muscle with nothing more specialised than a dull kitchen knife—dragged out her guts and torn the foetus from inside her, only to burn it later in a barbecue like any old piece of meat?

An answer suggested itself but her train of thought was interrupted by her grumbling belly. Her recent spate of stake-outs with the requisite snacking had left her stomach wanting constant feeding. Her body had become a conveyor belt. She hit the cafeteria—it was mac 'n' cheese 'n' chips day. She could smell the school-food aroma it gave off from way down the corridor leading to the canteen. Her nose wrinkled but her stomach moaned.

The young lad behind the counter—a cap on his head and net over his beard—gave her a smile when she asked for an extra scoop of the plasticky yellow food, which she attacked the second her bum touched the seat. The congealing, savoury goo was a sticky ambrosia and she stuffed her face, letting her mind go numb.

She was so deep in her food trance that the sound of the chair opposite being scraped back across the lino floor was the first indication she had of the body looming over her.

"Anybody sitting here?" A middle-aged man, any trace of potential handsomeness being sapped by a cheap, non-specific, grey haircut and the thin chain that joined the legs of his glasses together, now hanging on his chest. Mr Itchy Unofficial, the silent superintendent from her interview last year.

McCoist shook her head, mouth stuffed with the soft mush of overcooked macaroni.

The man sat down. He didn't have a lunch tray or even a cup of coffee. He was in uniform, no lanyard. "I expect you know why I'm here," he said.

McCoist swallowed the food in her mouth without further chewing, feeling the lump slide all the way down her throat into her gut. "Sir?"

"The rags in the rubbish bin found outside that Spanish restaurant a while back—that's your case?"

The mac 'n' cheese wasn't sitting so well now. "If you could call a bag of bloody rags with no body to go with it a case."

The man smiled a textbook interrogation smile—disarming, deceiving. "No other leads?"

Something stank and it wasn't just the shite cafeteria food. "Nothing has shown up yet, sir."

"Oh, see, I thought the rags were related to this car-wash business."

Shit. Who the fuck is this guy? Anti-corruption? Mob squad? "Oh, you mean Bell Street? I'd been there on a few occasions to follow up on reports of threatening behaviour—the owner is a bit of a screwball. One of his workers then turned up injured in A & E—I thought his boss might have had a go at him, wanted to keep an eye on them."

"And that's it?"

"That's it."

"Well, did you see anything interesting?"

McCoist felt everything unravelling. She decided to play dumb, which would at least feel plausible to anyone familiar with her earlier work. "Nothing yet. Maybe I was wrong."

"Mhmm." His manner, once again, reminded her of a soft-spoken librarian. There was something naff, a bit Sunday school, about him. His next words, even and smiling as ever, bright like ice, undercut this impression: "Speaking of being wrong, have you heard the news yet?"

"Sir?"

"Stuart Knightley's mother died."

Despite the ongoing treatment of McCoist as a pariah, her colleagues all seemed to carefully avoid ever alluding to Knightley around her. Never directly, always in whispers at her back. To hear the man's name casually spilling from the mouth of a senior officer sitting in front of her made her cringe, shuffle in her chair with physical discomfort. It took her right back to that interview, when she'd last seen this man smiling his benign smile from the sideline, perched against the windowsill, surreptitiously scratching himself. They'd raked over her work, conducted a thorough audit, and officially concluded she couldn't have done anything differently but privately sentenced her to public humiliation and hard labour. "Was she ill?"

"Yes, the kind of dementia she had… Anyway, the day after the news was broken to Knightley—this morning, in fact—he was stabbed to death by a fellow inmate." He leant back in his chair, deliberately displaying open body language: informal, trustworthy, textbook. "It was an old metal Scrabble rack, sharpened at one end; L-shaped cross section, impossible to close the wounds. Though there were twenty-seven of them—eye, throat, chest, gut, you name it—so maybe that doesn't really matter." He shrugged a *"what can you do, eh?"*

McCoist fought to keep any reaction to this particular detail from her face. "Are you saying these things are related? Knightley wasn't exactly well liked, sir."

"I'm saying that it's all squared away. No chance for Knightley to recant his confession now. Maybe, with his mother not needing to be cared for any more, he might have had something new to say to us, an alternative story to the one he told you, but…" He turned his palms up, smiled, then folded his hands in his lap.

McCoist pushed macaroni around her plate, no longer hungry.

"You sure you don't have anything else to tell me about the car wash, Inspector?"

McCoist couldn't meet his eyes, continued to stare out her cooling food, congealing like a wound, as she spoke: "The rags they use to clean the cars are like the ones found in the bin bag—they also use the same kind of bags. So I decided to stake the place out. Paul McGuinn is a regular customer. Probably a lot more than a customer." She managed to cut herself off there. That was enough trouble without mentioning the face-to-face chit-chat with McGuinn and the possibility he'd had her followed.

The man beamed at her—full-on kind old teacher, *Now doesn't that feel better to tell the truth?* "Thank you for your help, DI McCoist, and for your work up to this point."

"Up to this point?" Her eyes shot up to meet him. They couldn't take this away, they just fucking couldn't. This was her chance—

"The case is being handed over."

"To who?!"

"If you're going to use that tone, at least finish with 'sir'." There was a brief frown turned to a smile.

"Sir."

"Doesn't matter. You don't need to worry about it any more, you've got bigger fish to fry." He stood up and pushed his chair back under the table. "Enjoy your lunch."

Dejected and ashamed like a child with a note sent home to her parents, McCoist dragged herself back to her desk. As promised, DCI Robson immediately called her into his office with another dead-ender. He continued to shuffle paper around his desk, speaking to it instead of her. "I have a suicide for you to look into."

"If it's already deemed a suicide then what's there to look into, sir?"

The gaffer deigned to give her a severe look. "The body is unidentified. You're a detective, identify it."

McCoist dropped her eyes to her shoes and mumbled a "Sir".

"DI McCoist." He stopped her with her hand on the door. "It's no small matter telling a family their loved one has killed themself. They never believe you. We need to be completely sure. Now off you pop."

JUNE

JUNE

50

Croaker was waiting for Davey inside the pub, two pints already on the table, his own half empty.

It took Davey a minute to find him: it was a crowded old-geezer place where everyone had scraggly grey hair and forty-fags-a-day voices and thick, ratty clothes that whiffed of decay. Needle in a haystack.

"We cannae dae this oer the phone?" Davey glanced over his shoulder before he sat down. He was speaking low but although there was no music and no television playing, the roaring conversation of half-deaf drunks would easily make their conversation inaudible to anyone out of nose-touching distance.

"Phones can be traced, tracked, recorded…"

"Aw aye, but the pub's secure as GCHQ, is it?"

Croaker laughed into his pint glass. "Naebdy's followin ye, naebdy knows yer here, so just relax, huv a drink."

"An how dye know that?"

"Cause Mince followed ye aw the way here." He wiped a foam stache from his upper lip with the back of his hand, allowed himself a flash of a grin.

"Naebdy's followin me?! Fucksake."

"Naebdy *else*. He's just watchin oer ye. Daein ye a favour, really."

"Yev done me enough favours. Tell him tae stoap." Davey wondered how long the boxer had been on his trail. Did he know about his return trip to the high-rise with Paulo? Christ, had he seen him go to Lennox's office in the Saltmarket? Though it had been some time since Davey had been there, at least—their last contact had been over the phone. Lennox sounded almost in a panic, although that seemed alien territory for the baldy old lawyer: hard to imagine him not just slobbing around in his office, leaning back in his chair drinking coffee and eating bickies. He'd flat-out told Davey to give it all up this time, either walk away or just keep his head down and get on with being Paulo's crime-cleaning stooge. Something had spooked him but he wouldn't say what. Not that Davey wanted his help any more anyway—that plan was in the bin. Now there was a new one.

Croaker pointed at Davey's still-full pint. "Neck that, am gettin two mare."

"Ma round is it?" Davey huffed but took a long pull of luke-warm lager. How long had Croaker been waiting there? That couldn't have been just his first pint he was finishing. There was a loose clumsiness to his movements, his eyes focusing like a slow camera shutter.

"Nae worries, yer auld Da is buyin, so fill yer boots." Croaker took his empty glass with him to the bar.

Davey choked down his Tennent's, playing catch up, watching the old pissheads as if suspicious one of them might whip a shotgun from inside his coat like the Terminator. It was a proper boozer, this place. Brass foot rail along the bottom of the huge, scarred horseshoe bar, dartboard on the wall, the surrounding plaster peppered with pinholes, double house whisky for three quid. Not so long ago there would have been sawdust on the floor. The punters all drank half-and-halfs—glasses lined up like chess pieces—the lifetime drinker's choice, a necessity when your liver, bladder and prostate are all fucked.

Croaker came back with two more. "How's the faimly?" he said.

"Fine," Davey said. "Fine" as in "end of discussion".

"Am separatet fae the missus an aw. The relationship died wae Becca, truth be telt. A mean, there wis a load ae other shite too—ye know wit it's like—but eftir oor wee girrul died we just… geed up tryin tae be thegether any mare." Croaker looked round the room and back at Davey, a look that pulled them all in and said, *We're aw the same here.* All men, alone. Cut off for one reason or another, maybe through choice. "She wantet tae forget it aw, get back tae huvin a normal life. An a couldnae. Av goat this instead. Revenge."

"Ye still miss her? Becca, a mean." Davey watched the man's eyes, hoping to read something there, as if he were Derren fucking Broon. He'd tried to ask Lennox during that final phone call if anything had come from his enquiries into the daughter but the lawyer had only bulldozed through him, saying there was a maybe on the girl—a Becca *Coleman* whose story chimed—but ultimately Croaker (*Alias? Liar?*) was just one more reason for Davey to drop it or, better, disappear.

"Every day, son, every day. A miss the baith ae them…"

Croaker drank fast, was nearly finished another pint before they spoke again.

"Sean's away oan his holiday next week, aff up north tae try a bit ae fishin." Paulo had offered Sean the use of his villa in Tenerife but Sean declined—he wasn't a deck-lounger guy, so he said. The fact he spent most of last summer taps aff on his folding chair outside the car wash went unmentioned. "He's geein me the keys Sunday night."

"We're oan, then."

Davey swallowed hard. "We're oan awright."

They ran through it again and when Davey finished his third pint he used it as an excuse to leave. As he stood, Croaker reached across the table and pinned his hand with a powerful, knobbly and broken-knuckled claw. "Davey Boy… Don't fuck this up."

Outside, the fresh air made Davey feel boozy, his legs like rubber. He clocked Mince hunched by a lamp post and gave him a wave.

51

"Pretend this is a real dug," Annalee started.

"It looks fierce!" Davey warded off the stuffed, bead-eyed toy Annalee held up, giving it the full parental am-dram effort.

"Naw, naw, it's a puppy—pretend it's a puppy. It's oor wee puppy."

"Ahh it's goat ma finger!"

"No!" Annalee squealed and laughed. "It's just a puppy! It doesnae—it doesnae bite!"

"Aw naw, it's taken ma whole hawn!" Davey pulled his hand into the sleeve of his hoody. Annalee howled.

"Is Daddy bein silly?" Sarah set down the mugs and biscuits on the coffee table.

"Yes!" Annalee dropped the stuffed dog, attracted immediately to the plate of custard creams.

"Ye can huv two," Sarah said, stern.

Annalee took one in each hand.

"Can a huv two an aw?" Davey asked. Sarah slapped his hand away from the plate with a smile.

"Yel spoil yer dinner," Annalee said through a mouthful of biscuit.

"Is that right, aye? That's me telt."

She nodded, no longer able to speak at all because she'd stuffed the entire remainder of the first custard cream into her mouth.

"Eat nice," Sarah chided. "An stoap walkin aroon, yer gettin crumbs everywhere. Stay in wan place, will ye?"

Annalee grunted something that sounded like agreement but continued to roam about, picking at her toys, rummaging through everything she had out.

"She's yer daughter awright," Sarah said.

"Ye wouldnae change her, but."

Sarah looked as if she were thinking this over, then smiled.

Davey helped himself to a biscuit. "Am better only huvin wan anyway—aff tae ma maw's fir dinner eftir, she'll huv made enough mince an tatties tae feed the whole buildin."

"We're sposed tae be seein her the morra, actually. Will ye tell her al gee her a call in the mornin?"

"Aye, sure. She's no bein a pain in the arse, is she?"

Sarah laughed. "Aye, but she's always free tae babysit so it's worth puttin up wae."

"Al tell her ye said that!"

"Who's she gonnae believe, eh?"

"Fuckin fair point."

"Davey!"

"Sorry!"

Annalee whirled to face them, scandalised. "Daddy swore!"

Davey held out a custard cream. "Here, if a gee ye an extra yin will ye forget aw aboot it?"

She nodded and snatched the biscuit from his hand.

Sarah jabbed him in the arm and glowered—maybe pretend, maybe a little real. "Here, why don't ye come roon here fir yer dinner wan night? Could get a takeaway or somethin."

"Aye, aye that would be… good. A cannae hink when ma next day aff is—Sean's away oan holiday oan Sunday so it won't be till eftir he's back. Al let ye know, but."

"Cool. Where's Sean aff tae?"

"A dunno exactly. Away tae sit by a fuckin puddle or somethin."

"Davey!"

"Daddy!"

"Sorry!"

The thought of Sean's holiday burst the cosy bubble Davey had built around the moment. The plan would be going into action then. As soon as the keys were in his hand. Christ, there were so many fucking ways it could all go wrong. Getting back into the flat and seeing Annalee again had been an uphill crawl—a real Shawshank of shite to swim through to get there, to play with Annalee, to make Sarah smile like that. His old life was just within reach—not even his old life, a better one—and the thought it could just be snatched away again…

Sarah had sensed the change—he was spacing out. Her voice dropped, soft and quiet. "How are hings goin then, wae the… ye know?"

The question seemed to come from far off, took for ever to register and digest. He waited too long; his answer wasn't believable: "Aye, goin well, aye. Doin better. Much better."

"Been seein yer pal Paulo?"

Davey swallowed with a dry throat, nearly choking himself. "Aye, he's bin at the group an that."

"Ye didnae take him up oan his offer tae talk? Seems he cares aboot ye, Davey."

The absurdity of the idea of sitting down with Paulo to talk about his feelings almost made him laugh out loud. And the earnestness in Sarah's voice—Christ, she really believed it, she'd been taken in completely. Davey had always thought of her as a good judge of character but, then again, she'd ended up staying with him for years, so maybe not. Maybe she just wanted to give people a chance, believe in the best of them, and at the moment that seemed to extend to Davey too, which only added to the constant feeling of queasy guilt eating at him. The whole thing was making him sick. All these lies were concrete boots—even if he made it through the plan unscathed, what would it take to chip them off before he drowned? "No yet but a will."

"Good."

They sat in silence for a moment, too close together on the couch. Davey wanted to move back or stand up but it would have been weird. He steered their attention back to Annalee: "Yer camera bin workin awright, doll?"

"She loves it!" Sarah said, rushing to fill in the unsettled quiet. "Go oan an show Daddy aw the photies yev bin takin!"

The scroll of fuzzy images they flipped through only made him sink further inside himself—blurry, unreal. He had to push on and get through it. Get it done and get back to his family. Back to the way things should be. No Paulo, no Croaker, no bloody big teuchter following him around—Mince was sitting in yet another different motor across the road from Sarah's. Davey was halfway down the street when he heard the engine start.

52

Suicide by complete self-annihilation: Nile's ankles, knees and back had all broken in various places from the fall. He'd then gone over the bonnet and roof of one car, then under the wheels of another. There were tyre marks on his neck, head barely holding on, glass in his eyeballs, every one of his limbs churned and broken, ribcage shattered, organs within mulched, guts strung out from his burst belly. Roadkill.

McCoist had seen plenty of bodies—Dannie Gibb's excised uterus had been a career-high horror—but this one took the prize for outrageous style. The sharp ends of broken bones erupting from the skin were particularly effective at making your lunch climb back up your gullet.

She'd only seen him the once—didn't recognise him then, no surprise considering the state of the corpse—then happily relied on the coroner's notes. She thought of those content warnings at the beginning of films: "injury detail". Right enough.

He had no ID on him and his phone was in a similar state to his body. It was only when she had a check through recent misper reports and saw Fred Nile's face looking at her from her computer screen that it clicked. The middle finger from the right hand had torn completely off—nicotine stain on the side of the knuckle. She shook the image from her mind.

The wife, Heather, had to be brought in to identify him. Poor cow. McCoist had to stomach a second viewing. Heather

Nile didn't manage quite so well, spent a good half-hour in the bathroom afterwards retching while McCoist handed her paper towels under the door.

The gaffer had been correct—Mrs Nile did not believe her husband would commit suicide. The business was expanding, they were looking forward to a trip away to Mexico in July, they were on the market for a new house—"Gettin the fuck oot ae Sighthill"—and he'd just quit smoking because they were thinking of beginning fertility treatment. Then a few nights ago Fred didn't come home.

"You said his business was expanding. That might have been quite stressful?"

"He wis workin lang oors, aye, but it wis aw goin well, ye know?" Heather Nile's face was a modernist painting of running mascara and smudged make-up. Every so often she would stop talking abruptly and hold her fist to her mouth, either holding back a sob or a boke.

"Would he tell you if he was having trouble with the business?"

"Wis he?"

"There was nothing in his accounts to suggest so but three days ago his warehouse was raided due to an anonymous tip-off. A fair quantity of heroin was found there."

Her shock seemed genuine. McCoist's had been too. She'd searched the records again for Nile on autopilot, muscle memory taking her through the steps. And where there had been nothing at all before there was suddenly a raid, seized drugs, arrest and questioning. Populated fields on the PNC and CHS. It gave McCoist the disorientated feeling of looking at an optical illusion—trees in a forest becoming tiger stripes. He jumped a few hours after leaving the station. Made sense—he was facing serious time.

She could have shut it down there, and her disappointment with the car-wash case almost made her do that, but something had been rekindled. She could feel there was more to it and, almost surprising herself, she wanted to find out what.

The man in the empty office in the Carnaby Centre—Nile's pal Tam from the pub. That was a load of shite. She knew it back when she first questioned Nile but she hadn't really cared. Heather—who Nile said disliked this man so much she wouldn't have him under her roof—confirmed it when she denied any knowledge of him at all. So who was he? Rough as fuck, for sure. Criminal? Well, Nile must have got the heroin from somewhere. And at that amount we're talking organised crime.

She went back to the Carnaby Centre. She got a warrant to get herself into the office this time, had SOCOs in disposable onesies and bootees give the place a makeover. ("There are some prints? No match on the record, though?"; "Bupkis?"; "I wouldn't say that?"; "Wouldn't you?")

McCoist spoke to the man at CyberGrafix across the hall, who confirmed he'd seen Nile on the night of his death. "He was looking for that guy that was staying in his office, the one I called about. The dirty guy who smoked all the time, stank the place out."

"He wasn't there?"

"No. I told the guy—Fred, was it?—I'd seen him leave the day before and he never came back."

"When was that?"

She gave dates and times to Findlay and packed him off to Eastgate with a description of Tam the Squatter, a tenner for the coffee machine and instructions to search the CCTV footage all around the Carnaby Centre and beyond until his eyes fell out of his head. "Then give them a dust, plug them back in and keep going. Find him."

Digging into Nile's background was difficult and threw up more oddities—she had financial records going back three years and nothing else. A business address book but no apparent friend or family ties beyond his wife. He was an only child, his mother and father both dead, according to Heather. There was no record of them. McCoist recalled the list she'd scribbled down of the places he'd worked before starting his own business and gave them a ring—none of them had hired or even heard of Fred Nile.

It was the lawyer who dropped the whopper:

"He had a new identity…"

The lawyer, Lennox, was a shabby middle-aged man, bald on top with shaggy grey hair at the back and sides like a medieval monk. Not the power-briefcase type most of them were. This made McCoist tiptoe around him, at least until she could decide if he was an ankle-biter or a pit bull. "He cooperated with the police in exchange for early parole. A new identity was part of the deal—for his own safety."

"Who was he giving up?"

"Maybe it would be best to speak to the police officers I liaised with at the time. I've been trying to get through to them but it's been difficult. They know the details already and it is very sensitive…"

McCoist could feel this one slipping away too. Reassigned to DI Baw-Jaws or DCI Dobber. She took a punt: "Did it involve Paul McGuinn?"

Lennox's whole body stiffened. "I really think we'd better wait and—"

"You don't think your client committed suicide, do you?"

"I wouldn't care to speculate."

"You don't. That's why you're here right now. The bridge your client jumped from is notorious—but not for suicides."

Lennox wiped his mouth, then spread his hands on the table. He looked down at them—they were hairy and ink-stained. "Mr Nile was given a new identity for his own protection. Hours after leaving a *police station*, he is dead in the road. I would like to speak to the officers who handled him as an informant before we go any further."

"Your client said he had no idea where the heroin came from and I'm having a hard time pinning that down myself. It just shows up in his warehouse, we get tipped off about it and pull him up, and the next thing you know he's dead at a well-known ambush point. Hauling him in put him back on the radar—whose radar?"

The lawyer stayed silent.

"Look, we both think he was set up, don't we? Did Fred Nile inform on Paul McGuinn to get out of jail three years ago? Talk to me."

His eyes were hard, grey and sad like a blind dog's. "I can't trust you, Inspector McCoist. I know who you are. I know the Dannie Gibb case," he said. That was a twist of the knife. There were those who didn't think she was just incompetent but had actively steered the investigation away from McGuinn on purpose. That throbbing wee erection of a sergeant from the inquiry was one, and there were plenty more. The suspicion of corruption was as painful as the embarrassing truth of her failure. Both had similar stinks that clung like cigarette smoke and were as hard to cover up. She nodded as if to say *fair enough* and consoled herself with the fact that she could tell from the look on his face that she was right.

Being right didn't count for much. It wasn't evidence. She kept working on the lawyer but it was slow moving—bound in red tape that was sticky and double-sided. The search for "Tam" was going nowhere either. Findlay had nothing yet (but would be interred at Eastgate until he did, the poor sod, skin going translucent from days in the dark with no sun, only the low blue underlight of the Operation Centre and the harsh white of a computer screen). The fingerprints at the office were probably his but with no record they wouldn't be useful for finding him, only for placing him there once he was caught—that's if he was involved in some way, which McCoist strongly suspected but, again, suspicion wasn't proof.

She questioned the wife and the employees again and scoured the warehouse and the offices old and new. Work and home computers came back without anything useful. ("Bupkis. There's some porn on there? But it's hardcore by definition alone? Pretty tame?"; "If you say so, Specky"; "Did you just call me—")

McGuinn was at the centre of it all. She circled him—every keystroke of her computer would be logged and traceable and she didn't want anyone to know she was back on him. Not after what happened with the car-wash thing.

Bell Street... That was the nutcracker. She'd had something there for sure. She tormented herself with it again, at work and at home. She forgot to fill the fridge for the kids, who were coming to stay at the weekend. She missed parents' evening before the schools closed for the holidays. Mark was pissed—his natural placidity and "cool dad" thing cracking as he let loose at her for letting the kids down. (Really, he was probably more annoyed at having to talk to the teachers on his own. McCoist was always good backup when it came to dealing with some of the fussier little tyrants in the classroom.) Cam was angry too but Tess took it with a kind of sad acceptance—you can't be let down if you have no expectations—and that hurt the most. The cost of getting her arse off the bench, one she didn't want to pay but was helpless now that she was back in the game with that relentless drive pushing her. She'd missed it.

That morning, McCoist was chewing through a KitKat Chunky at her desk for lunch when her phone rang—Mark. *Speak of shite and it hits you in the face.*

"Hiya."

"Hi Alison, are you working just now or can we have a quick chat?"

A quick chat. That wasn't good. McCoist's chewing slowed down. The idea of swallowing the wad of churned-up biscuity chocolate was suddenly not so appealing, her stomach no longer able to cope as it had dropped out onto the floor. "That's OK. I'm on my lunch."

"Cool, cool. Eh, look, my mum was wanting to take the kids away to the caravan this weekend. I know they're supposed to be coming to yours but she already said to them—sorry, she didn't run it by me, she just dove in, you know what she's like—and the kids are really keen to go—"

"Tess is really keen to go spend the weekend in a caravan with her gran?"

"Yeah, I mean, she said—"

"Look, just tell me they don't want to come round. Don't give me any bullshit, I get enough of it at work."

A sigh rattled across the airwaves. "Alison, that's not what happened. Really, my mum offered to take them, she's been spending a lot of time with them since Dad... She needs it, you know?"

McCoist closed her eyes and pinched the bridge of her nose, tension throbbing behind her eye sockets. "Sure. It's fine. I'm not going to stop them going—I can't force them to come to me, that would be..."

"They'll come over next weekend. I promise."

She hung up, dropped her phone and chocolate bar onto the desk. A weekend in front of the telly loomed. Going to the shop. Getting dragged round the neighbourhood by Bruce. Edith's face over the fence—"The weans no comin tae visit this weekend?"

Fuck it. She dove back in—called up Davey Burnet's home address. She remembered the way he'd behaved at their last meeting at the car wash, trying to get her out of a confrontation with McGuinn. She saw his terrified, desperate face. If one of them was going to spill, it was him. Solve the car wash, solve Nile, put Paulo McGuinn behind bars. Get a big cake made for everyone to share at the office that had "Fuck All You Cunts" piped on it in icing around a picture of her own smiling, smug face. Maybe she could even get a slice sent to HMP Barlinnie for the Big Man.

53

He wouldn't have to hurt this one. A couple of broken PC monitors and the boy's nappy was overflowing. Paulo was disappointed. Look at this pathetic streak of pish, blubbering at the mere sight of Paulo and his cronies, face red and knuckles white just having to share space with them. Paulo wanted to hurt him—the wee gimp was practically begging for it with his scrawny little body, specky face and virgin haircut—he felt it almost like a craving, like his body wouldn't be satisfied until he had his hands around that skinny neck, pressing his thumbs on the too-big Adam's apple bobbing up and down as he swallowed his nerves over and over. But it wasn't good business to hurt civilians, best avoided if possible. And in this case, it was very possible.

"S-sorry, I don't know any more, eh, I mean he was just there for a wee while, I, uh—" He was sitting in his office chair, hands just about ripping the armrests off, two of Paulo's biggest lads—faces like an old bar top—perched on desks either side of him, sitting where the computer screens had been before, now in a heap of cracked crystal on the floor.

"That's awright, son, yev bin very helpful." Paulo smiled and imagined himself forcing a pen right through the lens of the lad's glasses and into his eye. Fantasy would have to do for now. "So eftir yer unwanted bin diver ae a neighbour goes oot, an Nile who owns the shoap across the hall comes tae speak tae ye, there's nae sign ae him again?"

"N-neither of them. Just the police. They, eh, came to ask me some questions." He swallowed hard again, knowing the word "police" was a dangerous one to utter.

"Wit kind ae questions?"

The wee guy's knee was going wild, bobbing up and down, making the chair squeak. Paulo crouched so they were at eye level and put his hand on the web designer's shaking knee. He thought about sliding it up his thigh and grabbing hold of the man's tiny, atrophied bollocks, squeezing until he felt them pop, twisting until he felt the tubes snap and the scrotum tear. *Wid be good fir the human race, stoappin this sad wee cunt fae breedin.* But he didn't. "Wit kind ae questions?"

"Just the same kind y-you are. About the guy across the hall, a-a-and Fred Nile."

"Ye mind who this polis wis?"

He nodded, breathing hard, licking his lips before he could speak. "Y-yeah, it was the same one who had come before. To speak to the guy o-over the hall. The squatter. Her name was Alison McCoist. Stuck in my head, y-ye know? Like A-A-Ally Mc—"

"A get it." Paulo stood and gave the signal for his boys to get moving. The wee virgin's face was painfully hopeful at this. "Here, pal, a bin hinkin fir a while aboot revampin the auld websites fir some ae ma businesses. Maybe al be in touch." The hope died. "Nae worries aboot a cerd, a know where tae find ye."

54

She parked outside after five—he wasn't in so she waited until he showed up in wet clothes a few hours later. She hopped out and met him as he unlocked his door.

"Hello, Mr Burnet, it's—"

"Ally McCoist, aye a mind." He was spooked. He was looking beyond her, checking the corners.

"*DI* McCoist, please. May I come in?"

He didn't answer immediately—obviously deciding whether it would be better to say yes and get her in off the street quickly or to refuse and risk getting embroiled in something lengthy at the doorway if she wasn't going to just fuck off, which she had absolutely no intention of. McCoist reached inside her jacket for her ID to speed him up. "Aye, if ye must," he said, and had another look around before holding the door for her.

The close smelled of stale urine and bins. The panels in the front door had been broken and recently replaced with planks of chipboard. The lock looked new. They went upstairs and Burnet let them into his flat.

She'd seen worse living conditions. At the high-rise brothel, for instance. Everything was orderly, if dusty, and the smell of car soap clung to everything like a sheen of wax on the surface, which was maybe better than yesterday's cooking and damp. Burnet pulled his sodden hoody off and threw it over a clothes horse by the radiator.

"Am huvin a cuppa if ye want?" He went over to the kitchen counter on the far wall and filled the kettle. His movements were awkward: he was trying not to fully turn his back on her, not to let her out of the edge of his vision. He opened a cupboard to get a mug and as he closed it again he slipped a blister pack of pills, which had been sitting out on the counter, inside it.

"No thanks."

"Water? Goat some ginger in the fridge an aw."

"I'm all right. I came to ask if you knew a man called Fred Nile?"

"Doesnae ring a bell."

"He wasn't a customer at the car wash?"

"Could well huv bin but there's regulars a don't even know the names ae."

McCoist handed him the photo of Nile from the misper report. He shook his head. "Sure?"

"Sure. How come?"

"He's dead. I think Paulo McGuinn had him killed."

Burnet stopped stirring his tea—frozen.

"You know McGuinn." Unsaid: *You know what he's like.*

Burnet took the spoon from the mug and set it carefully in the sink. He turned to face McCoist—didn't pick up his tea. "He's a customer."

"A bit more than that from what I saw last time I came around. What was he doing in the office? Is he pals with the gaffer?"

Burnet was leaning against the counter now, hands braced against the Formica. "They get oan awright, a guess, wouldnae call them pals or anythin."

"So it's a business relationship then?"

He shrugged.

"Does Mr Prentice buy drugs from him?"

Burnet chewed on this. He was deciding what to give away, what to lie about. It was all over his face. "Naw... Sean has his ain dealer. Actually, he's geed it up noo."

"Good for him. How's the arm doing?" She pointed to the edge of red scarring visible just under the sleeve of his T-shirt.

"Fine, aye. It's no sare any mare."

"You know what would be sore? Falling from a bridge and landing twenty-five feet down on the motorway below then getting hit by two cars."

"That wit happened tae yer man?"

"Fred Nile. Yes. He had a wife; they were trying for a baby." She turned the screws.

Burnet licked his lips. He turned away again, finally picked up his tea. He blew on it but then set it back down without taking a drink. "That's rough... But like a says, a didnae know him, an av nae idea wit Paulo McGuinn hud tae dae wae it or anythin."

McCoist's jaw ached from clenching, molars turning to powder. This was the guy, this fucking eejit, a trembling wee ruin of a man dicking her about. He was the key. He knew something, something big, and right then McCoist wanted to crack him open. She got a handle on herself, deep breath before speaking, voice gentle: "David... I know something's going on, I know you're caught up in it. You're no gangster, you're not like these guys. They'll eat you as soon as they don't need you any more. Listen, I know what it's like to be in over your head, to make such a mess that you think there's no way back. Believe me, I've made my own mistakes, I've got my own shitty marriage and disappointed kids. Think of your daughter. Annalee is it?"

His body went stiff, jaw jutting out. His eyes were only trying for anger—they betrayed fear. She had the Vulcan death grip on him, fingers in the precise pressure point. "Annalee, aye." He sipped from his mug to distract from his discomfort.

"She's with her maw full time now, isn't she?"

"Aye, nae visitation rights, nae weekends, nae holidays, nae even a trip tae the park. Nothin. The *cow* stuffed me good an proper." It was the longest sentence he'd said so far, the most communicative McCoist had seen him in any of their short, terse conversations.

"When's the last time you saw her?"

"November," he said.

A lie. A very deliberate one too—he was waiting to see how she responded. He was watching her over the rim of his mug like a trench-coated Cold War spy with eyeholes cut in a newspaper. What was he up to? He either didn't want her to know he'd been in touch with his family or was probing to see if McCoist already knew he had been. She decided that playing along for now was the safest route: "That's hard. I've got mine every second weekend or so, depending on work, and that's difficult enough. I can't imagine, you know, going so long without..."

Bingo. He seemed to ease a little. "How many weans ye goat?"

"Two. Twins: Tess and Cam. They're teenagers now. Christ, the time just passes so quickly. Especially only seeing them once a fortnight, it's like watching them on fast forward when you're missing those bits in between. You blink and they've shot up another foot."

"At least ye can make the maist ae the time ye do get."

McCoist felt that one in her gut. She knew getting in close to someone necessitated opening yourself up a bit but she was still shocked at how deep that hooked her, and he didn't even mean it. "You'd think so." Bitter smile. "But the reality is... All the reasons I ended up divorced and my kids going to my ex, they've not changed. I've not changed. You must think I'm an eejit..."

He mulled this over. "Dae ye hink yer a bad parent?"

"Do you?" she snapped back, harder than intended.

He drummed his fingers on the side of his mug. "Naebdy does, really, dae they? Naebdy hinks they're a bad parent, though there's plenty ae them. Am no the best, al admit that, but am tryin. Tryin harder than a ever huv before. Cos av goat nothin else, really."

November, my arse. He'd slipped, or he'd judged it safe to let the lie go. "Good, David, that's really good. That's the best thing you can do and you should keep doing it. Don't make the same mistakes I have. You want to be there to see her grow up, don't you?" She'd turned it around. She had him. "Tell me what's going on and let me help you. Get you out from under, get you back to your family where you belong. Think of Annalee."

He was blinking, trying to keep tears out of his eyes. He wanted to confess, they all do in the end...

"A am hinkin ae her, an *you* should be hinkin ae yer ain. Please leave, av goat nothin tae say tae ye."

"Come on, David, you tried to help me at the car wash that day, I know you did. Help me again. *Please.*"

"A dunno wit yer talkin aboot. Time tae go." He pointed to the door with his mug.

. . .

McCoist stepped out of the close into a fresh drizzle, pleasant after the Lush bomb of Burnet's flat. She'd pushed too hard using the kid—with more blowback than expected—but she'd be back for another try. He was primed to break—his suspicion of her must have been fairly powerful to hold him together in the end. She wondered if he'd heard something. Fuck, maybe he was just scared. He was right to be if he was in the thick of it with a monster like McGuinn. What kind of protection could McCoist really offer? She thought of Fred Nile turned into a human accordion. She thought, as Burnet had suggested, of Tess and Cam.

There was a car parked behind hers that hadn't been there before. In the flash of her hazards when she unlocked the doors, she saw a man sitting in the driver's seat. Spike of panic: a shiver of adrenaline zipped through her. He looked down at his phone, a soft blue glow lighting his face—eyebrows thick with scar tissue and a crooked, flat nose. Not Anorak Man.

55

McCoist hadn't gone far, just passing the abandoned cattle market across from Bellgrove Street Station, when she saw a blue Focus at the side of the road, its hazards on, its front passenger door hanging open, blocking half the pavement.

She pulled up behind it. The street was quiet. She couldn't see anybody inside, though the back window was tinted and spotted with rain. Maybe they'd gone to flag down help, or to the nearest petrol station. But why was the door left open? The hazards continued to pulse and she felt the back of her neck prickle.

Somebody might be needing your help and you're sitting here freaking yourself out, she chided herself. Fancy detective or not, you're polis, you're supposed to help people. But everything with the car wash and McGuinn—*and being tailed, for fucksake!*—had left her paranoid, unsure of everything. The fright she'd got leaving Burnet's place minutes ago did not at all help. So call it in then, get some backup. That's what she should do. *Backup for what—somebody stopping by the road to go take a piss in the field?*

But somebody could be in trouble, the still-responsible part of her said. What if they're hurt? What if you drive off and it's something serious you've just walked away from? A whole different kind of Fuck-Up. Compound Fuck-Ups.

She swore, felt in her pockets for her CS spray and her phone, not sure which one to be ready with, and stepped out into the fresh haze of summer rain, the sun bleeding into the sky.

"Hello!" she called as she approached. "Anyone there?! I'm a police officer." Christ, if it was just somebody with a puncture or trying to find their phone under the seat she was going to look ridiculous. She screwed herself up, stepped to the door and looked in. Driver and passenger seats empty. Couple of half-finished water bottles in the footwell and some scrunched up pay-and-display tickets in the pocket by the handbrake but otherwise tidy (McCoist not really fit to judge). There was no immediate sign of anything off, just—

"HELP!"

McCoist stood up so fast she cracked her head off the roof of the car.

"HEEEELP!" A woman's voice, shrieking, animal, like a fox in the night, somewhere behind her, in the overgrowth of the old cattle market.

Adrenaline flooded through her, making her body powerful and light and her brain short-circuit. Heart pumping, giddy. "Hello?!" McCoist ran for the fence as the voice called again, no words this time, just screaming. "Where are you?!" She threw herself at the rickety, shoulder-high fence which had been erected around the wasteland—bleached, weather-beaten and battered through over the years, all missing spars, splinters, broken wood and bent, rusty nails. Fuck, the irony of getting caught on one and slicing herself open now, her brain rattled, flush with fight-or-flight chemicals. She tumbled over the top and landed on her arse in the weeds, scrambling upright, her jacket tangled in cords of fuzzy, spiny vegetation, thorns seeking skin to scratch. She yanked herself free. "Police! Where are you?!"

The screaming came again—the direction of the auction house's remains. "Police!" McCoist wheezed as she sprinted for it. One arm pumped furiously, the other tried to get her phone from her coat pocket, at least some non-lizard part of her brain still functioning, still thinking about protocol.

The warehouse was skeletal, with so many strips torn from its corrugated-metal skin that McCoist had no trouble finding a way in. The place was a dumping ground. Any hint of its former use had gone with the majority of the roof some time ago. Burst settees, old tyres, buckled shopping trolleys and traffic cones were scattered among a carpet of broken bottles, remnants of fires and used paraphernalia that littered the trodden-earth floor and the hardy, ugly plants growing through it. The place smelled of earthy rot and scabby burnt things—pish damp and viciously lonely, a passing-through place near the too-abrupt end of the line. Even the local vermin would find it a bit grim.

The woman was standing in the centre of the mess, grey hood up, black body warmer and leggings melting into the growing murk of shadows under the bleached wooden bones of the ceiling beams. She was no longer screaming.

"Police! Are you all right?!" McCoist approached, picking her way through the detritus, casting her voice clear and loud, projecting confidence, control, authority. "What's going on? Are you hurt?" The woman remained silent and McCoist felt the prickle on her neck again.

Sound of scraping metal behind—

The man pushed his way through the same gap between the peeling, ribbed sheets of metal McCoist had. He had his anorak on again, hood up, though the rain falling on them through the remnants of the roof was little more than a fine misting, giving everything a dewy shine. He had a large knife in one hand—a cleaver whose purpose echoed the past of the cattle-auction warehouse.

McCoist spun back towards the woman, who now held a knife too, long and thin like a spike, glinting pink in the dying light.

She saw it all now: Anorak Man lying hidden in the back seat of the car, waiting for her to appear at the door, a text signalling the woman waiting in the warehouse to scream. Cheese, mouse, trap, click.

56

Croaker ate a cheese sandwich he'd bought from a petrol station. It was the first meal he'd had in over twenty-four hours. His stomach couldn't handle much any more. His body was fuelled by coffee, cigarettes and an assortment of caffeine tablets and illegal amphetamines. Among the other pills he carried in his holdall were genuinely prescribed medications (albeit written out to a false name), over-the-counter sleeping pills for when he got to the stage where he needed to sleep or die, and street Valium for when they just wouldn't cut it. His mind was fuelled by decades of dead girls and dodgy dealing and living life in the blackened-brick bush of the Glasgow underworld, surrounded by ferocious trophies, beastmen, vipers and poachers, with nothing to rely on but his own cunning and fleet-footedness, base camp miles and years behind, home wilfully forgotten. A guy who got the job done, no paperwork, no bullshit, no going back.

He was in the back of a rusty serial-killer campervan in a scrapyard—he'd blagged the site manager into letting him kip there for a week. People who wanted to be helpful were the easiest to manipulate, God love them. Speaking of which, Nile's pus had been all over the papers—it had all gone down faster and harder than he'd anticipated, a roll that had come up sixes. Long overdue for that scummy bastart, Croaker had thought, skipping the shite about his grief-stricken wife and her plans for future wee Niles flushed down the bog. His concern was saved for whether Nile had actually talked, the silly fucker, or if the corruption within the polis had festered and spread even further than he already knew. A bent polis getting word out to Paulo that his old mucker had finally shown his face was a possibility. A juicy kink to follow up on after the main event was over. The scrappy was a little out of the city but bumping into his brother had impressed the need to lie as low as possible, and that meant staying well away until the kick-off. He had Mince updating him regularly from the touchline anyway—an interesting knot in proceedings had him in need of a favour.

He'd called the number, let it ring three times then hung up. He switched between taking bites from the sandwich and draws from a fag while he waited for the callback.

Sunday night, Davey Boy was getting the keys. Monday night, he'd have Paulo McGuinn. Done and fucking dusted. The sacred tiger skinned and made into a rug, his bastart head mounted on the wall, eyes gouged out and replaced with shiny buttons. Then what? Retire. Die. Who gave a fuck? Killing the Big Man wouldn't bring any of those girls back—it wouldn't save Dannie Gibb's parents or Becca Coleman's parents from a lifetime of torture. So why do it at all? Because he was too far in now, and too good to stop anyway. No, it wouldn't be death or retirement, it would be on to the next one. There was always a next one, and Croaker couldn't give it up. He wasn't a dog that could be called off. He was a wolf.

The phone rang. He waited for three rings before answering: "Bullfrog's special delivery."

"What have you got to deliver?"

"The Big Man's heed in an Aldi cerry-oot bag."

"I thought I'd been clear about this."

"Double or quits."

"You've said that before. I need you to stop."

"There's nae stoappin. No till it's done, an it's gonnae be done."

There was a long pause. Croaker could hear breathing over the line. "Why? What are you going to get out of this? You know there's little I can offer you now."

"Call it professional pride."

"If you genuinely believe that then you *have* fucking lost it."

Croaker rasped out a wheezing laugh. "OK, hows aboot revenge then? Or justice?! Aye, justice, fir aw the innocent girruls who didnae deserve the endin he gave them."

"Is that what you're telling yourself now?"

"Look, a enjoy the phone sex as much as any cunt but a need tae get doon tae business. Am goin ahead wae it…"

A deep exhale overloaded the speaker of Croaker's cheap phone, making a static crackle that hurt his eardrum. "What are you needing?"

"Am huvin some trouble wae that Rangers legend again."

"Tell me what your move is and I'll see about that."

57

The knives closed in.

She wondered if Fred Nile had ended his life caught between two blades like this. Images of his shattered corpse reeled through her head. Was that better than the alternative? *Stabbed, slit, slashed, pierced, penetrated, chopped, severed, gutted, opened up.* Had Dannie Gibb been lured into no man's land for her body to be torn apart by vultures?

Stalking closer.

McCoist knew the damage they could do, had seen it plenty of times. She'd faced a few in her uniform days too—the bulk of a stab-proof vest providing little comfort but bolstered by the baton in her hand, her fellow officers at her side, always there in every tour of duty, in body armour and polished boots. Now she was alone, facing two of them, a closing pincer around her, her jacket not even waterproof let alone stab-proof. *Plugged, shanked, sliced, striped, ripped.*

Closer.

McCoist's hand went for her pocket and came out with nothing but crushed receipts and petrified tissues. Shite, *shite*, the pepper spray must have fallen out when she clambered over the fence. Her other weapon then—her phone. She swiped a finger across the screen, bottom to top, to bring up the emergency call button. The camera switched on instead. *Fuck! Back, back!* She jabbed at the buttons, the screen now slick and dotted with specks of rain, not responding.

Now!—they darted forward, seeing her phone light.

McCoist was off a second later, as if fright from the starting gun had delayed her launch from the blocks but now she was moving, in the race. She went sideways to get out of the pincer manoeuvre, both of them having to fall in behind, too far to close the distance in formation.

Not far enough though. Anorak Man was on her heels, hand reaching for her collar.

McCoist ducked forwards as his hand came down, just missing her, and snatched the remains of a glass bottle, tossed it as she turned. A hard throw, it walloped the man's coupon at nearly point-blank range, bursting into shards and diamonds and glitter. He screamed and hit the deck, cleaver dropped, hands over his face, blood already seeping between his fingers. The Screaming Woman tripped over him.

McCoist would have been away then but her toes caught on something as she turned back around, the bottle throw barely breaking her stride, and she found herself, with a shocking plunge of the stomach, on the rubble of the warehouse floor, knees and palms cut.

She didn't feel any pain, heart pumping too hard, adrenaline lifting her from the ground in seconds, muscles grinding, guttural howls coming up from her belly and out her throat.

The Screaming Woman caught her by the hair and they both tumbled again, McCoist getting a face full of landfill—the ground Tetanus City. The long knife came down but McCoist bucked and twisted, throwing the woman off her back, then planted a hard, heel-first kick right in the tit which left her gasping. It was dirty, but when you think you're going to die the rule is "anything that works". Go for the eyes, the throat, the soft, tender parts. Use your nails, your teeth. Fish-hook them. Bend their fingers back. Give them a fucking Chinese burn if you have to. Kick them when they're down—which is exactly what McCoist did. She put the laces through it, made the woman taste shoe leather, foot crashing into her jaw and teeth, bursting the cheek and the lips and the tongue, throwing her head sideways, rattling her brain off the walls of her skull. (Send them homewards tae think again, if they're still able.)

Then she grabbed the woman's wrist with both hands and bit her knuckles until her mouth was full of the ancient-green-penny taste of blood and the fingers around the handle of the long knife went loose. McCoist snatched the blade and ran as fast as she could still manage, her body burning now, nauseated from the exertion—peak fitness many years, miles and Mars Bars, as well as two weans, ago—out of the building and across the field as her pursuers gathered themselves together. Threw her body over the fence, took a picture of the blue Focus's licence plate after she locked the doors of her car, whitied in her lap—the Screaming Woman's blood she'd swallowed coming up with it—wiped her mouth and fired up the engine. *Choke, choke, choke—come on—vroom!*

Then Away.

Alive.

58

Extraction had gone smoothly. The wife was home so they took her as well. They left her a free hand so she could hold the cup of tea Paulo had the boys make her—the other one and her ankles were taped to a chair.

Findlay had lost Croaker on the CCTV trail—the old man seemed to know what he was doing, knew how to keep himself well hidden, but the bloke who stopped him for a chat not far from the Carnaby Centre on the day of his departure certainly did not and had carried on his day oblivious to the cameras which followed him everywhere. Findlay then got his name, address, car, job, family, hobbies and anything else he bothered to look into. Easy-peasy. Information the freshly assigned detective constable kept from his new workmate, DI Alison McCoist.

The thought of her brought a wry smile to Paulo's face. His troops had taken a pasting (Babs would be eating nothing but soup for months and Walker looked like a Bond villain—he should've known not to underestimate Super Ally) but the message would have got across, and that's what mattered. He didn't care if she'd been killed or maimed or got away with nothing but a brick in her knickers, she—and her brethren—would know not to fuck about with Paulo McGuinn. To Paulo McGuinn, the polis were the same as any other gang in Glesga. Nobody was off limits, nobody free from reprisals. *Grasses get cut, curious cats get killt, and any cunt who makes a direct move against Paulo McGuinn will be hunted doon and exterminatet.*

Which brought him back to "Tam" Croaker and the bloke he'd been seen with, who was sitting—similarly trussed up— opposite his wife. Sweat was visible on his scalp through his number-two cut, dripping down his forehead. His lip wobbled, making the excess flesh around his chin jiggle. The initial yelling had stopped and now both of them sat in stunned silence, like they couldn't believe what was happening to them, like it wasn't real, only some shared hallucination. There was a certain hardiness to them Paulo couldn't help but admire, but then it was born out of ignorance. A chiselled-from-granite gangster would be sitting there in his own filth by now because he knew what he was in for. But these two were civilians—Paulo knew it as soon as they ripped the hoods off them. So best behaviour.

Paulo laid out the small cutting tools without intending to use them: scalpels, Stanleys, a razor blade which was mostly just used for chopping up lines. Nothing heavy-duty but all highly suggestive. At a closer look, one of the implements was just a dental scaler, though Paulo could probably find an interesting use for it if need be—*Imagine that hing jaggin through yer cornea and intae yer pupil, or hooked intae yer jizz slit?* No. Best behaviour.

"Hows the brew, hen? Need mare sugar? Yev no touched it." Her lips were clamped tight, her body racked up. There was no way she'd manage even a sip. She couldn't meet his eyes. "A admit it's a bit oan the lukewarm side but a couldnae be geein ye somethin scaldin hot, just in case. Here, Sandy…"—he addressed one of the trackie-clad Russian-doll head-breakers who were looming around—"…find the wummin a biscuit tae eat, will ye? There's a tin up in the office somewhere. Cannae have a cuppa waeoot a bicky, can ye?"

When Sandy came back with a half-finished packet of soft ginger nuts, Paulo had him dip them into the woman's tea and attempt to feed them to her, mushed-up biscuit crumb smearing all over her lips and chin as she started to snivel and cry.

"Stoap that! A said *stoap!*" The husband was shifting in his chair, working his wrists against the thick layers of duct tape keeping them fixed to the armrests. Hardy indeed, Paulo thought. "Just tell us wit this is aboot, ye don't need tae—"

Paulo put a printout on his knee—a fuzzy image of the husband standing talking to Croaker. "A want tae know who this guy is, why yer talkin tae him, wit yer talkin aboot, an absolutely anythin else a hink tae ask. Otherwise al cut a hole in yer missus' throat an stuff that packet ae ginger nuts doon it till she chokes, see how she likes the tea then. Awright?"

His brother. Estranged, not spoken to him in years, hadn't seen his nephews since they were knee-high, doesn't even get a birthday card. "Don't even know where tae send wan." It didn't take much work for it to spill. Poor Johnny would really have done anything to stop Stacy being harmed. He wanted to take all the licks himself, he really did. But Paulo wouldn't allow it. Not at first. Not till he'd wrung everything out, what little there was to wring.

But there, among the family history, was the key, and Johnny gave it up barely realising what he'd given.

"Yer no gonnae hurt Tam are ye?" The look was desperate. The man knew what would happen, yet he still wanted someone to tell him otherwise.

If he hadn't said that, if he hadn't crumbled into pathetic denial, would Paulo have just let him go? Could he have walked away without letting himself feed this time? He was a civilian, that would have been proper. But no—as soon as the man said he was Tam's brother, Paulo knew there would be no end to the violence he'd have to unleash upon him. The things he wanted to do… Happy days.

Paulo picked up the dental scaler.

59

The car's engine gave an emphysemic cough and sputtered out. It took three goes before it finally caught and settled into a shuddering rattle that echoed throughout the station's basement car park.

A knock at the window made McCoist jump.

She'd been edgy to the point of having a heart attack any time Bruce barked at the window since the attack the night before. She'd driven around for hours after, hounding herself in circles over whether to report it or not, whether to call in with the number plate of the blue Focus. (She'd checked it herself at work that morning—stolen, only a matter of time before it reappeared black and crispy somewhere.) First though, she'd called Mark from the car and told him to take the kids to his mother's—maybe another trip to the caravan would be a good idea. ("For how long? I can't stay stuck in that thing with my mum for more than a weekend. Three days tops—"; "Just do it, I'll call you again later.") She eventually parked away from the house, crept in the back door, and sat up with Bruce at the window until she passed out from exhaustion.

The day had been one of sore eyes, too much coffee, little work and swithering over the angles and options until she was dizzy. So McGuinn had tried to kill her then. Or at least put her in hospital. Did he know she was working the Nile case—was she closer on that one than she'd realised? How did he know? Had Davey Burnet tipped him off? No, he had no way of knowing she would come to see him at his flat, and the ambush was too soon after—they must have been set up already, followed her earlier. So should she tell *him*—was he now in danger too? His ex, his daughter? Or should she tell Robson? She might be number one on his shit list but surely he couldn't ignore an attempt on her life... Wait, if Burnet hadn't been the one to tip McGuinn off that she was investigating Nile's "suicide", then who? Who knew? Well, outside the police, there was Nile's widow, the lawyer, Lennox, the web designer from the Carnaby centre. *Inside there was...*

Fuck. Her thoughts chased their own tails, piled on top of her. A respectable time to leave the office eventually came around with relief. She headed to the car and in her mind was already home with Bruce when the chap at the window spoiled everything.

"Sounds like it needs a service," he said, muffled through the glass. His coat was covering his uniform insignia this time, his librarian specs hung at his chest.

"Needs to be crushed into a cube more like, sir," McCoist replied.

"Can I get in? I need a quick word." The passenger door opened and the sound of McCoist's car shaking itself apart kicked up a few notches then dulled again as the nameless high-up got in and slammed the door shut. A pleasant, clean scent came in with him, along with his air of quiet authority. He gave his crotch a quick scratch, getting comfortable.

"Mind if I keep the engine running, sir?" McCoist asked. "It might not start again if I switch it off."

"Of course. I have no wish to cause you inconvenience, Inspector." He smiled, bland and unthreatening, as everything about him seemed carefully designed to be. McCoist imagined this figure was just the bait dangling at the end of the tentacle of some monstrous deep-sea creature with a black-hole maw. She shuffled in her seat, uncomfortable, couldn't decide if it seemed more natural to rest her hands on the wheel or in her lap.

"What can I do for you, sir?"

"I want to ask why you were looking at David Burnet's file again." The smile was gone. He looked less Sunday-school teacher now, more Demon Headmaster.

Shit. That was fast. "I… eh…"

"I told you that case was being handed over and that you were no longer part of the investigation."

"Yes, sir—"

"Yet you are continuing to look into suspects in that case."

"No, sir, I—"

"No? Then what were you doing? If there is something you have to add that we may have overlooked, now would be the time to divulge it."

McCoist looked down at her lap, taking too long to answer, her mind choking like the car engine. *Who can you trust and what can you trust them with?* Maybe she should tell him all about it—the Nile connection, the attack, everything. He would take over this case too, no doubt, but it would be worth it to go back to a place of security, wouldn't it? A place where thugs with knives didn't try to kill her, where her biggest worry was mouldering away with boredom at her desk among a stack of tedious cases. Was that even possible now? Did she even want that? She had the chance to do something good, something big, something that would change lives. But what about the cost? Her thoughts churned. She almost spoke when he did first:

"Detective Inspector McCoist, last year you attended a raid on a house linked to an illegal dog-breeding farm."

McCoist felt her belly drop in surprise—amongst all that had happened, she'd almost forgotten about the crime she'd committed herself—then the panic began to build. She bit into her lip.

"While there, you *stole* one of the animals. Evidence in a much larger investigation into organised crime."

Fuck, fuck, fuck. Fucking Mannan must have grassed. Had to be.

"This is a matter of gross misconduct, especially considering your rank as a detective inspector. So I will tell you one more time: stay away from the car wash, stay away from David Burnet, stay away from Paul McGuinn. Do you understand?"

"Yes, sir."

"Do you want to keep your job and your dog?"

"Yes, sir."

"Do you want to let me out of this piece-of-shit car? The door is stuck."

"Yes, sir."

McCoist picked up a bottle of wine and a pizza on the way home, hands still shaking as she tried to get the keys in the lock while balancing the wine on top of the pizza box in her other hand. The keys fell. She pressed her forehead to the door and closed her eyes. "Stupid bitch," she hissed. As she scooped her keys from the ground she spotted Edith's face watching from between the slats of her blinds. She flushed, heat in her face and on the back of her neck, embarrassed at being caught in a moment of such intimate self-loathing; then her anger turned from inside to out and she gave Edith a look that would, with any hope, give the old curtain-twitching cow a heart attack. (If the knife thugs came to her home, at least Edith would see it and maybe call someone.)

Bruce came bounding over. She put everything on the floor and knelt down, welcoming his licks and his whipping tail. "Hey, no pools of pee today, good job, boy!" Tears started to run down her cheeks. She'd snatched Bruce with some ridiculous notion that he'd improve her relationship with her kids—and because she'd hit a rut in her job and convinced herself she didn't care if she lost it or not. Turns out she did care after all. She needed it. She needed the respect and the authority, the self-esteem and the rush of a life lived at the seams of society, the righteousness of locking up killers and rapists, of doing what little she could for those abused and abandoned. Christ, last night she'd literally fought off two armed gangsters. Not something you'd get in most jobs. But the rediscovery had driven an even deeper wedge between her and her family and she was about to lose it all for good because of the dog. What a fucking mess. Another Fuck-Up after all.

The hot shame of sitting in that car with her eyes on her feet—*yes sir, no sir*—washed over her again. Who the fuck was he anyway? The visible body of something much bigger. Its flesh and blood facade. She could see the shadow behind him but it was too vast even to have an outline. She didn't even have his name and she had no one to ask, no colleagues left to confide in.

She opened the bottle, stared down the barrel of the empty weekend ahead. *Should have bought more than one.*

60

The weekend had been a busy one. Colin was away to a music festival—not that his presence would have made it much easier. Davey and Sean burst their arses from eight to eight both Saturday and Sunday—though the Orange Walk making its way down High Street bought them a bit of time to have a breather on the Saturday as it cut off the traffic going past on Bell Street, causing a jam that stretched past the car wash, under the railway bridge, and all the way up the hill beyond. Sean got out on the road and went from motor to motor like some crazed American bum offering valets to anyone who could turn their car round.

At least it meant Davey didn't have to listen to any of Sean's usual pish. As the sun was setting on Sunday he even felt nostalgic for a bit of "RT gees ye the real fuckin news" or "The elites are aw a big fuckin paedo ring". Being sober hadn't changed Sean's attitude much—decades of dope paranoia can't be undone in a few months.

A number of Paulo's boys had stopped by for their usual free valet—always keen to take advantage of a perk and rip the arse right out of it—but nothing too bad as far as it went with that crowd. *You're no gangster, you're not like these guys.* The poliswoman, McCoist, was right. Davey had been tempted to tell her everything right then—her concern actually seemed genuine. But it wouldn't help. The polis would only make things worse—and that was just the honest ones. He had no idea how many of them were in Paulo's pocket, and though he believed DI McCoist wasn't one of them—Paulo's reaction to her when she showed up at the car wash, plus the way she didn't seem to know anything about him going round to Sarah and Annalee's place, was decent proof—it was still too risky. No, he'd made his deal with Croaker, and it was too late to back out now.

"Fuuuck." Sean stretched his arms up in the air. He held his right shoulder in his left hand and slowly moved his right arm in a windmill, the joint grinding and clicking as it swivelled, as if it were full of grit. "Fancy a cuppa before we clean aw this shite up?"

"Aye, al get the kettle oan," Davey said, feeling the stiffness in his own back and shoulders. He should probably get his own cool-down routine like Sean but it looked fucking stupid, like he was pretending to be a footballer coming off the bench.

He filled the kettle up in the bathroom sink—his eyes drifted to the panel of false tiling next to the toilet, the edges loose. Back in the office, he clicked the kettle on and started rolling a cigarette.

"Help yersel," Sean said, his stretching finished. He opened a cupboard and got out his strong painkillers.

"Am gonnae be needin those masel if the shifts keep comin in like that while yer away," Davey said. "Colin's gonnae be nae fuckin use."

"Ye gonnae be awright wae that cunt while am gone?"

Davey hadn't told Sean he suspected Colin had bumped his wallet and given it to Paulo—or that Paulo had then popped round to politely threaten him (or about the clean-up at the brothel with the offer of more work in that shit-liquidising, repulsive vein). "It's only a week, al try no tae put bleach in his tea."

"Don't even fuckin joke, Davey Boy." Sean got out the milk and the biscuit tin he always kept well stocked. "Nae doubt he'd drink the fuckin hing right doon but ye saw wit Paulo wis like when ye goat his motor explodet. Hink wit he'd dae if ye killt his nephew—even if he is a useless prick."

"Am sorry, Sean… Aw this fuckin shite."

"Well, av bin dockin yer pay a wee bit each night an puttin it away fir ma holiday, so…" He shrugged and dunked a ginger nut in his coffee.

"Wouldnae notice, pay's so shite as it is." Davey grinned.

"Watch it."

Part of Davey wanted to tell Sean not to come back from his trip, to do a runner. But that would mean telling him about the plan—and there's no fucking way he'd go along with it. "If he knows nothin, he's goat nothin tae tell," Croaker had said. "Better fir him if it comes tae it." He didn't say what it might come to, but Davey imagined something involving teeth and pliers.

"When ye leavin the morra?"

"First hing, soon as the sun's up."

"Why don't ye head aff eftir yer coffee an al shut up the night? Ye can get oan hame."

"Cheers, Davey, that'd be class." Sean took the keys from his pocket and tossed them at Davey, who caught them left-handed, no fumble. He felt like he was holding a hot coal. That was it. The beginning.

They finished their drinks and said goodnight at the shutter.

"Enjoy yer holiday!"

"Cheers, Davey Boy. Look eftir the place, an don't call me."
He laughed and turned away. He sloped off down the street,
hands in the pockets of his hoody, shoulders hunched.

Davey held the keys tight in a fist. He went back inside,
waited five minutes until he went into the bathroom to the
false panel.

Croaker and Mince were waiting round the corner to collect.

61

Davey wasn't a talker, wasn't good with telling tales, or subtlety, or nuance, so the plan Croaker had come up with played right out of his hands. At least the mark was an easy one.

Colin was using the space inside the unit to perform a kata. He made whooshing noises with his mouth as he chopped his fists through the air, yelling every time he came to a stop, feet sliding into place, arms rigid.

It had been a busy day and Davey said he wanted to keep the place open for a few hours that evening, though nobody had come by for some time. "We'll show the gaffer how tae make a bit ae money." He forced a laugh. Colin didn't care, though he had a bit of a petted lip at having to stay late with Davey. "Get oan up the road, if ye like," Davey had said, knowing full well Colin would have to refuse. Bored, the lad practised his karate. Silly noises aside, Davey was impressed enough to be worried. More worried than he already was. He'd been popping his tranqs like Tic Tacs to get a handle on the panic attacks, and the truth was he was now a bit out of it. Floating just a little.

Davey cleared his throat, working up to beginning. "A guess a bloke like you, knowin aw that martial-arts stuff, doesnae need tae worry aboot toolin himsel up, eh?"

Colin whuffed and grunted, pounding invisible enemies with balletic grace. "Ye cannae rely oan weapons, really. A knife or a bat or witever can be taken aff ye, turnt against ye.

But if yer hawns, yer feet, yer body are yer weapons, ye cannae be disarmed."

"Is that right, aye?" Davey said, then reminded himself he'd be better off trying to sound actually impressed and dialled down the *"listen tae this gobshite"* in his voice. "Wit aboot, ye know…"—he winked and made a finger gun, clicking his thumb, *pow-pow*—"…that Paulo dropped aff a while back?" He motioned over his shoulder towards the bathroom—slowly, carefully—making sure Colin clocked the direction his head moved in.

"Even those arenae a match fir a man who's disciplined in the martial arts."

"They're pretty cool though, eh?" Davey raised his eyebrows, big mischievous smile, reeling him in.

"Fuckin right!" Colin stopped his performance and moved in close to Davey. He looked over his shoulder towards the open entrance of the unit, then towards the bathroom before landing on Davey. "Dye know where they're hidden?"

Davey gave the room a performative eyeball and dropped his voice when he answered: "Sean wouldnae tell me but a saw him sneakin a peek a few weeks ago, checkin it's aw still there, a guess. Ye know wit Sean's like. Para as fuck."

Colin wore the smile of a schoolboy who'd found a window into the lassies' changing room. "Hink we could huv a look?"

Davey inhaled through his teeth in perfect imitation of a repairman about to give you a substantial quote. "Aw, a dunno aboot that, Colin. A mean, we'd huv tae be careful."

"We'd be careful!"

"We'd huv tae make sure we put everythin back *exactly* right."

"We will! Moan, Davey, don't be a shitein cunt, let's huv a look!"

Davey led the way to the bathroom. He hadn't seen Sean checking on the guns, but Sean's hiding place for his weed was an open secret. Guilt roiled in Davey's stomach. If the plan went tits-up, there was a high chance it would fuck Sean too. And—bottom line—despite all his bullshit, his anger issues, the endless spiel of tinfoil-hat political theories, he didn't deserve that. Especially not from Davey. The plan will just have to go right, Davey told himself.

He pulled away the false tiles and crawled into a dark space between the gyprock walls of the office and the damp stone of the building. The gap was a little larger than the toilet itself and stuffed with old and damaged crap, like someone's attic. Davey always said the *Antiques Roadshow* should stop by. There was another door here—locked and blocked by the aforementioned useless crap—that led out into a dead alley behind the unit. By the door, in a box covered by a moth-eaten net curtain underneath a broken sewing machine and various knick-knacks, was where Sean had stashed the shoeboxes full of bullets. The case containing the guns was on the floor covered by a folded-up, mouldy duvet cover, which in the light of Davey's phone torch was a smelly shade of yellow. Davey had worn gloves the night before, when he had to touch it in order to steal the guns.

Davey made a show of kicking around in the dark for a few minutes, then started to spit and swear.

"Ye awright, Davey Boy? The fuck's goin oan in there?"

Davey crawled back out, covered in dust and plaster crumbs. "It's no there."

"Wit?"

"They're no there. Maybe Paulo picked them up?"

"Nae chance. The deal isnae set yet." Colin's eyes almost crossed with the effort of thinking. "Let us huv a look." Colin crawled into the space between the walls, his own phone out. "Must be aroon here somewhere."

"The case wis under that big duvet there."

Colin thrashed around, kicking things over, catching his elbows as he rifled among the detritus. He picked up Davey's swearing chorus. "Fuck, fuck, fuck, fuck, fuck…"

Davey shat himself as Colin came crashing out of the wall, pinning him up against the mirror over the sink. "Where the fuck are they, Davey?"

"A dunno, Colin, swear oan ma life!"

Colin took a fistful of Davey's hair and slammed his head back into the mirror; a flash of pain in his skull, the sound of breaking glass.

"Where the fuck are they?!"

"A don't know fir fucksake! Swear oan ma daughter's life, a don't know!"

Colin let go. Davey felt something warm trickling down the back of his neck.

"Then that mental fucker Sean must know. Ye know wit he's like. He's goat his ain dealer pals, willnae touch oor weed. He's bumped them an made his ain fuckin deal, hasn't he?"

"Sean wouldnae dae that, Colin, a know the guy. He wouldnae dae somethin as fuckin stupit as that." Davey raised his arms, *calm doon*. It was going well, maybe too well.

"Comin fae the guy who nicked ma uncle's motor an goat it torched?"

"Look, al go roon tae Sean's, a know where his gaff is. Al see if a can get in, huv a wee look. Maybe he's no left fir his fishin yet."

"Fishin?!" Davey guessed this was the first time Colin had ever felt like he was the smartest person in the room, and it was glorious. "He's no goin fishin, ye daft cunt! He's done a runner. Am callin ma uncle. You stay right in that fuckin spot there. Move an al break ye in hawf." Colin stormed from the bathroom.

Davey bunched up a fistful of toilet paper and pressed it against the tender spot at the back of his head. It came away bloody and Davey started to feel a bit nauseous, though that could have been down to the toxic cocktail of adrenaline, acute anxiety and diazepam swirling about inside his system. He heard Colin's voice echo off the stone walls of the unit.

Shortly, Colin returned, a sheen of sweat on his forehead. "Paulo's comin doon right noo, we've tae wait fir him in the office."

This was the tricky bit—getting Colin to fuck off. "Hows aboot *you* wait fir Paulo, an a head oer tae Sean's an see if he's aboot? A bet this is aw just a misunderstawndin. Ad gee him a ring but ye know Sean, he doesnae even huv a phone."

Colin gave him that *you dumb fuck* look again. "Misunderstawndin, aye? Naw. We wait here fir Paulo, he'll say wit tae dae."

"Aw aye, an he'd be happy wae that, will he? His nephew just stawnin aroon like a lemon daein fuck aw when there's a crisis happenin."

"Wit wis that?" Colin shoved Davey, hard.

"Nae offence, pal, am just sayin we could go oer tae Sean's an see if we can sort this oot afore yer uncle gets here and skins oor baws tae cook his haggis in."

Colin paced the unit, jaw tight, fingers clenching and unclenching. Colin thinking was like watching an old television heat up. "Right, here's the score. You wait here fir the Big Man. Gee us Sean's address an al head oer there tae take a look, be back as fast as a can. If yer no here when am back…"—Colin pinched Davey's chin with his finger and thumb in a way that might have seemed intimate if it wasn't for the pressure—"al rip this aff yer face when a catch ye, awright?"

62

Davey stood by the open shutter, shivering although it was a warm night. Headlights punched through the growing dark of the empty street and the engine noise of a monstrous, petrol-fuelled animal roared through the tunnel under the railway bridge, the stone amplifying and reverberating.

Paulo's monolithic motor lunged from the mouth of the tunnel and, with brakes and tyres squealing, winged around in a wide arc across both lanes and bumped up the kerb into the unit.

The engine dropped to a throaty rumble, idling. The unit filled with the stink of exhaust fumes, blending with those that came from the pressure washer. *Wait till he switches the motor aff.* Those were Davey's instructions. Wait till he switches the engine off...

The headlights and brake lights died. Then the engine puttered out, a beast falling asleep.

...Then close the shutter.

Davey hit the button and the shutter slid down in its tracks—slow, painfully slow—raining flecks of rust and paint, its electric motor whining under the strain. Davey had cursed the bastart thing on many a cold night as he waited for it to shut so he could lock up and go home, now he was screaming inside his head, as Paulo climbed out of the driver's side and it was still half open.

Paulo looked deadly. His flabby, middle-aged face was the colour of a stop sign.

"Wit the fuck's goin oan here, Davey?!" He slammed the door and strode forward, Davey bracing himself for another meeting with a wall.

"Just thoat we might need some privacy tae talk, naw?"

Paulo looked confused, then appeared to notice the shutter as it coughed down the last foot to the ground. "Wit? No the door, ye daft prick. A meant: wit the fuck's goin oan wae ma guns? Where are they an where the fuck is Sean?!" Paulo moved round the car—squeezing his bulk between the wing mirror and the stone wall of the unit—and kicked open the door of the office. "An fir that matter, where the fuck is Colin?!"

"Oan his way tae Possilpark wae his heed up his arse," came a dry voice. Paulo turned to find Croaker and Mince emerging from the tiny bathroom as if it were the TARDIS. Davey had let them in the disused back door after Colin went charging off. Both were armed with guns—Paulo's guns.

The look Paulo gave Davey hit him like a gut punch. He felt as if his body had liquefied and he was about to collapse into a puddle on the floor. Then the switch flipped and the smile came up—just for a second. "Nice wan, Davey Boy," Paulo said. "An eftir a very kindly didnae huv ye turnt intae a cheese grater fir nickin ma motor an aw."

Davey bit his lip to stop himself from saying sorry.

"Leave the boay alane, McGuinn," Croaker said. "He made a smart decision fir wance, let him be proud ae himsel." He pointed his gun at Paulo. "Oot the office an up against the brick, please."

"No a bad place fir it, actually," Paulo complimented as he strolled over to the brickwork, seemingly unconcerned.

"Secluded, nae windies, concrete flair, jet washer, an plenty ae cleanin products. A knew this place hud bags ae potential when a took it oan."

"Great minds an aw that pish," Croaker said.

"Ye want me turnt tae the waw or are ye gonnae manage tae look me in the face when ye plug me?"

Mince came forward. "A want tae see ye fuckin greet fan a blow yer bollocks aff, ye shitehawk!" He aimed at the appropriate level.

Paulo turned the shark-tooth smile on Mince, seemingly unconcerned by the threat of castration by speeding bullet. Davey could sense the unease this had on his comrades; as for himself, the Voice of Reason had lost all reason and become a squalling klaxon of animal terror.

"We've no met, but fae the shape ae yer pus an that accent am guessin yer related tae that other sheep-shagger, the wan a had churned up intae dug food no so lang ago."

"Cunt!" Mince bellowed and pulled the trigger—it made a slick, metallic click, nothing more. "Fit?" The bodybuilder turned the gun, which looked like a toy in his meaty hand, this way and that. He tried again. *Click. Click.*

Paulo didn't flinch, not even the first time. He started to laugh, looking from Mince's confused face to Davey's, whose mouth was catching flies, body seized up and vacant.

"Fit's wrang wae this piece ae shite?" Mince asked Croaker.

Croaker didn't answer, didn't feign confusion.

"Guns at high noon is much easier when the other lad has nae bullets, right Filth?" Paulo said.

"Filth?" Mince turned his useless gun from one man to the next, not even willing to turn his back on Davey, who by now was shivering uncontrollably, starting to breathe loud and sharp through his nose.

"Aye that's right, yev been hangin aboot wae a polis, ma sheep-shaggin pal. Ye should always check the fine print oan yer wage slips, see who's really payin ye."

"Fit's he talkin aboot, Croaker?"

Croaker continued to hold his silence, brushed his lank, grey hair from his face.

"He's bin undercover fir years, so he has," Paulo continued, "tryin tae get me any way he can. Desperate fir me as a single forty-year-auld wummin at the end ae the dancin. Gone too far intae the deep end though."

"He's talkin shite," Croaker said. Mince didn't look convinced.

"Yer brother a liar then?"

Something twitched across Croaker's face then he had it under control again, fingers reaffirming their grip on the pistol. "Fuck up."

"Says ye joint the polis straight eftir school. Nae disco for wee Tam, couldnae wait tae get his bunnet an boots oan, swaggerin doon the bad streets ae Glesga like a big man. He didnae huv much tae tell me eftir that but wance a knew, there were dots tae join an threads tae pull, ye know? Course ye dae, yer a detective yersel, right?"

"That's enough, McGuinn," Croaker finally interrupted. "Time tae say cheerio."

"Croaker, fit's he sayin? Is he tellin the truth?" Mince's brain was burning trying to turn it all over. Davey was so far over the edge he could barely comprehend, barely follow the conversation.

"Ye no gonnae ask how yer bro's daein then?" Paulo said. "A know yer no close, but that's cauld. He's actually no keepin so good an aw."

"I said fuck up!"

"Eftir a hud his eyebaws oot, a decidet they best hing tae replace them wae wis his—"

"FUCK UP!"

Before Croaker could pull the trigger, Mince charged him with the scream of a man doing a three-hundred-pound dead lift. Croaker spun, fired—inside the enclosed stone walls of the unit, the sonic boom of the bullet going off was like having a white-hot poker stuck through one ear and right out the other.

Mince fell on top of Croaker; Paulo lunged forward and joined the dogpile.

Davey also hit the deck when the gun went off, closing his eyes and covering his head. He scrabbled across the white-washed concrete on his hands and knees, sliding himself past a huge tyre and under Paulo's car, which was taking up most of the space. As he crawled towards the rear wheels, he heard the gun's report a few more times, the shots muffled under the whining in his bleeding ears. He cracked his head on the exhaust pipe as he sprung out the other side—another dent to his skull—and slammed into the shutter, where he fumbled the switch.

The shutter creaked upwards, rising slower than ever. Davey looked over his shoulder to see Paulo moving around the nightshade four-by-four, gun in hand. "Your turn, Davey Boy, ye fuckin rat ye!" His voice was underwater, reaching from a great distance through the hiss and whistle of tinnitus in Davey's ears.

Davey yanked the car door open and dove in as a bullet whined over his head, a mosquito zip as it passed by and buried itself in the wall with a puff of brick dust. He pulled the door shut and hit the manual lock on the door handle. A second bullet hit the glass on the door opposite, sending a shockwave through the car, which rocked on its axles. But the window didn't give. A spider's-web crack formed around the impact point where the bullet had come to a stop in the glass—*bulletproof.*

Davey could see but couldn't hear Paulo cursing himself and his stupid fucking expensive car. He went for the door handle but Davey was there first. Paulo switched on his grin, eyes darting to the next door handle along—the front passenger's side. Davey shoved his hand between the front seat and the door, managed to hit the button just as Paulo snatched the handle. The gangster squeezed his bulk past the wing mirror and threw himself over the bonnet, the whole front end of the car dipping down on its suspension as Davey scrambled over the handbrake and into the driver's seat to meet him—

Thunk. The door locked. Paulo screamed and pumped his impotent fury into the windscreen, three shots popping like fireworks.

Through the shatter patterns on the toughened glass, Davey could see Croaker and Mince tangled on the floor together. There was a lot of blood.

Paulo rapped his knuckles on the driver's side window, holding up his keys for Davey to see. He gave them a rattle as if trying to entertain a baby, shark smile on his face. The button for the keyless ignition winked in the corner of Davey's eye. Just close enough.

Paulo clicked his button and there was the unified snick of the locks opening—Davey hit his and the engine roared to life. *Drive, fuckin drive!*

Paulo grabbed at the door handle but was yanked off his feet as Davey slammed the car into reverse. There was the teeth-breaking screech of shearing metal as the shutter—still grinding its way up—caught the roof of the mobster-mobile and tore away from its rusted housing.

The motor launched out onto the street, Davey spinning the wheel hard and fast, swerving it round to face the road—

Crunch of metal on metal, collapsing crumple zones. Davey was juggled like dice in a cup as the SUV slammed into another car coming down the street. Pain erupted all over his head in tender lumps. He tried to shake the ringing from his ears, confused and lost until Paulo's face appeared at the window and yanked open the door, giving him an ugly reminder.

"Get the fuck oot ma motor, Davey Boy, unless yer plannin on geein it a hoover right noo." Davey's eyes met the black-hole muzzle of the gun.

"Could gee yer windies a polish an aw, eh?" He held his hands up and tried to smile.

"Good time tae grow a sense ae humour. Get the fuck oer here!"

Davey fell out the door and edged towards Paulo and the gun. "A didnae know he wis polis, honest, Paulo." His voice broke and cracked as he spoke, fear sending his balls back up inside him, climbing into his throat.

"But ye did know he wantet tae kill me though, right?"

"A didnae—" Davey didn't get to finish the sentence. Paulo chopped the butt of the handgun into his face. The bridge of his nose caved in, shooting blood from the nostrils. His top lip mashed against his teeth and popped like a burst leech. He hit the deck, a scream muffled by his hands over his face. His internal organs exploded at the penalty kick Paulo drove into his belly.

"Eftir aw av done fir ye, Davey Boy!" Paulo spat at him. "Ye don't deserve tae go the easy way." He dropped the gun to the ground—the plastic casing making an insubstantial clatter against the tarmac.

Paulo stomped and kicked and punched until he had to stop to catch his breath, face red and pishing sweat. Davey was curled up in a ball, eyes closed, pretending to be some shelled, boneless creature.

"A hink av broke ma fuckin hawn," Paulo panted, giving Davey another kick because it was all his fault. He dragged Davey back inside the unit by his collar. He stomped over to the pressure washer and unravelled a length of the hose plugged into it. Then he wrapped the hose right around Davey's neck, so his head was stuck inside a loop of tubing—one end connected to the pressure unit, the other to the lance, and Davey's throat tangled in the middle.

Davey—punch-drunk, fading in and out of consciousness—let it all happen without much of a fight. Then he heard the choking sound of the Kärcher's engine starting up, smelled the cough of its petrol exhaust, and started screaming. "Don't! No! No! *Pleeease!*"

Paulo squeezed the trigger of the lance and the hose pulled tight as the water flooded through it at high pressure, hosing out the other end in a sharp, narrow arc that blasted the walls and ceiling. Davey's air was cut off. The rubber tube bit into his neck like a bear trap. His screaming stopped, replaced by a sick gargle as his tongue tried to escape his mouth and his eyes became too large for their sockets, blood vessels bursting. Paulo swung the lance down towards him, blasting Davey's body as he clawed at his own neck, nails gouging bloody troughs in the skin.

Lights were flashing, colours popping and curling in Davey's vision. He could hear Paulo's twisted, braying laugh over the sound of the engine and the jet spray crashing against the walls and the floor and Davey's battered, bloody body.

Then there was a noise—far away, a dull snap like somebody clicking their fingers or flicking a light switch—and it all stopped.

No more laughter. No more water. The hose around Davey's neck went flaccid and loose. Paulo sat down in front of him in a heap. There was a deep, dark hole in his head like the finger hole drilled into a bowling ball. It was leaking blood and brain matter.

The room came back into focus as Davey gulped in air through his burning throat.

DI McCoist was standing over Paulo, smoking gun in her hand, a spray of blood across her slack, unbelieving face.

Somewhere nearby, a phone was ringing—a tacky polyphonic rendition of *William Tell* from a cheap old mobile. It stopped—in the silence it left, the reverberations of the gunshots, the smell of the cordite, the after-image of bloody violence began to dissipate—and started again.

"Ye gonnae get that?" Davey wheezed.

63

Mince was now nothing more than his namesake—important bits and pieces were missing from his head, including his ear, a portion of his skull, and a tubular section cut from his brain, as if dug out by an apple corer. A trail of blood scraped along the floor away from the body and ended in a pair of legs sticking out the bathroom door.

"Police! Stop right there. I'm armed." The detective was trembling—there was a deep cut across her brow, blood leaking into her eye and mixing with the blowback from Paulo's burst melon. Davey wasn't sure she could pull the trigger again if she had to. All the same, he didn't try to make a run for it just in case—plus, his legs wouldn't carry him far in his battered state.

Croaker wasn't getting far either. He wheezed and grunted as he inched along the floor, blood trail oozing from his belly like a snail. *William Tell* was coming from somewhere in his long, ragged coat.

He held up one hand in surrender. "P-p-polis," he said, stuttering, drool spraying from his lips. He wheezed with every breath. Air was escaping from somewhere. "Undercover. Am… am under… c-cover."

"Paulo wis tellin the truth then?" Davey said, too tired to be angry yet.

"Polis…" he mumbled.

"So that shite about yer wean wis aw bollocks then."

"Back off, Burnet," McCoist said. She was swithering on the edge of panic, her body a twitching bag of ticks. The gun was in her slick hands, not pointing at Davey but there between them all the same. She'd just shot a man dead. A bad man, for sure, but there was no escaping she'd just taken a swan dive into the shite head first.

The *William Tell* ringtone started again. Croaker waved at her, flapping with a stiff arm, his face contorted with the strain required to lift a bus. "A-answer... it. Phone..." He half rolled onto his side and lifted the lapel of his coat. The shirt below was saturated with blood, the colour washing out from two ragged, black epicentres in his chest and gut.

McCoist fished the phone out of Croaker's inside pocket. Deep breath. She hit answer, held it up to her ear, waiting...

The conversation was a whisper, Davey only catching the terse tone of McCoist's side of it, words lost under traumatised eardrums, though he was sure he made out his own name on her lips. Her face was creased with confusion, eyes staring through the whitewashed brick of the wall, lost. She hung up and tucked the phone into her jacket pocket.

"Sirens oan the way?" Davey said, every word a rasping pain in his throat.

She wouldn't look at him. Her eyes were wet, jaw jutting out, face starting to twist and shrivel as the tears came. The relief of oxygen rushing back into his brain, the adrenaline of the fight and the pills before had left Davey floating, everything a dream, unreal, but now he started to come back down at the shake of her head. He licked his bloody lips, felt his stomach and legs start to loosen and wobble as his heart picked up speed again, churning the dregs of fear and anxiety through him.

"Wit's goin oan?" He could see her knuckles white on the grip of the gun. She certainly wasn't on the McGuinn payroll—that was for sure—but it didn't mean the only pay packets she got were PAYE.

"David, you need to go." Her voice was hard to hear, muted and far away, his ears fucked from the shots. She still couldn't look at him.

"Wit?"

"You need to leave here."

"Yer lettin us go?" A dribble of hope in his words fought against the unease in his body and the scoffing of the Voice of Reason.

"I don't mean the car wash. I mean Glasgow. Scotland, even. The whole fucking island, maybe. You need to leave and never come back."

"Ye know a cannae dae that. Annalee—"

"She'll be fine. As long as you disappear and keep your mouth shut, nothing will happen to her."

Davey started to cry too. Sobs racked him, his chest and shoulders shaking with it. "How dae *you* know, eh? Are ye wae them, is that it?" He gestured to Croaker bleeding out on the bathroom floor. "Fuckin bent polis, just like him."

McCoist finally looked at him. "I'm not… I'm not like that. I—" But the gun was coming up now, slowly. "No more questions, David. Leave here right now and don't come back. Don't think, just do it."

"Ye gonnae shoot us, Ally McCoist?!" Davey's voice was high and unhinged. Months of fear and anger and hopelessness came screaming out of him. Punched and kicked and threatened and humiliated, made to clean up death after death—Mealy in the boot of the motor, the people treated like cattle in the back of the lorry, the girl battered and plugged in the shag pad. All of them used and abused, and poor wee Davey too. "Ye gonnae fuckin shoot me, are ye?!" He slapped his chest then stuck his hands in the air.

"Christ, if I wanted you dead I could have just let McGuinn kill you a minute ago. Go, David, just go, and I promise you Sarah and Annalee will be fine."

"Don't say their fuckin names!" he screeched. "How can ye say that?! How dye know they'll be fine?!"

"I can—I could, I—" The gun dropped to McCoist's side.

"Would ye be sayin this if it wis yer ain two? Yer twins? Go oan an leave for ever, hope fir the best. Hope naebdy goes eftir yer faimly tae get tae ye." Tears were streaming down his cheeks, snot mixing with the blood from his nose and lips.

"I'll watch out for them."

"Is that a promise, aye? An wit's a promise worth fae a bent polis?"

"I'm not—" Her shoulders started to shake; she pinched the bridge of her nose to try to stop the tears which came out anyway, everything trembling and aching. "It's not like that, David. I'm not... not what you think."

"That so? Heard that afore."

"I-I don't know." She put the gun on the ground and slumped gracelessly onto her backside. Davey followed suit, crumpling down, wrapping his arms around his body, which started to feel cold, shivering uncontrollably. "David, if you stay, you'll die. Someone will come after you for this. They'll find you. Then there's no way back to Sarah and Annalee. If you run now, there's a chance."

"A chance a could come back later?" His voice was weak, not just from being strangled.

"I don't know. Maybe. If I can sort all this out, then maybe. But if you don't go then…"

"Ye sound awfy sure about that." He spat blood on the floor. "Will ye let me know?" he asked.

"If it's safe?"

He shook his head. It hurt. "How they're gettin oan."

"I'll try."

He scraped himself off the floor and stumbled towards the street.

"Davey?"

"Aye?" He rested against the power-washing unit, already exhausted from a few steps.

"How the fuck did you end up involved in all of this?"

Davey's sniffling sobs turned into a laugh. "A stole the Big Man's motor. Cause am a fuckin eejit."

"Big bastart Range Rover?"

"Aye—nae way a could afford tae pay back the money that hing cost, so…" He shrugged, his glance around the car-wash unit brushing the corpse of Paulo McGuinn.

Half a weary smile crossed her face. "Wouldn't have cost him anything, it was nicked. Numbers and plates changed."

Davey wiped blood from his face and laughed, hysterical and ugly, as he headed out.

64

McCoist had to step over the dying man to get to the sink. He wheezed the whole time she scrubbed at her face to get the blood spray off—she was having a hard time of it, took her a while to notice some of it was her own, pouring out a gash on her forehead. There was no pain yet, that was still to come.

The man's throat was rattling, like a can of spray paint being shaken up. Chunder rose in her gullet; she closed her eyes, swallowed it down, gripping the sink and trying to slow her breathing, but every breath was tainted with gun smoke. She dared a quick glance and he started coughing blood, which dribbled weakly down his chin and made bubbles in the corner of his mouth as he tried to say something. The car wash was full of rags and towels and shammies and all sorts of things that could be used to staunch the bleeding. All she had to do was step next door. Dial those three digits. He'd already lost a lot of blood, but what if?... His eyes were no longer focused, rolling back up into his skull, his attempt at speaking becoming a low groan.

"Fuck," she hissed. She looked back out the door to the unit where she could see the slumped bodies, one of them she'd killed by execution. How would she explain it all? Like the truth would matter if the man on the end of the phone with the bling on his shoulders was against her. "Fuck." When it comes down to "he said, she said", "she" always loses by default, and with McCoist's sterling reputation it would be no contest. Mr Itchy Baws had put it much the same way on the phone. The story was whatever he said it was. She could have a good role or a bad role. "Fuck."

She used toilet roll and a crusty bottle of Carex to try to clean up the gun, which was only maybe pointless, and had to step back over him on her way out of the bathroom. It was a stretch to avoid stepping in the blood now, which had formed a large, viscous puddle. It made her think of Cam and Tess when they were wee, leaping from couch to couch, the floor being lava. McCoist had played that game too as a wean. Funny that, and what a practical skill it had turned out to be. She laughed at the thought, which led to more tears.

Outside, she passed her wrecked Skoda, the front end mangled together with the side of the night-black beast peppered with bullet holes. The thing had come flying past her earlier, where she was parked on the hill beyond the railway bridge, and she had sunk deep into her seat behind the wheel, her mind starting to agitate itself into uselessness as her gut realised something was going on. She'd tried to move as soon as she heard the first shot but the car wouldn't start. She didn't know then if she was going to go down there or do a burly and get as far away as possible. More shots followed—her heart leaping with every blast, cringing with the embedded childhood fear of loud, sudden noise—and the engine of the Skoda whined and coughed.

It caught and she slammed the car into first gear, nearly stalled as she came off the clutch too rapid, jolting down the hill, revs screaming as she did an ugly shift into second, still moving towards the car wash rather than away, mind blank.

She blinked and hit the SUV that came barrelling backwards out of the half-open shutter.

The airbag swallowed her face. Everything was fuzzy, swimming, fine glass raining down on her from the broken windscreen, like being inside a snow globe. When she dragged herself out the car—the driver's side door was fucked and the passenger's side needed a good kicking to get it open—she found Burnet being strangled, water hosing everywhere, the King Kong frame of Paul McGuinn standing over him, battered and bloodied... and the gun on the deck.

She'd screamed at him to stop but he wouldn't. Her cries were lost under the waterfall fizz of the jet spray, the engine rumble, a roomful of deaf ears. Or maybe he just couldn't stop himself now until his victim was dead. That's what he was like. And when he was done, what then? Would he see her and put his hands up? Would he turn around and let her put the cuffs on? The crash seemed to have rattled her outside of her own body; her thoughts were slow, out of sync with reality, and her movements far off, the feedback subdued.

She'd never fired a gun before. It was easy. No thinking involved, not much pressure, just *click* and a hole punched itself right through McGuinn's head, warm spray from the blowback misting her face, stinging her eyes. The smell the burnt gunpowder made wasn't unpleasant. Bonfire Night, a doused campfire. She stood there, lost in the sensation until Burnet's wheezing voice brought her back to the car wash full of dead bodies and the ringing phone.

She recognised the voice on the other end of it: "Tam? You there? If you're there but can't speak, press a button once..."

"Tam can't come to the phone," she said.

And the voice recognised hers. "DI McCoist... So you couldn't leave it alone after all... Is Tam hurt or?..."

"Aye, you could say that."

"Don't fuck around, Inspector. Tell me what's happening."

"He's hurt badly, shot twice."

"Will he make it?"

"Not unless I get off this phone and call an ambulance right away, sir."

"Anyone else?"

She took a long, rattling breath. "Paul McGuinn is dead. There's another one I don't know. Dead too." He was familiar though—the man in the car outside Burnet's flat. Another one of McGuinn's? Or working with Tam? Christ, if he was polis too it wouldn't have surprised her.

"Give me the short version of the story—and assume any lies you tell right now I'll figure out and use to nail you for any number of offences you may or may not have committed."

McCoist did as she was told, not doubting his abilities of detection or the reach of his power.

"Listen carefully, Inspector... Are you listening carefully?"

"Yes, sir."

"You're not going to call an ambulance."

"What?"

"You're going to hang up this phone, dispose of it, then leave. Do not tell a soul you were ever there. Not your colleagues, not DCI Robson, not your own mother. Don't even confess it to your fucking dog. Go home right now and wait. Understood?"

"But, sir—"

"*Is that understood?!*"

McCoist flinched. She was still keyed up, agitated and in disbelief. The neat report of the gun, the perfect, geometric blood spray fizzing out the back of McGuinn's head like a twisted firework display—the after-image stuck on repeat, sparkling behind her eyelids. Now she was being asked to let another man die.

"Look at it this way, Inspector, either you find yourself on your own, talking to an inquiry about a gangland shootout you were inexplicably involved in, or you're with me and the likelihood of you losing your job, going to jail or ending up dead from a reprisal hit significantly lowers. Now tell me: is that understood?"

What choice did she have? Her frazzled brain was barely capable of scraping around for even a shred of an idea right then. "Yes, sir," she murmured.

"Good."

"My car's knackered though—crashed at the scene."

"Report it stolen in the morning, it'll get sorted out."

"And what about David Burnet?"

"He's there?"

"Yes."

"Injured?"

"He'll be OK."

"Tell him he's free to go. And emphasise the 'to go', all right?"

"Yes, sir."

"Good job, DI McCoist. Time to clock off. Head on home, I'll see you there soon." He hung up.

65

"Fuckin prick, fuckin wee pothead prick," Colin hissed as he drove back to the car wash empty-handed. He'd kicked down Sean's door with a very solid *mawashi geri* (*hee-yaaah!*), but the wee stoner wasn't in. He'd done a runner already. It occurred to Colin while he was digging around Sean's poky flat for *clues*—the ceilings and wallpaper all smoke-stained, the carpets oozing the stench of grass and rolling tobacco, strands of the stuff everywhere, DVDs stacked floor to ceiling against a wall in the living room the only indication of individual taste or personality, everything else just cobbled together second-hand furniture like some halfway house—that Davey might also have done a runner while he was gone, even though he warned him not to, that maybe Davey *wanted* him to leave. That dick wouldn't be stupid enough to pull something like that on Uncle Paul, though, would he? He was a workhorse sort of guy, a knuckle-down-and-hope-for-the-best type. *Fuckin pathetic.* What would he even do with the money he'd get from selling guns?

Colin turned onto Bell Street, approaching the railway bridge, and noticed light spilling out of the unit's shutter and, in the middle of the road, two crashed cars.

He kerbed it and approached the scene. Uncle Paulo's motor—the roof all scraped, silver lines gouged through the glossy treacle paint, windows spider-web shattered, door lying open—had been T-boned by some clapped-out old Skoda. Shite, Paulo will be pissed, Colin thought. He'd probably torch a cunt's house just for keying his car, never mind crashing into it. But where was he? Something wasn't right. Colin's brain was starting to hurt as it tried to process what he was seeing. A bad feeling trickled into his stomach.

Despite the chaos of what was in front of him, it seemed absurdly quiet—no noise coming from inside the unit, nobody getting yelled at. The shutter door had been wrenched completely off and was lying among the debris of the car crash.

"U-Uncle Paul? Ye there? Davey Boy?"

He stepped inside. Usually, the unit smelled of car soap, degreaser and the exhaust from the Kärchers; instead, the air was heavy with the thick, nostalgic smell of exploded fireworks. Underneath it was a whiff of something rank, like a backed-up drain.

Paulo was sitting on the floor. "Uncle Paul?" There was blood drying on his face, a dark hole in one side of his head and a much bigger one on the other, where a large chunk of his skull was missing and something gooey had dribbled out, bits and pieces of grainy-looking organ matter sprinkled on the floor. "Wit? Fuck. Wit the fuck? Wit the—"

Past him, there was another body lying on the ground and a trail of blood leading to a pair of legs sticking out the bathroom. Neither of them looked like Davey or Sean.

"Jesus fuckin Christ. Wit the—" Colin ran his hands through his close-cropped hair, palms slick. "Uncle Paul. Uncle Paul, are ye?…" He shook his uncle by the shoulder. "Paulo!" He gave him a shove and his uncle tipped over, hitting the floor like a bag of tatties. Something heavy splatted out the big hole in his head and onto the slippy red floor. "Wit dae we dae?"

He heard sirens. "Uncle Paul, wit dae we dae?!"

Outside, blue lights were strobing against the scrubbed sandstone of the old factories that lined Bell Street. Colin ran out to meet them and froze, dazzled by white headlights screaming towards him from every side. At first he couldn't see anything through the blinding lights, deafened by the ear-bleeding siren noise. He formed into a *kokutsu dachi*, hands ready to chop, but flailed this way and that as each car came skidding to a stop and doors were thrown open, the sound of feet hammering towards him. Backlit shadows at first, then he could see their armour, their helmets, their guns. His legs wobbled in their ready stance. Despite the wild pumping of his heart and his arms so rigid they were shaking, he felt his stomach muscles relax. Warmth spread down his thighs and his bulge-accentuating tight briefs filled up, getting even tighter, as his bowels emptied as well. The powerful, sewer-pipe stench of his own fear wafted up to his nose.

A voice screeched: "Down on the ground! Down on the ground!"

He put up his hands—his deadly weapons—and knelt down in a puddle of urine.

66

It was only riding in the bus home, her reflection looking back at her in the black window, that she began to shake. He'd be dead by now. She'd snapped the SIM and tossed the burner into a bin on her way to the bus stop. Definitely dead, not much more blood in him. Could she blame herself for him too? She saw the hole appear in McGuinn's head again. Instant death. It wasn't a case of the light in his eyes fading, more his bulb being burst by a power surge. His expression was the same, exactly the same, just dead. No such luck for the other man.

Bruce gave her his usual welcome, as if nothing had happened and nothing would ever happen. She embraced him, smelled his fur, let him lick at her until she realised he was slurping at her sleeve and cuff, where she hadn't cleaned the blood off.

She stripped everything off and tossed it in a bundle. She ran the shower and let it heat up. The thought that she should get a bin bag to put those clothes in drifted into her mind. She'd have to throw them out. Too bad, she quite liked that jacket. She whitied in the toilet. Bruce pawed at the door, concerned.

The water was burning, turned her skin red and stripped off the smell of death and car soap. The cut on her head nipped. Her stomach was sore from clenching, her muscles tight. She let the piss run down her legs, indistinguishable from the hot water.

Wrapped in a dressing gown, she sat in the kitchen with

an empty wine glass and an unopened bottle until somebody knocked at the back door.

He was there in his librarian specs, his plain but well-made coat, expression flat like the surface of a reservoir that swallowed someone every summer. "May I come in? And please, Inspector, put that knife down."

McCoist set the paring knife down on the counter—she wasn't much of a cook; the stubby little blade was the only one she had in the kitchen—and stepped back to let the man in. He closed the door after himself.

Bruce bounced all over him. He clearly wasn't a dog person, failing to understand that the quickest way to stop the dog pawing him was to give it what it wanted and clap it.

"Here, boy." McCoist got out a treat and sent Bruce diving into the living room with a throw.

"You've had a bit of a night," he said, sitting down at the kitchen table, a quick itch at the testes before folding one leg over the other. "You want to fill me in on the details?"

McCoist stayed on her feet. Part of her felt self-conscious at standing there in just her dressing gown, but another part was beyond all that. Fuck him, let him blush if he has to—she knew he wouldn't. She went through what happened, the long version this time; he listened politely, sitting folded and trim with the odd scratch at the crotch like a twitch or tick.

"So you executed one of the city's most notorious gangsters—that's something to be proud of, but for the sake of keeping things neat, let's just say that Tam Croaker got him."

"Who was Croaker?"

The man sighed and rearranged himself on his seat, a big question. "He was trouble."

"He was one of us?"

"In simpler times, yes, but really he was more just one of himself. That's all he could be. Undercovers who go out that deep, that far, they are their own entity... Some money still came from us but he had other sources too, brokering information mostly. Mind you, I took the liberty of expunging his records from our files when everything started to look dicey after the Knightley thing. He was so sure he had McGuinn when he found the location of Dannie Gibb's body that it really cracked him up when it slipped through."

"The baby... it was McGuinn's?"

"Gibb had been more than just a regular fuck for McGuinn. She had moved out of the high-rise, had her tattoo removed, but she wouldn't agree to getting rid of the baby. Croaker thought that with the body found, he'd have McGuinn strung up. Guess he hadn't banked on your unique skills."

"Unique skills?"

"Fucking things up." His smile was cold. "And I'm going to need you to make use of those skills again until this whole thing is buried."

"Sir?"

"The Nile investigation. Looks like he was involved with Croaker—but you already know that, don't you?" He seemed quietly impressed.

"Nile put Croaker up in his office for a while. Croaker disappeared from there when the tip-off was called in on Nile, just before Nile was killed. Nile had been given a new identity after turning informant to get out of prison three years ago—Croaker must have known him from back then or before.

"It's certainly intriguing—however, I want it shut down. I need you to run it into a dead end so tangled and seemingly banal that the term 'cold case' seems too hopeful. I want it in the fucking freezer. I don't want it to appear on some fucking true-crime podcast in ten years' time."

McCoist's mouth was dry. What he was asking of her was beyond corrupt. This wasn't just nicking a puppy from a dog mill. But what could she do? She'd killed McGuinn. She'd left Croaker to die. *You saved David Burnet's life, though, and that's surely something.* Wouldn't count for much in this game though. *Fuckin bent polis*, he'd said, his bitterness, his disappointment, a mirror of her own. Her pathetic reply: *I'm not like that*—as she tried to point a gun at him.

"While we're at it—I have another one for you. Body parts were found in a quarry that match the DNA of your bloody-bin-bag-rag mystery. You'll be taking the lead. Do what you do best."

"What if I just resign?" she croaked.

"No, you can't do that, Alison. Not now you're getting the chance to make yourself useful again." He did his Sunday-school smile. *Aren't you a clever wee girl, well done you.* He stood and went to the door. "Oh, and congratulations, you've just been promoted. Take a few days off, celebrate with your kids." Mention of the twins brought Burnet's words back to her: *Hope naebdy goes eftir yer faimly tae get tae ye.* Her chest tightened: she could feel the cage around her. The man's smile floated as an after-image in McCoist's brain for some time afterwards. She was unable to blink it out.

She sat frozen until she became aware of Bruce licking her palm, his big, slebbery tongue coating her hands in fishy dog-breath-smelling saliva. "At least I've still got you," she said with a wry smile, drying her hands off on his head as she clapped him. They hadn't taken her dog away. And they knew nothing about the half-promise she'd made to David Burnet. If I can sort this all out, she'd said. Big if. Big, big, humongous if. Yet she'd finally solved the Dannie Gibb case, hadn't she? Maybe she could do this too…

Paulo's burst head appeared in her mind again and she had to check her face in the mirror, make sure she'd got every last speck of blood.

67

The knock at the door woke Sarah with the feeling of falling from a great height. She shot upright in bed, heart pounding, something like fear in her belly—she used to have the same reaction when Annalee was a baby and woke, crying, in the night.

"Who the fuck is that?" she hissed to the dark, checking the time on her phone. It was past midnight. It must be a mistake, she told herself, and pulled the duvet up around her shoulders, inhaling the sweat-smell of sleep. Maybe it was the neighbour's door? The knock came again. Definitely hers. *Fuck!*

She grabbed her dressing gown and eased out the door, tiptoeing past Annalee's bedroom and downstairs into the hall. She hunched, trying to keep herself small as she approached the door, her phone held tight in her fist, ready to call the polis if she didn't like the look of whatever was on the other side of the peephole.

Sarah didn't like what was on the other side but she let it in anyway.

Davey was soaking wet, shivering in his sodden work clothes, arms wrapped around himself. His nose was mashed flat and crusted with dry blood, as were his lips and chin. Bruises were already taking shape around his eyes and swelling up on his cheekbones. Worst of all was the red-raw ligature mark around his throat. Sarah's immediate thought was that he'd tried to hang himself and a sick fear jolted her nerves. That didn't explain the rest of the damage though.

"Wit the fuck's happened?"

"Am awright, am awright." Davey waved her away, slumping down onto her couch, soaking into the fabric.

"Awright?!" She wanted to yell but she didn't want the wean waking up and coming down to see her father sitting there as if a bus had run over him. "Ye turn up at ma door in the middle ae the night beat tae fuck an yer tellin me yer awright? Well, good fir you, cause am certainly no awright!"

"It's no as bad as it looks."

"It's No As Bad As It Looks: The Davey Burnet Story."

"Look, Sarah, a just came tae say a love ye, an a love Annalee, an am sorry… Sorry fir aw the bollocks oer the years."

"Yer scarin me." She readjusted her gown, pulling it up tight around her chest and neck.

"Listen, av goat tae go."

"Wit, yer just poppin by? At this time in the mornin. Bleeding aw oer the place. Ye bin drinkin?"

Davey shook his head. Tears were running down his cheeks. "Naw, av goat tae go away, a mean."

"Away? Away where? Christ, why the fuck now?! Why? When hings huv bin… gettin better."

"A dunno where yet. Av just goat tae leave Glesga fir a while. Maybe longer than a while."

"Am—am gonnae call yer maw, awright? Get her tae come an pick ye up an we can talk aboot this in the mornin."

Davey lunged forward and snatched the phone from Sarah's hands. "Am sorry, darlin, but a cannae let ye dae that. Naebdy can know am leavin, a just came tae say…"—he wiped tears and snot and blood from his face—"…bye. An a love ye. Baith ae ye."

Sarah was cowering away from him.

"Can a, can a go oan up an see Annalee quickly? A willnae wake her, a promise. A just want tae peek in the door, just…"

Sarah was crying now too. Her jaw jutted out—defiant, furious—as she shook her head. "*You* don't go near her. Go, if yer gonnae go. If yer gonnae miss her, then ye can start right noo. Get tae fuck oot ma hoose. Go oan noo."

Davey dropped Sarah's phone on the couch as he stood. He was sobbing, snivelling. His eyes burned as bad as his throat, which was so swollen it choked his words and he didn't say anything else.

Sarah's parting shot hit him in the back: "Ye fuck up everyone ye meet, ye know that, Davey? Ye just make a fuckin mess an leave everybody else tae deal wae it."

He walked out the door and he was gone.

EPILOGUE

EPILOGUE

1

Lennox was dying. He'd had leftovers of last night's Chinese for breakfast and the heartburn was killing him. He chewed two Gaviscons with his morning coffee, then took the bus to work feeling dicey indeed, every bump in the road a potential disaster.

In his hurry to get the door unlocked and let himself inside the office for a second round on the bog that morning, he almost missed the lad waiting for him outside. "Hiya, Tim. You're early today. Always keen as a bean! Good thing actually, I think I'm going to need you to pop down to the shops for some toilet rolls and air freshener—mind and keep your receipts—"

Tim, the uni boy they had doing work experience for them, was holding an A4 Manilla envelope. The lad's own name was written on it in a messy scrawl that was maybe familiar. "This was under my door this morning."

"What's that?"

"It's from Davey Burnet."

Lennox froze with his key in the lock, vital mission suddenly forgotten. "How do you know Davey?"

"Maybe we should go inside for a chat," Tim said. His entire demeanour was different. He looked tall, his back straight, and the pained, sheepish smile he constantly wore—a sure sign of a helpless people-pleaser—was gone.

Lennox's belly gurgled, his guts cramping with sweet-and-sour acid. "Yes, I think we'd better."

2

Not a single bite in fucking days, man. Not once since Sean left Glasgow had he eaten fish for his tea. He took a sandwich from the cool box where he kept his dwindling supply of brave Sir Galahads (Aldi tinnies), unwrapped it and took a bite. Mother's Pride, thick butter, dinosaur ham—the king of pieces. He tore a corner off and put it on his hook. "Here ye go, ye wee bastarts, come an get it!" He cast the line into the river, breaking the surface, ripples catching the sun, glittering.

He was choking for a joint. He'd had a few cans this morning—crushed at his welly-booted feet—and now he felt desperate for a smoke. It had been months since he'd had such a powerful craving, and if he hadn't been in the middle of fucking nowhere—the closest thing to civilisation being a hamlet with a single shop that sold food, drink and fishing gear a few miles down the road from where he sat on the bank—he knew he'd have cracked by now.

It was Rusty who had put him in mind to go fishing—not that he'd seen the geezer since Paulo put him off. He used to go all the time, said it was pure magic, sitting by the water, chaining joints all by yourself, catching fishes to put on your wee barbecue. Bliss. "Closer tae heaven than ye can get in any church, man," he'd always say.

Shite. Sean had a sore arse from sitting on a camping chair for days on end, he was being eaten alive by the midges, and the closest thing he'd had to barbecued fish was a sweaty service station tuna baguette he'd eaten on the bus on the way here.

"Fuck yeez!" he shouted at the water. "Yer probly aw full ae fuckin mercury an aw sorts ae shite anyway." He stood, unzipped and took a pish into the water. "Drink it, ye wee slags!"

"That yer last worm, Sean?"

Sean jumped, sprinkling urine onto his wellies. "Fucksake! Jesus Christ, Davey Boy, the fuck ye daein here?" He tucked himself away. Davey had a sports bag over his shoulder and a blue plastic bag that looked as if it only had cans of lager inside. He wasn't dressed for a fishing trip. His face was a grotesque masterpiece, the whites of his eyes peppered with bloody spots, a livid coil of fresh, full bruising around his neck. "Wit the fuck happened tae ye?! An who the fuck's watchin the car wash? Don't fuckin tell me yev left that doss cunt Colin in charge for fucksake. Davey?"

Davey held out his bag. "Take wan, yer gonnae need it."

Davey finished telling Sean his story. He told him everything he'd been up to—the notes, the lawyer, Croaker, McCoist, cleaning up at the brothel and, finally, the showdown at the car wash. Croaker, Mince and Paulo all dead, shot to shit, the polis surely lying in wait, wanting to speak to them. He finished and braced himself for it—for the explosion.

But it didn't come. Sean took a mouthful of lukewarm lager and sparked a fag he'd been rolling while Davey spoke. He took a deep lungful, sucking away half the cigarette in one go and then blowing smoke at the midges that circled them. He fixed Davey with his cracked, manic eyes, bloodshot and set deep into prematurely wrinkled sockets. "Ye know wit, son? A wis hinkin ae burnin the gaff doon anyway."

Sean smiled and Davey burst into laughter. "Can a tap a fag aff ye?"

"Yev taken everythin else, so why the fuck not?"

Davey punched him on the arm and he threw the pouch of tobacco at him. They sat drinking and smoking and watching the river in silence.

Then the line moved, cutting across the water, reel spinning. They had a bite.

END

ACKNOWLEDGEMENTS

This book would not exist without the love and support of my wife Lisa. I owe everything to her and our children, a constant source of wonder and inspiration.

Thank you to my mum who has been my first reader ever since I began doodling stories on paper, my brother for his advice on gross injuries, my sister the evil twin, my friends and family.

Thanks also to my editor Daniel Seton, Harriet Wade, and everyone at Pushkin for making *Squeaky Clean* what it is, for seeing a novel in an acorn of a story and giving it a chance.

And to my agent and champion Emily MacDonald for her unwavering belief, sage advice, editorial input and countless other things which brought this book to publication.

Lastly, I'd like to thank my old gaffer Steven, who is The Don.

Introducing

PAPERBOY

A new case for DI McCoist coming soon from
Callum McSorley and Pushkin Vertigo

PROLOGUE

The King is dead.

Paul McGuinn, Paulo to his friends and enemies, his slave girls and lieutenants and errand boys. Fraudster, drug runner, people smuggler, murderer. His wife stood at the head of the stone in an expensive black dress, holding her daughters' hands. The crowd around them was thick with black suits and Rangers scarves.

Two polis in high-vis hovered near the cemetery gate, tense, as welcome as a fart in a sleeping bag. A woman in plainclothes office-drabs turned her nose up at the hearse parked at the kerb, appraising the floral tributes in the back which spelled out PAUL on one side and DAD on the other. "Tasteful," she said, catching their eyes as she passed them into the stone-lined path. One of them recognised her and murmured "Ma'am" with a slight bow of the head.

McCoist was attending because it was her duty—she was the DCI investigating the gangster's murder and she was the one who'd put the cunt in the ground.

She could still feel the moment, the screaming rush, then the shocking silence following the thunderclap of the gunshot. Dead ears—a dentist drill whine and a waterfall of white noise. Squeeze of the trigger, flash of the explosion, so fast it seemed to precede the movement, like it wasn't even her who did it. Inevitable. A slap on the face with warm blood spray. A black hole in the head, punching through hair gel, skin, bone, and brain. In and out the other side. The Clyde tunnel.

Case closed.

Not that McCoist could let anyone know it was that simple.

She watched from a distance as the Rolls Royce of a coffin was lowered into the earth. The reverend was saying something but she couldn't hear him. What do you say when you believe the deceased is going straight to hell? *Bury him deep, boays, save him the taxi fare.*

The wife threw something into the hole. Folded paper. A letter, maybe. The daughters, both of them taller than their mother in bigger heels, did the same. Surrounding them, a who's-who of Glesga's criminal underworld bowed their heads and clasped their hands like schoolchildren. The impression wasn't of praying though, it looked more like they were waiting for something. A sign.

Long live the king.

She had only been able to think of two words to write to her husband:

Fuck You

And she'd written them over and over and over again until the page was full. Lottie was never much of a writer. Not her chosen method of expressing herself.

The letters had been Gemma's idea, and she was so sincere when she came out with it that Lottie had to go along with her. Her older daughter, Ari, had agreed it was a *"wonderful"* idea, but her eyes betrayed something, maybe envy, like she wished she'd thought of it first. The floral letter tributes had been her suggestion—her little sister's paper letters were both more heartfelt and cheaper. Paulo would have appreciated that. Rich men are cheap. Never spend when you can steal.

Lottie had a fleet of Mulberry handbags in her wardrobe she'd always known better than to ask the provenance of. A lot of lorries turning carelessly.

Ari stepped forward and dropped hers in—God knew what she'd written—then returned to squeeze between her mother and sister, taking one of their hands in each of hers. Gemma had read her letter out to them in the morning, tears in her eyes. Beautiful in that moment, though if Lottie was honest her youngest had too many of her father's genes to ever be considered so in the conventional way. Ari, however, was her spit. An unsettling double.

The reverend was droning and the dirt was sprinkled in—a handful at a time at first, later to be finished by the excavator, reversing its earlier work.

The men didn't know what to say. Not yet. They'd find the words later on, down at the pub after a good scoop. Pints and whiskies, drinking the money she put behind the bar although she didn't plan on attending. Hoovering up something stronger off the toilet cisterns. Paulo wouldn't have minded. It's not disrespectful, it's what he would have wanted. A night out in his honour. Maybe even a club later. Or the casino. Girls. Violence.

She wondered if talk would turn to revenge. There was no way any of them believed her eejit nephew Colin had killed him as the polis claimed—put a bullet through his uncle's head after being caught making deals behind his back in a brass-bawed attempt at taking over the firm. No, the only coup young Colin could ever conceive of ate grass and said "Moo". Though maybe it would be easier for them if they pretended to believe it. Less trouble. She could understand that. She'd had to ask her own sister not to come to the funeral. Appearances needed to be kept up.

For now.

Fuck You Fuck You

The best part of a year later…

1

"TRNSMT?! I wonder what else gets transmitted there that isn't just music."

"Gads, Alison. She's only—"

"She's a teenager. You'll have to accept that soon."

"She's our daughter. We can trust her to be sensible."

"I can't trust her to do her own washing or bring the mugs down from her room. Who are *you* talking about?"

"She's not silly, when it comes to the big things—"

"Like her exams?"

"Here we go…"

McCoist was on the phone to her ex, arguing about the twins again. Not the twins, really, just Tess. Her standard grade results had been unexpected. Unexpectedly shite. A good slip down from the prelim results. A sign of trouble, they both knew, but what to do about it they couldn't agree on. And now she was whingeing about going to TRNSMT Festival with her pals next week and the tickets cost a lung and pair of a kidneys, so McCoist wanted to say no but Mark questioned if that would seem like they were punishing her and could risk further alienating… and so on and on. Soft touch.

"And you know what else there is at music festivals to go with the sex and rock 'n' roll?"

"Don't say it."

"Drugs."

"Stop."

"Mountains of the stuff. There are more dodgy pills floating round a music festival than fucking bucket hats. Plus the dodgy geezers who sell them."

"Hats or drugs?"

"Shut up."

"Could you switch off your polis-brain for a minute?"

"That's not polis-brain, it's parent-brain, you should get one."

"Nice. Very clever. Very grown up."

The sight of the corpse stopped McCoist from saying something she regretted. "I have to go," she said instead, hanging up although she could still hear Mark speaking. He was used to it. One of the reasons for the divorce, probably.

The body was on its back, lying in a gulch between the wall of a motorway on-ramp and the overgrown embankment beside it. A strip of torn fencing separated the two. Beyond a flapping hole in the fence, a path had been trod up the embankment over time.

She almost whistled. "Rats?"

The photographer nodded. The thing that had once been a person had no eyes or face left. The cheeks were hollow in the literal sense, not the sickly avant-garde film-star sense. The sinews had been chewed through, clean to the bone in some places. Stripped of everything else, the former-face's main feature was its lipless teeth. Large, yellow and animal-like in black, receding gums. Quite the smile. Wriggling things were living in it.

"I heard on this podcast—"

"Every time you start a sentence with that it costs me a thousand brain cells," McCoist said.

The DC tagging along as her gofer, Gaz Travis, grinned, undeterred by the practised weariness in his boss's voice. "I heard on this podcast, right, that there's so much coke floating about down there in the sewers in Glasgow—in people's pish and getting flushed down or poured out and that—that the rats are more geared up than Maradona. Makes them super aggressive."

The photographer was staring at DC Travis now, eyes narrowed. "Rats on gak..." he murmured, cogs visibly turning in his brain.

"And polis on acid, apparently," McCoist snapped. "Can I speak to someone sensible about this?" She motioned to the decaying, feasted-upon body. It was in a suit, as if ready for the funeral. Long overdue for it, actually. The suit too—past its fashion sell-by at some point in the eighties.

It reeked and she had to try hard not to pinch her nose. More than just disrespectful, it was amateur, and McCoist would not allow herself to be seen that way. There were enough rumours around her promotion to DCI already. Plenty of sniping and whispered accusations of affirmative action. A leaked WhatsApp chat had recently embarrassed Police Scotland and led to a good number of polis—bicycle bobby and senior detective alike—getting the boot or made to take early retirement, including her former boss, DCI Robson. She wasn't surprised that fat, baldy shitehawk had been involved—his contributions to the group chat had been racist, sexist and poorly spelled—and she wasn't sad to see him go, but the truth of her ascension was more complicated than convenient optics. The cost to her had been great too.

A SOCO detached herself from a group of paper-suited colleagues scouring the surrounds—the graffitied concrete temple under the on-ramp littered with broken bottles, empty baggies, cigarette butts, needles, crisp packets, clues—and pulled her mask down to speak, a glove off to shake. "Amy Caruso."

"DCI Alison McCoist." She held out her warrant card.

"I've heard of you…" Caruso's eyes went scary wide, a smile pulling her face apart.

McCoist gave the woman a look that said the next words out her mouth better not include a reference to a particular ex-Rangers striker.

"…You worked the Car Wash Case!"

Caruso was impressed, as if this other McCoist in front of her was also a legend.

"What little work there was to do. The lad was found at the scene of the crime."

Three dead bodies, including his uncle Paulo McGuinn, in bits on the floor of a grotty wee car wash in the east end. Poor, thick Colin, just in the right place and time to take the fall. McCoist had railroaded the boy straight to Barlinnie. Her guts knotted at the thought. She'd been bouncing between Imodium and Lactulose ever since it happened. Fear, guilt, and anxiety were hellish on the bowels. The Car Wash Case. Car Wash Catastrophe, more like. McCoist had really cunted it this time, worse than all her previous mistakes combined, and there were a lot of those.

"I know, but, scary people to deal with, eh?" Caruso's voice lowered to a conspiratorial stage whisper.

"None as scary as DCI McCoist," Travis chipped in with a grin, fully expecting the withering look McCoist slapped him with. It had no effect, nothing did with him, he was fully assured his puppyish charm would let him get away with it. After all, the gaffer was a dog person.

"Speaking of scary, your man here with his Hallowe'en mask on too early." McCoist shifted the subject. "What can you tell us?"

You could almost hear the switch of Caruso going from star-struck to professional. "He's been here about twenty-four hours. Strangled, from what I can see in situ. Reckon he was dumped off the side of the ramp."

"Not dragged through the hole in the fence?"

"Not likely—no obvious evidence of that but we'll take a closer look. The PM will confirm if he was dropped down but we're searching the road above anyway."

"Good." A couple of uniforms and a van were waiting to bag him up once the photographer was finished with him. "Anything interesting around here?"

"Not unless you're keen on outsider art." Caruso jabbed a thumb at Travis, who was taking in the graffitied pillars as if he were in a gallery. "This is a dump site. He was killed somewhere else."

"All yours." The photographer stepped away from his subject and the two uniforms sucked foetid air in through their teeth before approaching with the black bag, neither one of them thrilled to be het for this task. "Rigor's still in effect, and he's nice and flat for you, shouldn't be too bad."

"That right, aye? Ye offerin a hawn then?" One of constables said.

"Sorry, pal, bad back." The photographer smiled.

They took up a position at each end. "Wan, two, three—" They lifted "—Fuck!" Congealed blood, stained fluids and rotted brain matter slopped out a hole in the back of the corpse's head and splattered onto the constable's shoes.

Caruso nodded in approval. "He was dropped."

2

Everybody called him Chuck though his name wasn't Charles. He had curly ginger hair and wore corrective NHS specs throughout his school years. His pals were wee pricks. Despite him now having a shaved, balding dome and favouring contacts, the nickname had stuck. He didn't hate it anymore though. He was nearly thirty now. He was at peace with it. It was a fact of life. It was his name. Secretly, he liked it better than "Stuart" and its attendant nicknames: Stu, Stewie, Stu Pot, Stupac Shakur. When anyone asked his name he replied, "Evrybody caws me Chuck."

"Because that's your name?" replied the old boy with a quizzical eyebrow tick.

"Because ae *Rugrats*. Ye mind that? Chuckie wae the glesses, ginger hair?"

The man shook his grey head and let Chuck into the house—not a place where children had ever lived judging by the furniture and decoration and complete lack of photographs, so it's no wonder he'd never heard of the kids' cartoon. They went through the kitchen—Chuck had been asked to come to the back door—and into the hall. "The stairs shouldn't be a problem for a strapping lad like you," the geezer said, creaking his way up the staircase, a brown, threadbare carpet runner down chipped, white-glossed steps.

"Depends how many trips it takes." Five years of hauling towers of confidential waste papers and the shredded hay bales his machine turned them into had taken its toll on Chuck's knees and back.

"Just a few boxes for you. Having a clear out." They entered a bedroom which smelled of Eau De Auld Geezer and astringent bar soap. The room was spartan: a wicker chair coming to bits in one corner; a night table at the side of the yellowing bed with a few well-read paperbacks and the Bible; net curtains which gave the place a sepia filter, as if glimpsed through a brown medicine bottle.

A fitted wardrobe the length of one side of the room was open. The clothes hanging on the rail were divided in the middle into black vestments and civvies. The large, cardboard boxes were on the floor of the wardrobe. There were five, each one marked with a decade, sixties to noughties. "Just these, cheers," the minister said. "Would you like a cup of tea? Coffee?"

"Naw thanks, pal, this willnae take lang."

The first box was heavier than expected. Bad things twitched in the small of his back as he huffed it up to his chest. The stairs were precarious. He couldn't see over the box, had to come down sideways to watch his steps, caught his knuckles against the wall—*bastart!*—as he turned at the bottom to head back out through the kitchen.

His van was parked at the garden gate, decal on the side reading:

SIMPLY SHRED

Secure Document Destruction

Mobile On-site Shredding

He opened the side door and fired up the machine inside. The rolling blades at the bottom of the hopper churned together with relentless force, a gnawing, savage hunger. Chuck often thought of himself as a zookeeper, and it was feeding time. He hefted the box up and tipped it in.

50 lbs of glossy pornography tumbled into the hopper. Naked women being stuffed from all angles were chewed and swallowed by the shredder, its appetite as apparently insatiable as their own. Among the churning, ripping flesh were disembodied organs: shining nipples, a probing tongue, a cock as big as a baguette with rippling veins, dripping at the tip.

Chuck looked again at the writing on the box: '60s. Vintage. Lifting his jaw back into place, he went back upstairs. Seventies next. He almost wanted to lift the flap a little, take a keek at what a fifty-year-old scud book was like, but resisted. Confidentiality was the name of the game after all. Discretion. Legally-binding discretion. And would he really want to touch any of these stiff, old jazz mags which had been kept by the minister for half a century? *Should probly gee the machine a good rinse oot eftir*, he thought.

A few more jaunts up and down the stairs and he'd caught up to the contemporary filth. Job done.

Almost.

"These too, son." The minster held two laptops. One old, based on how thick it was, one a bit newer.

Chuck felt something cold trickle in his stomach, his world shift a little off kilter. He had a special hard-drive shredder in the van, it was part of his services, but it was usually only businesses that asked for it. One-off Joe Public punters like this were rarely in need of it. It was the smart thing to do, considering all the things Chuck had learned about identity theft since getting into the shredding game, but most people just left their old laptops in a cupboard to gather dust. Chuck had a healthy prejudice against the holy professions to start with. Add in the dirty book archive and the question of shredding the computers, along with whatever was on them, raised the hairs on the back of Chuck's neck.

He almost asked why. But he didn't. Because not asking was part of his job, and reliability was everything. He knew another guy in the game once—Harvey MacNeil, a small business solo-operator like himself—who let slip a few quiet words about a customer he thought might be a nonce. And this boy, this wrong yin, found himself strung up by a vigilante mob, who battered his maw's door down and dragged him into the street in the middle of the night, kicked every Dulux sample of shite out him and put him in a coma before the polis could show up. Justice done, maybe, but Harvey was out of business by the end of the year. Nobody could trust him anymore. He ran a leaky ship and everybody knew it now, even if they felt he'd done the right thing.

Chuck was running enough risks as it was through his trading deal with Mr Jamieson, so he took the laptops without comment.

"Cheers, son."

He held his phone under the wheel and flicked to refresh over and over, quick look up as he joined the expressway back towards town, then a glance back down. *Moan tae fuck, moan tae fuck*. Three minutes of stoppage time coming to an end. *Fucksake. Fuckin bastarts*. He prayed for a miracle. *Please*. Final whistle.

"Fuck!"

He slammed the wheel, causing the horn to blare and the driver in front to swerve slightly. *Shower ae useless pricks!* Fucking nil-nil. Hundred quid down the Tommy Crapper. He threw his phone into the stack of paperwork on the passenger seat, causing an avalanche on Mt Admin. Heart pounding, he crushed his teeth together and made growling animal noises, dredged up from his queasy stomach. Punched the horn again. The driver in front flashed their hazards and pulled onto the hard shoulder. A wee face in Chuck's passenger-side wing mirror screamed, "Wit the fuck?!"

Chuck signalled left and the wee face shat itself, thinking he was stopping to have a word. Instead, he pulled back off the expressway at the upcoming exit, headed to the petrol station at the nearby retail park.

He filled up and stomped inside to pay. It wasn't much because the tank was three-quarters full. He also bought a ten quid scratch card. He had a green penny which lived in the dookit of the dashboard which had once proved itself lucky.

Not today.

The scratch card was tossed on the pile of paperwork. The silver rubbings lay dead in his lap. The coin went back to its home. He took slow breaths, feeling calmer. What was ten quid anyway? *Couple ae pints. Didnae need those anyway, bad fir ye.* There were other bets ready to pay out anyway. Ones that would eclipse the ton he just dropped. (Plus the ten spot.) And if all else failed, there was The Great Accumulator. A pension pot. A take-the-wife-and-fuck-off-to-Cancun pot. He had *the feeling* about this one, bubbling away in the background.

A horn peeped from behind. "Awright, awright." He raised his hand, saluting with every finger rather than just two. Back in control. He'd need it to get through his last appointment of the day.

"Ye winnin, Chuck?" Not a greeting, and not meant as a joke. Jamieson was flatly serious. Always was. He was the only man Chuck had ever met that didn't consider himself to be funny. Easily mistaken for a lack of ego, but it certainly wasn't that. No, it was something else that was missing, something more vital.

"No yet, Mr Jamieson, but there's always hope." Chuck licked dry lips, forced a smile which was not returned. Jamieson's face was a slowly rotting tumshie lantern carved with a blunt knife.

Jamieson's secretary, a Michelangelo's David with the added bulk of a stab-proof vest under his suit, pushed Chuck down into a seat across a busy desk from the boss man, who gave a hint of a sigh. "Useful as ye can be, Chuck, av come tae hate seein ye here."

Chuck didn't know what to say to that, so he adjusted and readjusted himself in the chair, making the leather squeak like a sneaky fart, comfort impossible. Marble loomed over his shoulder, apparently with no seat or desk of his own to do his admin on.

"Ye goat somethin fir me?"

"Aye, slipped some bits an pieces fae that new rehab place oot Bearsden way—thoat ye might find somethin interestin, a hear they've goat politician's weans an fitbaw players' wives an aw sorts bein banged up there." Chuck held out the paperwork to Jamieson but it was intercepted by Marble, who then passed it on. Checking for papercut potential, maybe.

Jamieson leafed through, nothing to read on his face. As ever. Chuck had only managed to scrounge some random papers while the bloke who was supposed to be supervising the shredding fiddled around with his fags and lighter, so likely it was all useless shite, nothing to further Jamieson's cause of acquiring information about everyone and everything which made Glesga turn. "Security & Investigations" was printed on Jamieson's business cards. Rumour said before he became the business card-carrying type he was in import and export: drugs, guns, women, anything to turn a profit. Now he dealt purely in information. His taxes were on the legal side of creative. He had an office with a listed address in the Merchant City where Chuck sat sweating.

He found himself speaking without meaning to. "There wis also this auld boay…" Desperate to break the silence, to give Jamieson something of worth. Because that was Chuck's end of the bargain. Jamieson's end—well, that hundred quid Chuck had lost on the fitbaw was just a scrap, arse-wiping money really, to what he owed to the various jackals Jamieson kept in line as a favour to him. A favour to be returned. Not a favour. A deal. One that could not be reneged upon unless Chuck won big soon or decided he didn't really need thumbs anymore.

So despite Harvey MacNeil crying a warning in his head, Chuck told them about the minister, the boxes of smut, and the laptops.

"So?" Jamieson said.

"Wit if he's a paedo? Wit if the church know awready? Could be somethin." Chuck was warming up to it now that he'd started. Fuck the old man. *Pervy bastart.* He deserved whatever he got.

And Chuck deserved to have thumbs. "Maybe they're makin him get rid ae it. The big heed yins wantin tae cover it up."

"Maybe he's just auld an depressed," Jamieson suggested.

"How?"

"Ye know wit they say."

Marble answered for his boss: "Tired ae wankin, tired ae life."

Chuck had never heard anyone say this and looked puzzled between the two men: Marble as sure and solid as his nickname, Jamieson nodding sagely in agreement.

"Wit?"

"Did ye save the laptoaps?"

Chuck felt his cheeks getting hot, taking a beamer, his pale ginger's skin so easily flushed. "Naw. He wis right there next tae me."

Another sigh from Jamieson. "Al huv a hink aboot it. If that's aw…?"

Chuck made to stand up. Marble halted him at first, then let him go. He was just into the waiting room when Jamieson called: "Best ae luck."

He wasn't joking.

AVAILABLE AND COMING SOON
FROM PUSHKIN VERTIGO

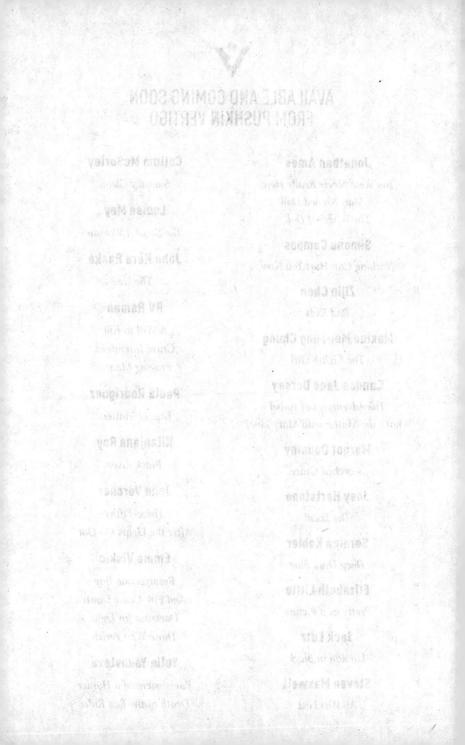